6

MEADE'S REPRISE

Major General George G. Meade

★ ★

MEADE'S REPRISE

A Novel of Gettysburg,
War and Intrigue

John Duke Merriam

POSTERITY PRESS

Posterity Press, Inc.
PO Box 71081
Chevy Chase,
Maryland 20813
www.PosterityPress.com

Printed in Iceland by Oddi Printing

Library of Congress Cataloging-in-Publication Data

Merriam, John Duke.
  Meade's reprise : a novel of Gettysburg, war, and intrigue / John Duke Merriam.
    p. cm.
  ISBN 1-889274-18-6
    1. Meade, George Gordon, 1815-1872—Fiction. 2. United States—History—Civil War,
1861-1865—Fiction. 3. Gettysburg, Battle of, Gettysburg, Pa., 1863—Fiction. 4. Generals—
Fiction. I. Title.
PS3613.E775 M43 2002
813'.6—dc21   2002071522

Front endpaper:
Camps; Looking East from the Capitol; lithograph by E. Sachse & Co. 1861.

Back endpaper:
Washington, D.C. View of the City (west from the Capitol); lithograph by E. Sachse & Co., 1871.

Picture Credits
Cover and frontispiece: National Archives, #11-B-16
Front Endpaper: Historical Society of Washington, DC
Page 15: Library of Congress, LC-B8171-7951
Page 16: Equator Graphics, Inc.
Page 131: Library of Congress, LC-B8171-7252
Page 132: Equator Graphics, Inc.
Page 255: Library of Congress, LC-USZ62-39407
Page 256: Calligraphy by Stephen Kraft
Back Endpaper: Library of Congress, LC-USZ62-19371

In memory of my father, Lawrence Merriam,
who passed on to me his fascination with the Civil War,
and of my late wife, Barbara;
and for our children, Jeffrey, Claire, Matthew and Andrew,
who joined us so many times when we
"drove out to see history."

"Meade in my judgment had the greatest ability. I feared him more than any man I ever met on the field of battle."

General Robert E. Lee CSA

as quoted by President Calvin Coolidge

at the dedication of the Meade Memorial, Washington, D.C.

October 19, 1927

CONTENTS

BOOK I

At the Breaking Point
page 15

BOOK II

Ending the War
page 131

BOOK III

The Wages of Peace
page 255

Maps

The Potomac Region: USA and CSA Forces, June 1863
page 16

Meade's Reprise: Gettysburg Battlefield, 4:30 p.m., July 3, 1863
page 132

Author's Note and Acknowledgments
page 325

PREFATORY NOTE

———————————► ☆ ◄———————————

The Battle of Gettysburg happened; it is fact. The personages of President Lincoln; Secretary of War Stanton; Generals Hooker, Sickles, Sherman, Grant, Lee, Longstreet, Gordon; and other commanders named here are historical. Into this real cast, I have introduced fictional people, such as Major Fitzpatrick, the heroic African-Americans Josephus Alexander and Henry Prediger, the schoolgirl Flossie Muelheim, Toddy Bates of the 7th Tennessee, the socialite Fannie Morris, Madame Alice, and especially the beauteous Maeve, briefly called "Maizie," as well others just as real and contemporary.

I have altered some facts, notably those relating to General Meade's actions at the end of the actual battle and thereafter into his future. Meade's many detractors, and many historians as well, have criticized his pursuit of Lee after the battle. These included at the outset both President Lincoln and Daniel Sickles, who was undoubtedly the anonymous newspaper columnist "Historicus." Armchair generalship has victimized Meade ever since. His own attempts to set the record straight until his early death in 1872 were pedantic and widely unheard. Recently, students of the battle have taken a more charitable view, noting that Union troops arrived on the field exhausted and that Meade's pursuit of Lee was pretty much what he could do in the circumstances. Until Appomattox no victorious general, including Lee himself, was able or even tried to press his foe to a final defeat. Let it also be said in Meade's defense that, from Gettysburg on, he retained the perilous seat of commander of the Army of the Potomac, and his enemy kept moving southward until the end of the war. Meade's orders on June 28, 1863, as stated here, were to take command of the army and defend Washington and Baltimore. His detractors argue that he should have counterattacked more aggressively at Gettysburg; had he done so, the course of the Civil War, and history, might have been altered—possibly as I have speculated.

DRAMATIS PERSONAE

---☆---

Historical characters in roman type; *fictional characters in italics*

WASHINGTON, CAPITAL OF THE UNITED STATES OF AMERICA
Abraham Lincoln, President of the United States
Mary Todd Lincoln, the President's wife
Edwin M. Stanton, Secretary of War
Maj. Gen. Henry Wager Halleck, General-in-Chief, USA
Col. James Allen Hardie, Asst. Adjutant General, USA
Major James Edward Van Arsdale Fitzpatrick Jr., assistant to Hardie,
later aide to General Meade, etc.
Senator Benjamin Franklin Wade (R Ohio), Chairman, Committee on the
Conduct of the War,

ARMY OF THE POTOMAC
Maj. Gen. George Gordon Meade, commanding officer
Margaretta Sergeant Meade, his wife (in Philadelphia)
Maj. Gen. Joseph Hooker, previous commanding officer
Maj. Gen. Daniel Butterfield, Chief of Staff
Maj. Gen. Marcena Patrick, Provost Marshall
Brig. Gen. Henry J. Hunt, Commander of Artillery
Col. George H. Sharpe, Chief of Intelligence
Capt. George G. Meade Jr., aide-de-camp

First Corps
Maj. Gen. John F. Reynolds, commander, at the outset
Maj. Gen. John Newton, subsequent commander
Maj. Gen. Abner Doubleday, subsequent commander

Second Corps
Maj. Gen. Winfield Scott Hancock, commander

1st Division
Maj. Gen. John Gibbon

Third Corps
Maj. Gen. Daniel E. Sickles, commander
Maj. H. E. Tremaine, aide-de-camp

1st Division
Maj.Gen. David B. Birney,

2nd Division
Brig. Gen. Andrew A. Humphreys

71st New York Infantry Regiment
Sergeant Tucker
Corporal Edmundson
Private Macintosh

Fifth Corps
Maj. Gen. George Sykes, commander

12th New York Infantry Regiment
Third Sergeant Liam O'Bannion

Sixth Corps
Maj. Gen. John Sedgwick, commander

Eleventh Corps
Maj. Gen. Oliver O. Howard, commander

87th Illinois Infantry Regiment
Private Heinrich Landsman

Twelfth Corps
Maj. Gen. Henry W. Slocum, commander

Cavalry Corps
Maj. Gen. Alfred Pleasonton, commander

1st Division
Brig. Gen. John Buford

3rd Division

2nd Brigade
Brig. Gen. George A. Custer

CIVILIANS

Journalists
Aloysius Brennan, New York World
Herman Meyer, The New York Times

U.S. Sanitary Commission
Mrs. Clarissa Scott
Miss Fannie Alice Morris

Doctors and Surgeons

Camp Followers
"Alice's Special Services"
Madame Alice Lee
Miss Maeve McConnaughy or "Maizie,"
Miss Sigurd McConnaughy or "Flame"
James, hired hand

Gettysburg and Surroundings
Miss Flossie Muelheim, school girl
Mr. Henry Prediger, hired hand and freedman
Mr. Josephus Alexander, escapee

ARMY OF NORTHERN VIRGINIA
Gen. Robert E. Lee, commanding officer

Staff aides
Junius, manservant and slave

1st Corps
Lt. General James Longstreet, commander
Lt. Col. Porter Alexander, deputy chief of Artillery

3rd Division
Maj. George E. Pickett, commander

2nd Corps
Lt. Gen. Richard S. Ewell, commander

2nd Division
Maj. Gen Jubal A. Early, commander

1st Brigade
Brig. Gen. John Brown Gordon
Fanny Rebecca Haralson Gordon, his wife

26th Georgia Infantry Regiment
Pvt. Beverly Stuckey

4th Brigade
Brig. Gen. William F. 'Extra Billy' Smith

3rd Corps
Lt. Gen. Ambrose Powell Hill, commander

1st Division
Maj. Gen. Henry Heth, commander (at outset)
Brig. Gen. James Johnston Pettigrew (subsequent)

Archer's Brigade
7th Tennessee Infantry Regiment
Private Toddy Bates

James Harrison, actor, scout and spy

RICHMOND, CAPITAL OF THE CONFEDERATE STATES OF AMERICA
Jefferson Davis, President of the Confederate States of America
James Alexander Seddon, Secretary of War
Colonel George Washington Custis Lee, aide to President Davis
Miss Elizabeth van Lew, spinster, property owner and spy
Miss Mary Bowser, freedwoman and servant in the Davis household
John Wilkes Booth, actor
Cuyler Rutledge, attorney from Savannah

WASHINGTON (LATER)

Maj. Gen. Ulysses Simpson Grant, commanding officer, Armies of the West

Julia Dent Grant, his wife

Brig.Gen. Lafayette C. Baker, commander 1st DC Cavalry,

Provost, agent and spy

Senator Everett Van Huysen (D. Delaware)

Mr. Frederick Douglass, journalist and advocate

Rev. Benjamin Turner

In addition: code clerks, orderlies, doormen, chambermaids, streetfolk, prostitutes, politicians, journalists, Members of Congress, and other denizens of the capital.

MILITARY UNITS AND THEIR SIZE

Both armies followed the standard U.S. table of organization. Confederate units were larger and consolidated, while Union units were many and varied. According to the best historical estimate, the Union had roughly 93,000 men engaged including cavalry, the Confederacy 70,000. The breakdown was:

Corps

The Confederate Army comprised three corps of 20,000 to 25,0000 men. Union Army comprised seven corps of 10,000 to 15,000 men.

Division

Each Confederate corps had four divisions. Two Union corps had two divisions, the rest had three. A Confederate division could have nearly 8,000 men, nearly as many as a Union corps.

Brigade

The smallest unit commanded by a general, hence the basic unit of command. In both armies, brigades were originally composed of 1,000 to 2,000 men, but were often fewer.

Regiment

Each brigade had at least three or as many as eight regiments. These were recruited locally, often on a political basis, and shrunk as casualties occurred. The South sent in replacements for casualties, while Union units faded with attrition and were consequently smaller.

Book One

AT THE BREAKING POINT

After the battle of Antietam, President Lincoln meets McClellan and his officers; the bearded general behind him has been identified as Meade.

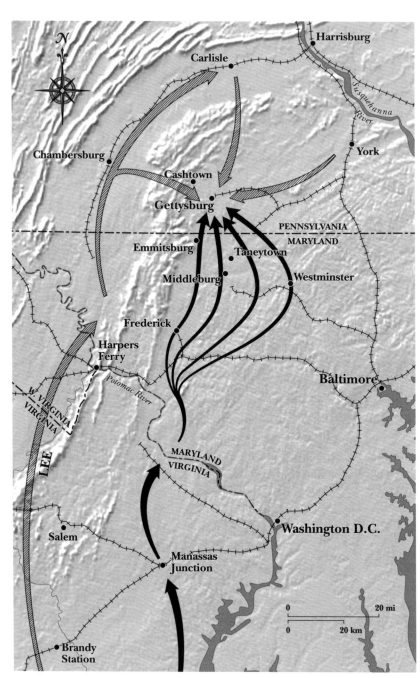

The Potomac Region
Movement of US and CSA forces, June 1863

16

STATUS QUO ANTE

June 27, 1863

In first high heat of a hot summer, tempers in Washington City frayed, and in the streets men spoke warily of panic. The enemy had marched deep into Pennsylvania without firing a shot. Rebel cavalry raided Rockville in Maryland, twenty miles away. The Confederate Army led by Robert E. Lee was poised to sweep down on the capital and end the war at a stroke. Foreign embassies were packing up, and British diplomats talked openly of going to Richmond. For President Lincoln and his party, the end seemed near. There would be no continuing. Everyone asked, "Where is the Union Army?"

Slowly, its men struggled northward to meet the Rebels. Their commander, Maj. Gen. Joseph Hooker, no longer a public darling, had lost his nerve. Men were leaving in gangs as enlistments expired. Hooker balked at orders from the capital, evaded civilian superiors, and late in the afternoon sent a telegram to the Secretary of War.

CHAPTER I

Lord, give us a leader to bring us out of Egypt, Abraham Lincoln, 16th President of the United States, prayed as he trudged over mud and gravel west of the White House toward the blazing lights of the War Office. Damp night air rose from shrubs and puddles along the path. *And our slaves, too,* he added, the folds of his face breaking along lines deepened by worry and fatigue into the angular grin critics reviled.

Minutes before, the Secretary of War had sent an urgent message: "Jackson's old corps stands across the Susquehanna from Harrisburg. In the eleventh hour, Hooker wants to quit."

Lincoln felt the tension in the city. He had already ordered troops to the railroad station to stop mass flight. *And worse, the British, curse them, are making noises again about recognizing the Confederacy.*

Hooker must go, whatever his game. Bad enough to lose the general just when the battle starts. . . . No time to think. . . . No time for ceremony. . . . Hesitate. . . . Lose an hour, and they'll come down on us. Final disgrace. . . . prison perhaps . . . chains for the freedmen.

Five men. . . . We've had five generals lead the army, one twice, and every one failed. Now Lee makes the Rebels invincible. Oh, that he'd taken my offer! Command is our Jonah.

Foul smells floated up from the river and the canals, from slaughterhouses on the Mall, and horse droppings everywhere. A lone sentry saluted as the President stepped into the light; he answered with an airy wave, and passed up the steep stairs to the Secretary's office. As all Washington knew, Lincoln depended on William Stanton, lawyer, politician, controversial and unhandsome, but versed in the ways of the East and more recently of military politics.

I'll wager he'll want Meade, the Philadelphia aristocrat. He pushed the door open.

From his standing easel, Stanton glanced up without greeting and went back to his papers. "No time to lose on Hooker. We've got to put someone in command. Going over it, I find no alternative to Meade." He looked up again and, seeing no response, talked on. "John Reynolds would be more suitable, but he demands complete independence. We can't risk that, now."

Lincoln took off his coat, hung it on the back of a chair, and sat in shirtsleeves at a table in the middle of the room. Sweat seeped through his collar. "I tried giving Hooker his head. In the end he wouldn't stay in the traces. He has some wild notions, like letting Lee ravage Washington while he chases off to Richmond." He shook his head.

"Reminds me of a story I used to tell on the circuit." Lincoln grinned at Stanton, then dropped his smile. "But no time for that." He waved a bony hand before his face. "Will Meade take orders?"

Stanton went on. "Others lack experience. Meade has a solid record. Handles troops well. Other commanders respect him. And, by all accounts, he follows orders." He paused, waiting for a question. "There's no time to bring anyone from the West."

Lincoln stared out the window at the dim lights of the White House. "Yes." He spoke slowly. "Grant's got Vicksburg in front of him. That may be the saving of us."

Stanton smiled, and his muttonchops shifted.

The President sighed, "No, Stanton, I can't disagree. When Meade came to town a while back, he seemed a thin rail. You couldn't judge the make of him, except he ate politely. Didn't have a lot to say. But men speak well of him, and he appears to keep clear of politics, except for Mrs. Meade's family." Lincoln picked up a pen from the inkstand and toyed with it. "Though I hear from Philadelphians she wants the job. That's not a recommendation I can altogether quarrel with." He sighed, looking again toward the White House. "And he's from Pennsylvania. He'll fight well on his own dunghill."

The Secretary of War winced.

"Let us be swift. The sooner Meade feels the reins in his hands, the better. You don't think he'll shy, do you?"

"No, he's a good soldier," said Stanton. "I've got a steam locomotive from the Baltimore & Ohio to take Colonel Hardie and Major Fitzpatrick to Frederick posthaste. They should find Meade before dawn. Halleck is drafting orders telling him to protect Washington and Baltimore, and to assure him he'll get no petty guidance from here."

Lincoln toyed with the wooden pen, staring at it. "Let's think for a minute. We wait until we're near disaster and say, 'Here, Meade, you take it.' What does he do if he wins? We don't know, do we? He hasn't been taken into the fold. We haven't appointed a man without a proper ceremony before." He looked over at Stanton. "Still, a federal army under a trained commander ought to trap Lee up there, and whip him."

The Secretary of War handed him a short letter. The President dipped the pen in ink and quickly signed it. "Let it be so, and let us now say our prayers for General Meade."

Stanton struck a gong by his desk, and an orderly brought in two men in plain dark suits, the sort travelers wore. The older, Colonel Hardie, was his trusted adjutant; the younger, his assistant Major Fitzpatrick, tall, dark, and emaciated. He grinned sheepishly. Both seemed to feel they were in costume.

Stanton handed Hardie Lincoln's letter along with another relieving Hooker. "Find Meade. Take him to army headquarters, oversee the transfer of command, and report back immediately. Make sure Hooker understands you come from the War Office. He ought to recognize you, even in that suit. Let's hope he's sober."

The men in mufti withdrew, quick-stepping down the hall to the open door of the General-in-Chief, where Henry Halleck stood waiting. "This may be difficult, Hardie. We don't know where the Rebel cavalry are. Jeb Stuart's troopers have been as near as Rockville in the next county." Halleck handed over the official orders and paused to stare. "Do you really need Fitzpatrick? Won't two men be conspicuous?"

Hardie turned to his companion, still gray about the eyes where recovery clung to him. "Fitzpatrick was with Meade at Fredericksburg, sir. He'll get us through the camp. With his honorable scars and my age, any Rebel will take us for a couple of commission men, unfit for anythin' else." He winked.

The General-in-Chief squinted over his spectacles. "Well, Hardie, I rely on you. None of this is pleasant, especially not for George Meade. I can't imagine a more difficult order." With a tired flick of his hands, an unusual gesture for a punctilious man, he dismissed them.

The two saluted smartly and rushed down the stairs and away from the building. Hardie felt silly. He had spent his life in uniform, and had worn nothing else since the war began. The clerks joked that he slept in one. At first he had wanted command, and knew he could be a major general by now like the rest of his class at the Military Academy. Running a complex war machine fascinated him, as the interference of politics annoyed him, and he saw his duty lay in the capital. Others respected him for the choice, especially the young major, two ranks below but far behind in experience.

Neither liked the disguise. Fitzpatrick found a cab, and in it they huddled out of sight all the way to the station. A battered wood-burning locomotive hooked to an aged passenger wagon waited at the end of the platform to speed them to Baltimore, where it would have to wait for priority to chug over a choked, overworked line toward the army in western Maryland. They found the car littered with food wrappings, newspapers, and other trash from soldiers, the stench overwhelming the steaming interior.

The two sat side by side, rigid on hard wood benches as the train bumped over ill-fitted rail joints. Hardie tried to relax. This was his biggest task of the war. He knew better than anyone else how the generals were feuding, about their ambitions and the crowd of politicals who clung to Joe Hooker.

"Meade will depend on John Reynolds." Hardie's Scot's burr thickened in private. "They've fought together through it all, and there's a bond o' trust between 'em."

The major kept silent, as he always did, respecting Hardie's out-loud thoughts, which he shared when they were alone.

"Did your family know the general in Philadelphia?" Hardie breathed noisily through a small dark mustache.

"He was with my father in school. But the Meades fell on hard times, and George Meade had to leave. After that, father seldom saw him."

Hardie took off his soft brim hat and mopped his brow, eyes searching the depths of the empty car. "The President had no time to consult the Cabinet. That won't help a new Commanding General. He'll have enemies the minute they know his name."

Fitzpatrick stood and took off his jacket. "Begging pardon, sir, I don't suppose dress matters?"

"There's na point in it. I'd sooner march behind a mule in the Sierra Madre than ride in this thing." Hardie also took off his jacket and rolled up his sleeves. "I have the uncanny feeling we aren't going to be alone. There's too many know what we're about. The capital's a sieve in the best o' times, and the threat breaks down discipline. Nothin's secret. Spies must have sent word to Richmond as soon as we left." He mopped his forehead with a large handkerchief. "A man can hardly breathe. That may keep a few folk away."

He turned to the younger man. "Did you ever meet him?" Fitzpatrick was going to be his gift to George Meade, from one professional officer to another in time of trial—a good staff man, from the same city and class, and, most of all, savvy in the ways of headquarters.

Fitzpatrick glanced at his left hand, stripped of all but thumb and forefinger. "The general visited me after Fredericksburg and wrote home I was safe. I gather he does that sort of thing—the proper courtesies. A lot of men fear him, but I've only seen him be decent."

Hardie pulled out a cigar and bit the end. "He's dyspeptic, they say. Well . . ." he paused to spit out the end. "Everyone's got something. Lincoln's constipated. Stanton, asthmatic. Most o' the generals have the diarrhea. One Rebel has a wooden leg. Lee has a bad heart. Why shouldn't Meade have a stomach?" Hardie stared at the mess of the floor of the car, and wiped bits of moist tobacco from his lips. "Military life is no' easy on the insides."

"If they expect a magician, they may be asking too much," said Fitzpatrick, staring into the night forest.

"Do you have doubts, major? Meade will want you on his staff." Hardie tried to see his face. "I would, if I were him. You're one of his kind, educated, and a social peer. He can trust you."

Fitzpatrick looked down at his boots, slowly moving them back and forth. "I'll go where I'm ordered, colonel."

"I'd want every loyal man I could find." Hardie went on. "He needs reliable liaison with his corps commanders. Many will resent him, and they'll test him. It's no' goin' to be easy. What would you say to it?"

Fitzpatrick nodded knowingly and smiled. "I couldn't say no, could I?"

Hardie raised his voice near parade-ground level. "Laddie, your role could be very important. Do you know how an army truly runs? Men have to take orders. Bull Run was a gang fight because no one knew what to do. We chased Beauregard and went too far, beyond reach o' command. Jackson's men obeyed all down the line, and the Rebs held. Ours didn't, and we lost. Meade's commanders have got to respond, or the army don't function."

The train paused at a siding. Hardie stared out at troops loading ammunition crates by lantern light. "I hope they dinna make mistakes just now. Everyone hurries too much.

"Reynolds, of course, is reliable." He spoke as much to the window as Fitzpatrick. "And his good word will help. He's fine."

As the train pulled away, Fitzpatrick stared into the darkness. "I can see Meade will need their confidence. But in God's name, colonel, I can't understand why anyone would buck him now, before the fight."

"You know who to worry about, don't ya, laddie?" Hardie's eyes locked on his assistant. "Major General Sickles, late of Tammany Hall, don't play by the rules. His pal Hooker lets him do it. Lincoln laughs at his jokes. He defended the Mrs. when she was caught fiddlin' the White House books. Did you know that, laddie?"

Fitzpatrick grinned and stared at the dirty planks, shaking his head. "Everybody talks about Sickles—how his savvy lawyer kept him out of jail, a lawyer who now happens to be Secretary of War."

"Mr. Stanton's no fool. He sees Sickles using the war to rise, and sees him playing hero to the press. In the bargain he'll try to make Meade look a fool. The devil of it is Hooker's men will follow his lead, including Butterfield, who'll be Meade's chief of staff. The new man's got two, maybe three, days before the fight; he's not time to replace 'em."

Hardie's eyes followed Fitzpatrick. "Eighty thousand men can't be led by word of mouth. It takes good staff to make commanders do what the chief wants." Hardie held his eyes on Fitzpatrick.

"Look at us, laddie. We're charged with changing the command of the Army of the Potomac. What if Hooker says he don't recognize us?" He turned his palms out as if to show off his suit. "He could say we've no authority? What if Meade says he won't do the job? We lowly fellows have to make the President's word stick. That's good staff work. It's not aw dancing and dining at the generals' mess."

★ ★

Before midnight the train pulled to a stop far out in the Baltimore yards. They waited in their boiling suits, looking out at a shifting array of cars of all types and sizes loaded with war stuffs to go west. Some carried troops.

"We're stripping every garrison for miles around," said Hardie. "I hope the secesh folk don't think this is their chance. We keep a full division here to hold on to the city. If Lee gets close, the town will rise."

The unexpected "special" brought officials to check Hardie's authority, and after an hour's delay the tracks were cleared. But not before a dapper, mustachioed major general in a well-tailored uniform swung himself aboard. Neither had a moment's doubt who he was.

"A cheerful good evening to you, colonel, I heard a 'special' was going out. It was damned hard not to hear, they're making such a to-do about it. Not a good thing for Johnny Reb to get wind of. You might get trapped." Dan Sickles took it as a matter of rank that he didn't have to introduce himself, and offered a self-assured smile. "Not much to worry about. Stuart's men are miles to the north."

The general shot a glance both imperious and disarming at Hardie. "I need a ride. I've got to get back to my troops—unless there is some objection?" With the certainty there could be none and without waiting for a reply, he sat down, pulled out a pack of cigars, and offered them.

"Nay objection at aw, gin'ril," said Hardie, waving off the cigars with a forced smile. "Fitzpatrick and I shall be glad o' your company. It will help us forget the heat."

Fitzpatrick kept silent as Sickles told one joke after another, smutty old saws from the music halls. He marveled at Hardie's skill, keeping up his end of the banter, telling polite Scottish stories, avoiding war talk and any allusion to their mission.

Sickles hinted he knew all about it. He had spent the day visiting friends in the Congress and calling at the War Office and the White House, mentioning by name the men he'd seen. He pretended to complete knowledge of events in Washington City, as well as in New York, where he had spent several days "rallying support for the Union."

He thinks everything is going perfectly, Fitzpatrick mused. *His friend in the War Office is certainly not the General-in-Chief. Stanton?*

"The war is a great stimulus to the nation," Sickles said. "Does wonders for our democratic genius. You should see New York. You'd never know we're fighting a war. The galas and the yacht races go on just the same." He spoke as if this were a very fine thing.

No need to tell Sickles anything, thought Fitz. *He'd say he already knew.*

While Hardie did a two-step with Dan Sickles, adding a mite of conversation to every two of the general's, Fitzpatrick took stock. Able-bodied but unfit for troop duty, he was assigned to Washington. This meant long hours of work in campaign season and boredom in winter, dancing with senators' wives and daughters, carrying papers to embassies and the Capitol, attending tea parties, and consorting with dandies who bought their way out of military service but had the temerity to stay in town.

The family wanted him to come home and marry. His fiancée pressed, and her parents had talked to their congressman about a discharge. Fitzpatrick resented the interference. He wanted to do his duty like other men.

Hardie's talk about Meade did not displease him, even if it meant being a mere staff officer. *Thank God, I can sit a horse. They'll accept a man riding around when bullets come.*

Sickles noticed him. "I suppose, young fellow, ah, major, you're on your way back to duty? We've all got to be there for this one.

This is where we show the Rebels what the Union is made of."

"I'm ordered to Washington, sir, with Colonel Hardie."

"And I need him, general," Hardie broke in before Sickles could demand Fitzpatrick be sent to him. Dan Sickles would be hard to refuse on the eve of battle.

The general's deep, dark eyes looked knowingly at each man from under strong eyebrows and a heavy array of face hair. "These are great days to be alive," he said, staring at Fitzpatrick as though weighing up horseflesh. "We'll be busy tomorrow. I'm going to see if I can get some sleep." He stood, walked down the car, took off his coat, and, carefully folding and laying it on a bench beside him, stretched out and dozed as though he had nothing on his mind.

Hardie and Fitzpatrick continued in silence. Neither slept. They were disciplined to the endless hours demanded when the Army of the Potomac was on the move. A cat nap would enhance the exhaustion they lived with day after day.

CHAPTER II

Gettysburg, a college town of 2,400 people, lay on a checkerboard of fences on a fertile greensward a dozen miles into Pennsylvania. Surrounding farms produced grain, fruit, and cattle. In town, small workshops turned out an array from saddlery and candles to ironwork and intricate gadgets. Roads out radiated to bigger places, up to Carlisle and Harrisburg, east to York, south to Frederick and Baltimore, west through steep defiles in the mountains to Chambersburg and Hagerstown. Through these passes teamsters picked their way with care, and soldiers, when they came, looked up anxiously at rocky outcrops.

Reports of Lee's whereabouts were received, and contradicted, hourly. On June 26, men from Ewell's corps came and laid down a heavy requisition for supplies. After prolonged bargaining, they took what they could get and moved north. On the 27th a small cavalry detachment passed through. For the second day in a row local militia quietly disappeared. Rebel troopers got leave to dismount and visit the stores.

Gentlemanly fellows, but filthy, and not awful bright, wrote Flossie Muelheim in her notebook before she went to bed.

When they came into Papa's store, most couldn't read the labels. I had to help, and they wanted everything, specially clothes and shoes. They all talked to me.

It was good Papa was there. He was very angry we had to take Confederate money. For the past three nights we've buried stock in the basement. Hardly anything is left on the shelves. Papa is sure they'll be back, and he wanted Mama and me to go over to Hanover on the train. But the rail bridge is out, and the cars stopped running. A lot of folks have left. Hundreds, I think. Mama fears the battle will be right here. Papa tells stories about wars in the old country that singe our hair.

One of the Rebels saw Henry, our hired man. Very quietly in a corner where the others couldn't hear, he told me, "You better get that nigger outa sight. If the provosts catch him, they'll take him back to Dixie where he belongs. You understand me, Missy?" Fortunately no one saw us.

When I told Papa, he put Henry on our mule and sent him down to Uncle Yokum in Taneytown. It took a lot of arguing to get him to go. He's sweet on Fat Sally across the way, and wanted her to come too, but we didn't dare tell anyone what we were up to.

Henry says Maryland is still a slave state, but he went when I explained what I'd heard. He could tell he'd better go by the way the Rebs looked at him.

Now that Henry's gone, it's the quiet before the storm. The other side of the mountains is busting with Johnny Rebs heading up to Harrisburg. I told Papa they're bound to come here because we've got so many good roads. He huffed, saying women didn't know anything about military matters.

It's plain logic, as we learned from Teacher Schulman. He says girls are smarter than boys sometimes.

George Meade had found the ride back to camp invigorating. Green fields on the banks of the Monacacy glistened fresh from rain, and he could hear birdsong. Goldfinches and buntings darted in and out of bushes along with towhees and sparrows. The heat of the day softened with the sinking sun.

He rode onto a small knoll to survey the landscape, using skills honed over years as a survey leader to assess gradient, contour, elevation, and watercourses. From his tunic he drew a silver watch. *Sundown will be quarter before eight. We can fight on a clear dry day until quarter to nine.* Meade pursed his thin lips, pulled a hand through his thin beard and took a deep breath.

His journey was fruitless. No sign of the Commanding General. At headquarters north of Frederick, no one knew anything. Hooker had circulated no plans. No one knew where Bobby Lee was. His men were out there, somewhere.

Lee is heading north for the Susquehanna. We've got three corps going west to South Mountain. The wrong way! It will take a full day to get them back. He sensed disaster, and so did the men. Everyone knew when a commander lost his grip. The provost marshal said reports of desertion came in hourly. *Hooker's morals are loose. His sense of order is scarcely better.* Meade shuddered, remembering Chancellorsville.

The tents of corps headquarters stood away from the creek and the troop bivouacs. Yet the stench of camp—sweat, horse manure, latrines, coal oil, and burning wood—reached them. Meade handed the reins to an orderly and, after a short conference with the adjutant about orders for the next day, called for food in his tent. There, with paper on his knees, he vented frustration in a note to his wife, his closest confidante. He ate, removed tunic and boots, put his spectacles and watch under the pillow, and lay down on the camp bed.

Worries kept him awake, about Hooker's mindless march and his boisterous henchmen who couldn't see a military problem if it bit them. He worried about changes. *Who would take over? Reynolds? Would he pay for the disaster? Would there be charges and courts-martial?* Gas rose in his stomach. He wondered about sleep, something he needed but failed to get during a campaign.

As night deepened, breathing came smoother. The hobgoblins dispersed, and he dozed off. Lying on his side, with knees drawn up to the edge of the bed, Meade's tall body extended over the end. Aroused in the night, he heard noises. A horse neighed in the distance, a common waking sound. Muffled voices approached. An argument? A stranger was in camp! Lanterns skewed shadows on the tent walls.

Meade rolled onto his back, eyes open. The campsite was unfamiliar. He blinked to clear his mind of a troubling dream. Reality surged back. *How will it end? Surely, in disaster up some country lane.*

The sounds grew louder, heavy footfalls, voices speaking with authority. Light flooded in as the tent flap opened. "General Meade," said a soft Scot's burr. "I'm Hardie from the War Office. My apologies, sir, for rousing you so early."

Meade sat up, disoriented but recognizing the grinning man in odd, civilian clothes as an aide to the Secretary of War. *What was he doing here dressed like this? At this hour?* He managed a formal, "Good morning, colonel."

"Good mornin'," chuckled Hardie, "I've come to give ye a bit of trouble."

Meade missed the humor, if any was intended, and guessed some strange working of army politics had put him under arrest. "My conscience is clear, colonel." He searched for his spectacles and watch. "I'm ready for whatever comes."

"Of course, general. I've come to give ye an order from the President. He has appointed you Commanding General of the Army of the Potomac." Hardie held out Lincoln's letter, "As of receipt, sir."

Meade perched spectacles on his nose, reached for it and stared at the signature, "A. Lincoln." *Bona fide, so was Hardie. Extraordinary!* He repressed the memory of his dream. *Margaret will be pleased. Maybe she's the only one who will be.*

Hardie hooked the lantern on a tent pole while Meade reached for his soiled blue tunic. The colonel explained that Hooker's sudden resignation had forced his midnight mission.

"You made good time, colonel." Meade sat on the bed buttoning his coat. "How did you find your way?"

"The War Office arranged a special car and sent young Major Fitzpatrick as my guide. He served with you at Fredericksburg. His family owns a property in this area."

Meade shook his head to banish errant thoughts and reached for a bowl of warm water and a towel handed through by an orderly. "That's all very well, Hardie, but surely there are others better suited than I? What about Reynolds?" Meade completed a cursory toilette, ran a comb once through his beard, and stood up stooping, his soft cone hat pushing against the tent top. "Colonel, I must wire Halleck and beg to be excused. I know nothing of the army's whereabouts, not a jot about Hooker's plans, and less about Lee."

Hardie smiled. "They've anticipated you, general. What I gave you is the President's direct order. I am to escort you to Hooker's camp and witness the change of command. They're a bit nervous in Washington City just now."

"I understand that at least." Meade pulled back the flap, his head bowed so he could pass unobstructed, and motioned for Hardie to precede him. "Well, I'm hardly dressed for it," he said standing at last at a full six-three with hands on his sword belt in the early light.

"I suppose, then, I've been tried and condemned without a hearing." He grimaced at the awkward eloquence, and wondered if this was the way he was supposed to sound.

Odors of brewing coffee drifted from the mess where Fitzpatrick waited with others, including Meade's son George, who served as an aide. Hardie introduced Fitzpatrick while the staff stood around smiling and proud. At a long plank table they sat down to an early cup and yesterday's bread as the day grew brighter. Meade warmed, joking with officers he was about to leave, and gave final orders to the adjutant. He spoke to Fitzpatrick about Fredericksburg and Philadelphia and was glad George Jr. seemed to know him.

When their general rose to leave, the officers filed slowly past, shaking hands. Baldy stood saddled and waiting. Meade mounted. The adjutant stood close by and saluted stiffly, face taut. "Just go on as you've been, general, and we'll all be right."

Meade reached down and said, "Thank you," showing as much emotion as he dared.

"George, you'll ride with us," he shouted over his shoulder. "I think I need a witness. You can talk with Major Fitzpatrick. Perhaps he's ready to come back to us."

Hardie stifled a smirk as he checked his stirrups. The small party trotted off, and, as they wove through camp, soldiers lined the way cheering and waving.

"He may look like a goggle-eyed old scarecrow," said 3d Sgt. Liam O'Bannion of Company D, 12th New York Infantry, waving his cap, "but he knows how to fight men, and he don't waste 'em. We can be glad of that much."

As Meade rode toward headquarters, the last of the Army of Northern Virginia were crossing into Pennsylvania. Ewell's corps of 20,000 men approached the Susquehanna, and Stuart rode through central Maryland. Reports of these movements had reached Meade and others through unofficial sources. From Hardie he learned the War Office knew little more. He glanced frequently toward the mountains and Sharpsburg. One year ago, he had taken over

Hooker's corps from its wounded commander and fought Lee's men to a draw over there on Antietam Creek.

"It will be bloody again," he told Hardie, as much to relieve the tension as to think. "Lee will attack because he has to. He can't stay up here long without it, not as long as we can fight him. He must destroy us. He's looking for the *coup de grâce*."

Fitzpatrick and George Jr. rode well behind, talking about mutual friends. George seemed to look up to the older man, and Fitz was glad to talk of home, but astonished to hear George knew he was engaged.

"It was not announced," Fitz said firmly. "It's one of those war situations. Casualties mount. Risks are high. I've been wounded twice. I begged off the announcement. But both families want a wedding. So does Mable, of course. There's something about war makes women want marriage. Makes no sense to me. I don't want to leave a widow with a baby at her breast."

Passing through Frederick they saw scores of men sodden with drink sitting dazed, some lying down, on the wooden sidewalks. Provosts tried to round them up, but there were too few police and too many drunks. A good number had to be carried off in ambulances. Out from the edge of town they passed a park of Conestoga wagons brightly decorated with signs proclaiming "Alice's Special Services." Women waved from the backs of the wagons.

Doing his best to look away, George blushed. "Father will put them at a distance. The provosts are going to be busy. Of that you can be sure. He doesn't believe sin and fighting mix, a point on which he disagrees with General Hooker."

A radiant redhead in a black velvet dress bowed to show her bosom. She was young, probably still in her teens. She eyed Fitzpatrick, and bestowed a provocative smile as he passed near. "Come back and see me, major," she warbled, toying with a yellow silk handkerchief as she swayed her hips. Fitz blushed deep red, lifted a hand a few inches from the saddle, waved, and immediately spurred his mount. When he looked around, he found George laughing.

"Hie thee from temptation, soldier," he mocked with unconcealed delight. "Or father will never speak to you again."

General Hooker received them in full dress as they rode up, dour yet trying to chaff about passing on a thankless burden and how glad he was to shed it. Slowly, he read Halleck's letter assigning him to Baltimore. "I suppose under the circumstances that's a good place to be." He forced a smile and hastened to offer refreshment.

Meade refused politely, thinking he meant whiskey. Hooker stared at him as if he were a schoolboy and snorted, "Then I suppose we'd better get through the formalities."

Meade motioned George along with Hardie and Fitzpatrick to follow into a large tent where headquarters staff waited stiffly to receive their new leader. Butterfield, the chief, arrived late, spouting apologies.

Hooker and his men tried to pinpoint the location of seven Union corps and estimate Lee's strength and position. Chewing on a cigar, he confidently put the Rebel force at 100,000, though he admitted to hearing reports it might be as small as 80,000. Three Rebel corps had been definitely spotted, plus Stuart's cavalry. A long string of wagon trains was moving up from Winchester across the Potomac and up the valley on the other side of the mountains. Farmers coming to market gave them most of this information. Under prodding from Meade, Hooker admitted he wasn't sure where Lee was.

"Perhaps Stuart's on one of his larks," suggested Meade, "avoiding Lee as well as the Yankees? Have you seen Rebel cavalry reconnoitering our positions?"

Hooker's rambling answers suggested he knew little about Stuart at all. He spoke of Lee's "intentions." "He sure isn't going to go into Harrisburg. He doesn't have bridging equipment. We know that much. The locals will burn the bridges over the Susquehanna, and that'll force him to turn south, probably toward Baltimore." He laughed as he relit a dark brown cigar. "Wouldn't that be a turn?"

Meade knew ground. He demurred. "When the water goes down, he can cross at the shallows above the city."

Hooker grumbled, puffed, and laughed as though inspired, "Well, with the amount of rain we've just had that isn't likely." His chuckle indicated this was a great gaffe. A few officers smirked. Chief of Staff Butterfield joined but stopped, looked embarrassed, and turned away.

No one wanted the conference to last. Meade understood Hooker would offer very little. The man was bitter. He had no precise plan, no strategy, some intelligence worth the name, but worst of all, no accurate maps. Lee's force was about the same as his own, or maybe larger. The number would have to be determined carefully. He jotted in a small notebook and nodded to the Chief of Staff. Hooker brought in two personal orderlies, introduced them, and took his leave. Officers followed to say farewell.

Meade asked Butterfield to remain behind. From him he rapidly confirmed an impression of the slack state of headquarters. The two had never been on easy terms. Meade was church-going Philadelphia of established stock. Butterfield, a well-dressed New Yorker, man of business, and a smooth article. Meade told him he must stay in his post for the coming battle, and mentioned reassignment afterward. He didn't tell him that even before coming to headquarters, he had quickly offered the job to someone else who had refused.

Nor could he bring himself to offer the vacancy in the 5th Corps. Taking off his spectacles, he said, "At the rate things are moving, we could all be in other jobs in a few weeks." A few months before, Meade had asserted seniority to snatch the 5th from Butterfield's hands. He expected restitution. Meade was firm. The Chief of Staff didn't hide his disappointment.

Clarissa Scott, head of the women's section of the Sanitary Commission, was delighted with Meade's appointment. The women despised Hooker's louche ways. Some, before the war, graced the best salons of Philadelphia, New York, and Boston, and they welcomed a man of kindred spirit. Her able assistant, Fannie Morris, she knew, felt the same. *Why shouldn't she? She'd known George Meade like an older sister since he was in swaddling clothes. She'll be a great help getting him to help us.*

But still she was wary. Fannie was a woman who had refused offers of marriage to follow her own restless spirit. She spoke, and often acted, like a man, unlike Clarissa, whose husband was years in the grave. *She'll be running the army if she can.* Clarissa sat rolling bandages from a wicker basket by the side of a square, stubby wagon that served in combat as an ambulance and at other times as their home.

"I suppose you'll want to call on General Meade first thing, dearest Fannie? I shall make a list of things we need. The army can certainly get farmers to give us space to lay out the wounded." She kept her eyes on the basket, waiting.

"I'll give him a little time," said Fannie, sitting a few feet away, writing a note of congratulations to Margaretta Meade. It was bright midday. They had learned of the change hours before.

"Lord, I can think of a thousand things he won't be able to do anything about." Clarissa looked up. "I hope you don't have too many notions about running the war. Maybe I ought to go with you." A smile rearranged the features of her gaunt face.

Fannie chuckled. A large woman with large black eyes beneath abundant hair piled on her head, she radiated both purpose and energy—one of many reasons Clarissa tolerated her unconventional ways. "Never fear. I'll stay on safe ground." If she had other thoughts, she hid them.

"We're going to have ten thousand wounded," Clarissa went on. "We can assume the running water will be fouled. They'll be hardly any to wash with, much less drink." She looked up at a large dark cloud above the tree.

Fannie finished her note and began to put her writing things away. "I just wish the Almighty would leave more men with their full limbs. All the surgeons know is cut and saw, as if it were part of the compact, a completion like a rite at the end of a battle."

Clarissa put down her bandages to appraise her friend. Fannie's reach always went well beyond the ideas of others. Who knew what she'd think up? "My dear," she said, "patience."

CHAPTER III

George Meade went by the book. Everything else relied on trusting men he barely knew, who probably resented him or played roles in the intrigues that dogged the army. He hated schemers, but with a fight coming he could not make changes he would like. They had to move on. Within hours of taking command on June 28, he took over the army and laid out plans to stop Robert E. Lee. He needed everyone. The Army of the Potomac was half the strength McClel-lan led to the Peninsula a year before. Trained veterans were leaving in droves.

Command was a problem. His seven corps each had more than 10,000 soldiers, half as many as Lee's three, but still large enough to be slow-moving and cumbersome. Commanders like Dan Sickles might not know the book, but their men obeyed. In an army where orders went astray, that was vital. Sickles was an undependable opportunist, a military upstart like Butterfield and the rest of the Hooker gang. But few were complete incompetents, and he could not remove them and meet Lee at the same time.

Meade watched Hooker's entourage mount and move off. *The President and Halleck may have faith in me, and bless them for it. Yet I can't play God with my peers.* He returned to the tent and began to pore over reports with Butterfield. Several corps commanders came to congratulate him and wait for orders. The Chief of Staff hurried adjutants to and fro. Maps were no more than sketches showing rail lines, a few roads and streams, and no topography.

Meade looked for ground, rising ground where he could mount a defense. "Lee can't leave us in his rear and keep moving north," he told visitors. "He'll have to attack because he can't tarry without a military decision. If I know anything about Bobby Lee, he'll be looking for the chance to destroy us and win the war. We must find good ground. Depend upon on it. If we stay in his rear, he'll have to come back to us."

The generals nodded. It meant less risk. No one wanted another assault against ready positions like Fredericksburg. They knew what entrenched men with massed rifles could do to an army advancing over open ground.

Meade spelled out his immediate plan. "We will fan out northward with Reynolds on the left nearest Lee and the mountains. The rest will take position on a line running east with John Sedgwick and our largest corps on the right covering the route to Baltimore." The visitors nodded.

The tent stood in a small clearing shaded by high willow oaks and maples. As the day advanced, robins and meadowlarks took cover, green field grasses faded, and clear, bright shades of early summer gave way to a dull haze. Clouds of flies buzzed, a common nuisance like the smell of camp. Inside, the air was sodden and still, stifling to men in stiff woolen uniforms.

"This tropical heat will slow the march," Reynolds said as they left together for the noon mess. He had dressed carefully to honor his friend, though nothing could exalt his worn, dark blue uniform. The soft cone hats they both wore to shut out the sun's rays made them look like walking scarecrows.

"The men won't think about heat once the fight starts," Meade answered. "We're going to be on open ground in plain sight of each other. That will grip their minds." They went on in silence, knowing each other's thoughts.

He was a good host, but took no more than a glass of milk. He would gladly avoid meals if he could.

By nightfall, Meade had set the line of march, reorganized his cavalry, given emphatic orders to clean the drunks and whores out of Frederick, reviewed all available intelligence with Colonel Sharpe, and sent the engineers to scout a defense line to the north of town.

He sat alone in the tent. It was nearly dark when he called in Fitzpatrick. An oil lamp shining on his narrow spectacles highlighted a crook in his nose. At his table he sat upright, bareheaded, face drawn, scarcely moving the papers in his hands. By now he was tired, and spoke without a smile.

"I need men with brains and discretion, major. You went to the university, I understand?" He didn't wait for an answer. "You know about headquarters and the crotchets of generals. You probably know more about the intrigue in this camp than I do."

Fitzpatrick nodded, and found it frightening not to see the general's eyes.

"I'm going to gamble on you, Fitzpatrick. George says you're a good man and will be loyal. I don't have to tell you what a fix we're in. We fight with an arm tied behind our back, while the South is deadly serious. Some of our generals lack confidence. Others think war is a game. We could lose it all in a day." Meade was rail thin, skin pasted tight to his skull.

"I will receive information from time to time that I will entrust to you. For you only and for whomever I direct. No one else. Some will come to you first." Meade paused. "I'm not thinking about camp gossip, but about military intelligence.

"Colonel Sharpe will make reports. Many no doubt will be very good. But when it comes to using them, this army has never known how to winnow the wheat from the chaff. Were you on the Peninsula?"

"Yes, sir, with the 6th Pennsylvania."

"Reynolds's old brigade." Meade looked away as if staring into a campfire with his mind wandering. "You remember how McClellan kept calling for troops, saying he was outnumbered. It was absolute bunkum, of course. I think he knew it. Pinkerton gave him high estimates of Rebel strength. It suited his purpose in the end. Helped him skedaddle." Meade laughed suddenly and turned to share the joke.

"One of the good things Hooker did was organize the flow of intelligence. We know that the bulk of Lee's army is west of the mountains, though not exactly where and in what strength.

"I want to judge for myself when and where to act. I've told Sharpe you will be working with me. There will be reports coming from irregular sources. There always are. You will receive them and inform me. We'll let Sharpe know in time, but I don't want anything significant to be overlooked. Even the best of systems needs a check. Do you understand what I'm saying, major?"

Fitz nodded, "Yes, sir."

"You'll need to be close by. You'll share a tent with George." Meade smiled slightly and hesitated. "You've doubtless heard I have a terrible temper." He waited, and Fitz smiled.

"Alas, that rumor is true. In the tension we endure, I am sometimes consumed with rage, usually at stupidity. I suppose outbursts from generals are to be expected. Mine may be worse than others. But when I'm wrong, I admit it, and I often am." Meade laughed, and his face briefly lost its skeletal look.

"When the fight comes, you will ride by me. Others can dash off with messages. I'm counting on you because you're the best man available. You may think it's *faute de mieux.*" Meade, still smiling, watched Fitzpatrick's expression.

"Ah, you know the phrase," he said. The interview was over.

Dan Sickles stopped in the afternoon to pay his respects and rode on. By the end of the day, the 3d Corps, following Meade's orders, moved from west of town to camp 10 miles north. Sickles halted his men in a mile-long formation to hear the adjutants read out, regiment by regiment, the orders changing command. He rode along the line watching them, making no comment, then left for the mess tent. Staff officers joined him loudly condemning the loss of Hooker.

"General Halleck wants control in the field," Sickles told them, sitting relaxed by a table covered in white linen. "Down in Washington that's all anyone talks about. Lincoln and Stanton are not entirely pleased with Old Brains. If this new man don't win a resounding victory, there'll be another change, and jolly quick."

The officers nodded, looking with awe on their leader, who had special access to the powers in the capital and who, many believed, would be next in line. Few knew anything about Washington City, until war came. The bugles and the roll of drums, the gunfire, and the drama of battle had changed them. They had left humdrum lives in small towns and hard-worked farms. Sickles, a magic man, had showed them the world.

Life in the 3d Corps was somewhat different below headquarters level. The division commanders, with 5,000 men each, were divided. Birney in the 1st was a political appointee and a Sickles man, no admirer of George Meade. Andrew Humphreys, Military Academy 1831, was a staunch friend. The brigade commanders, with more than 1,000 men, were less involved, and the colonels in charge of regiments were prominent men from their own states and chiefly involved with the affairs of their troops.

In the ranks of the 3d, views varied. "Don't like these here changes," said Sergeant Tucker of the 71st New York, as he paced along staking out the bivouac, "If the generals can't get it straight, how in Hell are we gonna do it?"

Corporal Edmondson, at his side, said he agreed, and so did 3d Corporal O'Hara. "But old Lee," said Private Macintosh, behind them marking sites with a bayonet, "he's awful smart, and he did catch Joe Hooker nappin'."

"Don't you believe all that stuff," said his sergeant. "If they'd listened to Dan Sickles and Fightin' Joe, we'd a whupped 'em. Lee ain't no seven-foot giant. He's a little bitty guy."

Nor at army headquarters was the Chief of Staff happy. All day he itched to get away to think his own thoughts. In the quiet of sunset he found time to walk off into the hardwood forest.

A newsman from the *New York World* followed. "Ain't you the indispensable man now, General Butterfield?"

"Not exactly, Mr. Brennan." Butterfield stopped dead, standing like a statue, and spoke straight ahead as if addressing the trees. "General Meade knows what he's about. He's retaining me because there's a battle coming. No time to change."

"But you must concede, sir, we'll all miss Fighting Joe Hooker," said the reporter, trying to keep the statue talking. "Has Meade got the fire in his belly? He looks cold and uppity to me."

"I'd say he's more a book man," said Butterfield, at last looking at his pursuer in his rumpled brown suit and black bowler hat. "You won't tell the truth entirely if you call him an aristocrat. That's not all that makes him tick. He's like a scholar.

"Fire? Maybe not much fire." Butterfield put a thoughtful hand to his chin. "Maybe you're right there. We'll know better when we see if he takes the aggressive. Seeing the great chance, that's what made Hooker."

"And you think we may have lost the spark with this new schoolmaster? Is that it, sir?" Brennan took a pad out and began scribbling.

"Now, Brennan, don't put words in my mouth. We'll have to wait and see." Butterfield again looked away. A smile told Brennan what he wanted to know.

★ ★

General Lee sat at a field desk outside his tent at Confederate headquarters near Chambersburg. His man Junius brought in the evening tray. "Fine English tea, Mars' Robert. That's good for your stomach."

"Thank you, Junius," said Lee. He was pensive, having just received a group of local citizens complaining about theft from their homes, horses taken, even sleigh bells. His men could not get enough of the North. The temptations sapped discipline.

In many ways the march into Pennsylvania was a treat—plenty of fresh food, stores with things to buy, and a population usually sullen and resistant but not always hostile. *Didn't Ewell this morning receive a full report from friendly locals on the defenses of Harrisburg?*

The food was a bit rich. In his mid-fifties, Lee had to watch his diet. He had disciplined himself to Spartan meals. Good food tempted him, made him ill, and held him in camp when he needed to ride about. He watched Junius shuffle away and blessed him silently.

Harrisburg, the state capital, was his for the taking. What would he do with a city full of Yankees? *Where is the Union Army? They're bound to be half again as many as we are.*

A special courier had brought a telegram reporting Meade's appointment. Lee remembered him as a junior mapmaker on board the *Petrita* under enemy guns at Vera Cruz. *If the Mexicans had been better marksmen, they could have bagged us all—Meade, McClellan, and General Scott, too.* He sighed. *We were all brethren in peril together.*

A noise distracted him. Lieutenant General Longstreet, cigar in hand, strode out of the dark followed by a civilian. Lee frowned.

"General, this is Harrison, a scout and a patriot. He's been

41

behind the enemy lines and seen things we need to know about. The Union Army are just over the mountains."

"You've seen their formations?" Lee was caught between caution of the man and the force of his message.

Harrison, in a buckskin vest, filthy linen shirt, black pants, and torn riding boots, reeked of a spent horse. "Yes, sir, the lead corps this morning, several of them, were the other side of South Mountain Pass. But they turned back. Must be some response to the new commander." He pointed toward a map on the desk. "Some of their cavalry has moved north toward Taneytown and Emmitsburg. Headquarters is at Frederick, but I don't have any reason to believe they're going to stay there."

He speaks too well for a farmer or a common soldier, yet he's no gentleman. Where did Longstreet find this man, and can we believe him?

"He uses his talents," said Longstreet, a usually taciturn man, almost ebullient about his protégé. "He's an actor. This very morning, general, he mixed with the Yankees to find out what's going on. The change of command has sown confusion in the ranks, set the officers to doubting their commanders."

"You say morale is low?" Lee ventured.

"One knows when men are frightened, general." Harrison had no difficulty with words. "Mr. Lincoln did them no favor by withdrawing Hooker. The Yankee soldiers had faith in him."

"And not in Meade?" Lee concluded.

"No, sir, they don't know who he is. Some call him the Snapping Turtle because he gets angry at his staff, but there seem to be few who know the sobriquet."

"Thank you, Mr. Harrison, you have rendered a service." Lee nodded. "I need to speak with General Longstreet."

"Certainly, general." Harrison bowed and departed. Lee motioned to stools, and the two sat in the summer evening. A coal oil lamp hung from the tent poll below the tent fly where bugs circled.

"I couldn't see his face in the light," said Lee. "Do you believe this man? Is he a paid spy?"

"In a sense he is, general. He's been scouting the enemy since we left the Rappahannock. He has abilities as a scout we don't often find—well spoken, uses different dialects. He's been on stage with the Booth family, a dissimulator by his calling, perhaps, but loyal and brave. I trust his word. The Yankees are bound to have moved up by now."

"Stuart and his cavalry may be trapped on the other side of them," said Lee with a frown. "The detachment he left us hasn't reported a thing from the passes. Either they're useless, or your man is exaggerating. Still, I take your point. Washington will protect itself. They appointed Meade, a reliable officer—and now they press. Cautious and in order, I'll wager."

Lee stood and walked into the tent to get the map. "If your man is correct, we have only a short time to bring the army together. I'll recall Ewell, bringing him down the other side of the mountains, so we don't have all three corps using the same roads." Lee put the map on a table and leaned over it.

"Gettysburg, where the roads converge, is due east over the pass. We will concentrate there with our line of supply running back here to Chambersburg. This valley will remain free of enemy as long as we're in force."

He stood erect. "I don't know whether I'd trust your man at first sight, General Longstreet, but he's told us things that are probably true and, as you say, we need to know. I am indebted, sir."

Longstreet saluted formally. He had put away his cigar.

Henry Prediger did not ride all the way down the Taneytown Road. Except for leaving Sally, he was not unhappy to leave. He had work to do in other places. As one of the few Negroes in the area who could read and write, he thought he might have a role to play in the coming fight, and if the Muelheims were kind enough to send him off on a mule, that was all the better.

At a fork below the round rocky hills south of town, he reined right and took a narrow track west toward the mountains. It was nearly midnight when he reached a small cabin by a few apple trees and a tiny garden where tomato plants and a few short corn stalks showed promise.

Josephus Alexander came out, shotgun in hand, as soon as he heard the cracking of dry pine branches he had laid on the road.

"It's you, Henry. I was hopin' you'd come."

He dismounted stiffly. "The Muelheims got me away. I was lucky, but I couldn't bring Sally. She's stuck, and if the Rebs find her they'll take her away like they always do."

Josephus tied the mule to a stump. "There's a bunch they took over in the Valley. They all goin' down as soon as the bastards go back. We all treated as runaways even if we've got papers. They don't accept anyone up here. Maybe they round people up just to make sure we don't do nothin'. But I don't reckon they could know about our operations yet."

The word "operations" sounded grand and very military. Henry grinned, as Josephus put out his hand, shook his and pulled him into the house. "Let's don't spend time frettin' over what we can't do much about. Come on in an' set a spell," he said. "I'll fetch some cider."

Henry was glad to rest. The mule was slow, the saddle worn through, and his legs barely responded as he walked inside. He didn't know Josephus hardly at all, but the man had secretly organized the black people in these parts, and seemed to know what he was doing. Someone said he'd studied war down in Virginia before he got away. Henry felt safe in the cabin. "The Rebs keep comin'," he said. "I bet they use the Cashtown pass. I don' know much about fightin', but it seems that's the way it's gotta work."

Josephus poured two earthen mugs of cider, and handed one to Henry. "We're getting pretty well set up over there, using the old hiding places. You'd be surprised what our people can do. Old Mars Robert don't know how bad his menservants wants freedom. They takin' some big risks."

Henry sat and took a long pull. "I'm supposed to be goin' to Taneytown, and maybe I'll get there sometime tomorrow. I'd bet that mule the Union men are goin' to be comin' up the road soon. I was thinkin' I might try to sign with 'em if I can get anywhere near the general. No good talkin' to anybody but the boss man."

Josephus reached down in the cushions of an aged chair. Digging deep, he brought up a flat leather pouch. "If you think you can reach the Commanding General, get him to look at this. The man who took it would be flogged out of his skin if they caught him. It could help the Yankees. And be your way to a job with 'em." He handed the case to Henry.

Carefully undoing the webbing, Henry slid out two sheets of official-looking paper with a printed head, THE CONFEDERATE STATES OF AMERICA, HEADQUARTERS, THE ARMY OF NORTHERN VIRGINIA. Below were the names of generals and units—corps, division, brigade, and regiment—together with the numbers fit for duty on June 25, 1863.

"They calls that an 'order of battle,'" said Josephus. "It should be worth its weight in gold to the Yankee general, or so folks with General Lee say."

Henry wasn't ready to answer, though he quickly figured that, if Mr. Josephus said so and the numbers were right, the Yankees would know how to use them.

"From what I hear, one side doesn't know much about the other," said Josephus. "That piece of paper should give the Union a big advantage, if you can get 'em to take it."

CHAPTER IV

Early in the morning of June 29, Union troops marched north in columns two and three miles long well to the side of the muddy roads. An endless caravan of supply wagons struggled alongside through the ruts, while in between fast-moving horsemen rode up and down. Meade understood how the men felt about pointless countermarches, and hoped now to give them a sense of moving to battle. The thought of imminent action was with him night and day. His generals seemed to have caught it, but, *Can they carry it to the men? They have to feel excitement more than exhaustion.*

An orderly came to his tent. "A lady come to camp, sir, just outside. She asked me to give you this." He handed over a clean engraved calling card bearing in script the name, "Miss Fannie Alice Morris," and in the lower case at the left, "First and Third Tuesdays."

The Commanding General jumped up with a smile transfiguring his gaunt face and terrifying the orderly as he towered over him. Lifting the flap, Meade said, "It's only Monday, Fannie, but I am home to you."

"Thank you, general, you've always been a good boy," laughed the lady, bouncing past the wide-mouthed orderly.

"I see nobody's become familiar with you, George. I suppose a little awe is what the army needs just now." She draped herself over a camp chair, lost to sight in the folds of her skirt, and pulled knitting needles from her bag.

"I am delighted to see you, Fannie," Meade laughed, "as long as it doesn't utterly destroy my authority."

"That's what I've come to talk to you about, your authority.

Clarissa thinks I'm asking you for help. I've made you a list in her behalf." She reached again into her bag, and tossed a packet of papers onto his desk. "What I'm here to discuss is much more interesting, namely, George Gordon Meade's future beyond next week."

"You see me how I am, Fannie, I couldn't be happier. This is what He meant me to do, I think. Why should you be so concerned, you, who, alone here, knew me as a child?"

"Precisely, George, you're too nice for this position. You'll let men like Sickles dance around you, and you keep that viper Butterfield in your nest. They'll destroy you!" Fannie pointed a knitting needle at him. "And look at those cracker crumbs in your beard. You haven't brushed it out in a week."

Meade put his hand to his chin.

"You've got three possible paths, George. First, Lee defeats you, and you'd be better off dead. That's how you'd feel."

Meade nodded, thought about reaching for a cigar, and decided not to.

"Second," she pressed. "You win, but you win like McClellan and don't pursue. You don't destroy the Rebels. Lincoln will moan that you might as well have lost. The cannibals in Congress will do their dance, and a search will begin for yet another new man. They're not used to you and don't know you. So why should they be faithful?"

Fannie was absolutely right. She told a truth he hated to hear. His worst fear was to win without a military decision. Nothing would be resolved, and the war would go on as before. Senator Wade and his Committee on the Conduct of the War would effectively court-martial him.

"Third," Fannie raced on, knitting rapidly and looking up at him after each declaration, "and this is easily the most interesting, you destroy Lee and become our second George Washington."

"I have no ambition to be other than I am," said Meade chuckling. "I intend to destroy Lee's army. Consequences will have to look out for themselves. I have no interest in politics."

"That's all very well, George. If you do destroy Lee, you will be *sans pareil*. Politicians will come to you. Lincoln himself will beat a path to your door. You won't know exactly what to do about all of them, but like a child in the water you'll survive well enough."

Meade knew such ideas were hidden in his mind and begged for examination. "And you propose, Fannie?"

"I've thought about this a good deal, George. It's not often I am privileged to give important advice," she grinned and looked up at him. "I propose that you prepare for victory. If you don't plan, you won't have it, and if you're not ready, you'll fail as surely as if Lee shot you with a revolver. I am not only talking about the military side. That part is up to you." She sat back and held out her work to look at it.

"I have every confidence you will win," she spoke softly now, knitting again slowly, "and when that happens, the public will want to hear anything you say. *In fine*, George, you'll need to know what to say, whom to speak to, and how to say it." Fannie stopped to fix him in her sight.

"Journalists are hardly your cup of tea. From what I hear, you'd rather talk to a scorpion than one of them. You can't avoid the press, George, and you'd best take the initiative. Carry the battle to them." She grinned with enthusiasm. "I have a man, Mr. Meyer of *The New York Times*. He's reliable. He wants to work with you. He can guide you so you don't put a foot wrong."

The general leaned back in his camp chair and crossed his long legs, thinking about things he'd shunted aside in the rush to battle. Seconds passed while Fannie's needles made the only noise. "You speak the truth, as always, Fannie. I can't keep this command if I make enemies." He paused a full minute looking down at his knees. "But these newspaper people are so persistent. They ask about personal things or military secrets when I've got to be about my business. And I swear I can never think what to say.

"Hooker would tell them bad jokes, josh, and talk the worst brag about how the war will be over tomorrow." Meade sat straight up and began to make wide sweeps in the air with his hands. "He'd carry on for hours with them over whiskey and cigars. I can't do that. I have nothing in common with these men. They have nothing to tell me, and I naught for them."

"You're going to have to learn, George." She frowned. "When you win, you'll be tempted to think you can do what you wish. But that's not so. You can't get by with men like Captain Biddle and Major Fitzpatrick, though the last one knows the world a bit. You'll become a creature of the public's imagination. You must learn to speak to them, or they will make you into something you don't want to be."

Meade found this terrifying, and stared at Fannie. Again the tent was silent. *Everything has its price*, he thought.

"All right," he said reluctantly, "Bring on your man. I hope he doesn't tell me a joke first off."

The light of late morning lit up the tent walls tinting them a soft yellow orange. Fannie rose, glowing in triumph. "I'll warn him. I have him with me." She rustled out.

Meyer, fiftyish, wearing a brown bowler, a soiled brown wool suit, and a chocolate vest with a gold watch chain hanging across it, followed Fannie carefully and correctly. "I am very pleased to meet you, Herr General."

Meade waved him to a bench by the tent wall. "How long have you been with *The New York Times*?"

"Five years, Herr General. I came in '48 from Köln, or Cologne as you say. I was apprenticed in Germany."

"I don't quite understand what you and Miss Morris propose."

"I begin as a journalist, Herr General, writing a story about your life to now. You will see how I work. There won't be any quotation except what you approve. That would be the start. Then, I advise you on how to talk to my colleagues. But I will not judge them. That would be unethical, I think. Maybe later, if an arrangement can be reached."

Meade's mind raced ahead. He was not comfortable on this ground, but he knew where his powers lay. "You mean if I made you a personal aide, or something like that?"

Fannie rose, beaming. He knew what to do now. She left with Meyer in train, as the general said to him, "Look me up after mess this evening. There will be time then."

Meade stood by his table thinking about an encounter with Brennan the night before. The man tried to goad him to talk about attacking Lee. "Would he carry the battle to the enemy? Would he take the aggressive?" *Almost as if someone put him up to it. That would be*

Sickles, if he were in camp. Butterfield?

He could never stop his staff from currying favor with the press. He needed to know how to handle the likes of Mr. Brennan. *Meyer was welcome. Welcome, indeed! God bless good old Fannie!*

Maj. James Edward Van Arsdale Fitzpatrick, Jr. rode ahead with the staff to set up headquarters in Middleburg, a four-hour ride, 20 miles to the north. The general would arrive for evening mess. Three corps were to camp nearby. The roads were clogged with wagons and troops and by frequent backups for detours around huge mudholes left from the rains. He rode past men weighted down with full pack—bedroll, knapsack, haversack, rifle, ammunition box, and their few treasures worth toting in the heat.

Fitzpatrick rode into town and sought out a livery stable, where he left his horse with an obliging colored man, whom he asked for directions. At the city hall he made inquiries. No one had seen the Rebels, though many told tales of "bad things going on over the mountain" and "Rebels on the Susquehanna." Middleburg was a small market town. The few farmers coming in lived no more than a few miles away. None had seen a Rebel, though they gladly repeated stories they had heard.

In mid-afternoon Fitz came back for his horse. The man who met him was not the same who served him earlier. This Negro stood erect and looked directly in his eye and called him "major."

"Are you with the general?" he asked.

Fitz nodded, silent and wary, standing just inside the stable in view of passersby.

"You've been asking around about Lee's army." The Negro spoke quickly, assured but on guard, eyes searching the roadway. "I have information for the Commanding General, I guess that's General Meade. I need to get it directly to him. Can you help me? My name is Henry, Henry Prediger. I come from over in Gettysburg. We had Rebels in town yesterday."

Fitz had never heard a Negro speak to him directly. This man was no household servant. He was uncertain what to do, but decided to take a risk. Manners told him to put out his hand. "I'm Major Fitzpatrick of General Meade's staff. Pleased to meet you."

"And I am pleased to find you," said Prediger with a smile, relieved, not unctuous. "I have information for the general. I must be sure it is safe to pass it on. Perhaps we should move into the stable. It may not be wise to speak here." He stepped back, and led Fitz to the stalls, calling out to the man who had served him earlier. "He's a friend. He knows we have to be careful." His eyes met Fitzpatrick's, waiting.

Fitz nodded again, still unsure, standing next to his horse with a hand on the stirrup.

"What I have to say doesn't come just from me, you understand, major." Henry's voice was soft, almost pleading. "None of us wants General Lee to win, and we are willing to take chances to make sure he doesn't." He paused. Fitz kept silent. He went on. "I have information from the other side of the mountain about General Lee. My people want to be sure it gets to your general. Can you help?"

"He will be here this evening," Fitz said, and caught himself. *What danger is here? No sign.* But he wasn't sure. *The man is earnest.* Fitz raised a hand to hesitate. "Let me think. Will you be here late, after sundown? Is that convenient?"

"I'll wait until Christmas, major, if that suits. But I must keep out of sight. They don't know me here. I look strange to the locals. Johnny Reb got spies too."

"You mean they might think you're a Rebel spy? I doubt that."

The man shook his head and smiled. "I don't know what these folks think. But if they see a strange nigger in town, they're going to talk about it, and that copperhead who hears 'em might send a message. Plenty of 'em around, I expect. We don't exactly trust people in Maryland."

What the Negro said is fair. He can't trust people south of the Line, or maybe even north of it. If Mr. Prediger really has something to tell us about the Rebel army, General Lee's men would want to stop him. Fitz found himself thinking reflexively in ways he'd never done before. *A complicated business, spying.* He didn't know the drill.

"At ten o'clock I'll send an orderly to the stable here asking for the man who took in my horse this morning. Your friend can alert you, and they'll lead you to my tent. When you tell me what you know, and if it appears valuable, I'll take you to the general."

Fitz questioned himself, as he rode off to the old house on the north side of town that was headquarters. *What would a darky know that other men don't? The general will think I'm simple.*

But before evening mess, when he went in to tell the general, Meade gave him full attention. "These are the kinds of things I expect you to bring, Fitzpatrick. You never know who's going to have something. Was he a contraband?"

"No, sir, he was careful not be noticed, but I'd guess he's free." Fitz stood before the rough table that served as the general's desk.

"We've had reports coming from all points today." Meade poked a bony finger in several directions. "Stuart sacked a town twenty miles from Washington. Ewell's Corps has taken Harrisburg. Lee appeared in Harpers Ferry.

"Colonel Sharpe has been able to resolve them, I think. Rebel cavalry, that damned Stuart again, cut our telegraph at Rockville and tore up rail track. The rest is unfounded. On the other hand, what your man says about Gettysburg . . ." Meade paused to brush a fly from the papers before him, and point to the map board on the mantle leaning against the dark stones above a smoke-stained fireplace. "That was the town you mentioned? Sounds about right. If Lee's marching through those passes, he'll have to come there." Meade looked intently at Fitzpatrick to see whether he followed the logic. "Bring your man by late in the evening when camp is quiet."

Three hours later Meade was glad to talk about intelligence. He had just finished a difficult meeting with Sickles, and treated headquarters to an outburst of temper, overheard, he was sure, by adjutants and orderlies, and, God knows who else.

He told Sickles in withering terms that the 3d Corps had bungled miserably, blocking progress of other units on the northward march. Sickles, camped well north of everyone else at daybreak, was ordered to move ahead quickly and leave the road clear for the artillery reserve, another corps, and the headquarters column to follow. But he hadn't got his men through Middleburg even yet, a march of only 10 miles.

Meade didn't want to antagonize a corps commander. He'd have to apologize to the little martinet, not a good man to make an enemy of. He penned a note saying he knew how trying these days were for all of them. He read it over and tore it up. *I'm damned if there's going to be an apology! The man makes blunder after blunder, and no one calls him to order. That's going to change!*

George Jr. gave Fitz a different view widely shared by their colleagues. "Father didn't exactly call him an idiot, but he said in very angry terms Sickles didn't know how to march his men. I don't think the fellow liked it." George laughed. "Father has been furious with him since Chancellorsville, when he told a newspaperman father didn't want to fight. I suspect down not very deep he enjoyed his tantrum. A privilege of power, I suppose."

Flossie Muelheim wrote on the night of June 29:

People prepare for the worst, but talk as if it won't come. The Rebels were polite. But father says the cavalry are gentlemen, and we mustn't expect the same from foot soldiers.

He insists the battle won't come here because soldiers fight in open fields. We hear reports of so many men around us. Yankee cavalry have been to Fairfield. The Rebels are in York to the east and just over the mountains in the west. They seem to be coming this way. We are going to be at the center, or very near, I'm sure of it, and I'm not the only one. Many older women say the same.

But the men outdo each other to show how calm they are. Myrtle's father refused to send away his matched pair of carriage horses, saying no harm will come to them. I pray he is right.

Everyone hopes the Yankees will get here first. People are very excited. We have sold almost all our flags, keeping several to put out of the windows upstairs the minute we see them. I wish they'd hurry.

Mother worries about water. Our well is full, but she says the soldiers will drink it dry and keep it down. We store water in jugs in the basement. It's odd how everything goes down there, if we feel so safe. People say one thing and do the opposite. Everyone is stowing possessions below ground like rabbits.

This afternoon Father got a message from Uncle Yokum asking about Henry. He hasn't appeared. I hope he's all right. Fat Sally is begging the Morgans to send her over to Hanover, but they say there's too much work picking out the kitchen garden and safeguarding property. She's frantic, and doesn't know what to do. No one really believes the Rebels would make her a slave again. I've heard her begging, even screaming. But the Morgans insist. Poor

Sally can't go away unless someone helps her.

Henry Prediger appeared as requested. Briefly, he told Fitzpatrick what he knew, and showed him the document in his leather packet. "My people are careful, major." He sat on a bench in a tent next to headquarters house, and seemed more relaxed in the midst of the federal army. "I don't want to know where it comes from. I might betray somebody. But you can figure it come from a man close to the general, like you but on the other side. They all have slave order- lies, those gen'l'men. Can't break themselves of that habit, can they?"

Fitz smiled. "No, that would probably be hard." He stared at the astonishing sheet of paper. Clearly it was penned by a military clerk, who had carefully written the names of each Confederate corps, its commander, strength, and location on the night of June 25. Under each came the divisions and the brigades with the names of com- manders, their numbers, and campsites. "My God," said Fitz. "If this is correct, it's exactly what we need to know."

"I'm very pleased, believe me," said Henry smiling. "Can we see the general now?"

The outer office was empty. Meade didn't keep them waiting, and shook hands warmly as if it was something he wanted very much to do. "You are welcome," he told Henry and sat down to scan the document, running his finger down the paper line by line, commenting to himself. "This looks to be authentic. May I keep it?"

"I brought it for you, general," said Henry as if the question were unnecessary. He pursed his lips, hesitating. "We have a chain of people who carry messages over. That way no one is ever far away from where he belongs, and no one knows exactly who got it in the first place. I believe it's from Rebel headquarters."

Meade asked Henry to wait outside. "I want you to take this to Colonel Sharpe right away," he told Fitz. "Tell him to examine it carefully, but under no circumstance tell him where you got it. Say only that I believe it could be accurate. The numbers are as low as any we've heard. They alone make it suspect. But, if they are cor- rect line by line, we have gained a great advantage." He put the paper down and turned to Fitz.

"I want you to work with this Negro. Find him a job, possibly with the horses, somewhere where he can move about when he needs to and also meet with you regularly." Meade laughed. "Sharpe will be knocked off his pins when he learns the Negroes are doing this. He told me about a contraband at Chancellorsville who gave him fits. The information was the best we got, but we refused to accept it until it was too late."

They stood in the office-*cum*-dining room under dark rafters which nearly scraped Meade's head. "Major, you understand, this could be the most important information we get. On the other hand, if it's fake, we could be seriously misled. What else does your man say?"

Fitzpatrick's words spewed out. "He says Rebel cavalry from Jones's brigade were in Gettysburg yesterday passing through going north. He thinks they were looking for Stuart."

"You mean Lee thinks Jeb Stuart's lost?" Meade laughed. "That's a bit of a reach. Still, young Jeb is a showman." He liked the idea that the man might come a cropper who made the Union Army look foolish on the Peninsula by riding his troop all the way around it.

Fitz continued, "He also says Lee recalled Ewell's corps from the Susquehanna toward Gettysburg. Longstreet is on the other side of the mountains, and so is Hill, moving east toward the pass."

"That means Reynolds will run into them." Meade stroked his beard. "No, first it'll be cavalry."

"Sharpe must know right away. If our intelligence men think it right, we should inform Reynolds before morning. Trouble is, it will take time to prove your man's numbers." Meade threw up his hands. "Imagine, Stuart has cut our telegraph to Washington, and he himself may be lost. There's so much rumor."

Fitzpatrick left. Meade sat at his desk and smoked a cigar. These were the lowest figures on Lee he'd seen. The old man would conceal weaknesses. He always has. The black man's numbers could be right. Still, we mustn't let people know what we know, or where we got it.

Meade wasn't sure of the size of his force. With stragglers and reinforcements, Union rolls varied widely from day to day. *Bobby Lee has control. Of that I am certain.*

Slowly, he leaned over the desk, put down his cigar, and took up a pen to write Margaretta. He would be reassuring and tell her as much as he dared, remembering the letter might be captured. "By Jeb Stuart, by Jove!" He laughed as he began to write.

Headquarters, Middleburg, Md., June 29, 1863
Mrs. George G. Meade
Philadelphia.

My dear wife,

We are marching as fast as we can to relieve Harrisburg, but have to keep a sharp lookout that the Rebels don't turn around on us and get at Washington and Baltimore in our rear. They have cavalry destroying railroads, etc., with a view to getting me to turn back, but I shall not do it. I am going straight at them, and will settle this thing one way or another. I have made young James Fitzpatrick my aide. Do you see his family?

The men are in good spirits; we have been reinforced so as to have equal numbers with the enemy, and with God's blessing I hope to be successful. Good-bye!

★ ★

At 2:00 a.m. Meade mounted the steep narrow stairs to the dormer for the night, his mind deeply engaged in the events of the day. He expected no sleep as he went through his routine, taking off his boots and tunic, putting pocket watch and spectacles under the pillow and stretching out face-up over the blankets.

Musty air beneath smoke-charred shingles scarcely moved. From the road came the clop clop of hooves, curses of teamsters, and the whine of axles as wagons passed by in the night.

Pain rose in his stomach as Meade pondered Fannie's warning. Rolling onto his side and pulling up his knees, he dozed on and off. The faces of Sickles, Butterfield, and Senator Wade flashed in his head. A thundershower drummed on the roof. He nodded off.

Meade rode up Pennsylvania Avenue toward the Capitol astride a sleek black horse on a raw winter day. A single groom followed him. Ice crusted the branches of maples along the street. Thick mud forced the horse to labor and swerve so that he could barely hold his seat. The Committee on the Conduct of the War wanted him to explain why he failed to destroy the Army of Northern Virginia.

He tossed his body onto the other side of the bed, wakeful. Pain in his head and stomach bade him get up and walk, but, without opening his eyes, he forced himself to stay, and rest. Again he dozed.

In his dream appeared an orator in the House of Representatives, "Why, after all the money we have spent, does the war consume lives and treasure like no other conflagration in the history of man?"

Above and behind the speaker, a giant Chairman Wade peered through binoculars searching for scapegoats. Gas balloons with the faces of members of the committee peered down over the roar of cannon and thud of Minié balls, watching, uncomprehending.

Again he was on horseback, riding up to the massive entrance on the Senate side at a high facade of new white marble, and passed unnoticed through the ornate halls. His corps commanders stood waiting in the anteroom. No one acknowledged him. At the back of the chamber, newspaper men waited with pads and pencils.

"The committee will come to order." Wade thumped the gavel, and spoke without looking at Meade, his witness, alone at a very small table many feet below him. Meade sat in dress tunic wearing short sword and white gloves over muddy field breeches. Eight committee members glared down at him.

Meade talked about strategy. Specters of Sickles, Hooker, and Butterfield appeared, and the chairman bade them sit high with the committee. Sickles walked with a crutch, and greeted them as old friends.

Wade spoke, leering at his colleagues, "General Meade, it seems to me—I'm not a military man—if I had Robert E. Lee flat on his back, I'd finish him off." The other members grinned and chortled. "What were you thinking about, General Meade?"

Wade's head swelled and his eyes came down to Meade's nose.

Foul breath burst from Meade's mouth, and he sat up shaking his head, desperate to get rid of the nightmare. Supply wagons were still passing as the first rays of dawn appeared in the window. Birdsong relieved his mind. His head ached. Meade thought about getting up and drinking tea. "Must rest," he said aloud and lay back down, but pangs on his right side, from his year-old shoulder wound, told him it was useless.

The dream vanished. Meade opened his eyes and shut them again. Morning bugles sounded. One final tableau, half-seen— members of the committee waiting on President Lincoln to present testimony of Meade's enemies, and demand the recall of Fighting Joe Hooker.

CHAPTER V

The provost marshal sent troops to sweep Frederick clean of drunks, stragglers, and skulkers. Officers warned saloons and other places of entertainment, and shut a few.

A sergeant, known to Madame Alice from the old days as a policeman, and from the Old Sod, stopped by with a warning. She quickly took in the meaning of the new order and made a decision. "No use just followin' headquarters," she told her girls. "We'd be asking for trouble. This new muckymuck general would keep us well away, if he knew anything about us at all."

Alice ordered James, her black wagonmaster, to lead the train east along the National Pike, then due north flanking the main body of the Union troops on a little-used road paralleling the track of the 6th Corps toward the Susquehanna. By now she knew as much about military movements as any man in the army. The route put them in the way of good business, and out of sight of the new general. The men were due two months' pay at the end of June. She gambled on a good day or two tumbling them in the wagons before the fight started, and the girls looked forward to the bonanza. A long day's jolting trek brought them to a campsite in a grove of light green willows on Little Pipe Creek.

By late evening several soldiers passed by to look them over, though they could spend no more than 10 cents for a glass of beer. "None of the officers dare show his face," she told her crew. "It's not like the days with Joe Hooker. We gotta be smart." She put a bony finger to her gold incisor, grinning at blonde Sigurd, with whom she slept. They would be ready for business on the 30th.

☆ ☆

In the shower of reports coming in were drops of truth about Lee and his whereabouts. How to catch the bits that were true before they were lost? At sunrise, sipping coffee outside the mess next to Meade on a camp stool, George Henry Sharpe, the army's intelligence officer, cast scorn on the document mysteriously produced last evening. "Too precise, too detailed, and too recent for anyone but a genie to get it across the mountains so fast. The numbers are the lowest we've seen. The Pinkerton men think it's fanciful."

Sharpe, a college-trained New York lawyer, was skeptical of all strange documents. "Interesting thing is, it's not a final copy. Clerk's scratchings and mistakes are all through it. If it's genuine, it'd have to be something the Rebels threw away and forgot about. It's such a perfect way to mislead us, a faked official report. The Rebs are good at tricks like that."

He had been disappointed in Hooker after a promising start. Would the schoolmasterish Meade understand the ways of his business? He wondered why Meade decided to receive messages on his own, and why he refused to divulge the source of this paper. "Odd," he muttered as he put a steaming mug to his lips. Hot coffee wet his full mustache and stung briefly. He suppressed a wince. *Can't show weakness. The new boss is a statue. No telling what he thinks.*

"The organization table in that paper," said Meade, "gives us a gauge. You'll be able to verify or disprove it by observation of the enemy, whom we shall see very soon. You have methods of estimating strength, of course?"

It was a question an engineer would ask. Meade probed. Sharpe liked that. The general used his mind, like a draftsman perhaps, but he used it. Joe Hooker would turn on and off, and Sharpe couldn't be sure when he was serious. Meade was always serious. Sharpe wiped his mustache with a pocket handkerchief.

"There are two parts to it," Meade lectured. "One, the size of Lee's force. The other, their location. Some reports say the Rebels are coming across the pass from Chambersburg. That makes size most important." He put his cup on a stump, focused his eyes on Sharpe from under his cone hat. "There may be more coming from this source. I'll pass it on."

Buford's Union Cavalry brigade had reported a Mississippi regiment just north of where Reynolds should be marching that day. Word had come from the opposite flank that Stuart's troopers had dined last night at Westminster, 35 miles to the east. General Pleasanton, the cavalry chief, was skeptical, but others closer to the place were not.

These bits of information put Rebels on both right and left but not in the center. Meade could not abandon his right and give Lee an open door to Baltimore. Nor could he let go of the left and give Lee free access to the mountain passes. The distance from one flank to the other was beyond the army's reach.

☆ ☆

Meade ordered Fitzpatrick to ride to John Sedgwick's 6th Corps, pick up an escort, and question locals about Stuart. "If anything is over there, it will be cavalry," he said, putting the shank of his pen on his long nose. "We have no word of infantry. Your man Prediger says Ewell's corps is coming back toward Gettysburg. I think that's probably right. Lee will consolidate once he hears we're coming. I doubt you'll learn much, but I want to be certain." With a wave of the pen, he dismissed Fitz and went back to his papers.

Meade clung to the hope, cherished by all his senior men, that he could draw Lee into attacking them in prepared positions. The Chief Engineer had surveyed a strong defense along the south bank of Pipe Creek, running northeast along a ridge up to Westminster. Meade ordered Butterfield to draft a circular about it to corps commanders.

"We are proceeding well," said Butterfield with a resigned expression, standing before Meade's table. "What with these rapid marches and countermarches, the staff are working 'round the clock. The engineers have been most helpful. You should have a plan in hand by this evening."

"And a circular drafted?" asked Meade, looking up slowly and feeling a guilty thrill in twisting the bonds of servitude around Butterfield's neck. Fragments surfaced from last night's dream, and he struggled to suppress them. *Maybe I just don't like New Yorkers. Butterfield works hard. I'll just keep him busy.*

"Orders will be ready early tomorrow," said Butterfield. His forehead rippled.

"Tomorrow," shouted Meade, losing control, "may jolly well be the fight, for God's sake! Please," he caught himself. "See if you can't get a circular out by tonight."

"Yes, sir," said the Chief of Staff.

"Thank you, General Butterfield," said Meade looking down at his desk. "I'm sure you will oblige."

In mid-morning a young officer rode by Alice's wagon park staring intently at the vehicles parked under willow trees like a gypsy camp. "He wears no corps badge. He's from headquarters," rejoiced the blond Sigurd, who famously cherished the memory of every officer she'd met.

"We've seen him somewhere before," said Alice, squinting to follow the dark figure trotting toward the bend. "He'll be back," she said, getting down and walking over to Number 5.

Further along, Fitzpatrick fought with himself. The day was heating up, and he was sweating. His chest tightened, his throat closed, and for an instant he thought he might choke. An urging rose in his groin. *Go on! You have no business there.* The sensations persisted.

After a quarter-mile of torture, Fitzpatrick turned and galloped back. *I'll just have another look. Thank God, there were no soldiers.* He rode slowly around staring into each wagon with a scowl and no hint of greeting. He stopped at the one painted "5" in bright red.

She stood framed in the hoop of the Conestoga, dead still, wearing the same knowing smile. *I'm damned,* he thought, and pulled up close.

"You've come back, major," sang the girl. On seeing the him approach, she had quickly primped her bright red hair, squirted French scent at her breasts, and pulled on her black velvet dress. As Fitz came alongside, she bent forward, offering her breasts in a low-cut bodice, and reached out a slender hand. "Just hop across." She laughed through large green eyes. "Don't be afraid. One of our niggers will take the horse."

James Edward Van Arsdale Fitzpatrick, Jr., of Philadelphia, major of the Pennsylvania Volunteers, red-faced and sweating, froze in the saddle. To stop the turmoil in his body and brain he would have to obey. Caught between grimace and grin, he swung a leg over, grabbed her hand and jumped into the wagon. She pulled the curtain as soon as he was clear.

"I, I don't know what I'm doing, but I know why I'm here. I can't not come to you."

"That's honest," laughed the girl, unbuttoning his jacket. "And that's good. Now give me five dollars." With an impish grin, she put her hand out, "Please."

Fitz ungloved a shaking hand and took greenbacks from his pocket and gave them to her. "Too much," she said, holding some of them out, and quickly pulled back when he waved them away.

The girl hung his belt with its holster and his coat on a peg and bade him sit while she pulled off his boots. Then in a single move she undid her dress and stood naked before him, cupped rising breasts on a trim body.

Glorious! He stared at the hourglass curve between her hips and bosom. A machine on cue, he began to shuck his trousers. *Like a Dresden vase out of Christmas paper.* Cooler now, but heart pounding, and lacking all control, he took the hand she reached up to pull him down beside her onto a straw mattress on the floorboards.

"I knew you'd come back," she said looking up with a wide smile. "I knew it." And she giggled with mischief, making him grin like a schoolboy.

"I don't know what to do," he murmured, erect and swelling full against the foreskin. It hurt pleasantly.

"It's easy," she said softly in his ear. "I can teach you. Her hips seemed to swing again. "If it's learning you want, I'm what you need." Slowly she brought him on top and, with her hand, guided him into her. After some minutes, the wagon was quiet but for a gentle rocking motion.

The explosion that burst from his groin echoed in his head, and he went limp. Relief and shame took hold of him together with new thoughts. "I love you," he panted. "I oughtn't to say that, but I can't help it. I do love you."

"Of course you oughtn't." She laughed, mimicking his educated words. She seemed both pleased and radiant. "But it's all right," she purred, scratching his head. "There's no hurry. You've paid. We can do it again. I'm called Maizie. That's the name Alice gave me. We all have work names, like actresses. You have to ask for "Maizie," but my real name's Maeve. I'm not supposed to tell you, but I want you to know." She smiled, and Fitz thought she was almost shy.

"Just relax and wait," she said and pressed a hand on his chest. "You're not hairy, I like that." They lay together silently while his breathing calmed. After what seemed only a few minutes, she put a hand below his stomach, and he felt an instant tremor, and stiffened. "You'll like it better, this time."

Fitz stayed almost an hour. Dressed again, he held her in his arms and kissed her fully, almost formally, on the mouth.

"La, you don't have to that," said Maeve wearing the smile she'd borne since he first appeared. "Just being here and payin's enough."

The uniform called him to duty. He found his horse standing at the back of the wagon when she parted the curtain. He mounted swiftly and took leave with a short "Good-bye, *ma chérie*," and rode off.

"Come back," she shouted after him. A warm sadness clouded her face, and for the first time in the month since she'd been "with the wagons" she felt a touch of shame. She watched the horse gallop away. She knew he was what she wanted, and knew she'd never have him. Maeve wanted to cry but pulled in her feelings when she turned to see three girls scrambling into the back of the wagon.

Alice followed with her hand out. "A dollar'll go on your account." Her eyes scoured the road, as if searching for more men. "That was a good one. If he's from headquarters, maybe he'll keep that bastard general off our backs."

"Or maybe on our backs," giggled Sigurd.

The others simpered. Alice turned on them. "What am I supposed ta do with a buncha whores can't leave off the whiskey in the mornin'? It's fine you drink with the men, and they pay fur it. But ya oughtn't to be drinkin on yer own. It'll go down on yer books, and ruin yer looks."

Down at the creek, James, her black man, could hear her bray above the snorting of the mules.

A quarter-mile away, Fitz could not overcome turmoil. Maeve had given him total pleasure. Drained of passion, he felt morally lost. His family were Presbyterians with a Scots respect for sin. He was a fornicator given over to evil.

He nudged the horse into a canter to make up for time lost, came to the rail line at the advance supply depot, and rode down the right of way. Several engines together pulling long trains creaked forward, train after train burdened with foodstuffs, fodder, weapons, ammunition, and medical supplies west to the army. They chuffed and puffed of coming battle, duty, and the heavy labors of the Commanding General. *My God! What would he think?*

The more Fitz thought, the less he recalled pleasure and the more he felt guilt. *I am unworthy. I must never, ever see her again.* As soon as he told himself this, Maeve's happy smile-wreathed face came before him, and he knew he would. *I'm damned then. It's a consolation soon to be in battle, on a field of honor.* Atonement brought relief, and he spurred his horse.

He found General Sedgwick urging his divisions north and eastward over rain-soaked roads. "Uncle John" was pleased Meade was concerned about his flank and gladly furnished Fitz a fresh mount and a cavalry escort. Angry locals complained that Stuart had forced them to feed thousands of men the night before. They said Rebel wagon trains were ". . . up on the road."

By noon Fitz and his escort were far north of the main body of Sedgwick's corps. Coming to the top of a hill south of Hanover, they found scouts waiting to report unmistakable sounds of rifles and small cannon a few miles ahead. A look through binoculars told Fitz that Union cavalry had run into Stuart. He sent the scouts forward to fix the position, and, when they returned, was stunned to hear the Rebels were between him and the Union horsemen. A long string of captured supply wagons stood on the road two miles ahead.

"There's an awful lot of 'em," said the fuzz-cheeked escort commander. "What's your pleasure, major?"

"You weren't ordered into battle," said Fitz astride an ample bay. "My duty is to find Stuart. Well, there he is. I don't need to run up and hug him."

The cavalryman leaned forward in his saddle and laughed. "If you order us, major, we'll be glad to run right into them."

"Not much we could accomplish that four thousand cavalrymen can't do," Fitz reasoned aloud. "But we can learn a lot about Stuart's force, and what's in those wagons. Once we've done that, captain, you go back to Uncle John, and I'll cut across to General Meade."

Riding on country lanes under tree cover, going on foot to talk to farmers, and keeping their field glasses on the ebb and flow of battle, they formed a clear picture. It was a stalemate. Judson Kilpatrick and his able brigadiers, Farnsworth and Custer, had stopped Stuart's larger force from moving either west toward Gettysburg or even to the comparative safety of the north. The Confederates, encumbered by their prize train, would have to slide eastward away from Lee. No one picked up any sign of Rebel infantry.

Flossie stood waving the flag as Buford's dirty cavalrymen rode through town.

Union forces are here at last. What a thrill to all of us. Some girls have been downright foolish. One, whose name I'll not write, spent an hour in the barn with a trooper. Her mother doesn't know, and others say they'd do the same. I hope this is not a sign of things to come. The men had better not stay long.

A few came into the shop. Honesty forces me to say they don't look any better than the Virginians. Father likes them because they pay in greenbacks. That's better than Confederate paper, which is nearly worthless. None of it's as good as gold, he says.

The men from the Illinois and Indiana regiments seem to be the best educated. They can read and write, and they are also more patriotic. The Regulars are a strange group. Some look like criminals, as I imagine them. They have teeth missing and dirty faces with no manners. Even so, the women want to help the Union boys, and bake pies from the cherries in season. It's different from the forced work they had to do for the Rebels.

The officers are mostly gentleman. They say General Buford is a professional, a Military Academy graduate, but he looks grim. He stands not much above five feet, very thin and serious. He pays little mind to complaints about the Rebel requisitions, and says there is nothing the army can do.

The general pitched his tent behind the town on Cemetery Hill, where he and his officers sit looking through telescopes toward pickets who stand guard west of town. We are now indeed in the middle.

★ ★

In the capital, summer air was foul as ever. Afternoon thunderstorms did nothing to relieve the heat. Men walked about with their coats off, and ladies carried parasols and fans.

Interiors, even under high ceilings, were worse. The outer room of the Secretary's office was a sweat box. A crowd of politicians, newspapermen, and officers waited for a nod from Colonel Hardie. They seldom got one because the President, in shirtsleeves, spent most of his time inside reading messages and listening, no matter how much it bothered him, to military professionals. Like the rest, he waited for word from the north.

Away from the White House, Lincoln escaped the siege of men from Pennsylvania, including representatives of the governor, complaining that Rebels had plundered the state. Thaddeus Stevens, the powerful Republican congressman and abolitionist, claimed Rebels had burned his iron works west of Gettysburg. Fleeing citizens of Chambersburg moaned that Ewell's men forced them to pay tens of thousands of dollars in tribute. The mayor of Philadelphia issued daily orders to arm.

"Meade undertakes," said Halleck striding back and forth, "to cover all contingencies. He knows Ewell's corps has been in the north and that Lee is concentrated around Chambersburg. He must spread his troops out until he can join battle. At that time he'll want the advantage of good ground. That's something he knows about."

"But General Meade doesn't know where Lee is and neither do we," said Lincoln, anxiety poking through his normal calm. "With the telegraph out we don't know where he is, either. I get the feeling Meade vacillates."

Halleck persisted, "His last evening's dispatch arrived by a roundabout route an hour ago. It lays out a careful plan. He won't let a few pinpricks from Jeb Stuart divert him. He'll meet Lee in the next two days." He held his right hand fast in a pocket lest he wave it at Lincoln.

The President looked up. "Yes, but he doesn't say he's going to attack."

Halleck was on difficult ground. The President didn't like fighting on the defensive. "Meade wants to lure Lee into attacking him in a favorable position. His first task, Mr. President, as we ordered, is to defend the capital. The alternative is maneuver. He knows full well his corps commanders are no match for the Confederates when it comes to movement. Chancellorsville haunts us all."

"You mean when Hooker got the jump and failed to follow through?" growled Lincoln. "Well, I never was much of a soldier. I hope Meade realizes that if he beats them back, that's time to finish them."

Stanton stood at his easel, holding papers in both hands. He had tried to coach Halleck, but somehow the good general couldn't master the game. He watched the back and forth like a father hoping his gangly daughter would learn to waltz. Lincoln was impatient.

"We've had another dispatch from Vicksburg via Admiral Porter," Stanton said. "Grant is making progress and should achieve a victory soon."

"That would be consolation," said the President, smiling at last.

Colonel Hardie came in and spoke quietly to Stanton. "There's an urgent delegation outside from the Committee on the Conduct," announced the Secretary. "Chairman Wade is with them."

Lincoln stood, took his coat off a peg, and turned to Hardie. "Give me half a minute to look presentable and then you may show the luminaries in."

Ben Wade led in two others. "We are concerned, Mr. President," he spoke as soon as the door opened. "It seems General Meade has strong connections in the South."

"His brother-in-law was governor of Virginia," said Senator Chandler, moving out from behind.

"Good morning, gentleman, or is it afternoon?" said the President with a smile. "We've been keeping watch here so long I'm not sure. But as to your question, yes, General Meade has in-laws in the South now in the Confederate Army, as do I. Do you think me unqualified, gentlemen?"

Wade, Chandler, and the others hastened to demur. Wade, trying to smile, said he wondered whether changing leaders so near the battle was wise. "But, then," he said, answering himself, "I guess it's too late for that question."

"It is a big question, Mr. Chairman." The President looked at him with a winning smile. "And if we've got it wrong, none of us will survive long enough to debate it. Besides, you can all cheer up. General Meade was born in Spain. He can never run for President."

Wade looked at the floor. "His great grandfather was a slave trader. I suppose that wouldn't help in politics. But if he crushes Robert E. Lee, I don't suppose the people will care about either problem."

"I suppose not," said Lincoln. "The general is a soldier and has undertaken what we want him to do. From what I understand he is completely for the Union. I can reassure you on that point, at least."

In Taneytown, 12 miles from Gettysburg, Meade received more evidence Lee was massing. Butterfield finished the Pipe Creek circular and sent it off before evening mess with a separate note from Meade warning his commanders it was not to go into effect without a specific movement order.

For the Army of the Potomac the choice lay between swinging back to Pipe Creek or hoping to find good ground near Gettysburg. Despite Fitzpatrick's reassuring report that only cavalry were in the east, Meade could not shake from his mind the possibility that somewhere on his right lurked a Confederate force ready to pounce the minute he turned toward the mountains. It would be Chancellorsville all over again, absolutely the worst outcome, and the destruction of his army.

In his tent after supper Meade sat on a camp stool finishing a cigar and leaning over papers strewn on a rough table beneath a hanging oil lamp. He longed to have Reynolds to talk to. But he was alone. Battle was hours away.

Putting by his cheroot, he wrote in a careful hand to Margaret,

All is going well. I think I have relieved Harrisburg and Philadelphia. . . . I continue well but much oppressed with a sense of responsibility and the magnitude of the great interests entrusted to me. Of course, in time I will become accustomed to this. Dearest wife, Good-bye.

He then wrote final orders to the corps commanders to address their men "explaining the immense issues involved in the struggle."

The men were to carry three days' rations and 60 rounds of ammunitions, and to keep weapons at hand. Finally, in a harder tone he ordered "the instant death of any soldier who fails in his duty at this hour."

As he sat reviewing these steps, he heard a foreign, clearly civilian voice imploring his orderly, and stepped to the flap to find Meyer begging admittance. Meade would like to have sent him off, but instinct warned him. "Come in Mr. Meyer," he called, disarming the orderly.

Meyer was apologetic. "You see, Herr General, about this Pipe Creek business I must speak. The reporters know about it, and I wonder whether that was what you intended."

Towering over the little reporter, Meade flinched as if stung. "I assure you, Mr. Meyer, it absolutely was not. This is a grave breach of order. Lee has his spies. My God! Someone deserves to be shot!"

He cut himself off, and having no place to pace in the tent, sat down deflated. The word "treason" raced through his mind. "Damn!" he said, slamming the table with his fist, sending cigar ash over his papers. He lowered his voice and looked up at last. "Perhaps, Herr Meyer, you should tell me what you know."

"About an hour ago, Herr Brennan from the *New York World* showed me a circular to the commanders saying, 'He guessed "Ol' Meade" wasn't going to attack.' As far as I know, it was seen by Brennan only."

"This means," said the general, taking his glasses from his nose, "that someone on my immediate staff told him. That man must be court-martialed, and I will arrest Brennan to prevent publication."

"May I advise, Herr General?" Meyer stood visibly shaking, hat held in both hands over his vest. "I know this goes against military experience, but I think it might be better to think the reporters are patriots. Don't arrest Brennan, but call the reporters here, trust them, and tell them it would be a heavy matter in this moment about these things to write."

Meyer's goodwill was obvious. Meade saw arrests would not stop publication. Meyer's soft approach might succeed. He had no fear of what reporters might write after the battle. He must protect his strategy now.

"I'll take your advice," he said. "Bring the men to my tent in half an hour." Meade called an orderly to fetch the Chief of Staff and the provost marshal. "Tell them to get here as if the battle had started."

Maj. Gen. Marcena Patrick, the policeman, came at quick-step, and was outlining arrest procedures when, breathless, the Chief of Staff, arrived.

Meade was by now calm but frosty, and addressed Butterfield with a face as cold as his words. "General, your men have done well to get out the circular this afternoon. And they have done well on the other things. But someone, sir, is patently guilty of a betrayal of military information. The press has seen the Pipe Creek circular. And I am told, moreover, they are determined to use it to assault me personally."

Sweat globs grew on the forehead of the Chief of Staff. "My God," he stammered. "This is awful. We must find the culprit and punish him."

"No doubt, we shall." Meade enjoyed Butterfield's discomfort. "General Patrick will begin interrogations immediately. I doubt it will take long to get to the bottom of this."

"I shall assist the provost marshal in any way I can," said Butterfield.

"Thank you, general. Your first job is to stand by me while I assemble the newspaper men to discuss the circular. I shall not refer to a breach of confidence but assume they are patriotic citizens and ask for their loyalty. In that way, they will all be equal. What have we got to lose?" Meade was taken back by his own, sudden good humor.

"Yes," said Butterfield brightening, "that's a very good plan."

"And we can see to courts-martial later on," said General Patrick. Butterfield could not suppress a shudder.

CHAPTER VI

By sunrise July 1, it was hot. Lee didn't think his men ought to do a lot of marching in such weather, but he believed in giving his officers a wide latitude. He would not let himself fret, not in the presence of staff. Ewell's corps would soon be approaching Gettysburg.

The day before, when a brigade from Hill's corps marched toward Gettysburg, the commander found Union cavalry, possibly forces of the Army of the Potomac. Hill's staff were doubtful. "Probably a detachment of observation," said an aide, a view they all insisted on, even after a young captain who had stayed back to observe reported seeing well-trained troops.

The officers discounted reports of enemy activity. Everyone, Lee included, was enjoying good food and the beautiful countryside. No matter if it was a little warm, everyone welcomed the relief from foraging in the barrens of the Virginia wilderness. Western Pennsylvania was a land of milk and honey.

General Hill sent a message saying an unknown number of enemy cavalry had been spotted and that he planned to send men into the town. Headquarters sent back no objection, and a division marched off in the early sunrise. Hill was new to corps command.

Private Toddy Bates of the 7th Tennessee, Archer's brigade, didn't mind a short march if at the end he got a new pair of shoes. In town, men said, was a whole warehouse full of 'em. The Yankees had so much. A little heat was no bother, and maybe they'd find fresh eggs. There'd been plenty on the farms hereabouts.

Bates was 14, though he claimed 15 when he signed up. As he marched out of the mountains over one low ridge after another, his thoughts were the same as the veterans. *These were hardly what you'd call hills back home, just low-lying rolls, one no bigger than the next.* Bank swallows swooped over the marshes in and out of clouds of morning mist. The regiment moved up onto the ridge. Crack shots bragged about having duck for dinner. Bates wondered if the ridges had names. Marching in the third rank, he felt something hit his boot and looked down to see a bright, spent ball of lead fall to the ground.

A sustained fire came from a fence line 200 yards away. "Accurate for Yankees" grumped the sergeant. Orders came down the line. The captain wheeled the company abreast of others in battle formation close to the road. Bates marched in the front rank of the brigade as it faced the enemy.

On the Union side, John Buford had been moving men about since dawn. Four miles to the west of Gettysburg he posted a line of vedettes, scouts, and skirmishers to watch for a Rebel advance. Behind them along Herr Ridge he placed pickets every 30 feet in a line at right angles to the road. The bulk of his 3,000 cavalrymen he spread wide as dragoons, calvalrymen who fight on foot, in woods on a ridge to the rear. With this defense in depth he hoped to hold out until the infantry could come up.

Action began about 8:00 a.m. when the Confederate commander sent skirmishers forward in a wide swath. Buford told his pickets to fire resting their Sharps breech-loaders on fence posts to improve speed and give the appearance of a larger force. The Confederates formed into wide ranks, one brigade to the south of the road, another to the north, pushing back on the Union dragoons.

Buford saw the beginning of a general engagement, sent a brigade and six cannon forward, and hung on. Ten thousand men, some of the best in the Union Army, and John Reynolds were on the way. *For once we've got the right people in the right place first,* Buford thought, *and now we'll see what the other side can do. For the first time in this lousy war, we are going to play the opening gambit right.*

When Reynolds arrived, he found the cavalrymen outnumbered but in strong position. He raced a mile back to his own men and, finding a shortcut, ordered them to tear down fence rails to gain direct passage to the ridges west of town. He sent messages, one to

Howard to bring up his corps, and one to Meade saying the Rebels were threatening to take high ground west of town. "If pushed back, I will barricade Gettysburg and cede a foot at a time until reinforcements arrive."

The 7th Tennessee came on, rifles to the fore. A man beside Toddy Bates fell gasping, writhing, a stream of blood spurting from his neck. Others fell. The sergeant said for all to hear that casualties were light. He ordered Bates, the youngest in the company, to help a wounded corporal to the rear and return quickly with ammunition. "We ain't running low yet, but if more Yankees start making themselves targets, we soon will be."

The gray line swarmed slowly forward, taking an hour to push the Yankee men across Willoughby Run, and move up the low west slope of the ridge opposite. As a Yankee corps came into line, the balance shifted in favor of the Union.

Lead cut through the grass as Toddy gave his shoulder to the wounded corporal, and they limped away. "He sees them blue coats coming over the ridge," said the man. "Knows what's comin'." His breath came short. Sweat streamed from his forehead and oozed over his gray shirt-collar. He winced when his leg touched the ground, but insisted the bullet was "shallow," meaning he hoped the surgeons would get it out without taking off his leg.

Toddy told himself to say nothing and follow orders. He sweated too, and dust stifled his throat. If he didn't have the corporal with him, he might run.

"Sergeant wants you young 'uns out of the way. You might get hurt," gasped the man.

Down the road, an ambulance crew put the corporal in a farm wagon with a score of others, most wounded far worse. Bates waved good-bye and went on to find cartridges.

He wasn't sure what weapons the men carried. The clerk gave him 400 rounds of Springfield and 500 Enfield. Bates put the heavy load on his back and moved away slowly. "Archer's boys are giving them fool Yankees Hell," the supply clerk called after him. "You ain't the first to come for more."

Toddy struggled back to the ridge. The mist had cleared, and in its place were smoke and flame. Cannon boomed. Men yelled and screamed. Some ran toward him up the slope. Others stopped to kneel, fire, and come on. Columns in blue knifed down the far hill, surrounding men holding up their arms. Lower on the right, others splashed across the creek toward cover in groves on the near bank.

Men of the 7th Tennessee found little cover. Behind them were open fields of trampled corn and wheat. A stream of men filed up the road, many wounded, some limping along with help from comrades. Two men came carrying the sergeant, a bloody hole in his stomach. Bates tried not to gape.

"Don't lose them cartridges, son," ordered the sergeant, weak but steady. "We're gonna need 'em." They moved on. Bates remained still, looking after him.

"Better ya come along," said a passing veteran. "The Yankees got the general and whole bunch of ourn. They'll have to bring up another outfit. We'll reform behin' the ridge." He pointed west.

Toddy Bates, 14, bearing 70 pounds of cartridges, having seen killing, bleeding, and death for the first time in his life, having seen the mortal wound of his sergeant and the near destruction of his brigade, did what he was told.

☆ ☆

Henry Prediger and Josephus wakened to sounds of battle, how far away they could not tell. "Last year near Antietam Creek some places you could hear for miles," said Josephus. "Other places you couldn't hear a chain away. I guess we've been told it's started."

They sat outside at a rough-hewn log table drinking a hot herb brew Josephus called "coffy." "You'd best stay through daylight," Josephus put down his mug, straining to hear. "A black man does best at night 'cause the white man can't see him. Learned that getting away from Lexington. You gotta use cover, and we got some that's natural. When the fightin's over, you go back in the dark. Got to be Reb cavalry 'roun here now."

"Funny thing," said Henry, sucking his lips. "The front's not where you think. Moves in all kinds of angles. You think the North be on the north, an' the Confedercy be on the south. Today it's other way 'roun."

"Tomorrow it'll be someway else," said Josephus, satisfied he knew where the noises came from. "From what I read about ol' Napoleon, I'd say they're gonna be fighting on those ridges around town in order to hold the high ground. They'll fight all day and bring up more and more men. When they done, they dig in, and that's where they goin' to stay. Then we'll know how many the Rebs lose and where they are. And you can tell General Meade.

"This may be the last time you gonna be able to come. We'll have to use the signals." He chuckled. "The Rebs trained us a signal man. The Alexanders taught him so he could read the Bible—like the rest of us down at Fairfield. We snitched every jot of writing we could. This child was smart. Young Porter took him off to the army, and he learned the signals right under his nose. Then about two weeks ago, Porter beat him for stealin' pears. If he hadn't done, the man would still now be servin' 'em tea, instead a sendin' over his secrets."

Henry laughed. "What do you think 'Ol Mars' Robert would say if he heard two black men talking this way about his battle?"

"He'd think he'd lost the war for sure," snorted Josephus, leaning back in his chair, thoroughly tickled.

By noon it was quiet. Josephus said that didn't mean fighting had stopped, only that they couldn't hear. The two men walked up onto rock outcrops above the cabin where below they saw troopers moving around a village. "Reb cavalry," said Josephus taking an ancient telescope from his eye. "Where we stand now we're on their side. The Yankees are makin' no claim to this ground."

Meade rose early and sat on a log by the mess taking coffee with Patrick and Sharpe. He expected the fighting to begin within hours, and agonized over his lines strung out from Manchester 25 miles east, to Gettysburg, 15 miles west. If a full-scale engagement began, he would have to mass his troops in a hurry, meaning that a third of them would arrive spent and useless.

Stuart's romp in the east kept him off balance. He disliked cocky cavalrymen. Fitzpatrick's report yesterday was far more helpful than his Chief of Cavalry, Pleasonton, who merely said his men "did well" and nothing about Rebel strength.

Strength was what it was all about. The army had shrunk since last year. After the defeat at Chancellorsville, men were bitter.

Patrick got daily reports of men saying, "We'll just go home, if Bobby Lee wins this time." Meade wondered if Lee knew how close he was to victory.

"I found out who betrayed the Pipe Creek Plan," said Patrick. "Just one man. It didn't take long."

"Don't speak the name," said Meade, "I know who it was. We're going into battle. We can expect every man to do his duty, especially the senior officers." He enjoyed Patrick's amazement. "There's time enough for courts-martial, and forgiveness of heroes."

The provost marshal accepted this wisdom of silence.

At 11:00 a.m. a courier weaved his way through Taneytown's rutted streets past supply trains and marching men. Eventually he arrived with his urgent message at Meade's modest tents a half mile east. The fighting had started. Hill's corps of 25,000 men was attacking Reynolds with less than half that many. Meade resisted an urge to jump on Baldy and hurry off.

"Just like Reynolds," he grinned after the rider gasped out the message for the second time. "Let's get him some support. Where is that damned Butterfield?" Things got worse when Buford sent news that pickets northwest of Gettysburg met a second Rebel corps, probably Ewell. Lee was massing. Reynolds would be overmatched.

"The roads around that town are vital. If we lose Gettysburg, we're lost!" Meade bellowed orders to Fitzpatrick for Sickles at 3d Corps, and to George for Slocum at the 12th, telling them to hurry off.

Headquarters was tense. Officers avoided him. Before noon, Winfield Scott Hancock arrived with his 2d Corps. Meade was pleased. If Reynolds' men were good, these were possibly the best in the army. Meade calmed after a long talk with Hancock about plans. Hancock would not suffer nonsense, and his view of fellow commanders fit Meade's own. Sitting under a large maple tree away from the swarm of flies, they chewed over possibilities.

Before noon, ladies of the Sanitary Commission came and broke up their talk. Meade summoned his surgeon, and the generals took time to receive the ladies, pass the time of day, and assure them of support.

"We're desperately short of help," said Fannie, sitting on a stump too small for her seat. "We're going to have to take all we can find, including a few nurses you might object to." She watched Meade carefully.

"Camp followers are ever with the army," said Meade with a resigned smile. "Just keep them at work, and do what you can to relieve suffering. There will be a lot of it."

Fannie nodded, wondering if he would be so calm if he knew she had accepted Alice's girls as volunteers. "There are camp followers who do the laundry, and there are others. We're not going to try to weed out the trollops."

"I rely on your discretion," said Meade stiffly. "Perhaps the surgeon has a view?"

"If they are prostitutes," said the doctor, "I must inspect them. We can't take the risk of disease. Otherwise, I wager these women are used to men, and may be very helpful."

Meade blushed. It wasn't his type of parlor talk with ladies. "I see." He kept his eyes on the surgeon. "I leave this to you and the commission. I'll call off the provosts."

Fannie knew he'd avoid her gaze and signaled Clarissa they'd better leave. At the road they passed a rider galloping into camp, horse lathered, muddy-legged, and nearly spent.

☆ ☆

On the ridges west of town Reynolds urged his men forward, riding his horse in full view of the enemy as he exploited his advantage. North and south of the pike his men pushed the invaders back. Union strength would swell with the arrival of Howard's corps on his right. Reynolds rode toward the line a few yards behind the advancing 2d Wisconsin urging his men on. As he turned in his saddle to rally troops in the rear, a sharp blow hit him in the back of his head, and he fell from his horse. A Rebel sharpshooter had sent a bullet into Reynold's brain.

Before noon, a dust-covered courier arrived at headquarters to croak out the news. Meade took the man aside and questioned him, trying to find out whether his best general and his closest confidant might live. Later, he sat in his tent, unmoving. The camp stilled. Bustle ceased. Soldiers looked over at the tent in silence.

Meade could keep a calm face as well as anyone, though his eyes bulged behind his glasses. He thought he knew death, having seen a lot of it. Yet the loss pulled away a strong prop. He had counted on John Reynolds. Plans became senseless. He closed the flap of the tent. For a few minutes no one understood the sounds coming from it, except a few of the Irish, who distinctly heard a jumble of Latin. Butterfield paced the ground a few feet away.

Meade recovered as though overcoming a fever. He pushed the flap open and called for Hancock. The young general arrived in minutes. Meade kept him standing beside Butterfield while he barked out orders. "Go immediately to Gettysburg. Butterfield here will write the orders and give you all we have in the way of maps. Take an ambulance so you can read as you go. Get out there, look at the ground, and report. Do we fight there or pull back?

"And give my respects to Howard." Meade rubbed his nose as if trying to pull from his head all the things he needed to remember. "Tell him I know he's your senior, but in the circumstances I have chosen to exercise my power to supersede him because you are fully informed of my plans. I hope he takes no offense. Assure him of my high regard. You will be able to manage that." Meade smiled at last. "I'm sure you can."

In his clean white linen shirt with open collar, Hancock radiated energy. He saluted and left without a word. Meade penned an order to John Sedgwick to bring his 15,000 men with speed and report in person as soon as possible. Before the battle went any further, he wanted an understanding with the men he trusted.

CHAPTER VII

Late in the day sitting cross-legged on the earthen floor of the cellar, Flossie Muelheim wrote:

Everyone came out to cheer the long lines of our men marching through town late in the morning. They looked so strong we thought our saviors had come. The women carried water out to the soldiers. I went out at first, but father heard a man say bad words and made me come back.

Some people shouted German greetings to General Shurz's men passing by. A man said they were not brave, and would run again as they did at Chancellorsville, but they looked fierce to me.

Later we heard explosions, and a window broke on our second floor. Father sent us down to the cellar. We could hear bombs come close, but we could only learn what was happening when someone was sent up on an errand.

We could hear soldiers crowding through the streets leaving the field. Stragglers must have found our well, because later we found it dry. Mother said she saw large numbers of wounded, some limping along, some aided by comrades. Others went in ambulances to what they call "hospitals" down the roads beyond the cemetery. Around three o'clock men beat on the cellar door and begged us to hide them. They even offered to pay. Father was very angry, and called upon their patriotism. They smiled sadly and shuffled on.

Fitzpatrick was glad to get away from headquarters. Yesterday's rash encounter with "La Maizie," as he called her, filled his head, and he needed to clear it. The late morning air was steamy sweet, and he could see far over the fields, lush except where marching men had come.

Dan Sickles's reputation at headquarters was all Hardie foretold. He seldom followed orders, came late into position, and never went by the rule book. Yet senior men feared him. Recalling stories of Sickles's sordid dalliances, Fitz concluded he himself was no better. *He's no gentleman. No more am I, since yesterday.*

The night before, he had written to Mable asking her to break the engagement. The letter was evasive, saying that with all that was happening in the war he couldn't "make himself ready for marriage now. It was unfair. . . ." The prospect was never easy, and he felt relieved. Mable didn't excite him, but he felt shameful. He could never face her honestly again.

Distant cannon sounded as he approached 3d Corps headquarters. Men sat idle along the road. At shortly before one o'clock the staff were still at table. He had heard Sickles kept an elegant mess where fine wines flowed in quantity and whiskey was available any time after noon. The general was said to pay for much of it himself.

Sickles greeted Fitzpatrick as "the fellow from Philadelphia," meaning from "Society," leaving his aides to gather he got the job through connections.

Fitz parried this with a soft smile and repeated Meade's orders verbatim. Standing before Sickles who sat in a camp chair beside a white-clothed mess table puffing a cigar, he underwent cross-examination. Sickles probed for a loophole. He obviously bridled that Meade gave specific orders to his division commanders by name, bypassing him.

Fitz was firm. He'd memorized Meade's order, and was ready to repeat it endlessly. As he rattled out the words, he thought, *It's a matter of who's more arrogant, the swaggering general, or the school-smart major.* He suppressed a smile.

Fitz was repeating the order for the third time when a courier brought news of Reynolds's death, and Howard's call for troops on Cemetery Ridge at quick time.

"No conflict there," said Sickles, ignoring the tragedy. "Why don't the Commanding General hie himself over to the battle?" He addressed his staff, who laughed dutifully. Then, keeping his back to the messenger, and puffing his cigar, he said to Fitzpatrick, "I don't suppose you'd want to comment, but I'll tell you frankly this Pipe Creek notion is going to fetch George Meade a peck of trouble."

Lee received reports suggesting the start of a major battle. He was sure Ewell's men would swing the balance in his favor. What he didn't know was how either of his two new commanders would perform. At midday he rode alongside General Hill on a ridge west of Gettysburg, where he sat observing troops moving forward. The man was unwell.

"Heth's division has borne many casualties," Hill reported. "I have ordered Pender up. The Union cavalry has done well to hold their left. We have to go straight at them. General Ewell's corps will catch their right and swing the balance."

"In my experience, General Hill, one cannot count on the enemy to make mistakes." Lee turned in the saddle to look at Hill's gray face. The fine leather creaked softly. "Are you entirely well, general?"

"I am quite all right, sir. Just a little of the stomach complaint."

"Yankee food is too good," Lee allowed himself a chuckle. "It is possibly their secret weapon. Maybe that's why we find so much of it." Hill's condition worried him. Literally it seemed to take away his stomach for fighting. "Hold back a little longer. When the time is right we can go in *en masse*."

Hill pushed off to give orders. He would soon be back. One way to make no mistakes this day was to stay close to the commanding general.

⭐ ⭐

Battle sounds did not penetrate the thick maple and locust woods 13 miles away. Meade's headquarters worked at full speed. Breathless riders and horses came and went. Orders were sent, and reports received. Clerks held their noses down to their papers, or scurried between tents at quick time. Butterfield's staff could not keep up. The last telegram to Washington had reported Ewell on the Susquehanna. Everyone was busy and, with battle beginning, harassed. No one walked. Everyone ran.

Waiting was intolerable. Meade chewed into his long agenda—finding replacements, sending up ammunition, sorting out routes of march, finding officers for vacant jobs. This work had dogged him since his first hour of command. Getting on top of the army was a full job, battle or no battle, and George Meade was not a man to shirk duty.

Meade let Hancock take away the only reasonably good map. He reminded himself that his job was to oversee the work of his commanders and keep his army from being caught off guard.

He looked out into the forest. *Grant, they say, never answers telegrams, and he's very popular in Washington. How does he do it? His duties must involve an enormous amount of writing.* Meade picked up his pen and shook his head. *I will get on Baldy as soon as Sedgwick comes, and we'll hurry out together.*

Fitzpatrick appeared. It was a relief to talk with the young man, even if he only told him Sickles was recalcitrant. Meade's hopes were pinned on Hancock. *Hancock, I can depend upon, but he's new. Howard is unsure.*

Fitzpatrick entertained him with a droll description of Sickles's camp. Meade thought of Lee, the high-born captain he knew in Mexico. *Painfully correct, totally assured, Lee is out there with his generals, measuring out orders, each courteously received, passed along to respectful subordinates who idolize him. How perverse, that we, in the moral right, face such chaos: the wild Irish, the solemn Germans, the politicals, the stiff New Englanders, and the slick New Yorkers.*

Meade stepped out with Fitz behind him. The wind had shifted, and cannon boomed from the battlefield. He summoned Sharpe. Meade wanted to stretch his legs while his mind churned through the possible outcome of the day.

Pipe Creek is out. I wish I hadn't sent that circular. It will confuse the commanders now they are getting battle orders. Lord preserve me from being one of history's failures who can't command.

Is Lee really massing? Are all of Hill's men engaged? Is Ewell there in force, or are some still on the Susquehanna?

The trio strolled in silence, the Commanding General in the middle not speaking but nodding occasionally to passing aides. "Where is your colored man?" he finally asked. "We haven't had any further reports." By now everyone in camp was aware of Henry Prediger, the only black man who came and went at will.

"Prediger rode off yesterday telling me the battle was about to start." Fitz laughed, cutting himself short. "I expect him back after dark."

Sharpe smiled. "I'll have something too, I'm sure, from a man in Gettysburg. He may confirm your order of battle. Everything we have seen so far says the work is genuine, even if his numbers are low."

"It would be a blessing," said the general, "if Prediger's account were correct. The fewer Lee has and the more certain we are of them, the better I can fight him. Will your man know where to find us?"

Fitz smiled. "That's one thing I've learned about Henry. He has ways of moving in the woods we don't know about."

"Interesting," said Meade stroking his beard, "I shouldn't wonder that Negroes have long had ways of hiding around these parts. We are only a few miles north of the line. Runaway slaves must have built havens all over this area."

To Meade the fact of slavery was a matter of guilt and shame. His grandfathers traded in slaves. The Meades never spoke about it, though they proudly recalled his father's sacrifice of his fortune to finance the Spanish King against Napoleon.

Another exhausted rider appeared, and Meade quick-stepped back to the tent to hear of the retreat to Cemetery Hill. Hancock thought they could defend the ground, but in the context of his report were huge Union losses. The Rebels had won the day.

The urge to get going returned. The message was marked 5:30 p.m. Hancock said Lee gave no sign of attacking. Meade recited Macbeth, "What's done is done." The fighting was over, for now. His most important duty was to be the man of reason on a day when everyone else went mad. Things needed doing, and he needed to talk to John Sedgwick.

By twilight, in bivouac northwest of town, Private Beverly Stuckey of Gordon's Georgians wrote:

Dear Ma and Pa,

We whupped a whole Yankee division an tomara I expec we'll finish 'em off. General Gordon saved a Yankee general who wuz dyin in the field. The general sez we shudda taken the hill across town befor sunset but that don worry us much. We all know God's truth is that one of us can fite better than ten Yankees. We fot the Germans agin, and they run. My frend Bill More sez one more day fightin oughta do it. He sure is proud. Hope you are well.

★ ★

Flossie Muelheim finished her day's entry:

People have closed their shutters, locked their stable doors, and went into the cellar. In mid-afternoon the line of stragglers grew to a swarm. Papa said whole regiments came through, almost running, to get to Cemetery Hill. He said the Rebels would take the town before dark, and we became very frightened.

Before dark we came upstairs. Across the street Fat Sally came out the Morgan's front door and ran away. Mrs. Morgan shouted after her, but she wouldn't turn around. She just kept on running toward the Union side.

Several windows were cracked, but there was not much damage. Father went out to the well and said it was filling. The yard was strewn with clothes and things of all kinds, even guns. In the far corner a wounded soldier lay moaning on his stomach. We took water out to him and rolled him over to clean his face. He had a bullet in his arm. We carried him in. Mother took the bullet out with a clean kitchen fork and washed the wound deep with hot water and strong soap. The man yelled but then tried to stop for fear the Rebels would hear.

His name is Heinrich Landsman from the 82d Illinois Regiment in Colonel K's brigade. I can't spell the name. They were caught and unable to get through to the cemetery. He fears Rebel prison and begged us to hide him.

Heinrich is 17, not much younger than my brother who fell at Malvern Hill. Mother looked sadly at father. He'd rather not take him, but he knew she wanted him to stay. We bandaged his wound as carefully as we could, cleaned up the blood, and took Heinrich to the cellar. We piled things up around him, stock we didn't think the Rebels would want, like furniture and women's clothes. By then he was glad to lie down and rest. He'll sleep better than I do.

Rebel horsemen clatter by every few minutes. Sooner or later one will knock on our door. I am hiding this notebook under the eaves in hopes no one will find it.

★ ★

Well after midnight, Meade and his staff picked their way through the stream of men converging on Gettysburg. From the first hour he feared Lee might have a trick up his sleeve. Jackson's ghost haunted all of them. Somewhere, a full Confederate corps might be out there ready to storm unseen into his rear. *No one knows the exact whereabouts of Longstreet's men, except for the black man. How can Prediger really know these things?*

They rode unseen past columns of men plodding, heads down, shoulders hunched to beat fatigue. Many dragged muskets behind them. A few straggled out of line, to be forced back by officers on horseback. On the roads, empty supply wagons bumped and jolted to the rear. The stench of camp and wood fires was everywhere. Out of the humid night, clouds of eye-stinging smoke drifted over them.

When Meade reached the caretaker's building in the cemetery a few yards from the lines, he found Howard, Sickles, and others clamoring to tell about the day's fight. Their straining, dissonant voices could not keep from him that the day was all but a disaster.

Slowly, the truth emerged. Half of Reynolds's men were lost, along with their commander. In Howard's corps, half the men were gone, and Howard was finished as a leader. The Confederates had killed, wounded, or captured 10,000 men. Meade could not decide whether the retreat through Gettysburg was an orderly withdrawal or a rout.

Through the discord he heard that Hancock's energy had saved them from destruction. Working in uneasy tandem with Howard, he placed remnants of Reynolds's 1st Corps atop Culp's Hill, lined up other shattered units along the crest of Cemetery Ridge, and urged on Slocum's men to hold the right flank. Hancock had very likely held off a Rebel *coup de grâce*.

From time to time, Buford's name slipped out. His cavalry stood fast, took new positions as needed, and in the end, alone, thanks to Sickles's tardiness, secured the left, where Lee might have attacked over open fields from strong positions a half-mile distant.

Still, in spite of differing views and intense competition, the generals answered, "Yes" to Meade's repeated question, "Is this then good ground?"

"Then here we shall fight," he said, and left to walk off through the Union line to look down on the enemy's fires and trace the Rebel position.

CHAPTER VIII

Before first light, Meade left with Hunt, the Chief of Artillery, to set out a defense line he called "the Fishhook." The barb lay on Culp's Hill to the east. The hook came north around Cemetery Hill toward town, the shank running south along the ridge to the high ground his men were calling the "Round Tops." They were the eye. He left Slocum in charge of Culp's Hill and ordered Hancock to bring his corps into the center along the ridge with Sickles's men reaching down to the Round Tops. Meade wrote each commander, ordering him to draw a map showing the terrain, the placement of each brigade, and as much about the enemy in front of him as he knew. It was July 2, the second day of battle.

Fitzpatrick carried orders from general to general without break. They received him jovially, offering a joke and a drink before he moved on. The commanders accepted his self-control as assurance of supreme authority. They seemed glad someone else risked making decisions. He found he could joke easily with men in the ranks, a sign morale was not bad, considering the long marches and the day's losses.

In the dawn he met Henry Prediger walking up the Taneytown Road. Henry came alongside and handed up a crumpled paper penciled with numbers and diagrams.

"No need to fret, major. The Rebels took a licking too," he grinned. "Probably lost about eight thousand, though they gonna put a lot of wounded back in line. We got counts from burial details and medical stations. Those lines on the paper are where Lee's men went into camp last night along roads leading outa town.

"You can see they've put a lot of 'em over beyond Culp's Hill.

They're gonna try something there. But the real push will come down by the Round Tops on our left. General Lee ordered General Longstreet to attack with two divisions and part of General Hill's corps. Those are the Rebel orders for the day. Will you take that paper to the general and tell him what I said?"

Fitz glanced at a group of officers riding by and staring at the Negro. "He's off with General Hunt." His eyes returned to Prediger. "I'm sure he'll be pleased. I heard him mention Culp's Hill. I've no idea what's going to happen on our left. Captain Meade took a message to General Sickles. All his men haven't come up yet. I'll report to the Commanding General as soon as I can.

"Headquarters is at Mrs. Leister's place, up the road about a half a mile. Wait there until I get back." Fitz spurred his horse, then reigned in to shout back. "And thanks very much, Henry. I'm damn proud about this."

Henry Prediger walked on wondering what had happened to the widow Lydia Leister.

★ ★

Hancock's men came into position at dawn. So did half of Sickles's, though Humphreys's division didn't arrive until well after daylight, having nearly marched straight into a Confederate bivouac along the Hagerstown Pike. They abruptly changed direction in the middle of the night after a lone colored man stepped out of the forest to offer directions. In the darkness and sensing he was lost, Humphreys was to glad to see him.

"You'll find the rest of your corps two jumps over on Cemetery Ridge yonder." Josephus pointed into the dark with a stout cane. "Take the pike and go back to Black Horse Tavern, turn left back to the Millerstown Road. Turn left again." When he had delivered his instructions and drawn a diagram on the ground in the lamplight, the old man bowed graciously. The general thanked him, and Josephus walked away into the night.

Later, when he called on his friend the Commanding General, Humphreys said, "I coulda been wrong as Hell, George, but something told me to trust the old man. He was well-spoken and earnest. It was clear nobody put him up to it. He musta once been a major-domo in some fine Southern home. 'Thank you, sir,' I said, 'I am in your debt.' And he just bowed and went off the way he came.

"I took his advice without a second thought. Lord knows we would sure as Hell come to grief if we didn't find you. That old darky was a godsend."

Meade and Fitzpatrick questioned Henry, and Meade was still trying to decide how to act on his message. "Do you think Henry and Humphreys's old man are in league? The Negroes have a great stake in our victory, don't they?"

"I'm beginning to understand, sir," said Fitzpatrick. "We've seen the handwriting on Henry's map before. Someone in Lee's army is passing along information through a chain of slaves and freedmen. The man Humphreys saw was part of that chain." He stood before Meade's table unsteady on bowed legs, reeking of horse sweat. Neither had slept. The general, not a young man, sat before him almost bright as a day.

"Tell Prediger I'm grateful," Meade ordered, "and take his paper to Sharpe. His man in Gettysburg has confirmed most of the first report. Still, we have to be careful. The Rebels are clever about these things. They might think it worthwhile to give us information we'd eventually get anyway.

"They wouldn't want to fight Humphreys at night; so instead of trapping him, they gave him a good steer, thus proving the bona fides of the rest of their information. It could have gone that way. There's a twisted logic in it. The Rebels play tricks, and, hard as it may be for us to believe, some of their Negroes are very loyal."

"Yes, I've heard that." Fitz steeled himself to argue. "But you should have seen Prediger's face, general. He's too proud to be taking orders from a master. When he stood by my horse handing this up, he was like a young man in his first suit. He wouldn't feel that way acting under force."

"Yes, and he's a freedman." Meade pulled on his beard. "You know, major, we don't have time to think. That's Sharpe's job. It's time he met your man. You both talk with Prediger. Plumb the depths, so to speak. I'm sure he would betray his doubts if he has any. See if he knows this old man who steered Humphreys."

"Meanwhile I shall assume Longstreet will attack. George will go to Sickles again to see exactly where he stands. He is supposed to have men on those heights. I damn well don't want to see Johnny Reb looking down on the 3d Corps."

A rattle of muskets from Culp's Hill was followed by a rider with an urgent message from Slocum. Meade had to spend time looking after the Union right. Artillery boomed on both sides. Pulled from side to side, he felt squeezed. Unsure of Sickles, he ordered cavalry to scout and, as dragoons, to hold the area in front of the Round Tops.

The 5th, Meade's old battle-hardened corps, began to arrive along with couriers announcing that Sedgwick and the 6th were not far off. The advent of these men, a third of his force, improved his humor. Without them, he had fewer than 40,000 men to face half again as many Rebel veterans, cockier than ever after yesterday.

The Negro's order of battle played in Meade's mind. Everyone believed the Rebels outnumbered them. The Pinkerton men insisted Lee had more than 100,000. Sharpe doubted their figure but was loath to accept numbers from a colored man. *Why should they be any different? Should we just assume Negroes can't count?*

★ ★

Riding south from the seminary under the morning sun, Lee drew up in full view of the enemy to look over their lines. "George Meade is a student of war," he told an aide. "He knows the lessons. Whoever concentrates and attacks first, wins. General Longstreet knows that." The horse lurched, jostling Lee, and sciatic tremors shot up his back. He winced to force the pain from his mind. What bothered him more was that his senior commander seemed to have bogged down. He was supposed to have attacked in the early light.

He found Longstreet with his division commanders, and dismounted, pointing toward the Round Tops. "Our scouts report no Yankees on those heights."

Longstreet, bareheaded, collar open, disputed the scouts, arguing Union forces were now there in force. "We should take the men farther right around the hills to turn their flank." The division commanders seconded him.

"We must attack them where they are massed," Lee responded, looking with piercing eyes at each general in turn. He went to a large stump to lay out a map and describe an assault up the Emmitsburg Road, taking the Yankees by the flank. "Your men are fully prepared, and I am confident they can take that low ground over there, or anything else we need them do. Aren't you, general?" His eyes fixed on his senior commander.

Longstreet chewed on a cigar and looked away. Lee disliked the habit. He chewed, obviously choking down disagreement. "The men are ready. Yes, sir."

"I hope I make myself clear, gentlemen." Lee turned to peer through his binoculars, and pointed. "You will of course take those heights—after you have isolated the force there. I see no more than a few signalmen. I suggest you move your men. You have said they are the best fighters in the world, general. That's no argument to say they can't succeed."

Longstreet saluted as Lee turned to ride away.

Fannie worked through the night in steaming tents down the Taneytown Road. She collected surgeons' tools, cleaned them, gave water to amputees, and sent them off, hopefully to find a clean place to lie down once the cutting was over. *Nothing eases their pain,* she thought, *surely not the few drops of whiskey they get. They have to endure, and a good many won't.*

She stepped out to watch the sun rise across fields where wagons were unloading supplies. Rays struck the tent, and a wood thrush sang. *A bit of God's blessing on this horror.*

More were coming in—some afraid to be looked at for fear of losing a limb, some brought by friends or limping in from hiding places where they had avoided capture. The volunteers worked steadily and well. The farm women knew how to boil water over a log fire and where to find straw. The six young girls with the madame were a mixed lot. Most tried, though they had little skill, even for small household tasks like washing up or making fires. Some joked with the wounded, a little coarse at times, and sometimes they sang. *The men love that.*

But the redhead pitched in as if she'd worked with suffering all her life. She went right into the surgeries, and no one said a thing as though a young girl could know what she was doing. Standing by the surgeons for hours, she reassured the men, holding the limbs they were about lose as though they were precious. *Even cleaning up gore, she was cheerful. She couldn't be any more than seventeen. What was she doing in a brothel?*

An old surgeon came to the tent flap, a saw in one hand, a bloody rag in the other. "Whatcha say, ma'am? I haven't heard word about anythin' but cuttin' for the last eight hours. Musta done thirty more since I last spoke to a whole person."

"I was just thinking about the helpers," Fannie said. "Some are very good." She did her best to smile. This man needed cheering.

"That purty little redheaded girl," said the surgeon. "I've never seen the like. You don't 'spect young women to have the stomach for work in a place like this. But she knows what to do, all right. Someone in her family musta been a surgeon, or an undertaker."

"I suppose," Fannie said, "She has a natural vocation. Some women do, you know. We're just lucky to find one."

Alice, head wrapped in a kerchief, limped up to the tent, looked in, grimaced, and pulled back. "Stinks to Hell. Whew! Someone shit in here? Can't you douse it with cologne or somethin'?"

The doctor recoiled and walked wearily back into the tent.

"They do defecate, if that's what you mean," said Fannie. "One simply has to put up with it. I doubt all the scent in France would do much good. You don't smell anything after awhile. It just makes the air sweeter when you find it again."

Alice moved closer. "My girls, are they doin' okay? I want 'em to do right, you know, so the new general will appreciate us."

"Some do very well," said Fannie, turning away to avoid alcohol fumes. "I dare say one has found her calling. The red-headed young woman is very competent."

"That'd be Maizie," said Alice, steadying herself on a guy rope. She stepped forward, stumbling toward Fannie. "Pardon, ma'am, I just took a little drink. My nerves, ya know."

The odor of cheap whiskey overcame the stench of surgery. Fannie stepped back. "I suggest you find some clean water or hot tea. You'll need to keep a clear head."

Alice looked out through thick graying brows, eyes narrow and dull. "God, all we're doin' here and ya don' give a damn." She spat, looked away and stomped off heavy-footed and angry.

"It's a gamble, I suppose," said Fannie aloud, as she turned into the tent where the surgeon, with the girl's help, prepared to cut off the leg of a frightened young corporal below the knee.

As the sun rose higher on a bright clear day, the mists melted, and the two armies saw each other. Captain George Meade's boots banged onto the floorboards of the Leister House as he stormed in. "That damn man's asleep, father, and I couldn't find anyone to wake him or take my message. They're not on the Round Tops yet. You've got to do something about 3d Corps."

Meade looked up, always glad to see George, and smiled, then frowned. "All Sickles's men not in position? You're right. Something is damn well wrong. Nearly noon. I wonder how long we have? If Longstreet's going to attack, he should have been about it by now."

No sooner had he spoken than the source of worries appeared, as Sickles put it, "to clarify my orders." Meade received him courteously. Sickles asked how much latitude he had. Meade said he must cover the ground between the 2d Corps and the Round Tops. "Within those limits, you have room to maneuver." To avoid misunderstanding, he sent Hunt, his chief artilleryman, back with him to go over to the lines.

An hour later Hunt reported Sickles had moved his corps forward onto what he claimed was better ground. The argument was logical, Hunt said, except it left both flanks open and no force on the heights.

An orderly brought in a message from signalmen on the Round Tops reporting Longstreet on their front. Hunt suggested Meade ought to go see for himself. At the same moment, a courier came from the cavalry commander reporting Longstreet about to attack.

It was always Dan Sickles who didn't follow orders. God damn politicians! Where do they learn anything about ground? Meade ordered the 5th Corps to move onto the heights and cover the left flank of the army. "It's late," he said, pulling out his watch, "If an attack is coming, it's overdue."

Outside the house, he met Fitzpatrick, nearly out of breath. "The signalmen on Round Top report an unknown wigwag sending messages from behind enemy lines, general."

"More strange intelligence?" Meade seemed angry.

Fitz got a deep breath. "Sir, the message reads: 'Longstreet with two divisions marching on Round Tops, Hood's division directly, McLaws toward the peach orchard.'" He paused. "And this is the key, sir, 'where General Humphreys came through from the pike this morning.'"

"What does Prediger say?" asked Meade.

"Henry says the man who steered Humphreys is called Josephus. He has an associate who somehow learned signals while a slave to Col. Porter Alexander. He's the man sending messages."

Cannon boomed all around the Fishhook. Frustrated and now fatigued, Meade caught his breath and paused, standing on the porch with a dozen officers around him, and tried to think. His mind cleared. "I have to say that makes sense in an odd way. Former Lieutenant Alexander USA helped organize our signals and now serves with Longstreet. He set up the Rebel system." He would like to chew over a thing like this with colleagues around a campfire. But not now.

"We must assume Longstreet will attack right at the 3d Corps. We've got to get over there." He swore and his stomach churned. "Of all the plagues visited on the Army of the Potomac, Dan Sickles is the worst."

☆ ☆

The 3d Corps commander paced before a line of young officers outside the Trostle House, a lone frame building that served as his headquarters in a glade below the Emmitsburg Pike. "We are going to have a helluva fight today." The sword hanging by his side just missed a rock. "Old George Meade is no fighter. But, by God, the 3d will set the pace. We'll finish Robert E. Lee and those phony Rebel aristocrats."

The officers nodded and grinned to each other. In the north, cannon sounded and muskets rattled. In almost every direction, dust rose where horses churned up the roads. Down the lane behind a group of officers, all seemingly generals, rode toward them.

"General Sickles," Meade called. "I've come to look at your position. You're going to have a fight on your hands very soon."

Sickles smiled. "It's Longstreet with 20,000 men. I guess we'll have to stop them."

"That's a big order, general. Come with me and let us ride over the ground together. You may need some help. The 5th is moving onto your left."

They traced out the lines, including a field of huge boulders men were calling "Devil's Den," uncovered on Sickles's left. At the end, Meade was troubled. "You've left your flanks in the air, general. The 3d Corps was ordered to connect with Hancock on the right and anchor on the Round Tops on the left. You don't reach either. Furthermore, several positions are exposed by the flank. If Longstreet mounts the kind of attack he's capable of, and it hits you there, your men won't hold."

"My men will stand, General Meade." Sickle's humor was gone. "They can hold." He gritted his teeth and the mustache twitched.

"I'm sure they are excellent men, General Sickles. But you and I must take no unnecessary chance. Longstreet would be up on those heights before you can turn around."

Sickles stared at his horse's head, breathing heavily. Finally with a sigh he asked, "Do you want me to withdraw, general?" A spark seemed to reignite him. "Won't the men say we ordered a retreat?" He looked at his Commanding General.

Meade glared down at him. *The little man is trying a bit of blackmail.* "General Sickles, I will post two brigades, the 5th on the Round Tops and the rest of two divisions below, connecting with you. Your men will move to make room for them. The Chief of Engineers will mark out the lines. You will form deeper positions, particularly at that orchard on the pike. Longstreet is now on your front. If you look just to your left, you can see his cannon about a mile away.

"Tighten up the gap between your divisions. I will order Hancock to move on your right. And I suggest you not hug so tight to the pike. If we have enough men properly aligned, we can indeed stop them."

Sickles looked away. Resistance seethed through his words. "As you order, sir."

Meade's face froze. He desperately wished he could say something cheerful, crack a heroic joke, josh the little son of a bitch, and carry the day like a gentleman. Contempt held him back.

The brief silence was hard. "My men will do as ordered," Sickles raised his hand to his hat.

Meade returned the salute and reined his horse back toward the ridge. "General, I bid you the best of luck." Baldy moved off in a sidling trot well ahead of the staff.

One of Sickles's aides, thinking the Commanding General had lost control of his horse, began to laugh. Sickles rounded on him with a snarl. "Shut up, you young bastard, and get over to Humphreys. Tell him his friend George Meade don't want to take the aggressive today."

CHAPTER IX

In the afternoon sun, Sergeant Edward Tucker of the 71st New York stood in double line with his company in an open field behind the Emmitsburg Road. Cannon sounded right and left. He heard the rattle of muskets moving up from the south. "Skirmishers! They do that to discover our position. You hear that?" He raised a hand for quiet.

O'Hara nodded. He'd heard about it before.

"Them Rebs are sending skirmishers in groups one after the other," said Tucker, "Sending 'em over to find how we stand. They'll be some coming anytime soon right out front here. Keep your eyes peeled on our men in those woods." He pointed forward and to his left.

O'Hara made a face. "Glad we got a road here, but I wish to Hell the ditch was deeper. Don't give much protection."

Men in front returned fire from Rebel skirmishers. Shooting lasted a few minutes and slacked off. "Them Rebs found what they wanted to know," laughed Tucker. "They can see us anyway, plain as day. I say they'll hit first down through the trees, and come on us like a surprise. We're gonna have a hot time. You hear them cannons booming down there?" He paused. "And soon it'll be our turn."

"I know," said O'Hara. He wasn't smiling, and wondered why Tucker got so excited. *He seems to like it. Not afraid of dying or anything. Scary as Hell to me. Am I gonna remember to load? Powder stinks, tastes terrible. If the gun jams, I can clear out.* O'Hara had yet to face a full-throated Rebel charge.

Late in the afternoon the first of Longstreet's men came over the fields at the base of the Round Tops. Trained and cool, they advanced in order toward men of the 5th who had met Rebel fire at Fredericksburg and Antietam. General Sykes placed his men carefully in the wheatfield, on the rocks of Devil's Den, and on Little Round Top. Dragoons extended the Union line in front of Big Round Top. Skirmishers and sharpshooters kept low in front picking away at the advance. The men of the 5th were ready.

The attack surged in and out for more than an hour. Fire from the dragoons' breech-loaders bit into the Rebel flank. A Rebel's brigade wheeled to the right. No one on either side doubted the fighting skill of the Southerners, but the Yankees had better ground. Their left was secure. Longstreet's men, assaulting, withdrawing, charging, and recharging, could not dislodge them.

Minute by minute and hour by hour the fighting boiled northward as succeeding Confederate brigades slammed one after another into Union lines. Both sides suffered heavy losses. When Rebels crashed through the peach orchard yelling like demons, they had better luck. Sickles's men gave way. They retreated and regrouped and sent the Georgians back over ground littered with bodies. The Rebels reformed and attacked again and again, as lines thinned.

⋆ ⋆

Dan Sickles heard the roar of battle at the Trostle House. On the down slope below the Emmitsburg Road surrounded by trees, he had a limited view and depended on a steady stream of messengers.

First word from the left was encouraging. "They're strung out like we are," he told the staff, biting his lip. "We'll show George Meade and those damned Academy men." He raised an arm. "We stand to the fore! The 3d will take this thing head on. Hold on men, and victory will be ours."

A rider brought an appeal from General Birney for more men at the peach orchard. Sickles had already sent a brigade from Humphreys's division to support him. He pulled out a cigar, and an aide rushed over with a lit match. He puffed. Cannonballs whistled overhead, and one exploded near the house. He called for his horse. "I'm going to reconnoiter. Two of you go to the rear, find whatever units you can for General Birney. It's hot over there. That's where the battle is, and mind, it's our battle. Don't take back talk. I don't care what they wear on their shoulders. You have my authority." Sickles glowered. "I'm in command on the field. If Meade's got troops back there sitting on their ass, I'm damn well going to have 'em."

Wearing the unquestioned authority of their leader, Sickles's aides set out to find regiment and brigade commanders and order them in his name to send men to the peach orchard.

☆ ☆

By a copse on the edge of Cemetery Ridge, Meade watched with Fitzpatrick by his side. Among trees below, a mass of men seethed in the billows of smoke and fires. Men, cannon, horses and wagons moved in and out of chaos that was a pattern to Meade. He saw Rebels attacking along the line of the Emmitsburg Road from the south toward town. Two of Longstreet's divisions, plus a division of Hill's corps poised and ready, made a total of 25,000 men. He had about the same, if Sickles could hold. Slocum sent frequent messages saying Ewell's men still threatened his end, the barb of the Fishhook.

"It's clear now we were right to trust Prediger," he told Fitzpatrick. "Look how George Sykes and our old 5th do the job. They wouldn't have got into position so quick without that intelligence. Our left is going to hold. The outcome depends on Sickles holding the center." Below, stragglers from the 3d Corps streamed out of the trees in larger numbers. "No message from him. I suppose I shouldn't expect one." He smiled at Fitz, but raged inside. "He sacrifices men with gay abandon."

At the top of the Fishhook, Meade had put all troops under Hancock's command and ordered him to send a division to support Humphreys. He could see Rebel brigades lining up to carry the attack up the road toward town. "I'd put Humphreys under Hancock altogether," he told Fitzpatrick. "But, if I'm cursed with Dan Sickles, I must accept him. It's his moment, whatever he may do with it." Sickles's staff aides rode below in the smoke, but none came near—a bad sign.

In the woods below, Rebels appeared to have forced a breakthrough. Out of it men drained, some to die, some to tarry and pray,

99

but most to struggle back in spent groups of twos and threes toward safety. Meade turned to Fitzpatrick.

"Go to General Sickles. Tell him first that the Rebels are attacking all the way up the road. That may help him understand he's not alone, or entirely in command." He laughed.

"Second, tell him I have secured his flanks with men of Hancock and Sykes. Then, ask whether he needs help. Finally, ask if he has a line to fall back to. He won't like the last thing, but we've got to give him a chance to be modest." Meade chuckled. *Hardly something to laugh about. This young man has become my confidante. We understand each other.*

Fitzpatrick saluted and left.

From the wheatfield to the angle at the peach orchard was over half a mile. On good ground, two brigades could hold it, especially when backed by artillery. Sickles counted on crushing the Rebels with canister from 30 guns set to fire into advancing flanks. He was proud of his design, cannon along a lane at angles to the main road and set to fire into the Rebels *en enfilade*, while his infantry faced forward and fired volley after volley at the oncoming enemy. He liked French terms. They were professional, and he didn't hesitate to use "French" maneuvers.

He did not account for the mettle of Longstreet's men nor the skill of Porter Alexander's artillery. Following closely on an intense and well-aimed cannonade, two brigades, Georgians and Mississippians, advanced in repetitive lunges through the peach trees and broke the Union corner at the crossroads, sending the artillery racing to the rear. Birney's brigades fell back in disarray, as Mississippians pushed through.

Sickles returned from his talk with Birney and found his cannon pulled back, some even heading for the park behind Cemetery Ridge. He ordered what was left into line to staunch the retreat. In some places Rebels moved in disciplined lines toward his rear. He hated to think about it. *The center of Birney's line is breaking. The men fight well. They slow the Rebel advance, but they don't stop it.* He grasped for hope. *Perhaps there is time, if George Meade will send me troops.* He scowled, remaining mounted outside the Trostle House as bullets and shells whined and whistled around him. Orange flames etched in black smoke lit the scene on all sides. Sickles's eyes watered. Dimly in the gray-hazed forest he saw Fitzpatrick riding up—*the Commanding General's Benjamin.*

He saluted. "General Meade sends his compliments and says the Rebels are attacking all the way up the Emmitsburg Road to Gettysburg. He has ordered a division of the 2d Corps to move onto your right. The 5th stands firm on the left. General Meade asks whether you need assistance and where, if need be, you would want to establish a secondary line."

Sickles said nothing and stared at him dressed like his commander in plain blue. *Now he's wearing Meade's ridiculous hat. It nearly hides his face. Don't look bad on him. Where does this little son of a bitch get the gall to order me around?* Sickles took a loud, commanding tone, almost a shout. "My men will hold, major. Tell George Meade I'm here and intend to stay put. I've asked him for a division from the 2d Corps to support General Birney, who stands engaged at the center of battle. If that message hasn't gotten through, you take it back, major." Sickles scowled, drawing up his mustache and goatee as he saluted to wave off Fitzpatrick.

Fitz raised his hand to his hat. "I'll report your response, general." With lips taught and teeth clenched, he turned to ride off.

A staff officer yelled after him. "You tell the Commanding General we're here, major." Others guffawed.

A cannonball crashed in the middle of the area near the general. They didn't see it graze his horse. Sickles moaned and slid from his saddle, right foot caught in the stirrup. Aides ran up to hold the horse and free him as he fought to stifle gasps of pain. His right leg was in tatters.

Sickles babbled. He said he feared capture and asked his men to hide him in the rear of the barn to wait for help. After a few minutes he recovered and sent an aide to tell Birney to take command of the corps. He asked for a cigar.

An aide from 3d Corps cantered past Fitz toward Cemetery Ridge. At a dead run he caught up with the breathless lieutenant, who yelled, "I going for an ambulance to take General Sickles out of danger."

Meade struggled to suppress relief at having the little man out of the way. He had sent a division to staunch the Rebel flow. Now he put Hancock in charge of the 3d Corps, penciling a hasty note to Birney. Men were still needed to fill the hole. A messenger from Sedgwick announced arrival of the 6th Corps; 14,000 men had marched 32 miles in 17 hours, an exhausted gaggle, but they were 14,000 men. Meade ordered two divisions into line behind Hancock. He was now certain he could hold.

Fighting raged. Men stood face to face in combat. Neither side gave way. If a Union regiment fell back, or fell apart, another took its place. The lines held, and Rebel ammunition ran short. Fatigue took its toll. Two Rebel brigades withdrew. Along the lane by the peach orchard the battle continued, and farther up the Emmitsburg Road brigades of Hill's men struck at the 2d Corps. Through a gap, Wilcox's Alabamians reached the slope of Cemetery Ridge. Many fell, but they came on. A single Minnesota regiment of 300 men charged into them. After a half-hour's fight a full brigade joined to force Wilcox back. At dusk a final Yankee surge of men from four separate corps swept across Plum Run and took back the Trostle Farm. The Confederates fell back to the crossroads at the peach orchard. The sun set over the mountains long after 8:00 p.m., leaving dead and wounded men and horses between the lines to groan, stink, and cry out in the night amid smoke and raging fire.

On the earthen floor Flossie Muelheim wrote in twilight:

Rebel horsemen rode up and down in front of our house all day. They didn't bother us last night, except for a polite lieutenant who told us to stay inside and be ready to answer when called out. Early this morning teams of men came to search and take away food, clothes, blankets. They asked for Yankee money, though we were told they weren't supposed to. Fortunately, Papa buried his greenbacks days ago. I think the sergeant knew it because he wasn't pleased with what he got, and said angrily, "I'll be back."

They barely missed our Heinrich in the cellar. The sergeant asked what was in the pile of boxes. We told him "ladies' clothes and patent medicines," and he made a face and said, "I ain't got time to fool with women's gear."

They were probably too interested in plunder to care about a harmless wounded Yankee. We hear some neighbors have taken in wounded men from both sides. The Rebels don't seem to mind as long as the Yankees are badly off.

Heinrich sleeps most all the time, but he seems to be getting better. Mama fed him broth, and he thanked her much for it. I pray he will recover.

The Rebels caught Sally. Mrs. Morgan wouldn't help, and they marched her off screaming. I can't believe the Johnny Rebs are going to take her south.

The fighting was farther away than yesterday. We heard plenty of noise from cannon and, once in awhile, rifles. A ball exploded just down the street and damaged a store front. The Rebels have barricaded all roads up to the cemetery, even tearing down a cabin for timbers.

CHAPTER X

People in town heard sounds of battle all through the day and into the night, but could not distinguish between a furious artillery duel two miles away and urgent, deliberate fighting close by, where late in the afternoon Ewell sent men against the top of the Fishhook. In the dusk, Ewell's men gained a lodgment on the brow of Cemetery Hill. Farther east, others seized trenches on Culp's Hill abandoned by Yankees called away to defend the other side of the Fishhook.

George Meade felt pleased with the day's work. He had been in the thick of it, sending in men where needed, and once himself rallying a brigade to stop a Rebel charge. Even as fighting raged on, he knew his men would hold, and Lee had lost more than he. He was satisfied with his ground, and convinced Lee's forces were wasting away.

At nightfall, he met in the Leister House with Sharpe and Fitzpatrick. Battle sounds penetrated the room, but for the first time in days his stomach was calm. On a side table stood a bottle of whiskey.

"Have you heard from your man, Fitzpatrick?" Meade stretched back in his chair.

"Not yet, sir. We expect to see a signal tonight."

"What do you think, Sharpe? Prediger's warning gained us time. Are they giving us good numbers?"

"I've been trying to decide, sir. Everything we've got from our regular sources fits what they've told us."

"Can you guess how they get information?" Meade picked up his cigar case and held it out. The junior officers refused. He took one and lit it from the oil lamp.

Sharpe looked up from a paper in his hand. "Prediger says they have people working in hospitals and on burial details, but that wouldn't be enough. They must have well-placed men who serve senior generals, possibly Lee himself."

"You mean," Meade chuckled, "the man who shuffles in and says, 'Heahs yoah mo'nin' tee, Mars' Robert,' finds time to rifle his papers? Sounds unlikely. The Rebels know about this kind of warfare, more than we do. Surely, they'd think of such a thing."

"We know the Rebs have sent out warnings about this possibility, sir. But ties between master and slave are often very old, particularly with a venerable man like Lee. It might not occur to him he was taking a risk, and no subordinate would dare point the finger."

The lamplight beamed off Meade's spectacles. "Yes, that's possible. I know a bit about the South. We have Southern connections. They swear by their own Negroes, even if they're scared to death of everyone else's. I suppose you're right, by Jove. If a trusted servant in Lee's household were a spy, he might indeed go undetected."

He stroked the outer hairs of his beard. "We may know more about Lee's strength than he does about us, and his strength is much less than we thought. In fact," Meade held his cigar in the air, calculating, "if we've managed to maul two divisions from Longstreet, and all Hill's and Ewell's, we've cut into every one he has."

"Lee has one fresh division, sir." Sharpe looked at his paper. "Pickett, with three brigades of Virginians we haven't seen for a year. We observed his men coming up."

A loud knock made all three look toward the door to see Hancock bound into the room. White shirt open at the collar, he radiated energy. Meade's smile became a grin, "Hancock! the very man we need. Sharpe here says we're going to face George Pickett tomorrow."

Hancock took a chair Fitz vacated. A smile spread across his face. "Then it will be a medieval test of arms." He held his right arm wide as if holding a broadsword.

"Lee will come across to your front, if he's going to come at all. He doesn't have the men to outflank us. The ground before you might allow him concealment to come close enough to charge."

Hancock turned to Sharpe. "How many men do they have, colonel?"

Sharpe scratched his head. "General, if Longstreet lost thirty percent of his men today, I'd say, well, no more than fifty thousand, depending on how matters go on Culp's Hill."

Hancock pursued the point. "We've fought all their divisions but Pickett's. Is that right?"

"Yes, but in those we've fought, Hill has two brigades unbled, and our spies in town say Ewell has two."

Hancock waved a dismissive hand. "George, he may not be able to attack at all. That's defeat by any name for Bobby Lee."

Meade looked doubtful, "It's not the way he'll see the position. Lee must make one more try. It may be his one chance to win with a clean stroke. If he's forced to retreat, he can do it. He's an expert at vanishing over those mountains."

Meade stared at notes on his desk. "The 6th will be available for counterattack. God knows how many men Sedgwick actually has. Stragglers are still coming in."

Watching Hancock calmed him. He was sure an attack on the 2d Corps would fail, and, even without a counterstroke, victory would be his.

Meade dismissed the junior men, and continued talking with Hancock over whiskey and crackers. They spoke briefly of Dan Sickles, agreeing, as Hancock put it, his absence meant no loss of genius to the Union cause.

Hancock left Meade pondering his next message to Washington, now determined above all to keep his intentions secret from the enemy. Stuart's men might intercept him. He was cryptic:

Headquarters, Army of the Potomac, July 2, 1863

The enemy attacked at about 4:00 p.m. today, and, after one of the severest contests of the war, was repulsed at all points. One brigadier general was killed. Sickles and a number of other senior officers wounded. I shall remain in my position tomorrow, but am not prepared to say until better advised of the condition of the army whether my operations will be offensive or defensive.

George G. Meade

Major General Commanding

A procession of aides, bearers, and chaplains attended a battered ambulance carrying Major General Sickles. Stubbornly, his teeth clenched a lighted Havana. He babbled of approaching death. Loss of blood weakened him, and by the time he came to the surgery he ceased to speak.

The 3d Corps's hospital down the Taneytown Road was a barn surrounded by a half-dozen tents furnished with cots, benches, and rustic tables lit by oil lamps and candles skewered on bayonets. Outside, shadows of doctors doing continuous surgery projected against piles of bloody arms and legs, the residue of earlier work. Within a wide radius the stench was overpowering. An occasional whiff of chloroform gave faint hope that somewhere was solace.

The Chief Surgeon, warned of the general's approach, set a tent aside and assigned his best physician. At the 1st Corps hospital up the road, where surgeons were still dealing with yesterday's wounded, they told him about the amazing skills of a female nurse who might help the general in his crisis. She had had experience with victims of train wrecks and was particularly good during amputations, they said. He was astonished to hear of a woman working at an operating table, but war called for unusual measures, and he asked for her.

As soon as the general arrived, the surgeon ordered him into the operating tent. Carefully, Sickles's men put him onto an unsteady wooden table. The nurse prepared a cloth to give him chloroform. He looked up, pleased to see a pretty woman, and smiling a lusty smile passed out. The nurse and the surgeon prepared the wound, taking away a makeshift leather strap around the general's leg, replacing it with a proper tourniquet on the thigh, and stripping blood-soaked clothing from the skin below.

Shell fragments had gone into the leg. "It'll have to come off," the surgeon muttered. As spectators watched, mesmerized as much by the girl as the gory job, he calculated the cut. "Above the knee," he announced and swung his knife forward over Sickles's leg. Nodding to the men in the crowded tent to hold the general steady, he began carving away flesh. The nurse cleaned off blood so he could see. He picked up his saw and began to cut the bone straight through, grating. Men blanched and looked away.

The nurse stood close and solemnly pinched blood vessels so the surgeon could tie them. He finished in 15 minutes. She handed him a large needle with a strong thread to complete the ligature. Sickles groaned and gasped but did not cry out. The surgeon sewed the frayed skin into a stump as tight as he could. The nurse stood back, wiped her hands on her apron and silently waited with them folded over it.

"He must lie flat and rest now," the surgeon addressed Major Tremaine, the general's senior aide, "So the blood will clot. Mind you, he must not be moved for many hours, preferably days. His life depends on it."

The officers lifted Sickles onto a stretcher while Tremaine reached down for the leg. The nurse, Maeve, quickly picked it up, wrapped it carefully in cloth and handed it to him with a subdued smile.

"Thank you, ma'am, we must keep this," he said staring at her. Gently, they carried Sickles out and put him in the ambulance. It crept very slowly to a large house down the road, where in a stuffy, chloroform-stinking room, Tremaine and an orderly spent the night by his bed. Others sprawled on the porch. Two 3d Corps men stood guard at the gate.

At a late-night meeting, each commander gave his version of the day's fight, Meade from time to time adding his bit. The generals amused themselves with banter of a half-born victory. Butterfield took notes, and asked if he might pose three questions. To each, the commanders responded with a desire to stand and fight.

Meade had not set an agenda and did not want a council of war, which might tie his hands. It wasn't his way to cut Butterfield short. He made sure to continue the session and put his stamp on it. He laid on the table a sketch of the Fishhook showing where he wanted each corps to take position, reuniting all units sent away during the day.

"I am beginning to believe," he announced, "though I am by no means convinced, that, God willing, we'll have an opportunity to take the offensive tomorrow and do extensive damage to Lee's army. We must be ready." He paused, standing in the stifling room staring through spectacles at a paper in his hands. The generals nodded. Sedgwick dozed off, exhausted.

Meade was patient. They would take time to digest his ideas. Hancock would reinforce him. Birney and Butterfield nodded to each other. "I have been impressed," Meade continued, "by Buford's ability to maneuver dragoons. We must use cavalry." He nodded to Pleasonton, sitting on the floor nodding off.

The cavalry chief jolted awake where he was slumped against the wall and stood up. "We can certainly lead the attack, general. My men are ready."

Meade smiled. He was never sure of Pleasonton, except that he could bluster. "I have in mind using Buford's riders to break through and pin the enemy flanks as we make a hole in their lines. With carbines at close range, they can hold off a fair number of Rebels until massed infantry can crush them. It's rather a new tactic. One we must try with care, I'm sure. We shall talk about it with your commanders in the morning."

He had planted a seed knowing the infantrymen would be chary of a new tactic, especially one using cavalry. Some looked startled, almost outraged. Meade suppressed a grin, delighted in spite of himself. He'd not been an innovator before. In the hope of victory something heady, like wine, bade him try. Hancock in his white shirt grinned.

The generals left before midnight to pass along orders. All troop shifts were to be made before dawn, expected about 3:30 a.m. Meade lay on his cot, legs over the end, sleeping comfortably in the knowledge that he would waken to the rattle of rifle fire when Slocum's men moved to retake lost trenches on Culp's Hill.

★ ★

For surgeons, orderlies, and nurses, the night made no difference. Probing, cutting, and sawing continued in the fetid tents at each corps's medical group. Mounds of limbs grew, and so did the hospital fields down the Taneytown and Baltimore roads, where the wounded lay on open ground, each praying to make it through to daylight and some unknown deliverance. Chaplains moved among them, a few offering hope for life, others preparing men for the hereafter. It was a gamble which kind a man got, though to the women volunteers there was far too much talk of death.

Maeve returned to the 1st Corps Hospital, where Fannie and

Clarissa had established a base. Outside a recovery tent she found Alice with Sigurd. Both were unsteady, but Sigurd was drunk.

Alice spewed fumes, leering at Maeve. "Whad'ya think fer Chrissake? Yer the little angel of goodness. This dumb tart went right into a tent and took off her clothes. That rich friend o' yers was the one caught her, or we'd all be off down the road. Jesus Christ, as if anyone wants to be here anyway!" She spat.

It was hard to tell who put more alcohol in the air, almost a relief from the stench. "What happened, Sigurd?" Maeve's face showed pain held in all day.

"I did one of 'em." Sigurd hiccoughed. "A good-looking fella. Thought I could give 'em a little comfort." She smiled idiotically and swerved to grab a tent guy.

"Jesus Christ, you stupid whore, don't you know what I gotta do." Alice's face showed something like concern beyond her business worries. "You're going to have to go, and damn soon. I mean right now, before there's any more ruckus."

Maeve wanted to protest but saw it was useless. "Where?" she asked.

"I'll get her down to Sally's in Frederick. She can always use a yellow-hair. James'll take her tonight. You go pack your things, dearie."

Maeve gave Sigurd a hug. "Take care," she said, patting her stringy yellow curls. They embraced a second time. "I'll find you when this is over. Be brave."

Sigurd pulled away. "Don't worry about me," she said, and began to cry, as Alice led her away by the arm.

Maeve didn't want to think about it. Alice loved Sigurd, after all, and wouldn't see her come to harm. For two days she hadn't thought about men in that way, about "doin' the thing." Sigurd's crazy act brought back the mood of the wagons, where girls talked about "doin' it with a good-lookin' fella," and too often claimed they were in love, knowing they'd never see him again. In the weeks since she'd come to Alice's, Maeve had steeled herself. She saw the pitfalls.

"But that major!" the girls had said. "He's General Meade's right hand." She steadied herself on the tent rope. The major was the one man who had excited her, with whom, as the girls said, she'd "come." That hadn't happened before, though she'd been close. Now in the sight of sacrilege against human bodies, she recalled the moment almost happily. The memory brought her back to life. "But what kind of a life?" she asked, and caught herself.

The telegram reached the War Office in the early hours. The President in shirtsleeves was sleeping knees-to-chest on a cot in the Secretary's office. Stanton read the message over twice, pulling on his mutton chops, and handed it to the General-in-Chief. "Meade is being careful," said Halleck, looking over his spectacles at the sleeping figure and speaking quietly. "We know at least that he's holding Lee and wearing him down. Lee has to attack, and Meade knows it."

Lincoln yawned and stretched his limbs over the cot. "But, General Halleck, when is Meade going to attack?"

"At this point, Mr. President, this day's fight was for the best. On the first day Meade was caught off balance, briefly, before all his men were up. The army took heavy losses, but according to latest word, so did Lee. With Stuart on the loose, Meade and his men can't risk writing everything in their messages. It seems clear the day now beginning will be decisive."

Lincoln took the telegram and read it over. "Sickles is wounded. That can't be good. He's one of the few with fight in him."

"Yes," said Stanton. He preferred not to talk about his former client, and looked over at Halleck, whose owl eyes closed. Stanton, after long exposure to military order, had come to doubt Sickles's ability.

Lincoln looked up. "I know you prefer the professional men, General Halleck, but men like him add a little ginger to the mix. Don't you think?"

Halleck hesitated. The President was taunting him. "I think he can be replaced, in the circumstances. There are several officers who can fill the role. We don't know yet whether the 3d Corps is in condition to conduct operations. It must have borne the brunt of the day's fight."

"Well," said the President laying back, arms bent, cradling his head with his large hands, "I hope he's not badly hurt so he can tell us what happened." He closed his eyes.

The Secretary of War watched the General-in-Chief grimace and could not resist a smile.

As fighting calmed on Culp's Hill, Lee sent Ewell orders to attack first thing in the morning. Though Ewell's new wooden leg sent pains up his thigh, he was beginning to feel comfortable. Laudanum from the doctor helped, though at times he felt giddy and wanted to sleep. He was determined not to be slow again. His men kept their perch on Cemetery Hill. The corps was ready.

At the seminary by the Cashtown Road, Lee met in the cool of the night with Longstreet. He wanted the attack renewed on both flanks as soon as possible.

Longstreet's commanders had reported heavy losses. General Wofford, whose Georgians had nearly broken through, said flatly his men were not ready. Longstreet would rather chew nails than pass that to Lee.

"How bad was it?" Lee asked. Seldom was he so blunt.

"The men fought very well, general, and so did the Yankees. I would guess some brigades lost forty men out of a hundred. Not all, but some." Longstreet knew he was shading it. He did not include men returning with bandaged wounds, some with one arm, some who leaned on sticks as they stood. Hood's division, when he rode through, was not a pleasant sight. The men were down. He saw no sign of the confidence that made the Confederate soldier what he was. It had always been obvious. Tonight it was gone.

"We must mass artillery tomorrow," Lee went on. "You have young Porter Alexander with you?"

"Yes, Colonel Alexander is very good. I'm pleased to have him. He's bright as can be. Do you want to see him?"

"No, General Longstreet, but I want a heavy cannonade, like Solferino. You know, Beauregard broke up the Yankees that way at Shiloh last year. Artillery will overcome Meade's advantage on the ground. You will bring General Pickett's division up as soon as possible. I want the attack renewed in the morning."

Longstreet knew his own commanders thought like him—they

didn't want to report the worst. Honor required an officer to say his men were ready whatever their condition. He had taken the trouble to check the facts, but he was an officer and a gentleman. He didn't want to disappoint the old man. "Yes, general, I'll wait your further orders."

"No, General Longstreet, I want you to attack first thing."

CHAPTER XI

First light came. In open meadowland around the Fishhook, lingering night mists hid thousands, Union and Confederate, lying in the woods and grass, some able and resting, some wounded and dying, some cold and dead. On Culp's Hill the fog was lighter, and rifle fire pierced the dawn as soon as men could make out shapes across the lines.

Meade lay on his cot waking slowly from a dream where Reynolds on horseback led a long blue column marching in sunshine. Angels hovered above. The men were joyous and smiling with wounds made whole.

He heard wagons creaking by on the Taneytown Road, hauling stricken men to hospitals or to burial. It was too much to think about. He wanted to believe they fought willingly and gave themselves because they were men, because it was duty. That was enough for him. It ought to be for everyone.

He moved his head slowly from side to side. It ached, and his muscles were wooden. The hot room reeked of cigars. Stale whiskey soured his tongue. *Shouldn't have drunk a second glass with Hancock. Moderation in all things.* His eyes fell dimly on the bottle two-thirds full. He shook his head. He must keep it clear. This was to be a good day, and a lot needed to be done. Many commanders were not ready, and he had scarcely spoken to John Sedgwick. Spasms coursed through his stomach, empty since yesterday noon. He raised his body, rolled off onto his knees and softly began to say a morning prayer for strength and forgiveness, and for the men who would fight. "On both sides," he said in full voice, "when men pay the price of battle, let them be in glory."

As though he'd been listening, an orderly knocked. "An urgent message from General Slocum, sir."

Meade rose six-two onto his stocking feet, pulled long thin fingers through his beard, blew a foul breath from his mouth, blinked bulging eyes, sat back on the bed boot in hand, and shouted, "Come!" He read the message while waiting for a basin of warm water and a towel.

☆ ☆

Lee was wide awake and fully dressed. With a mug of tea in his hand, he walked to his horse, pleased to hear the rumble of guns on Culp's Hill. Ewell had moved. He mounted and walked his horse slowly south along Seminary Ridge in the gathering light, often in full view of the Union lines. Men rose in the ranks to salute. Many were seriously wounded. He reminded himself, *We must weed them out.* An excited aide rode up to say Longstreet was planning to take his men beyond the Round Tops to turn the Union flank. Lee scowled and spurred his mount.

He was pleased to see Colonel Alexander had placed cannon effectively along the low ridge of the Emmitsburg Road. Lee complimented him, asked about members of his family, and suggested the guns be pulled back a bit to make them less visible.

He met Longstreet and his entourage, and immediately ordered that no attack go forward without artillery support, adding almost as an afterthought that the army did not have the numbers to make a forceful turning movement. "Meade has at least one large fresh corps behind that ridge, and probably two others nearby. How many men do you have, general? Fifteen thousand?"

Longstreet looked away. "About that," he said, though his manner betrayed doubt.

"Is General Pickett up?"

"He's coming."

Lee frowned and dismounted, propping his field glass on his saddle to survey the Yankee lines. He had made his decision. "You see that copse at the north end, General Longstreet?"

"Yes, general."

"Our attack will concentrate on that point. The position is not heavily defended. Even with cannon against us, a deep and determined column can break through those lines. Your men will lie concealed behind the forward rises and the road during our barrage, then they will attack in line, closing together, extending and deepening the column as they move toward the trees." Lee traced the motion on the ground and looked up. "Do you follow my thinking, General Longstreet?"

"I do, sir." Longstreet's face bore a complaint, and so did his tone.

"Do you doubt, general, our men can take the position? I calculate they will charge over open ground as an average about four hundred yards. At quick-step that's no more than six minutes. Much of that time they will be shielded by the terrain.

"We shall lose some, but we shall gain the position, divide the Yankee army, and possibly destroy it. General Stuart's cavalry will make a demonstration in the rear. General Ewell is already taking ground on the other side of the ridge. We must risk it, general. That is what we are about this day." Lee knit his brows to look into the eyes of his subordinate. "I will give you men from Hill to go in alongside Pickett."

Longstreet looked at the ground. No one present could tell whether he was angry at being thwarted on the turning movement or unwilling to make the charge. He at length looked up and touched his hat.

Quiet descended on the western slope of the Fishhook. Hancock's men tried to build up the low stone wall that marked their line. The ground was hard and unyielding. They were not experienced in trenching, and had no digging tools, only bayonets. The most they could do was add a few inches to the two-foot wall.

The air was clear and the heat was not oppressive. Men could see for miles. Birds flew between the lines. Here and there squirrels scurried. Most striking was the silence. Few spoke. Across the lines men heard enemies in some places no more than a few hundred yards away mutter about mundane things, just like they did. Most of the time both sides went silently about their duties. Hancock rode up and down talking to his commanders and to the men, making adjustments, lending encouragement, confident an attack would come, and certain his men could repel it. Sharpshooters and skirmishers down the slope exchanged fire, and men begged him not to expose himself. He laughed. "Generals are supposed to take risks. That's why they're generals. How else do we lead?"

Looking out over the slope he saw sharpshooters leaving a barn they had used for cover. "Better burn that thing down before they use it against us," he muttered to no one in particular, and galloped off to give the order.

☆ ☆

Behind Seminary Ridge, far back and to the west of Confederate lines, Josephus and Henry Prediger stood on a secluded promontory looking out at the fields.

"The Rebs are going to attack today," said Josephus. "They got to. General Lee didn't come all this way just to go back south. Junius says he was certain of himself when he spoke to General Longstreet last night. They're not feuding, but General Longstreet don't want to make another straight-on attack. Mars' Robert, he's sure he can take the ridge. That's why young Porter's got all those guns out there."

Josephus enjoyed having someone listen to him after days of lonely thinking and planning. Years of secret reading about strategy at the Military Institute had prepared him. He understood war and its consequences. "That General Meade, what's he like? Does he know he's goin' to be a big hero 'fore this day is over? What's he goin' to do when everyone says he oughta be President of the United States?" What's this war's about is that folks knows how it oughta be are fightin' folks want to keep it the same." He sat down on a stump, hands on knees, and turned to his young friend. "Your general's changin' things whether he likes it nor not."

Henry scratched his chin. "I don't know exactly. But the general's seen black men before. He don't stare at me like I'm some kinda animal, like others do. I doubt he thinks nothin' much 'bout politics or bein' President. Major Fitzpatrick says he don't like the political generals. He a straight military man. Wants to fight."

"But somewhere back there in his head," Josephus broke in, "he's got an idea about black folks and slavery. Maybe he's for us or maybe he wishes we'd just go back to Africa. But he's got an idea,

117

an' I sure hope he's not one of those gen'lmen thinks the Rebs is okay if they wasn't so pigheaded."

Henry turned up his palms. "I got a glimmer of a feelin' he may be all right. That Major Fitzpatrick, he knew nothin' when I met him, but he learns. Pleased as anything to know the secrets." Henry sat on the ground below the stump looking out at the array on the battlefields in the early sun.

"We never going to see the like again," sighed Josephus. "They can't afford to waste men like they doin'. Goin' to have to dig more, move faster, get better weapons. It's easy to see they can do those things, if they'd just think about it a little."

As if reading Henry's mind, Josephus looked up. "It's easy when you look on from outside. We black folk ain't tied up with fancy ideas wrapped up in gold braid and red ribbons. If we try to see things clear, we have an advantage. That's all." He laughed. "Now how long it goin' to take you to get 'roun to the Yankees and take those numbers to General Meade? You got to be careful. If the Rebs catch you, it would be disaster for a lot of people."

"I got them in my head like I'll never forget them. They ain't goin' to find anything but a runaway nigger if I get caught."

Josephus chuckled. "That's a pretty good disguise. Later, when the big attack's done, I'm going to draw a little map of the Reb brigades an' try to get it across. Stay up high and look out for me. I'm not sure how we do this. But you see a black man comin' fast, you'll know. Understand?"

Josephus caught Henry short. "Don't take too many chances. We get past this battle, the problems only startin'."

The older man continued to chuckle, finally looking up. "Don't you worry none. It'll get through. The job today is all we can do. We got to get the Union to attack and attack hard. That's our job for today, and we got to push 'em."

Prediger looked at the ground. "I'll be lookin' out for the man." He put out his hand.

The older man stood to embrace him. "Keep you eyes open, and watch youself, brother!"

Henry turned and walked into the trees along the low ridge heading south on a circuitous ramble back to the Union lines.

★ ★

Meade watched early in the day on Culp's Hill where a college-trained brigade commander alternated units on the line so each Rebel attack met a fresh Union regiment. The tactic worked, and the enemy was forced back in spite of stubborn determination. Word came before noon that Ewell had called off his attack. The day was going well.

Meade rode up Little Round Top to talk to his commanders about a counterattack. They had a clear view to the top of the Fishhook. The issue was whether to move south around Longstreet's flank or "straight up the gut," as Hancock put it, between Longstreet's corps and Hill's once the enemy was repulsed. Between the two Rebel commands, they could see a long stretch protected solely by cannon. The position was vulnerable without massed infantry on its flanks.

Prediger arrived quietly in the rear, and recited his numbers to Fitzpatrick, who stood down the lee slope with Sharpe. Men in the ranks turned to stare at the black man.

Fitz carefully wrote down the figures, and questioned him about the dispute between Lee and Longstreet. Sharpe nodded as if to say "well done," but said no more. The place was too public.

When Meade heard the report, he stepped forward to peer over the rocks at Longstreet's men a few hundred yards away. He couldn't see much because of the trees, but the Rebs were surely there.

Men at the front yelled to get back. Sharpshooters were active, and rifle balls pinged off rocks around them. John Sedgwick standing at the hilltop scoffed, "At this distance they couldn't hit the broad side of a barn."

When Meade got back to his commanders, he said, "I think we can be sure the divisions in front of us are there to hold the flank for an attack in the center." He restrained himself. He didn't want to go too far on the strength of the Negro's report, but it was damned interesting, even exciting, to know so much.

"We can expect Lee to attack directly at Cemetery Ridge. His men below here are not lined up for a move by the flank, unless he's leapfrogging them, and I don't see him pulling out any of Hill's men." Meade looked at Hancock. "A column in depth to force our lines. That's what to expect. We'd better have a jolly good reception ready. I'll speak to Hunt about artillery."

He paused. It would come down to cannon and to Hancock's holding his line. The 5th Corps under Sykes and a massive assault by John Sedgwick and the 6th would carry the counterattack.

"When Lee is repulsed it will be up to you, Sykes, to pinch off these two divisions below with the help of 3rd Corps and cavalry on your flanks. We have good information that they're down to half-strength. Birney and the 3d will hold the high ground and support you on the left. That's the first step, sealing off Lee's left.

"Then," Meade turned to Hancock, "the attack up the gut, as you so elegantly call it, has a good chance." He looked at Sedgwick. "It's going to be our reprise, not just taking territory but taking back the initiative in this war."

A shower of Minié balls struck the rocks, striking an aide in the arm. A small tree branch exploded with a crack. Several generals jumped back, and Meade heard a moan like a child trying not to cry. John Sedgwick lay on the ground with a bullet through the middle of his forehead.

They stared down at the lifeless commander. Some took off their hats. Meade removed his, stepped to the body, knelt, put his hands together, looking down at his fallen friend. "Let us say a silent prayer for John Sedgwick." They all knelt.

Bullets zinged past, some coming close, as the commanders of the Army of the Potomac, feeling as if they were on stage, struggled with their thoughts. The men looked back from the lines, numbed. Except for occasional shots from each side, there was quiet. Meade did not tarry. "John would understand we cannot let this deter us." The officers nodded and moved away. He heard one of Birney's veterans on the line grump, "It may be nice to have a look-see from the big 'uns, but they draw too damn much fire."

On the lee slope from the rifle fire Meade continued the conference, ordering Newton to take over the 6th Corps, where he was familiar. Meade didn't dwell on John Sedgwick's death, though he felt a numbing effect. Only Hancock was left of the men he had known.

Lee's attack was due. Meade mounted with aides in tow and set out for headquarters. He found Meyer on the Taneytown Road, urging along a reluctant bay.

"*Ich muss!*" He was out of breath and excited. "I must speak with you, Herr General." Meade slowed. Meyer calmed. "There is a report among the newspaper men, Herr General. That you will abandon this position. I am told it comes from the authority of your Chief of Staff."

Meade's eyes bulged out from under his cone hat. Butterfield was talking again. "I will tell you, and you can pass it on. This is nonsense. Pay no attention to this palaver. It's the same old thing."

"I've told them that, but apparently Mr. Brennan has heard from his very reliable source that you still plan a retreat."

"Tell your friends." Anger and exasperation leapt from his mouth. "Tell your colleagues anyone who writes this on the eve of battle is guilty of treason. Tell them that."

"*Javohl, Herr General!*" Meyer raised his hand in a German military salute. "*Es wird gemacht.* It will be done."

"*Vielen Dank,* Thank you very much, Herr Meyer."

With a heavy tug, Meyer pulled the bay away and headed down the road. Meade turned to look at George and Fitz riding behind. "God bless him," he said. "We haven't lost all fortune yet." The thought struck him that stopping Robert E. Lee, so urgent on the 28th of June, might not do for the politicians once the battle was won.

★ ✪

At dawn, Toddy Bates stood in line north of Seminary Ridge with the 7th Tennessee, no more than 175 men, a shadow of its original strength. General Archer, the brigade commander, was a Yankee prisoner. Colonel Fry barked orders to get in line with the rest of the division, now commanded by Brig. Gen. James Johnston Pettigrew of North Carolina. Few older men were left. The sergeant died in the field hospital, where Toddy went to pay his respects the night before last. Once lowly corporals were senior. Toddy felt alone and a veteran.

About 8:00 a.m. General Pettigrew gave the order to march quietly south into a forest out of sight of the enemy less than a mile away on Cemetery Ridge. An officer told them to stay down and keep silent. Toddy could see men in position around them. Two of Anderson's brigades not yet touched by combat stood among the trees toward the front. Pender's division lined behind Pettigrew. Rumors flew: Longstreet and Lee were arguing . . . the whole army was going forward to take the Yankee ridge.

Toddy went forward with a message from the colonel to a friend in a Georgia regiment deployed in a sunken lane within rifle shot of the Yankees. As he came into the open he saw thousands of men lying in low ground to his right out of sight of the enemy. The whole army seemed to be crowded into a few acres.

The sun was intense. The air was clear, except when a gust carried the smell of dead and dying from fields to the south where Longstreet's men had fought the day before. Toddy knew what was coming. Veterans spoke softly of smashing through the Yankee line and cutting off Ol' George Meade's beard. Some told jokes saying the Yankees were pussycats and women, yellow, and ran the minute they saw a gray line. They were joshing, trying to hold onto their courage. Breakfast, strong coffee and hard biscuit, hadn't settled. His guts turned and he felt weak and sick.

Water was scarce. Willoughby Run was so clogged with garbage and horse turds that medical officers ordered the men not to fill canteens there. Water came slowly in carts from a long way off. By midmorning his canteen was near empty, but he felt a little better. The wait stretched on. Some joked about Old Bull Longstreet fussin'. The veterans' faces turned sour. Arguments among generals were not good. He tried to sleep.

★ ★

As Meade passed by 2d Corps, a third lieutenant ran up to invite him to come for lunch *al fresco* at the top of the ridge. They had found chickens. "No one vouched for their youth," he prattled in awe of the Commanding General, "but the general would be pleased to share them."

Meade thanked him happily. Officers did not draw rations. They had to fend for themselves. Lunch was the farthest thing from his mind, but this was a welcome break. He knew he would need food, and chicken was something he could get down. The staff of Gibbon's division had scrounged for miles around to find the birds, including a tough old rooster, a half-gone loaf of bread, potatoes, butter, coffee, and tea. Two Negro contrabands cooked and served. The breadloaf would have been whole, had not a hog got to it before the cooks could save it. The cooks stewed the chickens in butter in a large round pan with the potatoes.

Meade was glad of the chance to relax with Hancock. Pleasonton came with Newton. Behind the crest of the ridge, they sat on makeshift seats, sacks, boxes, and saddles, Meade on a roll of blankets. Staff sat on the ground. Someone said the bread served as toast with butter was more than passable. Meade raised his coffee cup to salute his hosts and the servants. The party became merry. They were happy and confident. They had united a shattered army to stand against an unstoppable Rebel onslaught.

Meade remembered the optimism before Chancellorsville, when the Rebs caught them off guard. *It's not the same. We had a good plan but were totally dependent on a commander who wouldn't act. Today we stand strong after two days' fighting, and know where the enemy lies—where he must come. Not the same.* He pursed his face in a half-smile behind his beard.

When the meal was done, they leaned back in the sun and lit cigars, offering them to the juniors, and talked of yesterday's fight. Meade gave his estimate of Rebel losses, guarding his sources, eyeing the cooks, wondering whether either was in league with Prediger.

Hancock thought Longstreet's men had put themselves in a trap. "They're too far forward to maneuver. They can't retreat, and can't move on our flank. Bobby Lee doesn't have enough troops for the length of his line."

"And after they've come up the gut," Pleasonton chortled in a loud voice, "We'll sweep down like the Assyrian from the fold, and scythe 'em like ripe wheat." He leaned back and laughed at the sky.

Meade blinked. He wished Pleasonton could contain himself. The counterattack should be kept quiet. How many men know about it, he wondered. Too many, but then maybe Butterfield has done us a favor. If the press expect retreat, they're not going to talk about an attack "up the gut." He left to go back to the Leister House, taking Newton and Pleasonton with him.

The 2d Corps men remained, lying on the ground, resting and

waiting. They did not stay long. At 1:30 p.m. by Meade's watch, two cannon shots sounded off from the Rebel lines followed by a barrage coming high over the lines, killing several horses tied behind headquarters.

☆ ☆

Before noon Porter Alexander had received a message from General Longstreet:

If your artillery fire does not have the effect to drive off the enemy or greatly demoralize him so as to make our effort pretty certain, I would prefer you should not advise General Pickett to make the charge. I shall rely on your good judgment to determine the matter, . . .

Alexander had no reliable gauge of his guns' effect. He had no idea whether his shells would explode. Yankee fire was fairly accurate, ripping into his caissons and horses. He could see shells falling among men in the fields below the road. The roar was unbearable. Far stronger than thunder, more than 300 guns fired at each other in the space of a mile. Alexander felt he was deaf. Smoke and fire, fumes, and gray clouds engulfed his guns and crews. Visibility was less than a few hundred feet. He had no idea how well the barrage was doing.

In front of Pickett's men behind the Emmitsburg Road, Longstreet rode, a bull of a man on a huge horse—larger than life in front of the ranks in full view of Yankee marksmen. Some shouted, "Get back. We can't lose Longstreet." He was their talisman of victory. The older men said it was atonement for an order he didn't want to give. At last, and to the relief of all, he rode off into the trees.

☆ ☆

Shot and shell struck everywhere on Cemetery Ridge though not heavily on the Union lines. A few men and cannon were hit, but most shots went high. Men of 6th Corps lined up behind got the worst of it. Shells struck the Leister House, taking off the porch, and blowing holes in the Taneytown Road.

Meade moved headquarters to a barn farther away. A burst sent a fragment wounding Butterfield in the hand. Orderlies took him off, and the work of sending orders almost stopped. Meade had to get the process running again in the hands of the deputy. An hour after the cannonade started he sent an order to Hunt to stop firing in hopes of provoking the Rebel attack.

The guns on both sides fell silent. On the ridge some stood up to see what the Rebs would do. Hancock and Gibbon on horseback ordered them down. Everyone felt the tension. Occasionally a man gasped or even sobbed. Then someone told a joke, and the laughter was loud.

On the Confederate side, George Pickett stood in the rear leaning on a small tree. Ringlets hung down over his collar from pomaded hair. He looked blankly out at the fields. Some of his thoughts were of his inamorata far away in Richmond, but not for more than a few seconds at a time. Today was to be glorious. If any had doubts, he was not the one.

A note arrived from Alexander:

General, if you're going to go, you'd better go now, else we'll have no ammunition to sustain the charge.

Pickett, the senior commander, strode before his men, signaling to Pettigrew, the North Carolinian, and Trimble, the Marylander. His voice did not carry along his line, and brigade commanders had to repeat key phrases. "Remember your wives, mothers, and sweethearts. Charge the enemy and remember old Virginia!"

Johnston Pettigrew invoked "the honor of the good old North State." Men in the ranks from Alabama, Tennessee, Mississippi, and Virginia took it as his right to lead them in behalf of his homeland. They lined up, Toddy Bates deep in his file, and moved forward in parade-ground order. Fences dissolved before them. No human power could stop them. Men in front reported a gasp of Yankee wonder when they came nicely into view.

Cannonballs from the front, the left, and the right ripped through the formation. Veteran file-closers tightened the ranks. They went at a quickened pace, and when they reached a bit of cover at the road they closed as Lee had ordered into a tighter, deeper column. They came on.

A man in front dropped his gun, grabbed his throat, gagged, and fell back, face covered with blood. Toddy stopped. The man behind said, "He's lucky. He's dead," and pushed him forward.

Cannonballs rolled through the ranks, sometimes passing among them on the ground, seemingly harmless but deadly to any they touched. Shells exploded overhead. Yankee shells seldom failed. A cannonball from somewhere far away crashed into the right flank of Pickett's division and was said to have taken down 30 men. Pickett's men passed the story back to Trimble's, who sent it on up to Pettigrew's.

Bullets came thick as they closed. Toddy felt a sting in his left arm and looked down at his sleeve. No blood appeared, and he could see from the trace through the cloth that the ball had passed on. Around him men were dropping, and some, skulkers, fell out to take wounded to the rear.

Toddy came close to the crest. Firing from both sides was intense. The file-closers gave up and took to their guns. Being short, Toddy couldn't get a clear shot, but after a few paces the ground opened in front of him. Men fell. Some turned and took their guns to the rear. He could see a low stone wall and masses of Yankees milling behind it. They stood forward and fired, sending forth sheets of flame and lead, then stepped to the rear as a new rank came up. Toddy's throat was dry, his eyes watered, and his stomach churned. He wanted to yell but his voice was gone. He ordered himself not to run, and bit his lips until blood came. He stepped on.

He could see on the right. Pickett's men captured a cannon. Here and there underfoot was a fallen Yankee. The ground became level. Toddy approached the wall, stopped to fire, and stepped over. There were no ranks or files around him, just men advancing. No officer or sergeant gave orders. Toddy bit his lips and kept coming. Men in front dropped rifles and raised their hands, walking forward but now toward a narrow passage between crowds of cheering Yankees, some calling out, "Come on, brother." "It's over." "You got nothin' to be ashamed of."

Meade worried when he heard yells rise higher and fewer cannon boom—tell-tale sounds of man-to-man combat. He mounted, trotting up the back of the ridge, passing 6th Corps troops. An aide came up with news that Hancock had been wounded. Gibbon had taken command. The wound did not appear to be serious, and Hancock had refused to leave the field. Bad news. As he passed the last of the reserve regiments, Meade ordered two colonels to follow him with their men to the lines. He lashed himself for complacency. *Such faith in Hancock. He's only one man. We're damn short of leaders. We can stop them, but at what price? I ought to have stood by Win Hancock, even if he didn't like it.*

Ahead, men suddenly broke ranks from the front and ran toward him yelling, a softer tone now, faces relieved—sunshine had burst through clouds. "The Rebs broke and ran. We've won! We've won! Hurrah for the Union! Hurrah for the flag! Hurrah, Hurrah for General Meade!" They crowded around looking up at their idol, radiating love and confidence.

"Meade for President," a man cried, and another took it up. Overcome by the turnabout and suddenly near tears, Meade reached out to take a Union flag in his right arm and rode forward. Men parted cheering "Meade! Meade! Meade!" He started to doff his cap and thought better of it, contenting himself to yell a loud "Hurrah," beaming at his men, as he clutched the flag and rode past.

Some of the wounded tried to stand with the help of comrades and salute. At this place at this hour, standing with the Commanding General was honor never to forget. No man doubted he was present at an exaltation of the Union, of Victory and of General George Meade.

No more than 20 yards away a Union soldier pointed his rifle at Toddy coming forward with an empty gun. "Better get along back, young 'un. Prison's no place for ya. Better go before I got to shoot ya or take ya prisoner."

Toddy Bates of the 7th Tennessee, standing beyond the wall on Cemetery Ridge, stared at the man for what seemed a long time. Frowning under his hat, he turned about and, gun in hand, ran as fast as he could, never looking back, until he reached the trees on the other side.

The cost of days without sleep and food caught up with Meade, elated and worn out. No aide was in sight. Fitzpatrick had galloped off to find Prediger. George was not back from Culp's Hill. On the ridge wounded and dead were scattered like corn stalks after a harvest storm. Blood was everywhere. Men seemed determined to celebrate and in no mood to go on.

Gibbon too was wounded in the final minutes. Meade had to award the 2d Corps to a brigadier general with less than a week in the Army of the Potomac. When the Chief Engineer came up to ask about the counterstroke, Meade temporized, "I can't find anyone to give orders to. How are we going to move through all this mess?"

He rode southward past cheering soldiers and fallen bodies. The army had lost at least 20,000 men. Commanders he knew and trusted, Reynolds, Sedgwick, Hancock, now Gibbon, were lost. *Strangely, I even miss old Sickles and his confounded aggressiveness.* His vision seemed to fail. A counterattack didn't look simple. *Bobby Lee's no fool. He's bound to be waiting.*

Meade rode down the ridge past a 6th Corps division dealing with two Rebel brigades stubbornly holding onto the hillside. Shooting was heavy. The fight was not over. Looking farther into the area around the Trostle Farm, he saw a lone horseman, clearly not a military man, burst between Rebel cannon and gallop furiously toward Yankee lines. Through binoculars he could see Rebel officers standing forward to unload their revolvers at him. The man's face was black—unmistakable. To the right Prediger was running down from the Round Top waving his hat. Closer in, Fitzpatrick on horse raced to meet the rider, clearly yelling to men on the line to hold fire. Meade spurred Baldy.

Down the main road bearers, a cavalry escort, two doctors, and an expert in transport bore the stretcher of Maj. Gen. Daniel Sickles toward the railhead at Littlestown a few miles away. Early in the day Sickles ordered them to proceed with an elaborate plan to get to Washington as soon as possible. He disregarded the surgeon's warning that movement might open his wounds.

Tremaine begged him to rest at least one day. Sickles rounded on him. "Think about it, my boy. Meade and Lee are going to finish this thing in a stand-off. I say that's a crime. The brave boys of the 3d Corps who stopped Longstreet dead in his tracks deserve the destruction of the Rebel army. It's in Meade's grasp. If he settles for anything less, I call him a coward." He pulled a cigar from his mouth and reached for medicinal whiskey. "We've got to get to the capital to see that justice is done to the corps."

The stretcher bearers, changing hands every few hundred yards, made four miles. They were still in earshot when the charge came and ended. They stopped at nightfall in a small farmhouse. On the morrow Sickles expected to be on board a waiting train, and in Washington by late afternoon—well ahead of the newspapers.

Book Two

ENDING THE WAR

General Meade flanked by staff: the officer at the far right, never before identified, could be Colonel James Fitzpatrick.

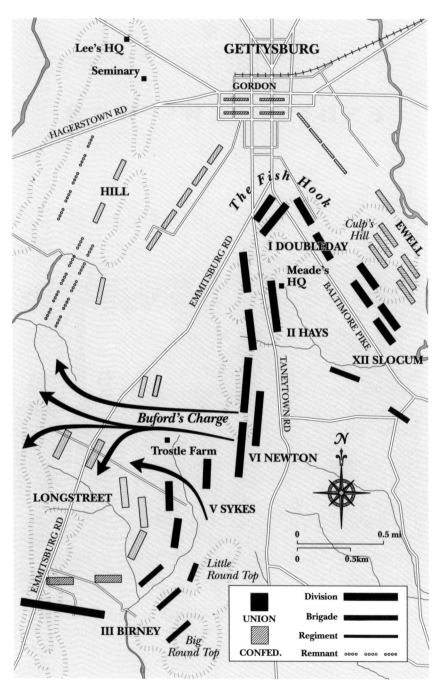

Meade's Reprise: 4:30 p.m., July 3, 1863

CHAPTER XII

In the early afternoon, Margaretta Sergeant Meade sat at a mahogany writing table in a small second-floor room in her Philadelphia home. Before her lay his last letter written three days ago and ending with an ominous "Good-bye." Morning papers reported a climactic battle in the western part of the state. She felt relief that the fight had come, though reports from railroad telegraphers along the Susquehanna suggested the army was losing men in large numbers. She shuddered at bloody deaths she couldn't imagine, and the enormous trial her husband faced.

Tomorrow was the Fourth of July. Patriots would march noisily through the city, their route passing the house. They knew she lived on Pine Street. The local garrison commander had posted militiamen at her door, and the soldiers called attention to it. She reflected on a quiet life a few days past when George was a modest hero, when she went about her life unnoticed except for the greetings of friends.

Now all Philadelphia claimed his skill and bravery, as though life itself balanced on how well, or badly, he fared. They believed that but for a heroic stand by George Meade, Lee and his Rebels would march through their streets in a matter of hours. Fear consumed them. Stories of rough Rebel behavior in western valleys and the arrival of Ewell's corps across from Harrisburg provoked panic. Prominent men beseeched her to write the President for more troops. She knew better—the right answer was precisely the opposite, and she told them so. Any spare men must go west to General Meade.

With the pen under her small chin, she hesitated. *God knows where he'll be when this gets to him. There's no sense worrying him about these fools. If the Union fails, we lose a great lot more than they do. The very men who most fear Robert E. Lee will lead the delegation to greet him.*

She bit her lip. Her thoughts turned to young George. *He'll be out there high on a horse where they can shoot at him. . . . No proper thought for the wife of the Commanding General. . . . He's far better off with his father. Good we took him out of the cavalry, away from the sort who become officers these days. The war has ruined social life in the army.*

She bit her lip again and put pen to paper.

My dear husband,

News of the battle reached the city yesterday. No one speaks of anything else. Our prayers are with you both. Whatever happens you will do your honest best. You are a good man, far better than Mr. Lincoln or any others in Washington know. We are on the verge of a great adventure. The prospect scares me sometimes. I think of Shakespeare, "Cry havoc, and let slip the dogs of war." Life will never be the same. This war changes the world, and now you, my dear husband, will be about seeing how it does so. God grant you His every protection and love.

Margaretta

Colonel Edward Porter Alexander CSA, Military Academy '57, grew up on Fairfield Plantation in Wilkes County, Georgia, raised by a Greek-loving father, who taught his Negroes to read the Bible. Such facts meant little where he sat astride his horse on the Emmitsburg Road looking over a sea of retreating men, except that brother officers even now unfailingly treated him with the respect due a planter and gentleman.

Alexander had given orders to reload three nearby batteries, nearly 50 guns, to repel a Yankee counterattack, preferably to blow it to Hell with canister, if it could be found. A superior had sent his supply train to some unknown spot in the rear to avoid the enemy's cannonade. Such was the style of the Confederate Army—officers were courteous, brave, and kind, regardless of how much blood was shed or how absurd the orders. He was angry. Generals could be damned stupid, though he couldn't blame a man for not having a military education. Most regarded him as highly learned—the man who organized the Signal Corps, the man Longstreet chose to direct the barrage. His father would urge patience and fortitude. Alexander ground his teeth.

Around the cannon, defeated and frightened men struggled, some hurrying, some hobbling by themselves or leaning on comrades willing to tarry in range of the enemy long enough to get them to safety. Above him Yankees shot at the backs of the retreating Confederates, shouting, "Fredericksburg! Fredericksburg!" On the slopes, groans and cries rose from trampled, bloody grasses strewn with bodies, some lying neatly in rows.

Not far away General Lee rode through the men followed by a British observer. "It's my fault. It's my fault," he told them repeatedly. "Now, let us quickly regroup and carry on." He tried to smile, but Alexander thought nothing was capable of erasing his sadness. Lee rode up to ask about the cannon and ammunition supply. He agreed that canister was needed immediately, and softly suggested again that the batteries move farther to the rear. Lee anticipated a Yankee counterattack coming down the ridge.

The Englishman spouted praise for Confederate bravery, a bravado Alexander found affected. Nor did he care much for the way the man spoke with his riding crop—"Magnificent, suh," waving the thing in the air. "Simply magnificent. With courage like that you're bound to beat that rabble." Lee ignored him, trying not to be discourteous. *No one can take away his dignity, not even this ass.*

At length the general sent regards to his family and, seemingly satisfied, raised a gray-gloved hand to his hat as his horse stepped off.

On the ridge Yankees danced and waved flags and bottles in the air. Alexander wished for a rifle to blow them to pieces. *But then, so long as those fools carry on, we've got time.*

Lee provoked images of Fairfield.

Josephus! Lord's sake! That darkey in the trees this morning was Josephus. . . . And trying mightily to avoid my gaze. What is that scoundrel doing here? He ran off from Lexington, got through the mountains. Maybe, we got him back at Sharpsburg? . . . Read everything. . . . the smartest nigger I ever saw.

Down the road near the peach orchard, pistol shots came from Moody's battery, as a horse and rider bolted down the dirt lane toward Yankee lines. Alexander raised his glass. The rider was black.

"Josephus, for God's sake!" He bellowed down the line, pointing, "That rider is a spy! Deadly as a moccasin. For Christ's sake, shoot that nigger! Shoot him!"

☆ ☆

Meade handed the flag into the arms of an astonished corporal, muttered about taking care of it, and galloped down the ridge. Passing massed artillery, where soldiers were aiming and reloading, he felt the call for greater effort seize him. It was oppressive. A shudder rippled between his shoulder blades as he thought of losses the cavalry would take. His stomach ached. The elation of victory slipped away.

He rode onto a hill behind a New Jersey regiment and pulled out field glasses to follow the lone rider racing toward him. An officer, probably Fitzpatrick, was yelling at a brigade commander, pleading, Meade was sure, to hold fire. *Who is that man? What does Fitzpatrick know?*

Another Negro came running to greet the man, a heavyset fellow hugging the horse's neck. He had to be one of the spies. Enemy skirmishers held up rifles and fired. A few bullets must have hit. The man slumped nearly flat on the horse's back.

Captain George Meade rode up. Hunt and Pleasonton came with others. Along the ridge toward town, men continued to celebrate. Meade pulled out his watch. *Nearly 4 p.m., time enough. How quickly would Lee reform?* Meade saw activity off to the right on Seminary Ridge but nothing that looked like a new formation. He was nearly spent, and his men must be near exhaustion. Days of endless work and sleepless nights furrowed his face, and he could feel strength draining away. Baldy, covered with blood, lather, and dust, carried him despite a half-dozen running wounds. The hot, wet air stunk of powder, sweat, blood, human wastes, and death.

Meade looked down and saw his son, and grinned. "We beat 'em, George." He pointed down the hill. "Bring Fitzpatrick and his black friends up as fast as you can come. I'd guess they've got something to tell us."

Gladly would Meade let the celebration continue, give in, and call it a day. Across the way yawned a mile-wide gap in enemy lines defended only by skirmishers and cannon. Reason, duty, and a whisper of personal interest said, *Seize this God-given chance to destroy Lee!*

"Half a league, half a league, half a league onward," he recited to Pleasonton. "Do you know Tennyson, general?"

"No, sir, I do not, but I know Buford and his brigades are pulling at the bit. Do we go at 'em?"

"The poet says they are going to ride into the mouth of Hell, general." Meade surprised himself. He was teasing the poor man about a serious matter. He turned to Hunt, "How many cannon do you count?"

"Not more than twenty can hit us." Hunt brought his horse next to Meade's, where they faced the field. "Half probably lack full crews. I can't guarantee a miracle, but if we pound them for fifteen minutes or so, we may cut that number back."

Meade decided. "Start your barrage immediately, and cease firing only when you see Buford's men pass the farmhouse down there."

Pleasonton sidled over. "God pray the artillery does its work, general. Buford remembers Brandy Station. Twelve Rebel guns stopped us." The man demanded his ear. "We'll charge in squadron front fifty men abreast. Buford knows what to do. I ordered him to ride with the second brigade, to stay alive. We'll lose a few, if the Rebs have canister. I thought I saw a wagon coming up. They're probably loading right now. Time is pressing, general."

Meade was stymied. *Pleasonton says the obvious, but I can never quite tell what he means. Of course the Rebels have canister. Has he thought the thing through? How is he so sure his men will press on when their front is blown apart? They're a "Forlorn Hope." He must know that. It's the infantry coming behind them who take the ground.* Meade shared the foot soldier's view—cavalry was mostly for show. Fatigue sent his mind onto rogue tangents, and he felt lightheaded. Batteries sounded off. The barrage began. The noise startled him.

Fitzpatrick came with Prediger leading a horse bearing a wounded man tied in the saddle. Fitz held out a soiled paper. "It's a map, general. It shows the exact position of the Rebels as they stand. Mr. Josephus brought it through from the other side. I think it will prove accurate, sir." Fitz was plainly pleased with his work.

Pleasonton growled. "How in Hell do you know about that, major?"

"Because," said Meade, voice rising as he stared at the map, "everything we've had from these men has been dead on the mark." He looked up and smiled a silent welcome as if Josephus were an acquaintance of long standing. He was too far gone to talk, but Prediger's face was wreathed in a grin.

While Meade studied the map, the two Negroes a few paces down the hill watched him expectantly. Prediger held Josephus onto the horse, his head resting on the neck staring up with a look of intelligence and pain.

"You see, Pleasonton," Meade pointed to the paper, "without this, you wouldn't know where skirmishers will be when you pass the farmhouse, nor that Kershaw's men, about one thousand able-bodied, will shoot at you along with cannon as you come up the hill. Nor that another brigade stands in the rear ready when you pass the guns. And perhaps most important, without this paper we would not have an exact idea of where the guns are." He handed the map to Pleasonton, who stared at it in disbelief.

The Commanding General leaned forward on his horse as if bowing to the two Negroes. "Your heroism is much appreciated," he said and turned to Fitzpatrick. "Are Berdan's sharpshooters in place?"

"Yes, general."

"Have them go to work immediately." Meade smiled and abruptly took the map from Pleasonton's hands, passing it to his son. "George, make a copy of the area in front of us right away, one for Hunt and one for Pleasonton. Be careful, but be quick." He overcame his doubts, and sent an aide for the corps commanders. He sent another with Josephus to the Chief Surgeon, then turned with a grin at Pleasonton. "We need to pow-wow."

The Yankee bombardment didn't surprise Lee, and he rode back quickly to the Rogers farmhouse where he had met Alexander. He thought he could see what Meade was up to. To his right down in the ravine in the trees, Yankee infantry were coming toward the peach orchard. *They aren't likely to succeed against Longstreet.* He sighed. *A bad situation could become worse.* Lee looked at the sun. *Meade has time. It's a long day. Really didn't think he'd move so fast. . . . not the same Meade I knew in Mexico, perhaps.*

He didn't see the Yankee cavalry. Uppermost in his mind was infantry, his own, to stop Meade's thrust. Men were scarce. He had only three fresh brigades. Lee turned in the saddle to search for Longstreet. Sciatica pain shot up his back. *Must remember not to do that again.*

Longstreet wasn't on Seminary Ridge, but Hill was there talking to his division commanders and Pickett. Lee spurred Traveler. *Meade has the men.* The horse broke into a canter, and Lee rode carefully to avoid running over wounded men—and to avoid pain. *The tables are turned. We stand on the defensive. We will find the best position.* By the time he reached the small group on Seminary Ridge, Lafayette McLaws, one of Longstreet's division commanders, had reported Yankees coming in force toward the peach orchard, possibly a full corps.

Lee's eyes were sad and, to the men he knew, betrayed a controlled anger. He asked Hill how long since Longstreet rode off, and was glad he would soon reach his men. He paused to think, then turned to Hill. "We must deploy on the best ground. I prefer this ridge. Can we extend farther south to meet Longstreet?" He pointed to five brigades standing half-concealed in a lane angling out from town below Cemetery Ridge, where they secured the left during the charge. "Or, do we form a salient here with our back on the ridge and a front with those men in that lane leading into town? We may need them where they are. Meade will very likely strike back along the line of our attack."

Almost without thinking he decided he could not count on Longstreet's men. "We'll fit them in when they come," he told Hill. "Scout the ground and show me what is to be done. If George Meade comes, he must find a stiff riposte."

★ ★

At 4:30 p.m., Meade gave the orders. George sat on a rock a few yards behind hurriedly drawing copies of Josephus' map. Meade gave them to Hunt and Pleasonton, then to Sykes and Newton, the

5th and 6th Corps commanders whose men would follow on either side of the cavalry charge. The 5th, which had taken losses the day before but had fought well, would strike on the left against Longstreet's flank, pushing his divisions south away from the main enemy force. Meade was counting on the courage of the men of his old command. The much larger, and unbled 6th would carry the main attack to the right. Men of the 6th were already pressing down the slope against two outnumbered Rebel brigades which had advanced without support. They would soon be overrun.

Meade leaned forward in his saddle to get a better view of Buford sending forth his riders. *The question now is how many survive to reach the guns? How many cannon will be ready with canister? How many men will they take down with each shot?* "Usually no more than three or four," he answered aloud, and continued speaking to surprised aides.

"Buford's men at a dead run can cover the distance in little more than a minute," he lectured the officers around him. "In that time fifteen cannon, if that's what's left when Hunt's guns subside, should fire three charges, or forty-five shots, each taking down four riders. Buford will lose one hundred eighty out of the first regiment of three hundred men. One hundred twenty men will be left." The aides blanched. "If they don't lose heart, they can take two batteries of four cannon. Seven guns will be left to fire at the next regiment." He stopped.

And then again, maybe they won't go on. No regiment takes such losses without giving up. It could be a disaster. Men fighting each other to retreat! Meade lifted his hands together above the saddle and put his head down. Some of the aides bowed their heads. "Oh, God, give us strength to win this victory, if you agree that our cause is just!"

Looking up, he found the binoculars, and got the horsemen into focus. The front rank broke into a run. Riders jockeyed to avoid obstacles. *Bodies! Bodies on the ground!* He could see them now. *Yesterday's dead, our dead—and wounded. How many do we trample? And kill? Hellish business!*

"Ride on!" He rose from his seat. "Go get them!" He waved his floppy hat. All around men cheered, and the yells of riders and the sound of bugles filled the ravine. The staff joined. They seldom saw their "old boss" so excited—except when he was mad.

The lead squadron came into range of Rebel guns. Riders swerved as horses fell before them. Many stumbled and threw their riders. More down! Cannon boomed again with greater effect. In the smoke the whole front—50 men—disappeared.

Alexander returned from corps headquarters at the Pitzer Schoolhouse where he went to trace his wagons. There, he learned that an unrecognized officer from Lee's staff had ordered cannon to the rear, and that McLaws had recalled his divisions to the peach orchard to repel infantry. Galloping back to the Emmitsburg Road, he found the Yankee bombardment had unwheeled one of Parker's guns and one of Rhett's. Shells fell every few seconds, and men had been hit.

Moody's battery, with four of Alexander's favorite 24-pound howitzers, stood at the end of the lane from the Trostle Farm, its guns loaded with double canister. Moody was a good officer. Parker's next battery to the north had three workable 12-pounders, but had lost an ammunition chest, the double explosion killing four men. Higher on the ridge, Rhett had three guns. Jones's battery of four had pulled far to the rear, and Frazer's and Manly's batteries, belonging to McLaws, were 300 yards away with guns trained toward Yankee infantry.

Alexander saw cavalry forming in wide ranks behind the Trostle House, clearly getting ready to charge toward Moody. *No one seems to see them. They'll charge any minute. I've got ten guns where I ought to have twenty.* He called to Moody and pointed down the lane.

Parker's guns were high. Alexander rode over and gave orders to resight them. A shell exploded in Moody's battery, killing one man, wounding three others, and unwheeling a gun. He had nine guns to repel the charge.

Through his eyeglass he could see Yankee officers raising their swords and calling orders. An attack in depth! Probably thousands of the bastards! The only hope is to kill enough to turn them back before they reach us.

In a burst of energy, he raced up to Rhett's battery, where the commander had been wounded. Little had been done. He checked elevation. The guns were much too high. Bugles sounded across the debris of yesterday's battle. He ordered a shot to get the range, saw that the aim was still high, and ordered a lower sighting. Parker and Moody's men went furiously to work.

To the south, Frazer's guns sounded. *At least they cooperate.* The boom of his cannon was now so loud he didn't notice the Yankee's guns had stopped.

Enemy riders came closer. The first shots took down a few. Moody's second salvo cut three gaps in the front rank. The cavalrymen closed at a dead run. He watched with admiration. *They're no volunteers. U.S. Regulars!* He was almost proud. *A tough lot!*

"Keep firing!" He rode behind the guns. "Keep on, as fast as you can!" he harangued, waving his sword. "Double canister. Double canister. You can do it." He knew they were short of shells.

Yankee bugles and riders' screams came louder, nearer and nearer. He could see the whites of the horses' eyes and flaring nostrils. Moody fired a third shot. A swath of riders went down.

An infantry regiment wheeled to the flank and were taking a fair toll. For a minute he hoped they might kill enough to stop them, and he jumped down to join Moody, ordering triple canister for a fourth shot. Only one gun had the shells. They fired, killing a line of Yankees. But they came on, screaming from the depths of their lungs, passing the battery.

Alexander pulled out his Colt. A bullet of the same maker struck his shoulder. He spun and went down.

CHAPTER XIII

Washington was sticky in the late afternoon. The air in Stanton's office had gone from bad to poisonous as cigar smoke, tobacco juice, and a crowd of unwashed male bodies mixed with foul odors coming through the windows. A late thundershower dowsed the city. It did nothing to reduce the heat, and added to the humidity, though it seemed for an instant to freshen things.

"The British call this the tropics," said the President, standing by a window in his shirtsleeves inhaling the damp of the rain. "I can understand why. The ambassador's summer uniform is of a light tan color so we can't see him skip over the Potomac for Richmond."

Generals, members of Congress and the Cabinet smiled weakly. No one cared much for the man's humor.

"This is the day," said the gangling Lincoln, turning to face them with his dry smile. "It all depends on General Meade. Would that we knew him better. His messages don't reveal much."

An orderly brought Stanton a telegram. "It's for you, Mr. President," he handed it over, "from Sickles."

The President pulled out his spectacles and read aloud:

I left the field yesterday with severe wound. . . . shall arrive by tonight and go to my house on F Street after a good fight. Am prepared with full details.

With Respect,

Sickles Major Genl, U.S. Vol.

"Not much respect for his Commanding General," snorted Halleck. "How in the devil does he think he's in charge of reporting to the President?"

Lincoln handed the telegram back to Stanton. "Sickles is a good fighter, general. I shall be glad to hear what he has to say, as I would hear anyone with news this day. It'll be a relief from wordless waiting."

Halleck was about to argue when Stanton cut him off. "Surely we will have a first-hand report, Mr. President, when General Meade is done with the battle."

Lincoln pulled on his cheeks, his fingers gripping the end of his large nose as they came away. "Well, I know Sickles is no professional," the twang stressed the second syllable, "but he'll have a report I'd like to hear."

Fitz followed Buford's men to the Emmitsburg Road. They had seized cannon and moved on to attack Wofford's Georgians directly ahead and Kershaw's South Carolinians on the left. Two regiments struck Wofford's flank 200 yards behind the artillery, catching Georgians unready. They gave way, streaming to the rear of the peach orchard looking for a place to reform.

On the left a division of the 5th Corps charged the South Carolinians, while dismounted cavalry with breech-loading carbines poured fire into their flank. On the right, to the north, the lead division of the 6th Corps had reached the Emmitsburg Road.

Toppled Rebel guns lay among dead horses and fallen men from both sides. Fitz trotted by a wounded Rebel colonel lying on the ground, and recalled later that he looked very much like Edward Alexander. Meade had given Fitz a copy of Josephus's map and 30 men from his personal escort to scout the rear behind Hill's corps, now the main body of remaining Rebels. Fitz was proud of Meade's trust even though he lacked a professional's knowledge of ground.

In columns of two they trotted west, then north, behind a Rebel aid station at the Spangler Farm. Enemy wounded barely noticed them. They trotted through a copse behind the farm, slowed to cross a pasture, and came to a small stream running down the back of the ridge into a wood lot. As the column came to the clearing, the lead rider raised his hand. Less than a quarter-mile to the north, near a staging area littered with haversacks, blanket rolls, and discarded clothing, Rebel soldiers were quickly limbering up cannon to haul them away. "Looks like they're pulling 'em out towards town," said the captain.

Fitz dismounted and walked down into a grove, where he found a ford of a larger stream. A wagon road passed across to higher ground in the enemy rear. He signaled, and in silence the men followed across the stream.

Not far beyond they found a Rebel soldier sitting by a cedar, holding his knees, rocking back and forth, face black with gunpowder. He stared back toward the lines, the whites of his eyes bulging. A rifle lay at his feet.

"What division you from?" Nelson demanded.

"Pickett," the Rebel barked without moving his head, unwilling to say more. He shivered in the heat, and kept pulling a tattered coat around his shoulders. A cavalryman picked up the gun, and they went on, passing more like him, alone, shivering and catatonic. They left each to his delirium.

When they reached an outlook toward the Rebel rear at the back of Seminary Ridge, Fitz ordered a halt, dismounted, and sent a scouting party farther along the high ground. Using the map as reference, he scratched out a report. Teams of horses were pulling supply wagons away from the rear to leave a clear field of fire.

"Why would Lee make a defense line to his rear?" asked Nelson.

"It appears he's building a bastion along the ridge," said Fitz, "trying to get the best defensive position he can with a smaller force." He ordered them to return, passing Pickett's lonely men and keeping well to the west of the stream to avoid detection from the cannon park.

Reaching a point he guessed was due west of the Union position, Fitz was about to order a sharp left turn when they ran into a small group of Negroes huddled in the forest.

The column halted, cavalrymen wary but calm, while Fitz went forward alone, calling out, "Is one of you named Parker?"

"Yessir, that's me," said a short woman, standing up in a soiled coat and light colored skirt.

"You'll be glad to know," said Fitz, "that Mr. Josephus got across. He was wounded, but we think he'll survive."

"Thank the Lord!" said Mrs. Parker. "Now, how does we get to the Yankees, too?"

Fitz pointed. "Wait until the shooting dies down and walk

straight that way. You're almost on Union ground right now."

She grinned. "Praise the Lord! Tha's wonderful. Now let me do you a favor, suh. The gen'ral's right back there at the school house, and nobody's much with him." She gestured with her chin. "Came about a half-hour ago. Hasn't gone anyplace since, 'cept to the outhouse. He be ready to leave shortly, I expect."

"Which general?" asked Fitz.

"The big gen'ral, massuh. Tha's Gen'ral Longstreet himself I'm talkin' about."

☆ ☆

Meade's fatigue dissipated as he trotted up the lane, weaving around dead horses and ambulances taking wounded away. Men saluted and cheered. *The happy look of victory*, he mused. *What a mess it might have been if "Someone had blundered."* Aloud, he recited:

Forward, the light brigade!
Was there a man dismay'd?
Not tho' the soldier knew
Someone had blundered.
Their's not to make reply,
Their's not to reason why,
Their's but to do and die.
Into the Valley of Death
Rode the Six Hundred.

"We didn't blunder, by God!" he shouted to Buford as he approached, and the cavalryman saluted. "You beat 'em, general, and you are to be congratulated." Meade reached out his hand. Buford seemed overcome. A rare moment had arrived when honor must be paid. It was Meade's obligation. They were not used to such victories. The flavor was sweet.

"We've lost about three hundred, I'd reckon." Buford spoke rapidly in his excitement. "They're the ones that blundered, by damn! We routed the Georgians before the 5th could get 'em. And flanked the South Carolina boys, too. That map was a godsend. I don't think the infantry lost any more than we have, and look at 'em." He pointed down the road, where the 5th was pushing south. "They're closing in on another Reb brigade. I'd guess old McLaws's division is pretty well finished. Look at that file of prisoners." He nodded toward a dispirited line of men walking down the road past the wheatfield.

Meade would remember this moment forever, the time when he truly gained command of the army. He could see it the their faces. Men he scarcely knew five days ago like Buford and Pleasonton had done his bidding because he was their commander, and he had succeeded without old friends like Reynolds and Sedgwick. From now on they would wait for him, wait on him, and watch his every move and word. He'd seen it with McClellan. It could be intoxicating. He must be careful.

Meade smiled. "What's your condition, general?" He pointed toward the peach orchard. "We must scout behind Longstreet and . . ." He turned toward the north. "I'm expecting a man back with a report on Hill's position. We'll need cavalry to go ahead of infantry. Have you forces ready?"

Buford smiled. "They're busting for more. I'll send Merritt off now behind Longstreet, and hold Gamble until you're ready." Buford saluted and rode out through a gathering crowd trying to hear their words and be a part of the victory .

The Commanding General pulled out his watch. After 5:00 p.m. Time to attack. He searched the woods for Fitzpatrick.

☆ ☆

Longstreet got to the Pitcher Schoolhouse just before Buford's men overran his artillery. The hillside and the trees masked the sounds. His thoughts concentrated on getting out clear orders to each commander. Time was pressing, but he thought the Yankees would be slow and deliberate as they always were. His men must withdraw carefully, fighting only as necessary, back onto Seminary Ridge and then north to join with the rest of the army.

He made the clerks take dictation. He wanted to be clear, and took the precaution of sending separate messengers on to each brigade. "This has to be done properly," he told the staff. "Nothing's harder than a fighting retreat." And then, giving himself a command, "I'd better get out there."

Two soldiers and an aide followed him toward the lines, turning left at the first junction toward McLaws's division. The road ran 300 yards past the Flaharty Farmhouse, then angled northeasterly through a grove of hardwoods to the Warfield Farm on rising ground a quarter mile beyond. Longstreet was surprised at the quiet. He saw stragglers in the woods. His concern mounted as he came closer, and he began a canter.

They were not far into the grove when six Yankee cavalrymen moved into the road ahead and pointed carbines at them. Longstreet turned in the saddle to see more to the right and left. Turning around, he found his retreat closed by men coming up in the rear.

A Yankee major came close and called out. "General Longstreet, you and your men are prisoners of General George Meade and the 1st Pennsylvania Cavalry."

Longstreet scowled. "He's smiling, the upstart son of a bitch!" He looked for a line of escape. One of his men raised a pistol and fired. Two Yankees shot back, nicking him in the arm. The Yankees closed in. "How many of these bastards are there?" he yelled. "They've all got their guns on me, except that damned major. Who the Hell does he think he is?"

Fitzpatrick came out of the trees. He had been schooling himself. They were all in awe of the man. Fitz had to keep his voice firm and avoid a smile. This was serious business. *Longstreet has to take me so, or the men will lose nerve. They're frozen in the saddle. Longstreet is seething anger . . . and danger, like a Shrapnel case in mid-air.*

"General, hand me your gun, and tell your men to follow," he ordered, slowly approaching on Longstreet's left. "I'm sorry about your escort. We'll have the surgeon look at him." He motioned for men to come for the guns.

"Damn! Goddamn!" shrieked the general, kicking his horse to surge forward.

Fitz caught the bridle, holding the animal down by force of will if not might, and tried to looked evenly into Longstreet's eyes. "You are a prisoner of the Army of the Potomac, General Longstreet. I am Major James Edward Fitzpatrick, aide-de-camp to Major General George Meade, the Commanding General."

Longstreet swung the ends of his reins like a whip at his face. Unseen, the cavalry sergeant raced up, reached out, and struck Longstreet on the chest, blocking his arm. "Damn you Rebel bastard, behave!" he shouted, a huge man as big as his enemy, signaling he was ready to kill. "You're our goddamn prisoner, and you'll come along." He held a pistol. "I've seen too many men die in this damn war to think anything of your goddamn worthless hide."

The general's horse subsided.

As evenly as he could, Fitz continued, "If you will kindly give me your pistol, sir, you may keep your sword, and we shall take you to General Meade."

Slow, reluctant, silent, and furious, Longstreet pulled his pistol from its holster, and, holding the butt by his fingers, handed it to Fitzpatrick. Aide and escorts followed suit.

"Now, general," said Fitz, eyes on his prisoner and talking constantly as he wheeled the horses around with aid of the sergeant, "we shall ride past that farm house and look for General Meade."

They formed a convoy, fore, aft, and down each side of the prisoners, and moved slowly forward in column, Fitz by Longstreet's side trying to think of something to say that might calm his mind. Finding nothing but the weather, he spoke of the heat, while the general grunted an occasional curse. As they came around the house, Fitz watched him intently survey the battlefield, amazed to see Yankee cavalry where McLaws's brigades had been. Union soldiers and guns were everywhere on the ridge, and artillerymen had resumed firing, with captured cannon in their batteries.

Finally Longstreet spoke, "I'm damned, major. What have you done with my corps? Where's McLaws?" He stood in the stirrups to see as far as he could, unwilling to accept what he saw.

Soldiers stared in disbelief at the party riding into their lines. The broad smiles of the cavalrymen told them who it was. No other Rebel general was that big. Men ran up to look, keeping out of the way, and lining out a path to where Meade sat his horse surrounded by a platoon of officers.

Meade watched them approach with as much astonishment as anyone, immediately recognizing the mountainous prisoner. No one who was in Mexico would mistake the "Hero of Chapultepec." "Major Fitzpatrick," he called out. "You have captured an army in one man. Well done." He nodded to Longstreet but did not to extend his hand. "General, you are our prisoner, and entitled to the courtesies of war."

Longstreet sat silent and numb, angry at being the focus of Yankee curiosity, and shamed by the sudden change of fortune. He knew George Meade, though not well. Seven years after Meade at the Academy, he had ranked him by two grades since 1848.

Meade spent little time on formalities. He summoned the provost marshal, who had come to talk about the growing herd of captives. Longstreet offered his sword. Meade refused it, saying, "General Patrick will take you to my quarters, where the orderlies will look after you. Your aide may go with you. Until later, general, when I hope we shall have a quiet time to converse." Meade touched his hat. Longstreet managed a bemused smile and raised his hand, as he and his three companions were led off.

Wounded men streamed into the "hospitals" in the rear—some seeking surgeons, some weary and seeking a place to rest and let nature cure them, and others abandoning hope and looking for a quiet place to die. Though supplies had arrived and water was more abundant, the stench remained overpowering, even for men who had lived in army camps for two years.

The Chief Surgeon recognized the amazing talents of the "red-headed girl" and sent her to nurse senior officers in special tents set aside for them. Ordinary soldiers lay in open fields, so did many officers. But they put senior generals under cover from the intense rays of the sun.

Hancock and Gibbon were among her patients, as well as Josephus. Orderlies put him in a special area in the large "generals' tent" behind packing cases where he had privacy—and where he would not attract curiosity. Hancock groused about having a black man with him, but the Chief Surgeon told him it was Meade's orders, and he was too far gone on chloroform to argue.

Maeve was happier each day to forget "Maizie," the flamboyant brothel name Alice had forced on her. She made rounds, brought water and food, tended bandages, and read to the generals. Newsmen, coming to see the heroes, were quick to notice the striking girl and began to call her the "Angel of Gettysburg," a title destined for their stories. They liked the artful way she dealt with their sallies, gently turning aside their ribald remarks, and would have taken her over completely had not Fannie shooed them away.

She was an irresistible puzzle. "How did a girl with no training become the assistant to the surgeon who took off Sickles's leg?" They asked. "Why is it she's so relaxed with men?" They debated these questions because it was fun and a relief from writing about the hard facts of war, especially about the wounded and dying.

When scouts returned the long, safe way around from Longstreet's corps headquarters to report a massive sweep of Yankee cavalry behind that position, Lee accepted it, but refused to believe Longstreet was lost. He discounted the story of his capture, though a scout had talked to witnesses who heard shots in the woods where he was taken. Lee counted on his best general to fight his way around that herd of the enemy he saw down the Emmitsburg Road.

At a mile's distance he couldn't make out much through his field glasses, though he was sure the stringbean figure sitting his horse like a skeleton was George Meade. Scores of officers milled around him. "Why do the Yankees need supernumeraries?" he asked Hill. "Surely, we can beat an army like that.

"We must assume they will attack soon. Hill, concentrate on the salient. Beat the woods for stragglers."

He was stunned to see the losses. Some officers got back a fair number. Most did not. From Pickett's fifteen regiments the yield was meager. Some men flatly refused to come even at gunpoint. In Garnett's brigade the officers found none at all.

Pettigrew, though wounded in the hand, led the search and had slightly better results. Three Tennessee regiments mustered nearly 300, including Private Toddy Bates. North Carolinians returned in about the same numbers. But an adjutant reported Davis's Mississippians and Brockenburgh's Virginians as ". . . highly reluctant to return to the field."

Of 12,000 in the attack, Lee could muster no more than 2,400, a loss fatal to any other army. His men had seen death, blood, and horror on every hand. They had lost the comrades they depended on. Yet, he knew they took pride in being outmanned. "None of us," he told Hill, "will leave Pennsylvania as free men, unless we hang together. We must assume the men think like we do." He sent an aide to Ewell to ask for two brigades posted in the town, and more from Culp's Hill as soon as he could spare them.

Meade would eventually strike at the angle where Confederate lines came together on the ridge. That way, he could take advantage of enfilading fire. Lee posted two of his best brigades at the angle, where he could move their men swiftly from one line to another. He salted another full brigade, regiment by regiment, among the remnants of the charge, placing them, along with cannon, behind stone walls and hastily built forts along the back of Seminary Ridge where the Yankees would have to attack across bad ground.

Although artillery ammunition was short, there was canister. Lee ordered the men to fill their ammunition cases, had water brought around, and suggested they eat what food they had.

Meade's main thrust soon came near the angle. Two, then three Yankee brigades charged into Posey's Mississippians and nearly broke them. Lee brought two regiments from the lane to stop the thrust. He sat on Traveler well to the rear where he could see the field. On lower, open ground 700 Georgians gave way. He reinforced them. After twenty minutes of desperate fighting, they were again about to break. He was delighted to see Ewell's men coming, and sent Louisianans into the breach. The enemy fell back.

A scout reported Yankees marching behind a westerly ridge toward the Hagerstown Road. Lee had anticipated an attack on his extreme right near the Seminary, and had strengthened the position. "If Meade thinks of repaying Chancellorsville," he told Hill, who kept constantly nearby, "we'll disappoint him badly. I've sent men to hold that corner down there." He pointed to the Seminary. "Even if he sends in a full division, we'll stop him."

The two generals sat side by side. Neither appeared to be well. Lee was tired. The day took its toll. He had not eaten, nor drunk water since early morning. Nor had Hill improved. Lee wondered about his stomach complaint. Rumors persisted he had a disease no gentleman would name. The lines on Hill's face were deep, those visible behind his face hair. At 38 he moved like a man of 50, and his sunken dark eyes lacked expression.

"General Hill," Lee turned his horse toward the road into town. "I'm going to see General Ewell about a withdrawal during the night. I'm sure you'll have more fighting and you will deal with it." Lee raised his hand to hat and rode off.

As George Meade, Jr., returned from carrying an order to Slocum, a shell fragment struck the side of his head and knocked him from the saddle. The horse dragged him a long way before men of the 12th rallied to catch it. They knew who he was, though his face was covered in blood, and carried him directly to the Chief Surgeon. Word spread quickly. Newspaper men came with a barrage of questions. Would he live? Where did it happen?

Meyer took them away, telling them that even the Commanding General did not know these facts. They must be patient. "Meanwhile, this fine young lady and the Chief Surgeon are seeing to *der junger* George." Meyer lied, "The doctors are very hopeful."

Maeve kept a straight face. The gash on the side of George's head was ugly. The surgeon had done what he could. Only the Almighty could save him.

Meade watched the fight at the angle. A messenger from the Chief Surgeon brought word that George had been struck in the head and was with the surgeons. Nothing more. He knew what that likely meant, and took it as calmly as he could. *George is my posterity—precious! Yet today everyone takes losses. It's not mine to pause, while I send thousands of others to die.* Once again weakened by heartfelt loss, he muttered a prayer and crossed himself. He hesitated while his breathing came again regularly, then signaled John Newton, watching him intently from a few yards away, to send in a third brigade. "Another thrust," he yelled, "and we should break them."

In a short time more Rebels appeared and threw back a savage counterattack. *Lee outthinks me. It's not going to go here. It daunts me, crossing swords with him. I've been lucky today, and I wonder whether I will ever know enough. How does one learn to think on horseback, calmly send men to die, and have faith? One learns by experience, and I will always be behind.*

Another courier:

To the Commanding General I have the honor to report no more than two thousand five hundred Rebels remain on the Rebel left. The 3d Corps and the cavalry have them surrounded. I have seven thousand five hundred men ready and able at your disposal, sir.

> *Sykes*
> *General Commanding*
> *5th Corps*

As Meade sat in his saddle almost in a stupor, caught in the currents of good news and bad, a wounded soldier called, "general, it's damn well worth it if we win the war today."

Not likely to win here. Lee uses his interior lines. He paused. *I have more men. Can we keep them stretched out, and strike at a weaker place in the center? If we envelop Hill, Lee will have less than fifty thousand, perhaps half that. Will the Gods of War stay with us?* He made up his mind and once again fatigue vanished.

"The men smell victory, Newton, and they will fight for it. You see how Longstreet's capture inspired them. Who are John Newton and George Meade to stop now, by Jove?"

His watch showed 6:30 p.m. Meade told Newton to watch for a signal from Cemetery Ridge. He had decided. The 5th Corps was to march up the Taneytown Road toward town. There were two hours to fight. With Sharpe and Fitzpatrick, he followed them, keeping out of sight. "We must surprise Lee again," he said. "If it works once, try again. "Major Fitzpatrick, find Pleasonton. We need cavalry."

☆ ☆

The next hour for Toddy Bates was tense and painful. Men fired across the lines from long distances. A Yankee brigade made a feint, only to fall back as Hill's men at the angle stood their ground. Along Seminary Ridge the men grew weary. The 7th Tennessee was down to 75 men as more went off wounded, died, or fell to heat stroke. News of Longstreet's capture spread soon after they started digging in. The loss, denied by their officers, troubled them. They remembered the bear-like general riding in full view of the Yankees before the charge, showing his contempt. How could they take him?

Later, Lee left the field, and word spread he was seriously sick. They were stuck with Hill. He was no replacement.

Toddy's face was frozen, his usual expression. He seldom showed anything, except when he used to laugh with his brothers and sisters back home. Since he'd been in the army, things had been mostly too serious to laugh about. Today, he had no idea what was going to happen, but it couldn't be good. When a Minié ball hit another comrade, Toddy thought the next might as well strike him. The army didn't seem to be doing things right.

☆ ☆

Pleasonton brought Brigadier General Custer to the ruined gate-keeper's house on Cemetery Hill, where Meade gathered his commanders. Inside was hot and crowded for the dozen he needed, but it kept away scores of others. Meade wondered at Custer glittering in gold braid and long blonde curls. *Not my sort of officer, but apparently he can fight. All these young horsemen are too eager.*

He outlined the plan.

"The 2d will attack the lane, concentrating on the end toward town, where Hill has thinned his forces. The 5th will continue toward Gettysburg on the flank of the 2d, and the 1st and 11th on its right will push against Ewell. Custer will attack at the end of the lane directly on the flank of the 2d, and sweep the Rebels back toward Seminary Ridge. He will join with other cavalry coming past the Seminary across the Hagerstown Road. That will complete the envelopment."

And waited for questions. There were none, and that bothered him. "Anyone who's late, or fails to move, can ruin the operation," he said. Still no questions. *It's not likely to be a disaster. Our numbers are too great, and Hill is isolated.* The heat in the room was overpowering. Sweat drenched their tunics. Meade couldn't hold them long.

He feared momentum might undo them. *They're eager for the kill.* "The first order is to destroy Hill. A final assault on Ewell must wait." He spoke slowly, looking at each man, making sure he understood. *Some will go after glory rather than finish their assignments. They all know Ewell would be easy prey once Hill is finished.*

"Ewell isn't a problem, yet." He went through it again, looking at each man again. "But bungled plans might make him one."

As they filed out, he called Fitzpatrick. "Major, take all Nelson's cavalry and follow Custer. When you get into town, turn away and reconnoiter. You'll know what to do." *Custer is the wild card. If anyone tries to do prodigies of valor, he's the fellow. All the more reason to send Fitzpatrick ahead.*

☆ ☆

By the time Lee rode into Gettysburg he was weary. He found Ewell in a building north of the square where Early's division had its headquarters. Here, distant sounds of battle seemed reassuring, though the citizens kept indoors. A few houses struck by shells were burning. The closest fighting seemed to lie toward the cemetery—ragged shooting, like sniping. *Probably sharpshooters,* he thought. *Nothing to worry about. This is one ability where we are superior.*

He found Ewell sitting in a chair, wooden leg propped up on the seat of another. Maj. Gen. Jubal Early, one his division commanders, paced the room. They seemed surprised to see him and said they were pleased all was well with Hill.

Lee complimented Early on his men at the angle and the Seminary. A stuffed armchair was brought. He sat heavily into it and closed his eyes. The other generals nodded to each other and kept silent, saying nothing as long as he slept. They knew a refreshed Lee was better to work with. Abruptly, he woke with a pointed question, "What provision have you made for holding the town, General Ewell?"

"Georgia sharpshooters are raising Ned with the Yankees when they poke their noses in. We've taken down a house or two, put up barricades, and have cannon ready to offer a whiff of grape, if they're persistent." Ewell looked at Early for confirmation.

"Sounds fine, General Ewell, but what about infantry? Do you have enough?" Lee gently persisted.

Ewell nodded to Early. "Brigadier General Gordon has put men into town, sir," Early said, glancing at Ewell. Gordon had sent only two regiments, concentrating most of his men to protect the flank of seven brigades below Culp's Hill. Early didn't have enough in town to stop a full-scale Yankee assault, but he couldn't say that to General Lee.

Ordinarily, Lee was quick to detect it when generals gave fluffy answers. He smiled and said, "Thank you, General Early, I'm sure you are right." His eyelids flickered, and he closed them again.

Fitzpatrick and the cavalrymen followed the last of Custer's riders around the Rebel flank. Custer and the infantry forced the enemy back toward the angle, opening gaps in their lines. The small party stopped on the Hagerstown Road to watch the fight.

As Custer's horsemen appeared in the open fields, both sides saw them. A revived and inspired 2d Corps pushed across the lane *en masse*. Everyone saw them break through, even the men across the way along Seminary Ridge.

A brigade of cavalry coming around the seminary swept across the Hagerstown Road and eventually joined Custer. For a while Rebels ran in all directions. Some came toward what had been the rear, only to meet their enemies behind them.

Fighting died almost as fast as it began. Both Yankees and Confederates knew the battle at this end of town was over. Hill's corps was finished, and his men captives. Hill himself was struck and killed immediately after the assault began by a bullet from a Spencer carbine.

Fitz watched a brigade from the 5th Corps wind slowly past Rebel barricades into town, and ordered his men to move ahead of them. Finding the streets empty and strangely quiet, they trotted toward the square. Most of the houses had been damaged. Several were on fire, and no one seemed to be trying to stop the flames. They held carbines in hand ready to fire. Here and there rear echelon soldiers, clerks, and supply men scurried away. Once or twice, one stepped from behind a building and fired a rifle in haste, then disappeared around it. They weren't good marksmen. Organized opposition in this part of town had crumbled.

The small force reached the square. To the east stood a large building with a line of horses in front, a Confederate flag hanging from the second floor. Fitz surveyed the area. The 5th Corps was far behind and moving carefully. To the right scattered troops retreated before them. To the left all seemed quiet. Two guards stood in front of the building. A Rebel messenger rode up in haste, ignoring or not seeing bluecoats 100 yards away.

Fitz nodded. Nelson ordered his men to surround the building. The two officers with six troopers rode up swiftly. The guards lowered their rifles, and one fired. The troopers fired back, wounding one. The other dashed inside.

Dismounting, Fitz, Nelson, and three men ran across the porch and into the building. A soldier behind a desk fired his pistol, hitting one of the men. They disarmed him and took three others prisoner, including the messenger. Fitz asked who was in the next room, but got no answer.

As a trooper pushed open the door, Early shot him with his pistol. Nelson fired back, striking the general in the chest. He dropped to the floor, unconscious and probably dead. Fitz, Nelson, and two soldiers stepped over him into the room, where Lee slowly rose from his chair, clasped his hands behind his back, looked up frowning. Ewell tried to stand by pulling up on a chair. They seemed more surprised by the sudden loss of Early than by anything else that was happening.

"Who are you?" demanded Lee in a commanding voice.

"I am Major Fitzpatrick, aide-de-camp to Major General George Meade, sir. You and the men in this building are prisoners of the United States Army of the Potomac." Quickly, the events with Longstreet ran through his mind. Neither Lee nor the other man, who had to be Ewell, was a physical threat. To the contrary, both seemed ill, stunned, and a little vague, as if they lacked the will to meet the situation.

He was about to ask for pistols, but seeing Lee carried none, hesitated. "You may keep your swords, gentlemen, for General Meade, who will come shortly. If you have small weapons, please give them to the troopers." Ewell unholstered a large pistol and handed it to Nelson. As he did so, footfalls banged on the porch and came into the building—the boots of a cavalryman.

Custer swung into the room. Outside, his men filled the street. He bowed theatrically to Lee, and turned to Fitzpatrick. "I see you beat me to it, major." He laughed as if it were a game.

Fitz could see the humor, but did his best not to laugh. Lee had to be accorded the honors of war. More important, they needed his authority to get others to surrender. "General Custer," he said, "If I may leave Generals Lee and Ewell in your hands, I will go immediately to bring General Meade to complete the necessary formalities." He wanted Custer to understand the need to follow protocol.

Custer stamped his boot, looked at the floor, and stared at the Confederates, who watched him fascinated as though he were on stage. Custer put his hand to his hat. "I guess you know best how these things go, major. It's an honor to defer to the man who captured Longstreet." He grinned and bowed again, this time toward Fitz. "I can do no better."

Lee came to life. "Then you do have Longstreet, general? Is he safe?"

"Yes, General Lee," said Custer, now alive to procedure, "Major Fitzpatrick has tucked him away in General Meade's headquarters, and I believe he is safe and unharmed."

Fitz nodded, "That is true, General Lee, he is safe and in custody."

"Well, I thank you for that much," said Lee sadly. He seemed at last to accept events.

The men of the 7th Tennessee stood up and looked to the rear, waiting. They could see the troops at the Seminary surrounded and beginning to surrender. In small numbers, men in other regiments began to withdraw. Chaos ruled the fields between the ridge and the lane. Men at the angle gave up when they saw cavalry in their rear. The ridge became quiet. No snipers' balls came over the forts.

Seeing Yankee cavalry suddenly turn and leave the field, a few decided to follow them. Toddy and two other men ran across the fields as fast as they could, stopping at one bush or tree, then another, taking advantage of what cover they could find.

"If we kin jist get inta town," said one of them. "Maybe we can jine up with Ewell."

That sounded to Toddy like the best idea anyone was likely to offer. Their only officer left had disappeared. They had no orders. Apparently it was right to get away, like he did after the charge.

They struggled through the open field, and were almost across, when one man was hit in the chest. Toddy wanted to stop, but the other said, "Leave 'im. He's probably done for, and if not the Yankees have as good of doctors as we do." It was an excuse to run, Toddy knew. He looked back and saw his friend's face was blue.

The man was lung shot. When he turned to go on, the other had vanished.

Toddy found a path into the streets and pressed north and east, thinking it best to keep to the outskirts of town, where there were fewer fires and perhaps no Yankees. He felt tired and fought off sleep. He wanted to lie down. He moved through back yards, behind livery stables and barns. He found a well, nearly down, but filling. The rope was gone, and there was no way to get the water up. Parched, hot, and exhausted, he decided to hide and rest in a barn, empty of animals, probably taken away by army drovers. He climbed into the loft, lay down beside his gun, and fell asleep.

When Fitzpatrick came for Meade, standing with other officers outside the gatekeeper's house, his commander's first words were, "Major, congratulations. I have not done this yet today, but I'm going to do a lot of it now. You, sir, are hereby brevetted full colonel from this minute forth. And you can be damned proud of it." He put out his hand. A gaggle of generals clapped and cheered.

Fitzpatrick took his hand and then saluted, for a moment speechless. The business of the day had been all too urgent. "If you like, sir, I will go to see how George fares." He paused. "After I show you the way."

"I would appreciate that, colonel. But right now I need you to ride by me." Meade's face glowed with triumph. "We must show the good people of Gettysburg their saviors have arrived." He walked to his horse, held by two major generals who had relieved his orderly.

They rode in procession down the Taneytown Road toward the square with Pleasonton, Hunt, the provost marshal, and two score senior officers. At first, only a few men stepped out to wave, then whole families appeared. By the time they reached the square, it was filled. Cheering came from every building. Many peopled waved pennants, and flags dropped from windows.

Meade noticed that most houses near the cemetery were destroyed. Some townsfolk were on crude crutches or carried their arms in slings. Yankee shells had done a great deal of damage.

He reached the hotel and found Custer standing up, trying to make amiable conversation with Lee, who looked up at him silently. He seemed determined to take no comfort from the young man's banter, but he stood abruptly when Meade entered, and smiled for the first time since the Yankees appeared. "Your hair is a good deal more gray than the last time I saw you," he said softly.

Meade grinned. "Most of that has come from chasing you." Officers crowded into the room, and Meade ordered them out, all but Fitzpatrick and Custer. The young general might need to learn something.

Meade wanted the fighting done. Darkness was near, and he could feel victory's chores closing in upon him. The fatigue that had never been far away pulled on his arms and legs.

Lee agreed to send an aide, as soon as one could be found, to carry a letter to Ewell's commanders telling them they might honorably surrender. "I cannot order them," he said, "because I am a prisoner. They are bound in honor to follow their own counsel."

Meade wouldn't temporize. Argument was unsuitable. "I have four Union corps surrounding eight of your brigades. It would be sad to continue needless killing."

"Sadly I must agree, general," said Lee. "Yet, honor holds the army together. I must not transgress." He managed a wan smile and indicated he wished to sit.

Meade saw how weary he was and quickly nodded. Ewell was teetering on his wooden leg, and Meade urged him to sit. He must wait for Lee to write his letter, and turned to converse with Ewell about Mexico.

☆ ☆

Brigadier General John Brown Gordon watched the Confederate Army dissolve with shock and dismay. No man on the field was angrier at Lee's mistakes. Late in the afternoon, after placing two regiments in town as a defensive screen, he was enraged to find his right flank open at the south when Early sent another brigade off to help Hill. Gordon rode out to the salient. Like others he discounted the capture of Longstreet, his fellow Georgian, and firmly believed the salient would hold, but after a brief meeting with Lee and Hill came away in fury and depression. He sensed the leadership was faltering. More than any other man come from civil life, Gordon found that intolerable.

As soon as he heard of Early's death, or capture (reports were unclear), Gordon took command of the division. When another commander was wounded, he took charge of his division well, massing 3,000 men. He decided to make a stand along with Allegheny Johnson's division when they withdrew from Culp's Hill. His plan failed when a Yankee corps cut off Johnson's line of retreat.

Lee's letter failed to reach Gordon. When Allegheny Johnson received it, he was torn. His men had fought for two days without cease. Unaware of Gordon, he couldn't determine whether to fight his way out or face up to the fact his men were spent. His brigade commanders split. Johnson bowed his head, bit his lip, and ordered surrender to men of Slocum's corps on the hill above.

Gordon had three brigades of men furious that Lee had been caught literally napping, as the story ran. He moved them across Rock Creek and up Benner's Hill, ordering them to dig in. He sent messengers calling on Stuart to send cavalry to relieve them. Surrounded, they fought doggedly past sunset, 2,500 against 20,000. From time to time Union men saw Gordon's gaunt figure moving behind his soldiers, calling on them to hold. In the last fading light, a Yankee sharpshooter dropped him.

An hour later, a soldier came out of the dark into Union lines with a message to "The Commanding Yankee General" from Brig. Gen. William Smith, a Virginia politician known as "Extra Billy" for padding his income at public expense. Smith, elected governor a few weeks before the battle, decided for the sake of his men to surrender.

CHAPTER XIV

Before going to bed Flossie Muelheim retrieved her diary from the eaves.

Soon after our soldiers marched into town, word spread that General Meade was riding to the hotel the Rebels used as their headquarters. People said they kept General Lee there as a prisoner. Papa and I ran up to the square.

Guns sounded to the east toward Benner's Hill, but no one was afraid anymore. It was as if the Rebels had vanished. People came out with flags to cheer the soldiers. Papa and I pushed our way through the crowd in time to see General Meade arrive. He is a tall, thin man, perhaps slightly awkward but graceful in a way. They say he comes from a rich Philadelphia family.

We made way when he dismounted from his huge battle horse. The general lifted his floppy hat to wave, and the rays of the fading sun struck his face with a fiery glow such as an artist would draw around the head of saint. Everyone who saw it will never forget.

A dozen generals followed him and jostled each other to keep close behind. But he ignored them and talked to a young aide at his side. People said this man, a colonel or a major, was a hero who captured several Rebel generals.

When we got home, mother told us Heinrich had left to find his regiment. Ladies called by to ask us to take in wounded. We have agreed to become a hospital.

As Meade met with Lee, word came that Stuart had broken camp, heading with all his force toward the pass over the mountains. Breaking off, Meade ordered his prisoners taken to the upper floors and made the ground floor room his office, immediately ordering cavalry to the foot of the mountains with infantry to follow from the 6th Corps, which was going into bivouac near the Cashtown Road.

The men would grumble about another march at the end of a hard day, but he reckoned they would benefit from better conditions away from the battlefield.

Reports poured in from harried staff officers, and Meade encountered a whole new set of problems. The Chief Surgeon sent word that George was resting in a coma. Stifling a parental urge, Meade realized he must deal with other urgencies first. Nor could he send Fitzpatrick off to visit him. The new colonel's sense of new circumstances was proving more valuable.

From town and everywhere around it they heard about the mess of battle—bodies of men dead, dying, and wounded, animal carcasses, burnt-out houses and farms, abandoned wagons, cannon, and stores—mostly Rebel, but some Yankee, possibly captured, no one knew. In the fields fighting had destroyed the crops, and the two armies had eaten almost all available food. Trash and dying men fouled running water, and wells were down. Railroad bridges were out, and, with Rebel cavalry still on the loose, reaching out to other towns was risky.

Meade drafted messages assigning the corps to positions guarding the town and field, and summoned, one by one, his senior staff. The quartermaster said he had rations for the Union troops but little for the prisoners. He fretted about looters and wanted, as soon as he could, to collect Rebel rifles and cannon, which lay everywhere in large numbers. The Chief Surgeon came to speak about George, and about thousands of others. He had co-opted his Rebel counterparts, now willing colleagues, and wanted to bring the wounded off the field, certain that wild pigs would molest and eat bodies, live or dead, in the night. Both sides were short of medical supplies. Sharpe wanted to separate Rebel officers from the men and question them about the defenses of Richmond. The town mayor came to express appreciation and quickly state his worry about water and to urge he engineers to repair the railroad.

Marcena Patrick, beset with 60,000 prisoners, wanted permission to call on infantry for thousands of guards. He had a special problem: the British colonel, an alleged observer, captured just before the battle ended. "What'll we do with that English bastard?"

Meade laughed. "I'm sure the Englishman was more than an

observer." He turned to Fitzpatrick, chuckling. "In this good company I can let my Irish show, though Mrs. Meade would rather I forget it." The others grinned, and Meade felt an intimacy he would never permit but for the victory, a Union victory. It was almost an elation, and he choked it back. This was business. "Put him in the hotel with the others, and tomorrow morning have an officer and two men take him to the nearest railroad with a parole to report to Washington City to Mr. Seward at the State Department. He's their concern." Meade hesitated, holding a puckish grin, "Take the men from Kelly's brigade. He best know we're no British satrap." Patrick left with a broad smile on his face as Fitzpatrick stifled laughter. It was heady stuff, like strong wine. Meade thought he'd better be serious before he was too tired to carry on.

Meyer came with a petition signed by dozens of newspaper reporters asking to meet with the general. Meade wanted to dismiss it until Fitzpatrick interceded. "Perhaps first thing in the morning a meeting would let you set the record straight as to who did what. That way, general, you can ensure credit goes where it's due."

Meade stared at Fitz wondering how he could be so wise while his own mind groped, then turned to Meyer. "He's right. If we don't tell it right, someone else will tell it wrong." He thought of Sickles, and Butterfield, wherever he had got to. "Tell them to meet me at 7:30 a.m. tomorrow. You and Fitzpatrick come with Sharpe an hour before so we can prepare." He slumped forward, head in hands in the overstuffed chair where he'd met Lee. "Who would dream victory brought so many problems?"

By the time the last Rebel had surrendered, Meade went from field commander to military governor, a role he barely understood. He knew what military methods called for, and ordered his staff to go by the book. The main task was to hold on to the prisoners. Victory would be lost if any number survived to fight another day.

He soon regretted his decision to keep his headquarters in the center of town. The hotel was fine for holding senior prisoners on the upper floors, and a good place for staff to oversee operations, but he needed to stay apart to concentrate on the next moves. The army was breaking into *terra incognita,* and so was George Meade, though personal thoughts barely touched him. He would like to write

Margaret and see George, but those things must wait. The precious opportunities of victory must not be lost. Too much blood had been shed for them.

The quartermaster found a large house on the campus of Pennsylvania College at the northern edge of town. There, half a mile away, he would be able to think. The elixir of victory was carrying them, but Meade knew fatigue would soon take hold, and tomorrow hardly a regiment would be ready for action. Nor would he.

The first move in the morning was to send troops over the mountains to recapture Union prisoners, seize Rebel supply trains, including loot gathered to go South, and to catch stragglers and small units north of the Potomac. This job was for cavalry, followed by men on foot.

Also important was to send soldiers into the towns in the valley to protect the citizens from angry Rebels, like Stuart's men, who might rampage. Meade telegraphed Harrisburg to hurry militia down to Chambersburg, and ordered General French in Frederick to seize the Potomac crossings.

To Washington, with the aid of Fitzpatrick, he sent his victory message:

Headquarters

Army of the Potomac

Gettysburg, July 3, 11 p.m.

To the President, the Secretary of War, and the Genl-in-Chief,

I have the honor to report the army today defeated and destroyed the Army of Northern Virginia. 10,000 Rebels lie dead on the field. 60,000 are Union prisoners, of whom about half are wounded. Genl Lee is taken along with Lt Genls Longstreet and Ewell. Lt Genl Hill is killed. All Rebel division commanders are prisoner, except for Maj Genls Early, Rodes, Anderson, and McLaws, who are killed. We have large quantities of enemy weapons, animals and stores including 200 cannon. Stuart's cavalry remain at large. Am in pursuit.

Union losses exceed 20,000, the number depends on how many prisoners we recapture. Maj Genl Sedgwick is killed. Hancock and Gibbon are wounded. The situation around Gettysburg is precarious. Water and food are low. Large numbers of wounded require attention. Requests for material aid will come sep-

166

arately. Have declared martial law and will bar from this area all persons having no legitimate business.

George G. Meade
Major General
Commanding

Fitzpatrick finished the copy before guns on Benner's Hill fell silent. Meade sent it off without hesitation, and then, thoughts turning to Washington City, realized that he had no peer to confide in, no one who could say a step was rash or wise, no one better than Fitzpatrick. Reynolds, Hancock, Sedgwick, and Gibbon were gone. Others, now battle-tested, were not confidants—nor anywhere near his age, save Andrew Humphreys, whom he would make the Army Chief of Staff. He would at last have a man who would not betray him. Fitz left with the message for him on his way to see George.

Meade rode to the white clapboard house at the college. Its well-ordered parlor was another world, and provoked other thoughts. Until walking into it, he didn't see his scarred boots or torn and stained tunic, nor the blood oozing from the back of his hand from the graze of a stray bullet. Somehow, the Rebels had left the house alone, probably because it was too far away. He thought of penning a note to Margaret, but lacked energy, and sat in a platform rocker and dozed off.

Fitz rode down the Taneytown Road searching for George. The moon had gone behind clouds, and in the gloomy night he could barely see the way. Thunder boomed in the west, and a light rain began to fall. Guided by men along the road, he found Fannie Morris's wagon. She was awake, and overjoyed to see the son of life-long friends, now such a hero. On foot they set out to find George.

She called him by childhood names, "He hadn't recovered consciousness when last I heard, James Edward. It's a bittersweet day for the Meades, and I pray for Margaretta. We've put George in a tent by himself, not far from Generals Hancock and Gibbon, and that brave colored man who rode so gallantly across the lines."

"How is Mr. Josephus?"

"He's not conscious, but I doubt his wounds are mortal. They've taken out all the bullets. If there is no blood poisoning, he should recover." As she trudged along, Fannie described George's situation. "There'll be a scar, but with luck he may chiefly suffer a deep concussion. He could awaken anytime. I've put our best nurse with him, a pretty, cheery redhead. If anyone can make a young man want to live, Maeve can."

Fitz was startled, *Redhead! Can't be the same girl.* He was glad Fannie couldn't see his face, as Maizie drove away other thoughts. Nothing remained, not the rousing acts of victory, nor fatigue, nor death everywhere, nothing. He was glad to be on foot lest he fall. When Fannie stopped to motion him into the tent, she had to tug at his tunic.

"I'll find someone with a light," she said and left him standing in the dark. The tent was large enough for a half dozen men. Fitz could see no one. Shapes appeared in shadows as lightning lit up the tent walls, a cot, and someone sitting by it. "Hello," he said softly, "I'm Major . . . uh Colonel . . . Fitzpatrick come from General Meade."

"Yes," came a soft familiar voice. "He's still asleep, but he did just take a little water." The woman stood up.

Her voice rippled through Fitz's brain. *It is Maizie! How does she get here?* He stepped forward. *Would she remember? What would she think?* "I'm glad you're looking after him. So well, I mean."

"I pray for him," she said, rising. "I firmly believe he will waken."

Fitz thought he heard a tremor as she spoke. "You're very kind to give him so much care. I'm sure the general would be glad of it. He's very busy and well, frankly, we're all pretty much spent."

"I know."

He saw her face lit by a lightning flash, wreathed in auburn hair, nothing ever so beautiful on a field of battle. "You know," he stammered. "I'm very glad to see you again. I'm Major Fitzpatrick, remember?" He put out his hand in what seemed a stupid gesture, but he had no say about what he did.

"I remember you very well, major," she said, and came toward him to take his hand, seeming no more than he to be aware of where they were. "We've been working as nurses. The woman who brought you, Mrs. Morris, she is kind. I like helping the wounded."

Fitz squeezed her hand, and wanted to pull her body to him, even began to do so when Fannie, light in hand, threw back the tent flap. "Ah, I see you two have met," she said, looking from one to the other. "Maeve has hardly left his side since he came. The poor wounded generals will be jealous." She laughed. "How is our patient?"

"Much the same," Maeve said. "He took some water."

"A very good sign, James Edward. You can report that to George Meade." Fannie's voice was official. "Now, I think it's best we leave young George rest, and you, Colonel Fitzpatrick, probably need some yourself."

The courier took two hours to bring the message to Hanover and another half hour to find a telegrapher. The man worked an hour before he could raise someone in Baltimore to pass it along. At a few minutes before 3:30 a.m. the first clicks sounded in the tiny room outside the office of the Secretary of War.

Tears welled in the clerk's eyes as he copied the words. As the first paragraph ended, he signaled Baltimore to repeat each sentence twice so he could be sure he got the words right. In the room the other clerk slept. For the moment he was the only man in Washington City with the news. Carefully, he rewrote the message in two copies, picked them up and silently carried the first in to the Secretary. "From Gettysburg," he stammered.

Stanton saw tears. "That bad?"

"No. Joy! Joy!" the clerk struggled. "We've won. Damn it, sir! We've won the war." He turned and ran out with the second copy for Halleck.

Lincoln stirred on his couch. "What's that, Stanton?" His voice was sharp. "What's happened?"

The Secretary of War stood erect, positioned the paper carefully on his easel, fixed eyeglasses on his nose, and read in an official voice. No one else was in the room.

"He's done it," said Lincoln, sitting up, rubbing sleep from his eyes. "Thank God!"

In seconds Halleck, wide awake, bounced in, a troop of others following. "It's a miracle," he said. "Meade has accomplished what no one else could do. He's destroyed Lee. The South is defenseless. The

169

road to Richmond is open."

"Meade is the great hero of the war," said Lincoln now on his feet, smiling, and shaking his head. "He's our new Napoleon, and we hardly know what to think about him. Remarkable, the workings of Providence!" He seemed almost not to believe what he said, and reached to Halleck for his copy. When he had read it twice closely, he looked up, convinced. "We awake to a new world."

Stanton showed the message to senior civil servants, staff generals and a few reporters. Sounds of life rumbled throughout the building. Lights were lit. Men ran through the halls and out into the streets to shout the news: "Lee is defeated. The Rebel army crushed. General Meade has won a great victory!" The news ran through the city like a wind-driven fire.

The Willards lit up their hotel as men filled the barroom. Torch lights appeared on Pennsylvania Avenue, and brass bands assembled to march toward the White House. Players ran to join up, pulling on their coats in the muggy, early dawn. On the second floor of the Willard, maids hung out flags. In the windows silhouettes of Lincoln appeared along with large letters spelling out "MEADE" and "Victory." A procession followed the bands to the White House, where the President had gone to wake his family.

As the crowd came up to the massive front, Lincoln stood in a large window on the second floor, bunting in the national colors hastily thrown over the railing. The crowd of men swelled outward into Lafayette Square.

Lincoln projected his voice as far as he could. "General Meade and the Army of the Potomac have won a great victory. At Gettysburg in Pennsylvania after three hard days' battle, Lee and the invaders of the Army of Northern Virginia met their match."

The crowd cheered. After the President read Meade's victory message, a man under the balcony yelled up, "Is the war over, Mr. President?"

"No, sir," Lincoln shouted back. "But with General Meade in command I have no doubt it soon will be."

The crowd roared and broke into a rousing cheer. A group took up a rolling chant, "Meade means Victory. Meade! Victory! Meade! Lincoln! Meade, Lincoln, Meade! Meade! Meade!" Endlessly they shouted "Meade," intoxicated with the name of their new giant.

Water dripped from the eaves over the porch. Mists lay thick in the fields as the first rays broke through from beyond the Susquehanna over Cemetery Hill and the town. The smell of death hung in the air, and occasionally a wounded man or animal cried in the distance.

The newspaper men assembled, sitting on damp ground before the house at the College, and waited to hear what had happened. Most had tried to send out word the night before, but no one was at all certain he had succeeded. The few who went themselves might have gotten ahead of the rest, but their stories wouldn't have much, other than to report a victory. Yet even now, after hours of retold stories, no one fully understood. They had seen victories before, but these made little difference in the grand scheme of the war.

Nor could they believe what they heard, hardened as they were to Union failure. The winners had lost, and the losers, won. Few would be surprised to see Jeb Stuart, or even Stonewall Jackson, ride through the mists and put an end to this illusion. Hardly anyone knew anything about this aloof scarecrow of a general, whom Southern reporters persisted in calling an "overcooked schoolmaster." "If the Yankees won," they asked, "where is Robert E. Lee and Pete Longstreet? Why don't he produce them?"

Still, the fighting was over, and their Southern counterparts sat with them, not on the other side of the field. Everyone could see the long gray lines of prisoners, along with captured flags and booty. Penned Confederates stared out behind makeshift walls and fences that Union men worked all night to build.

Their editors would want meaning, color, and personality. Was this the glorious end? What happened now? The public wanted to read about great events and great men, more than about details of battle. Reporters ignored bodies rotting on the ground. Busy with endless card games, their whiskey and special comforts, they tried not to see them.

It wasn't news that in the 5th Corps hospital down the Baltimore Pike 3d Sgt. Liam O'Bannion lay with his left leg off below the knee. Fannie Morris's crew had carried him from the field early the night before and got him through surgery and to the hospital in time to lie all night face up in the rain. This was a story for memoirs, not war reporters.

And only a photographer would go up the lane from the Trostle Farm to see Corporal O'Hara of the 71st New York. He fell wounded on July 2 and remained groaning for aid, dying suddenly the next afternoon when the hoof of a U.S. Cavalry horse stove in his skull. Reporters left grisly scenes to the artists and poets. They were fascinated by heroes and women, and wrote screeds about the nurses and the "Angel of Gettysburg," and they wanted to know what it all meant.

Two colonels, one mature, one boyish, came onto the porch and hung a sheet between the columns. On it limned in India ink was the battleground, prominently showing the Fishhook and the point of Buford's cavalry charge. A gust of wind billowed the sheet, and the colonels found bricks to hold it down.

A tall, skinny Maj. Gen. George G. Meade stepped forward— clean, shaven, bathed, rested and smiling. He had just finished the best breakfast of his life, prepared by a volunteer cook from the town with fresh eggs, milk, bread, ham, and fruit given by grateful citizens. His smile was benign.

Meade read his telegram to Lincoln. "This message," he said, "tells the story as of late last night. I can add that before midnight at Cashtown, Gen. Jeb Stuart's cavalry were caught between pursuing cavalry and other Union troops sent to head them off. Many of you probably heard the sounds of battle. Stuart, we estimate, lost a substantial number of men, and sought a hiding place in the mountains. We are in pursuit of all remaining Rebel units north of the Potomac. Mr. Meyer will see that regular bulletins are posted." He nodded to Meyer, who bowed to Meade and then to the newsmen.

Meade told the events of the battle in detail beginning with the first day, mentioning regiments which had fought well, avoiding criticism, but occasionally faltering and seeking information from one the men behind. When he came to the final attack his tone lightened, and he laughed as he recited Tennyson. "The Rebels must have thought we were insane. But we saw they were stretched out, and we could break them. We had to do it with speed and surprise,

172

before they recovered from Cemetery Ridge."

The reporters smiled and nudged each other, except for the Southerners, whose faces were grim.

"We felt victory come into hand when our cavalry attack succeeded. The proof came when Colonel Fitzpatrick here"—he nodded toward Fitz—"and a few men from the Pennsylvania Cavalry brought back General Longstreet. You could see the pride in the faces of the men. That's when we knew we had to dare all and go ahead."

The crowd, both from the North and South, sent forth sighs from time to time as if they had been allowed to join the action. The sun grew stronger and the mists less. Meade ceased to be awkward.

"I suppose," he said, "you have some questions."

"Where is General Lee?" yelled a Southerner. "And what have you done with him?"

"General Robert E. Lee is a prisoner and entitled to the courtesies of war," said Meade with a condescending smile. "He and Lieutenant Generals Longstreet and Ewell are in their chambers, along with other Confederate officers, under guard at headquarters near the town square. You may assure your readers they will be well looked after."

The Northerners guffawed.

"Will we be free to report our stories?" asked another Southerner.

Meade turned to look at Sharpe, who nodded. "Yes, indeed," he said. "It would be a very good idea for your people to understand what has happened."

Yankee laughter exploded, followed by cheers for Meade. "God bless you, general," some called out. "That's just the way to do it."

A man shouted, "What about the colonel here? Did he really capture both Longstreet and Lee?"

Meade's smile became a grin. "Perhaps you should hear about that from the man himself."

Fitzpatrick stood forward. "It was mostly luck," he said. "Without running across escaping slaves, we'd never have caught Longstreet. And yet, he would probably have been caught sooner or later."

"General, we hear rumors that the niggers played a big role in this victory. Is that true?"

173

Meade glanced at a frowning Sharpe. "As Colonel Fitzpatrick pointed out, there were instances where Negroes escaping from the Rebels were very helpful."

"Do you mean the slaves are working for the North?" The reporter glowered at the Southern colleagues.

"It stands to reason," said Meade. "Doesn't it? The slaves have a great deal at stake in the outcome of the war. And let me add they are fully capable of making a contribution." Meade tried to cut short this talk to protect Josephus and his group. Sharpe had picked up rumors from prisoners about a Negro spy ring.

A man called out, "Is the war over, General Meade?"

"Not yet, but we've taken a long step toward Richmond."

CHAPTER XV

Richmond woke to celebrate solemnly the Fourth as a day of sacrifice and patriotism as the citizens anticipated a great victory. The North was noisier, and cities grew festive as telegraphers signaled the news from Gettysburg. In the town itself people put out flags and bunting but found no occasion for fireworks and speeches. Among the soldiers fatigue set in. They lay in the shade taking their ease.

Flossie Muelheim got a holiday surprise:

Late last night a Union soldier brought back our mare. Someone told him she was ours. Papa sent me to the barn to get hay down. At the top of the ladder I stopped and stared at the soles of a filthy pair of boots. A sleeping Rebel lay sprawled out in the loft. As quietly as I could I climbed up, found his gun, and threw it down. There was a crash, but he didn't waken. I hurried back for help.

The Rebel sat up and put his hands over his head when he saw Papa had a gun. He was a young boy from Tennessee named Bates, and was scared as anything. He stank.

We told him he need not fear us if he behaved, and then we brought him in, and Mamma fed him. He leaned over his plate and ate without hardly looking up. He had no expression on his face, as if it were frozen. Mamma said he was probably trying to forget what he'd seen.

She felt sorry for him and took Papa aside, and then left the house. She came back with a sergeant and some armed men from the provost marshal's. They asked Bates what regiment he was from and such things. When the sergeant saw he was truly young to be a soldier, his manner changed a good deal. He told Papa that if we wanted to keep him with us to help with the wounded, Private Bates could sign a paper giving his word he wouldn't escape. So now

175

we have a real Rebel with us, and I think he is glad about it.

The morning was a release from strain and fear. Meade assembled his new housemates, Humphreys, Sharpe, and Fitzpatrick, in the parlor to talk about strategy. He didn't say aloud what he knew was happening. These men would be his Cabinet. The time for trusting senior colleagues and classmates was over.

Sharpe again urged a general interrogation of Rebel officers, saying he was amazed how frank they were after a drink of whiskey. Richmond was uppermost in their minds, but Meade was thinking, too, of Washington City, almost as alien and hostile. "You are a staff colonel now," he said to Fitzpatrick. "Your days of carrying messages are over. Thinking is what I need, and you seem to be good at it." He sat in the platform rocker almost smiling as he moved gently back and forth. "One of the first things we must do is talk with Mr. Josephus."

Fitzpatrick wondered whether more Rebels were camped north of the Potomac, or on the way. Meade nodded, saying it stood to reason some would be near the river, and told Humphreys to order two corps through the pass toward Hagerstown. The four men were bone tired and gladly would have spent the day working in the pleasant house. But Meade was uneasy about taking luxury while others had misery, and decided before noon to ride out with Fitzpatrick to see his wounded son.

As the surgeries emptied, Maeve spent more time watching over George. She needed to think. Miss Morris had invited her to Philadelphia to work with the city's poor. She was more than eager to leave Alice's, but what was she to do about Sigurd?

She had come to Madame Alice looking for her half-sister in the spring after their father, a drunken and bankrupt farmer, died in a small western Maryland town along the railroad. Sigurd, her only relative aside from a brother gone to the war, was a playful girl who hated work as a kitchen drudge and liked going with men to drinking shops near the tracks. Mysteriously she left town, leaving a note saying she had found work with a traveling show.

Maeve had nothing. The farm was gone. Not a stick of furniture, not a sewing basket, nor a thimble remained. Her employer, the parson who preached over her father's grave, tried to catch her in the kitchen and embrace her. The town offered nothing else. She sought Sigurd, and was not surprised at what she found.

From what Maeve knew of life she thought one way or another love was always bartered with men. That's all they seemed to want from women. Her mother's life was no different—bearing a child every year, most stillborn, submitting to a drunken man, harried, haggard, and toothless before she was 30, dead at 35.

Life offered few choices. Maeve knew what the parson would say, but he was a fake. And Sigurd seemed to be happy. Alice, anxious to get Maeve aboard her wagons, boasted of an exclusive trade with the officers. "The work's easy, sort of a party," she said, "and so's the money. We'll call ya 'Maizie.' They'll think that's wicked." Maeve told herself it was temporary. She might save enough to set up a shop of some kind.

Maeve felt no embarrassment in seeing Colonel Fitzpatrick. She expected to meet the men she'd been with, and felt no shame. The experience was rarely a pleasure, as it was with him, but, like the other girls in the wagons, she liked to think of giving joy to men about to die. They served the desperate, who came for love, weak and simpering, who told them stories of their lives and their fears. Up to the moment of climax they would give a girl anything. The work was often a party. Officers bought champagne, and if someone became nasty, Alice and James put them to rights.

Yet Maeve hated being a piece of flesh for any man to punch a hole in. One girl got an awful disease and was sent away. Another got pregnant and had to choose between a baby she didn't want or drinking poison to get rid of it. They talked about these unfortunates as if it would never be them, about the ugly ones and drunken derelicts in the rundown hovels of "Hooker's division," the whorehouse district of Washington City. They thought themselves above these evils, and Maeve tried not to think of them. With good whiskey and wily ways, Alice saw to it they were not discussed. But Maeve expected the dark side to turn up sooner or later. Already, Sigurd could not stop drinking. *God knows what'll happen to her!*

Colonel Fitzpatrick blushed when he saw her. "I've come to see

George again. General Meade is coming soon." He seemed not to want to look at her, but stared nevertheless, hardly looking at her patient. They talked of George, while Fitz sat on a camp chair by the bed, trying, but failing to keep his eyes on his bloody-bandaged head .

"Miss Morris asked me to go to Philadelphia with her," she said, as if the thought had just come to mind.

"That's a wonderful idea. She's just the person you want." He stopped, obviously trying not to speak of her trade, and his cheeks flushed. "I mean, I've known her all my life. You can depend on old Fannie."

His eagerness surprised her. "Yes, but you see," she stood before him, hesitating. "My sister Sigurd was with us, and, I'm afraid, um, she's been sent away." She didn't want to seem coarse, or flirtatious. She wanted help, if he could give it.

"Where has she gone?"

"To Frederick, to a place called Sally's. But she won't be there long if she drinks whiskey like she does. This Sally woman won't keep her anymore than Alice."

"Maybe we can find her," he said rising. "I'm no expert, but I know people who are." He seemed pleased to be able to help. "She'll probably go to a big city like Washington or Baltimore where there are soldiers. Would you like me to try and trace her?"

He blushed. Maeve marveled at the sky blue eyes circled by black eyelashes. She knew better than anyone else how handsome he was compared to other men. *My God! He's a grand hero now. Every girl in the United States of America will run after him.* Without intending to, she sighed, and he stood, ready to comfort her.

Horses came up. They stood still where they were and watched the tent flap come back. General Meade, paying no heed, hurried in to his son. George lay asleep while Maeve told the general how he was. She had barely begun when bustle outside announced the Chief Surgeon, who came in and took her role.

Meade seemed dismayed. There wasn't much to say, and the girl had done very well. *When George wakes up, he thought, he'd a damn sight rather see her than the surgeon. By the looks of Fitzpatrick, she's already captured one of us.* He asked to be alone, and sat by the cot, thinking. The time was sad. Dead men lay everywhere. Everywhere it smelt like a cesspit. Everyone was filthy, except him and his staff, and they all lacked energy. The time was good. The strain was gone. They reveled in victory and knew they would talk about it all of their lives. These were the fruits. Even sitting beside George, nothing overrode the elation. *He'll wake to a world where everyone knows his name.*

Meade had no doubt George would recover. *"I'm damned glad I sealed off the town. The men clamoring to get here I never want to see. The press can tell the others what's happened. The rest, except for the supply men, the relief troops, the railroad people—the rest can stay away. What we don't want is politicians. Thank God Sickles ran off! He'd be spinning webs for his special friends as fast as his little mouth could move.*

Meade dozed off, and awoke wondering if he'd spoken in his sleep. Rising and walking to the flap, he found his men waiting, Fitzpatrick talking to the pretty redhead. *Can't blame him. She's a lot better to look at than the mess around here now.*

Meade asked for Josephus, and the surgeons escorted him to the tent where Hancock and Gibbon lay. He spent a short time happily swapping battle tales with his friends, then left them with eyes agape as he walked back to spend a long time talking to their Negro tentmate.

✬ ✬

Major General Dan Sickles lay in his dirty battle tunic on a stretcher supported by benches in the parlor of a house on F Street east of the White House. The doctor fretted through the entire trip and now, a day after arriving, feared he was approaching crisis. He wouldn't let him be put into a bed. "The movement might reopen the wound. He needs absolute rest and quiet."

A young civilian came in the early evening to say President Lincoln was on his way. The general tried to sit up but was told to lie flat. "The visit will tire you," said the doctor. "I suggest we gently turn him away. He'll understand."

"The Hell you will!" shouted Sickles, and he sat up, lit a cigar, and lay back waiting with it clenched in his teeth, thinking of the coming conversation. "This is why we've made this risky trip, you idiot—to tell Lincoln how it was. Meade's won a victory, but he didn't finish them, not by a long shot!"

The President stepped in softly, and removed his hat. Beads of sweat dripped from the folds of his face drawn back in a pleasant grin. "Well, Dan, you are now a genuine hero. No doubt you played a great role in the greatest of victories, and are to be congratulated." He took a chair put it next to the stretcher.

Sickles struggled to smile. "Tell me the news, Mr. President." His voice was weak. "When I left the 3d two days ago, we'd made a vital penetration on the Rebel right. We gave Meade the opportunity. I wasn't sure he'd take it."

"It appears our attack began on the left somewhere near what they've dubbed 'the Round Tops,'" Lincoln said. "The papers mention the Trostle Farm, where the cavalry made its charge."

Sickles winced from pain, puffed on his cigar, and put it down. He smiled and blew out smoke. "I got this damn wound sitting my horse right in front of that farmhouse, sir. It was my headquarters." The words gave him pleasure. "They must have followed up the salient I built for them."

"No doubt," said the President leaning toward the patient. "Of course this victory is very welcome."

Conversation paused, as the President appraised the patient. "What do you think General Meade has in mind now?" He sat back looking away, as if asking someone else. "He seems to have captured Lee and all his generals."

He doesn't know the son of a bitch like I do, Sickles thought. *The Rebs aren't beaten yet*. He measured his words. "I suppose he'll move a slow pace toward Richmond, Mr. President. I have no sense of George Meade as a strategist. He's new to the business. Like his friend McClellan, he'll want to go back to the Peninsula." He coughed and reached for the whiskey.

"Not that again!" said Lincoln with a flash of anger.

Sickles hesitated, thinking Lincoln referred to the liquor, but, realizing he had McClellan in mind, went ahead and poured a drink.

"We've got to move quickly," Lincoln spoke as much to himself as Sickles. "I hope he's ready. We've got to scotch the snake while it's out from under the rock."

Sickles smiled. *He's got doubts. That's good enough for today*. "Well, Mr.

President," he said, "I'm very honored you came. How are things at Vicksburg?"

Lincoln smiled. "We pray for a double blessing. It's close." The doctor came in and nodded. The President rose.

In the cities of the East, and in the West as far as St. Louis, vendors sold newspapers as fast as they came. "Great Victory over Lee's Army," wrote the *New York World*. "Meade's Triumph a Second Waterloo," declared the *Philadelphia Bulletin*. "The Confederacy Finished," proclaimed the *Chicago Tribune*. People poured into the streets to celebrate as they had in Washington. The entire Union shared a glorious Fourth.

Individually, then in small groups in state capitals and in Washington City, elected leaders clucked over the victory—relieved that the Army of Northern Virginia was done for, pleased the ravages of war would soon pass, yet stunned by the suddenness of it and, most of all, perplexed and wondering about the man who won it. The wiser politicians noted how swiftly Meade's meeting with the press spread the news of his victory over the country.

It was another brilliant surprise. "I wonder if we know him?" asked Stanton, standing before Lincoln's desk. "Does he have some notion of politics we haven't heard about?"

The President sat weary and perspiring after walking back from visiting Sickles. The White House routine was nearly back to normal. Crowds of well-wishers begged an audience. Mary urged him to come upstairs and lie down. They could all be put off. The President needed time. "I was mightily relieved to hear these reports," he said leaning back. "And I still have trouble believing them." He yawned and stretched, looking forward to a night's sleep.

"The hardest thing in this world, Stanton, is to know your man. I had doubts about Meade. 'Schoolmaster' seemed pretty well right. Add 'haughty,' perhaps, though sometimes he seemed downright humble. 'Aristocratic,' I'm not sure about that. He doesn't appear to have much money. But then I don't know much about Eastern society. Mary would know." He ran his hand over his beard.

"I suppose he might even be dangerous?" said Stanton.

"Well, Dan Sickles don't care much for him." Lincoln fixed his eyes on Stanton. "I suppose we ought not make much of that. It's his ambition we need to gauge. Willy-nilly, he has power in his hands. The nation lies at his feet. If he's going to be our dictator, as some generals of our acquaintance once had in mind. . . ."

Stanton smirked.

"If he has power in mind, he couldn't have done better than hold that parlay with the newspapers. 'To give credit where it's due,'" Lincoln snorted. "That's well-chosen—modest, professional, and in the bargain he could be sure his name and fame went far and wide, overtaking everything else.

"As it stands, he could be elected President, I suppose, if he wants." Lincoln scowled. "Or, is he just an honest soldier? I'd like to meet one."

An aide came in to announce, "Six members of the Committee on the Conduct of the War demand to see the President." Stanton grimaced.

Lincoln swept his right arm wide in gestured grace. "Let them cool their heels, while the Secretary and I talk military strategy, John. And then we'll entertain them."

He overcame languor. "We need to see Meade again at first hand. Do you please arrange a train to take us up there tomorrow. No, in two days' time. First, send your Scotsman Hardie up to warn him we're coming. I shall declare a day of national celebration for the time. If in the meantime Grant takes Vicksburg, so much the better. It will be a distraction.

"We must keep this trip quiet, Stanton. We'll leave before dawn, before anyone knows what we're about. Every one of those sons of liberty out there will demand a seat in the car if he finds out where we're going."

★ ★

In the evening, Henry Prediger, sensing the disdain of Hancock and Gibbon for sharing their tent with a black man, arranged to move Josephus to the Muelheim House. Fitzpatrick supported the idea as removing him from questioning eyes of men too eager to know his secrets. Fitz's appearance at the Muelheims along with Henry as a war hero was enough to win their cooperation.

Josephus lay off the parlor in a small room. He was wide awake, not in pain, and pleased at the fuss. General Meade came again with the two colonels and was courtly. They seemed delighted to hear about his work. Josephus told him how, escaping from Lexington, where his master taught at the Military Institute, he managed to take away books about strategy by the Comte de Jomini and a German named Clausewitz. He struggled to learn enough German, but all he'd learned were the names of nine "Principles of War."

"That's more than most of us know," laughed Meade, slapping his knee. "You could be a general with that much knowledge. I don't know German myself. Few do, except Schurz and Von Steinwehr.

"So you decided how the battle would go before the rest of us did? Amazing! Your map was a godsend, and you deserve the thanks of the nation. Sharpe and Fitzpatrick and I will come again when your health is better."

Meade was surprised, when Josephus spoke of Richmond. The spy ring was broader than he thought. Josephus said merely, "We have people there who can help."

Meade needed to decide where the whole army, indeed the whole country, must go. Negroes were going to come into the war before it was over. Of that he was sure. He must find a way to give Prediger and Josephus status—perhaps as civilian advisers, possibly as junior officers. He would talk to Fitzpatrick.

As they left the house, an aged black man approached from the street and, seeing Meade, stood respectfully at the gate bowing like a butler. Junius, having found General Lee and brought him clean linen and a change of uniform, had come to see his friend Josephus.

By July 6, life in Gettysburg had moved slowly back to normal. Engineers repaired the trestle over Rock Creek, and rail cars carried away wounded and prisoners. Guards marched gangs of Rebels off to quickly prepared camps beyond the Susquehanna. The pressure of huge armies soaking up the wealth of the country eased. Trains streamed in with supplies, including hundreds of barrels of clean water.

The odor did not improve, but it didn't keep meadowlarks from singing over dead men left in the fields, or warblers and mockingbirds high in the chestnut trees from adding sounds of life. Soldiers pitched tents for their bivouacs, and most wounded were lifted onto makeshift beds off the ground. A visitor saw burnt-out houses, mass graves, and horses dead on the ground. What he didn't see he smelled.

In mid-afternoon a two-car train puffed into the station. General Meade came. A crowd formed to greet the "special," and gave Lincoln a lusty cheer when he stepped out.

Meade extended his hand. Both men smiled broadly. Meade showing the way like a courtier, they set off, riding side by side to the square, where Lincoln was to stay at the home of a local lawyer. Meade bade him rest and offered to call later in the afternoon.

"I'm not tired, general." Lincoln frowned at his mount, a short pony that forced him to push his feet well forward to keep them off the ground. "I would be very glad of the chance to speak with you. Is there a quiet room somewhere?"

Meade told orderlies to take the baggage and turned Lincoln and Stanton back up the Carlisle Road. The crowd tried to follow, but guards around the house held them at bay. In the parlor Meade offered Lincoln the platform rocker. Lincoln chose a straight Shaker chair and sat on it back forward. Stanton perched in the rocker, while Meade in clean boots paced on the oval rug in the center of the room. Fitzpatrick stood by maps on the wall.

Meade thanked Lincoln for coming and added a hope that this meeting would let him keep away from Washington. There was work to be done.

"That is commendable, general," said Lincoln with a narrow smile. "You must press on with the war. I support you. You have earned the nation's confidence; that's the least of it." His smile grew, and he turned toward Stanton, who nodded.

Meade pointed to the maps and began to describe, with Fitz pointing out positions, the three-day fight. He talked for some time, carefully mentioning the names of commanders, sparing criticism, giving praise where he could. "We were obliged to take the defensive after the first day. That was," he hesitated, "I can now say, a disaster. We lost Reynolds and half of two corps. If Lee had been ready, he might have destroyed us. As it was, Hancock and Howard

184

managed to put things aright."

"And General Sickles, where was he when things started?" asked Lincoln.

"His troops were not in position to engage." Meade avoided criticizing Sickles, the last man he wanted to talk about. *Why was he so influential?*

Lincoln moved on. "The loss of Reynolds was a severe blow." He bowed his head as if to think of a new topic. "What we all need to resolve here is what we do now. Your victory is most welcome and, I have to admit, a surprise."

Meade stopped pacing and faced him. "Every battle depends in some way on fortune, Mr. President. Take Colonel Fitzpatrick here, I sent him on a reconnaissance. He did the job, and brought back Longstreet. You can't imagine what that did to boost our spirits."

Lincoln turned. "A lot has happened since we met in the War Office, colonel. You were a major. How long ago?"

"Nine days," Stanton intervened, smiling at Hardie's former assistant. "He doesn't look any the worse."

Fitzpatrick blushed. "I've hardly been on the front line, Mr. President."

"Our colonel is modest, Mr. President." Meade was almost grinning. "He's been in the thick of it, I assure you. He attracts good fortune, and seems to know how to use it. I've come to depend upon him."

"You deserve high praise, colonel," said Lincoln, turning back toward Meade. "Now, how do we hold on to this luck long enough to end this war?"

"We have some thoughts," said Meade. He outlined a plan to assault Richmond with forces converging from several directions. "We'll need reinforcements, of course, at least one additional corps, and a large supply of breech-loading rifles. If we can get back to the Rappahannock in a month's time, we ought to be able to cross easily and move south.

"The Rebels may rally fifty thousand men or more, but their army will be hurriedly made up under a new commander. A good number will be militia, I'd guess. We need to have overwhelming numbers, and equipment to deal with entrenchment. I want breech-loaders because they allow men to fire faster and, more important, to load without exposing themselves. The enemy will have to dig in, if they choose to defend Richmond at all."

"Stanton will find you guns, I'm sure. The harder part is finding men. Thanks to you, I can cool New York City by suspending the draft. I'm hoping you'll help us raise volunteers. With this victory, and if Grant takes Vicksburg, we ought to be able to get men to join up in order to bring an end to it."

Meade looked at his protégé. "Fitzpatrick has urged me to speak to the Pennsylvania legislature to call for volunteers. The state has been aroused by the invasion, he thinks."

Lincoln paused. "I'm sure Governor Curtin would be happy to receive you, general. The idea might do." He appraised Fitzpatrick. "Colonel, why do you think this will succeed?"

Fitz took a step forward and cleared his throat. "At this moment everyone wants to hear from General Meade, Mr. President. The state is grateful. The tide is running in our favor. This creates a very different outlook. Men will come forward. We saw it in battle. When men saw we could finish the Rebels, they came forth with a will, even stragglers."

Meade continued. "This was an army that might have, indeed probably would have, run away, if Lee's final charge had succeeded. It was on an edge between regaining self-respect and giving up. Our defense on the second day began to turn the tide. When Lee failed, it all changed. The more we won, the more we stood to win."

"It's a fair analogy," said Lincoln, pulling on his beard and looking at Fitzpatrick. "As in war, so with other things. The more you win, the more you're going to win. You have given me much to think about, general." He stood to leave. "Would you be willing to appear in other places, like Albany or Columbus?"

"If that's what we must do to build up the army, of course. Just don't ask me to speak to the Congress."

Lincoln grinned and moved toward the door. "No need to worry about that. I shouldn't say it out loud, but I don't like speaking to those folks either. No man in his right mind should." He winked at Stanton as they stepped out.

★ ★

Returning to the square they met a large crowd gathered around a hay wagon halted on the far side and bearing a half-dozen Negroes. Prediger was arguing with the driver, a soldier bewildered by the attention and by Henry's anger.

Fitzpatrick rode over.

"They've brought back our people, colonel. That's my Sally in front," said Prediger. "This soldier here says he can't let 'em down because he don't have any orders."

Fitzpatrick looked from the soldier to the people in the wagon and back at Prediger. "How have they come back?"

"The Rebels took all of us they could find as prisoners," a man said. "They didn't care if we was freed people or what you call 'contraband.' They just took us as runaways. The soldiers must have caught up with this wagon going South, and didn't know what to do. They don't know anything about black folk."

"What regiment are you from, soldier?" asked Fitz.

"The 134th New York, Coster's brigade," said the man. "Eleventh Corps. We run onto these darkies, a whole bunch, maybe fifty or more, south of Hagerstown. They was all locked in a chain, two by two, like the animals going into Noah's Ark. General Howard gave orders to haul 'em here."

"Well, you've carried out your order, private. You can release them now. I'm Colonel Fitzpatrick, aide to General Meade. You can take my order." Fitzpatrick smiled to reassure the man, but was puzzled by his stubbornness.

"Okay, colonel, you'll have to answer to my commander if I've made a mistake." He nodded to his human cargo, and they scrambled out as fast as they could. Sally ran to Prediger, who lifted her off her feet, while Fitz directed the soldier to the quartermaster's office.

The crowd of spectators turned toward Lincoln and Meade across the square. "Isn't that the damnedest thing, Mr. Lincoln," shouted a man. "Here we're fighting to free the darkies, and our own men don't know it."

Lincoln smiled and dismounted. "Takes time," he shouted. "I'm sure we'll all come to understand, sooner or later." He bid Meade goodbye and walked quickly into the house before people could surge around him.

Meade sat astride his best horse, watching the performance. Fitzpatrick had done the right thing. But why had Lincoln run off?

One of the Negroes repeated. "Where's Massa Lincoln? Where's Massa Lincoln?"

Fitzpatrick crossed to Meade. "I never thought I'd see anything like this. Why wouldn't the soldier let them loose, general?"

Meade chuckled. "Not everyone has your self-confidence, colonel."

News of disaster came slowly toward Richmond. Late on July 4 an exhausted rider from Stuart's cavalry struggled across the Potomac to reach Martinsburg with a sketchy account. He was not an official courier, but the major in charge decided to send a semaphore message to Winchester, where a day later stragglers appeared in small groups. They came from so many line regiments, the garrison commander began to believe the report from Martinsburg. He telegraphed Richmond.

For two days no news had reached the capital from the army. Silence was ominous. A newspaper out of Baltimore arrived at the War Department about the same time as the telegram from Winchester. A more lengthy telegram came to the offices of the *Richmond Dispatch* from an unknown operator in the North. The style of the writer appeared authentic. Possibly, the editor thought, a Yankee hoax was underway. He could hardly accept the story, and consulted James Seddon, Secretary of War.

Seddon read the telegram carefully. "You should go ahead and publish this," he said. "Sadly, it just may be true. We need to notify the public."

The citizens of Richmond disbelieved the reports. A few days earlier they'd expected a great victory. The end of the war was not too much to hope for. Now they heard "disaster." Slowly shock set in, as officials in the War Department gave out what they had. The story might be true.

By morning came panic. Men of means hurried to Wilmington, North Carolina to bid for passage on blockade runners. Others took families to plantations in the Carolinas and farther away. Everyone buried valuables. Well-bred women consoled each other. Some were in hysterics. No casualty lists came. They were sure they would. The best they could hope was that their men were somewhere in a Yankee prison.

The news filtered quickly among the Negroes. A few trembled, fearing retribution from their masters. In the slave market, lines of men and women chained in coffles sang hymns and prayed. Owners fought for space on outbound trains, seeking to ship their assets to the cotton fields. Among household servants a feeling of joy was hard to suppress, and some waited expectantly for orders.

Jefferson Davis and his Cabinet went into continuous session, looking for soldiers and men to lead them. Davis, remembering the fight on the Peninsula, insisted Richmond be defended. He knew what Virginia meant to the Confederacy, not to ignore the Tredegar Iron Works and the web of manufacturing which supplied the army. Last year Lee had saved them, and now "Lee's Folly" had brought them to the verge of extinction.

Rivalries began to tear the government apart. Davis's enemies insisted on Beauregard, his *bête noire*, taking command. But the President, a Military Academy graduate, had no faith in his fellow South Carolinian. The alternative was Joe Johnston, no favorite either. The President's enemies in the Congress were determined to bring him down, even though they knew without him defeat was certain. To the staunchest minister, the case seemed hopeless.

CHAPTER XVI

In mid-July the last regiments marched out of Gettysburg for the Rappahannock. Meade ordered them to camp south of the river, train to attack entrenchments, and await reinforcements. He persuaded Stanton to overrule the politicians and allow volunteers to join old regiments, as the Rebels did. Recruits would learn faster working with veterans and, as Fitzpatrick suggested, men would join up for the sake of ending the war in a famous regiment.

Meade toured capitals from Columbus to Albany to raise troops and was obliged to learn how to be a hero. Bands greeted his special train and serenaded him in his quarters. A cavalry escort went with him, another Fitzpatrick idea, to make a show and encourage patriotism. Meade would have liked a smaller retinue.

Correspondence with Margaretta resumed. She was by nature a promoter and gladly would be his manager if he entered politics, if she were not a woman. She kept him posted as a good correspondent and former congressman's daughter had learned long ago. George recovered consciousness after a week-long coma, and was sent to Philadelphia to recuperate. The wound was ugly, but surgeons said it would heal.

Though saddened by his wound, Margaretta thought of his scars as a badge of honor. She delighted in Fitzpatrick, who came with him. James Edward was from a good family, and would have her husband's interest at heart. More important, he seemed to have the political intelligence her husband lacked. She began to share news and gossip with the Fitzpatricks, whose house was a block away.

Fitz took off a few days in Philadelphia, where he met a hero's welcome, surfeited with invitations, wined, dined, and became the most desired objective of young women and their mothers. His own mother saw that he held aloof, and put it down to embarrassment over his broken engagement. It might have been easier if he hadn't come back so soon. She also saw how his achievements tamped down gossip, and that the handsome fiancée had found quick consolation in a wealthy older man.

Fannie could see Fitz was serious about Maeve, nor did she think it wrong. Women, in her opinion, were straitened enough by the gear they wore and by social convention and the churches. Where real affection appeared, she blessed it, and had no lower opinion of her than that of the newsmen who called her an angel.

She took care to cover Maeve's tracks. No one knew, and few asked, where the "Angel of Gettysburg" had gone. Newspaper men left Gettysburg ahead of the army to chase other stories. Most went back to Washington City, and others, including the Philadelphians, followed Meade. Maeve had told them she was from western Virginia. They would not expect to see her in Philadelphia. Fannie presented her prim protégé in bun and smock without lace. Few reporters would recognize the orphan with few prospects who shared Fannie's passion for philanthropy.

Fannie deduced that Fitz had known Maeve longer than she, but did not dwell on it. To think they had coupled almost pleased her. She guessed they were in love, a thing she prized though few would know it. She was not surprised when he called with flowers in hand. Nor was she averse to giving them time alone.

Large Hepplewhite furniture an ancestor took from a bankrupt tobacco planter crowded her parlor along with odd knickknacks and scrimshaw from the South Seas. Maeve stood in the center of the room, plainer now, hennaed highlights fading from her hair. It flamed less, drawn behind her head, but it had not lost its luster, and gave her a penitent look. Her eyes with their natural lashes flashed excitement. She kept talking. "I'm surprised to see you. We've only been here a few days. It's all new to me. Running water in the house. These objects . . ." she held out her fingers as she walked in the room. "I don't know what they are." She stopped and turned to face him. "Oh, but Miss Morris is very kind. I wouldn't want anyone to think I'm unhappy."

"Maizie, Maeve." He used two names because the old one excited him, and he could not suppress the same stirrings he felt riding past her wagon by the creek, a lifetime ago. He must have loved her forever. People told him there was no past anymore, only future. *The battle changed the world. Why wouldn't that be true for her?* "I've come." He could see his uneasiness stimulated hers, and went on slowly. "I just came to say Colonel Sharpe got word from the provost in Washington. A woman like Sigurd, or who looks like her, is working in a house in 'Hooker's division.' I'll go there as soon as I can."

"God bless you, colonel," she put out a hand. He took it and without thinking pulled her to him. She made no resistance. He held her to his chest and put his mouth on hers, as she once showed him.

"God knows how I love you. I want you in every way a man can. I love you, Maizie, I mean Maeve."

She pulled her head back and kissed him on the cheek, then touched his nose with hers. "If it's Maizie you want you can always have her. She wants you just as much, I fear. And so does Maeve."

They kissed again, and stared at each other, close, almost panting. Fannie knocked, and opened to find them quickly parting, blushing and embarrassed. "I'll come back." She closed the door with a soft giggle.

"I mustn't compromise you," said Fitzpatrick. "I'll explain to Miss Morris that I'm deadly serious. You must understand my love is real and for as long as I live. I will come back when you've had time to settle, and I will find Sigurd and send her to you."

"Colonel," she said out of breath. "Thank you. I would be very grateful. I do not fear Miss Morris, or anyone I've met. She knows I'm not here to ruin the city." She smiled sardonically. "I've got to learn about proper women, I suppose." She used "proper" as if it meant something alien. "But where you're concerned I can't pretend."

Her smile, sweet and knowing, did nothing to calm him, and he wondered for an instant if he wasn't in evil hands after all. He moved his head from side to side trying to put thoughts ahead of emotions. "I don't really care about anything else, except to see you again and again, however long that shall be. Know that, and have faith in me, please." His eyes were pleading as he stepped back.

They waited without speaking for Fannie to return.

Thermometers showed 100° in the capital when a heavy-set, middle-aged major general stomped up the iron stairs of the house on F Street. Dan Sickles's friend Joe Hooker had come to talk politics.

"They do every damn thing George Meade says," he growled as soon as he came in the sick room. Hooker struck his dusty hat back and forth across his foreleg and took a straight wooden chair across from Sickles's bed. "The army's gone right across the Rappahannock as if there wasn't another Reb soldier standing. Damned if I know who's in charge down there. Meade's off making speeches."

Sickles, sitting up like a monarch at a morning levee, had regained color in his face. He motioned to the cigar box on the bed, which Hooker refused. Sickles was careful to defer to his old chief. "Meade's had one good piece of luck, general, but he's no different from the rest. That press conference was smart. I don't think he thought of it himself."

Hooker continued his grouse. "He's got dumb old George Sykes in charge down on the river. God! Even Pierre Gustave Toutant Beauregard could cut a swath through him. What in hell are they thinking of?

"Why don't they send you down there?" asked Sickles. "They could do a lot worse."

"I'm sure old George won't have me. I'm going out to Sam Grant. Bill Sherman's coming back. Sam's not happy about losing his roommate, but he and I'll get along. Meade's determined to purge the army of my people. He's chucked Butterfield, ya know. Somebody said he was going to court-martial him, but I guess victory softened the old bastard. Butterfield's going west, too."

Sickles waited for Hooker to extrude his venom. "The President's not happy about Meade's delays, and wonders whether he isn't another Little Mac. The Rebs will be digging like madmen around Richmond, and Lincoln knows it.

"And Meade makes odd remarks about the darkies, as if they're the hope of the army. Lincoln doesn't know but he's a newfound Abolitionist. He thought he was a lace-curtain Democrat, like his father-in-law. He probes me about Meade's politics, you know."

"I've always said we could use the Negroes, but I ain't going to lead the charge for them," said Hooker. "Meade's a fool if he gets into that hornet's nest."

"Let me tell you, general," Sickles leaned forward in confidence, "Meade planned a retreat all along, until he found he could attack from the salient I set up for him. Butterfield's sent me a full copy of a plan to run all the way back to Pipe Creek, a long way south of Gettysburg. I think the press has got wind of it."

Hooker grinned. "Well, Dan, I can't think of anyone better to know about that than you." He laughed and reached for the whiskey decanter.

Henry Prediger left Sally with the Muelheim family and went south to the army wearing an officer's uniform without insignia. He was now a recognized member of headquarters staff.

Rumors from Richmond poured into camp. Neither Prediger nor Sharpe had any way to sort them out. In late July in secluded offices, three tents in a swale south of the river, Sharpe received a visit from a lady refugee. She came with a heavy-set Negro woman and asked to see "Mr. Prediger."

When Prediger came in, the black woman rose from a bench in the back of the tent and greeted him in Yoruba. He smiled and responded in kind. The woman handed him pages of closely written text. Henry nodded to her, and she sat quietly.

The white woman was thin, with large deep eyes and a prominent nose. She sat forward in front of Colonel Sharpe's table. Henry thought her ugly compared to Negro women. "Matilda will stay on with you, Mr. Prediger. She knows by name and face all the people in our group. I advise you to regard her alone as your guide as to whom to trust." She spoke in the fluid voice of the Tidewater, but her expression was firm. Henry thought she'd be a tough mistress. He'd had experience with the type. She offered Prediger no name, yet was completely at ease.

The woman turned to Sharpe with the same cold look, though Henry sensed he knew something about her. "The Confederate leaders are in such disarray, colonel. We drove through Ashland without a question. They won't hardly miss us."

Henry thought she was the calmest woman he'd ever seen and smiled at Matilda, who grinned, exposing broken teeth. Though he now worked on almost equal footing with Colonel Sharpe, he felt it best to let the white folks do the talking.

"They are frantically digging trenches," said the lady, a spinster, Henry guessed, probably over 40 years, the way rich white folks live on. Her skin was tight around her chin, and she wore a fine lace collar at her throat without showing the least concern for the heat—a very proper woman. *From a slave-holding family, no doubt. Why would anyone like that help the North? . . . That's not bad.*

Sharpe asked questions about the defenses of Richmond. The lady answered with precision worthy of Josephus, and added, "General Johnston and President Davis have decided to bury the hatchet. Davis stays in office because there's no one else."

"Will they defend Richmond, Miss Van Lew?" Finally Sharpe used her name.

"I think so," she said. "We're not that close to the general. But we know," she nodded at Matilda, "President Davis is determined to stay, as he did when General McClellan came. General Johnston would prefer to retreat, but Mr. Davis believes Richmond is vital to the cause. That is probably guessing from what happened last year. Yet I have seen regiments coming in from the Carolinas and Georgia. Other states, we hear, are hesitant."

Sharpe seemed fascinated. "Are you going back to Richmond?"

"Yes. As soon as possible. My Union sympathies are known, but I'm not unusual. There are a number of us. As you must realize, colonel, Virginians do not expect women to do this work. I can explain my absence.

"My task is not yet done, and I worry about the prisoners, about what happens when you approach. I hope you'll try no foolish rescues. The guards at Libby Prison, and especially at Belle Isle, can be cruel."

"I shall report your opinion with my full support," said Sharpe smiling. "But how will you explain your absence?"

"We have been away for only one day. Lots of people are foraging. I will say Matilda bolted. She will stay to assist Mr. Prediger. If you will be kind enough to give me a few bottles of whiskey, I think

I can explain my little journey very well, colonel."

Prediger was amazed. She asked for nothing and revealed little, but Sharpe knew who she was.

The colonel asked, "Does your message ring true, Mr. Prediger?"

"It does, colonel. This lady has brought what Mr. Josephus told me to look for."

"There are at least two groups of us in Richmond, colonel," said the lady. "A white group with whom I work. We will reach you through the Negro network of Matilda and Mr. Prediger. They are very good, if I may judge such things, and they have people close to high councils of the Confederacy." She smiled finally, as if in triumph. "You will receive a steady flow.

"Oh, yes, let me add, I know very little about fortification, but I urge General Meade to move quickly. You can virtually walk into Richmond right now. But if you tarry, they will dig trenches deep and build parapets sky high. General Johnston is an engineer, you know."

"Thank you, Madam," said Sharpe, "I will tell him."

"Miss," she said, "and now, colonel, I must return."

She did not shake hands with Prediger but waved good-bye. He marveled at the meeting, like another herald of the great day coming.

★ ☆

The President fretted. Meade's tour was triumphal. Men were joining up. But, he was disturbed by the general's statements to the press.

"At least, he stood up for Grant," said Stanton.

The President had come again to check the wires and escape crowds at the White House. "Yes, we don't need any rivalry there, do we? I'll admit I wish Grant had bagged that army at Vicksburg, but he was right. It's worth their parole to take over the Mississippi. Meade was good enough to back him up. You wouldn't have heard that out of many others." Lincoln sighed, put down the dispatches and sat, leaning back in a straight chair with his boots on an embroidered ottoman. "I just wish he'd leave the Negro question alone. I've got scores of politicians telling me what to do with them, and I don't need lightning bolts from the reigning God of War."

Stanton stared at the ottoman, wishing the Lincoln would keep his feet off it. "To do him justice, Mr. President, he merely said he'd welcome Negro troops in the army. That's a fairly general sentiment."

"True," said Lincoln wiping his forehead with a soiled handkerchief. "But I don't particularly like him talking about our soldiers demanding an end to slavery. That's certainly not McClellan's view. Not that I agree with him. When popular generals talk about slavery, it hems us in. If Meade, who's the darling of the moment, wants an end to it, so does the public. Then he loses a battle, and they go the other way. We've seen too many come and go. We can't be consistent." Lincoln pulled his hand over his nose. Sweat beads appeared on his brow and he wiped it.

Lincoln was testy, probably not feeling well. Stanton thought better than to argue. "Looking on the bright side, Mr. President, he may only have one more battle to win. If he takes Richmond?"

"Yes, I know, Stanton. If he takes Richmond! Why is it when we hear the army is about to take Richmond, we halt. When does Meade get back to the Rappahannock?"

"He left Philadelphia yesterday, and should be in Fredericksburg at any hour. It's been a little over four weeks since Gettysburg. The army's got two thousand breech-loaders. We sent down a full new corps, and new men stream into the old regiments. They should be rested."

Lincoln seemed unconvinced. "We ought to have brought him here to talk about strategy. He can do little until Sherman moves inland from Norfolk.

"Good luck to him," said Lincoln staring at a large map of the Confederacy on the wall. "The only other place we face a big Rebel army is south of Chattanooga. Will General Rosecrans ever push ahead? He's another one with the slows." Lincoln crossed his legs putting the other foot on the settee.

Stanton watched him, concealing distaste. "I've sent a man down to urge him on. Rosecrans doesn't move fast, I'll admit, but he keeps a large Rebel force in front of him. That's what we need, Mr. President, to keep them occupied so they can't concentrate in Richmond."

"What would you think of putting Grant in charge in Tennessee?" The President looked at his feet as if his boots needed work.

Stanton knew Lincoln was testing him. "It would be a good move, of course, but Rosecrans is a victor, for all his faults, and if we removed him, some would charge it was because he's a Catholic. McClellan and the Democrats would have a fine time with it."

Lincoln let out a long sigh and slapped his large hands on his thighs. "The politics of war, Stanton, a fine art we had forgotten for a dozen years, since Mexico. You don't supersede a victor—unless you want to make him President."

"I doubt the country would make a Catholic convert their leader. Not against you at any rate."

"No," said Lincoln holding his hands together and staring at his fingers. "They wouldn't elect Rosecrans. But McClellan, or maybe John Fremont, might make a martyr of him. It would be very effective in the cities."

Stanton held his face blank. Meade's victory, however decisive, had greatly changed politics. Victory took pressure off the President and might assure his re-election, which Stanton strongly favored. But a quick end of the war meant a host of new problems and, with Meade, possibly new threats. The people were longing for great heroes. Lincoln had to be careful.

☆ ☆

Colonel Fitzpatrick wished he wasn't in uniform, and wondered whether bringing two soldiers along was a good idea. Major Lafayette Baker, an associate of Sharpe's at the provost's office, had insisted. At least he didn't look like a customer. Or did he? He felt like a hypocrite.

Hooker's division was a triangle of a crowded streets east of the White House down from Willard's Hotel. Before the war, government clerks and pensioners lived in the small houses. But when soldiers came willing to pay for pleasure, the madames moved in. They wanted a central location to show their wares. Some establishments became grand, and included several houses with huts trailing along the alleys behind, where the girls and servants slept, and the stores of liquor, drugs, towels, and barrels of water were kept. The streets were muddy, augmented by slops, and ran in the rain like open sewers. The business required a constant supply and discharge of fluids.

Nellie's was not grand. A broken screen covered the front door, where a fair-skinned Negro no more than 15 or 16 years old stood soliciting customers. She winked and grinned, but her face clouded when she saw Fitzpatrick and his escort.

"I want to speak to the proprietress," he said. "May we come in?"

The girl recovered and pushed open the screen, displaying as she did small, well-formed breasts. "Come in, gen'lmen." One or two teeth were missing.

A middle-aged woman approached in a pink silk robe with an abundant bosom hanging over a tight sash, her bulk filling the narrow hallway. She spoke with a voice sounding slaked with spirits, and exuded a sense of sin, making his throat tight. Girls in loose robes looked down through the narrow space between stairs, twittering like birds thrown feed.

"You have a young lady here by the name of Sigurd," he said. "I would like to speak to her."

"Of course, colonel, we are always ready to accommodate a gentleman." She was self-assured. "Would you be needing a room, or shall she come away with you?"

"The latter," he said, unsure whether it was wiser simply to buy Sigurd's time or force matters. Baker told him he need merely insist, yet he hesitated. *Will Sigurd come willingly? Can she? Will she be drunk? Those girls, their giggling . . . damned distracting!*

The madame called up, "Sigurd, get dressed, dearie, you're goin' out with a colonel!" She offered refreshment, meaning whiskey, which Fitz too swiftly refused. They eyed each other warily in the hall until he realized he would have to wait in the parlor as she suggested. Minutes stretched on and seemed like hours.

The madame smiled, hitched her bosom, revealing a good part of it, and leered at him. "I hope you officers have a good time. Sigurd's a good girl. How do you know about her?"

"A woman in Frederick named Alice had her, I believe." Fitz answered with a broader smile than he wished. There was something tempting about a brothel. It assaulted his sense of honor.

The giggling continued. Footsteps struck the stair carpet along with a rustle of skirts. "Ah, here she comes," said the madame as though producing a debutante. Sigurd in a tight blue velvet dress edged in black lace with a plunging bodice stepped sprightly into the room and hiccupped.

She's been drinking. I should have expected it.

She moved her hips. "Hello, colonel. Delighted to make your acquaintance." She held out her hand but stumbled slightly and withdrew it.

Lord help me, there is a family resemblance. She's drunk, and wanton. . . . if we were alone, I'd probably take her. He scolded himself. Heavier than Maeve, not so fine. Mountain accent is stronger. He stood. "We shall be on our way."

The madame coughed, "The money, colonel."

Fitz held out five dollars.

"Ten."

He handed over the bills, and took Sigurd by the arm. She followed him down the iron steps with a look of idiotic delight. The soldiers kept silent. They were obviously amused. He wondered what gossip this would spark. "Mrs. Dawson's boarding house on G Street," he ordered. *They'll see what it's about, or will they?*

Sigurd's response to his plan was disappointed surprise. "Oh, colonel, aren't we going to fuck?"

When he shook his head like a father with a naughty child, she seemed resolved. She would stay at Mrs. Dawson's while he arranged transportation. "I'll send a telegram to Maeve. She lives with Miss Morris now in Philadelphia."

Sigurd showed little emotion, merely saying she would be glad to see her sister again, and complained of a headache. "Last night's booze," she offered a rueful smile. "I don't suppose you'd buy me a drink, colonel."

He couldn't suppress a scowl. "Liquor? Whiskey at this hour! It's ten in the morning." He saw the soldiers on the box grinning.

"It's the only way, colonel." She spoke as if everyone knew. "The only way to beat the pain from this rotgut is more of the same."

Fitz stopped for headache powders, wondering what he was doing and why. *Still the girl needs saving, and she's Maeve's sister. A handful I imagine. I wonder how long she'll last with Fannie?*

Meade got back to the army in early August, and was pleased with the drills of the Pennsylvania Reserves using their breech-loaders.

Custer's new cavalry division, formed in less than a month, showed well in review. Sharpe's intelligence reports were helpful but ominous. The Rebels were recovering. Each day's delay meant lost lives, if not a long, weary siege. But matters were too complex to hurry them. He needed overwhelming force, and had to do it right, remembering what disaster would do to Union resolve.

Lincoln wanted the war over, and sent message after message telling him so. In Columbus, Meade went into a towering rage at being "treated like a subaltern." He wanted someone sympathetic to complain to, but Fitzpatrick wasn't there. He was glad to see him when he got back in camp, and listened eagerly to Fitz's account of Philadelphia, adding comments on his own stay. He liked talking about his home and family and sharing reminiscences in the mess with Fitz and other officers of his staff like Biddle and Lyman who shared his outlook. He told Humphreys to pass all messages from Washington to Fitzpatrick, who would be his buffer.

"I can't command with all this annoyance," he said to Fitz over after-supper coffee. "The more people involved the harder it becomes." He felt happier talking about the war. "Sharpe says Johnston's got forty thousand men, more than half veterans. They'll have ten or fifteen thousand more by the time we're ready even if we leave tomorrow. Sherman can't move any faster. He's reached Suffolk, but he's got to rebuild the railroad south of the James behind him as he goes. We won't take Richmond until he cuts the lines coming up from the south. Once he does, we've got them. But he can't go faster than a few miles a day. Remember that, and tell Halleck we're on schedule."

Meade scratched his beard and lowered his voice. "You know I rather like President Lincoln in spite of his crude ways, but he's a rank amateur when it comes to fighting. I think he looks at a map . . ." Meade tried imitating the nasal voice, . . . 'Well now, we can just go from here to there.' I'm dead certain those idiots on the Committee tell him we can just walk into Richmond." He sighed. "Would that he were right, but I'm not going to shed blood to prove them wrong."

CHAPTER XVII

The Union Army moved in late August after a brief fight on the North Ana that the Northern press hailed as a battle, and Meade dismissed as a skirmish.

Newspaper men pestered him—about conditions in camp, even though they were better than ever before; about his isolation in spite of Meyer's efforts to bring them together. "Why didn't he march straight for Richmond from Gettysburg?" It became a whine. Meyer soothed them, and kept them away except on carefully organized occasions. What seemed to Meade an impromptu chat was always well planned with chosen men. But for all Meyer's soothing they demanded blood.

More than 100,000 men were south of the Pamunkey, ready to face less than half that many behind Jeff Davis's ramparts. All was not going well. In the Shenandoah, cadets from the Virginia Military Academy aided by Wade Hampton's cavalry threw back a Union vanguard. Meade sent Buford to deal with Hampton, and gave up trying to hold the ground. He set a chokehold on the passes over the Blue Ridge. Memories of Jackson's sudden burst out of the valley haunted them all. Sharpe repeated streams of stories about Confederate regulars coming over from Tennessee.

South of the James, Bill Sherman grumbled about the way the army did things in the East. Meade saw through his bluster, trusted him, and sent him the newly reinforced 1st Corps. By mid-September Sherman, with 40,000 men, including two divisions of Negroes, was near Petersburg when the Commanding General returned from paying him a visit.

Meade insisted the key to victory was control of railroads. Two lines remained open, the Richmond and Danville from the south-west and the line from the south, which brought a steady flow of supplies through the Union blockade and the port at Wilmington, North Carolina.

"What I like about Bill is that there's no nonsense about him," he told Fitzpatrick as they found deck chairs aboard a river steamer leaving for their base on the York River. They sat alone under canvas on the afterdeck. In the late afternoon boats moved in and out over shining water carrying men and supplies.

"You can describe a plan in a few words, and he understands. He's moody as Hell. Anyone can see that. I suppose we all are. But he's always ready. Westerners don't say 'Please' and 'Thank you,' or write notes like we do. They're gruff, but they damn well do what's ordered. I wonder if all that's really 'Western?'"

Fitzpatrick smiled and gazed at the water. "I like the fact that there's no politics—at least as we know it. The closer we get to Richmond, the more problems we have along that line."

Meade relaxed in his chair as the vessel chugged into open water. "Sherman says they don't have much folderol out there. No European noblemen, no foreign observers, no congressmen, and hardly ever a lady." He laughed and leaned back against the railing. "I told him we came down just to shake them off." He pulled a hair from his beard. "I wouldn't know the army without them. Except before Gettysburg. We didn't have 'em then. Did we?"

"No, sir, they neglected us. And now we get attention."

"The winners win, my boy. And losers lose." Meade stared over his nose at the water from under his hat, head tilted back. "That's an iron law in this war. The world expected us to lose, and we turned it around. Now we've got to be damned careful not to let the Rebs repay the compliment." He liked the thought, for the moment pleased with life. He had been testy when he came back, but now he was putting on weight. They ate well at the H.R. Crawford plantation. Often at night he bade the staff come in dress, and they drank wine.

"I wonder if an army doesn't fight better with its back to the wall?" Fitz said.

Meade chuckled. "Colonel, your chief value may be impertinence. Yes, we are fat. And a good army ought to be lean. But we must exploit our material advantages. They save lives." He drew fingers through his beard and rolled his head to stare at Fitzpatrick. The low sun over the canopy of oaks and vines glared off the surface of the passing stream. Meade sheltered his eyes with his hand. "Along with technical superiority come the hangers-on, the sutlers, the photography shops, the madames and the barkeeps, as well as the idle curious, the political hucksters—a great long lot of people. I wish we could cut 'em off."

He sat upright, blinked, and looked around, waiting for sailors 10 yards away to move off, and said, "We can talk here. You know we'll lose thousands when we charge those ramparts. The odds are always poor. Our men may fail. Even so, they will hold Johnston in place and give Sherman a chance to move. The main assault comes down here when he strikes west for the railroad.

"Beauregard at Petersburg has fewer than twenty thousand, half militia. Johnston won't be able to reinforce him. If we turn Beauregard, the road is open. The Rebs will have to evacuate. The trick is to attack at the same time. We have set the operation for next week. God hope the weather holds. Rains will stop us dead in the traces." He poked his head out from under the canvas to look up at the sky.

Meade grabbed his hat lest it fall into the oily water, a floppy "Meade Conical," worn by every officer in the Army of the Potomac. The engine's thunk-thunk grew louder as steam built up. He pulled his head in, and his smile was gone. "I hate ordering men to die. They say Sam Grant doesn't. I'm a soldier, but I'm not made that way." He seemed to ask for sympathy.

Fitz kept silent.

"The correct thing," Meade went on as if quoting text, "is to send the reserves with breech-loaders in after the first wave draws blood, when we weaken the defenses, and know where the militia are. That seems right. We choose where to send the reserves when we see how the first men fare."

"That's war, general." Fitz found his voice. "The army, the President, the Congress, even the men expect you to find a way to win regardless of loss, because victory means no more death."

Meade's smile reappeared. "You've said it right, colonel. In the larger view, the loss will be less." He looked out at the water and said nothing for a long time. The boat chugged along. Men in the bow sang; one played a Jew's harp. The air seemed cool as the sun came lower.

Richmond papers raged at President Davis, Secretary Seddon, and especially at Robert E. Lee. Reports from Prediger said the Rebel leadership was in crisis. Davis and Johnston were at swords points. The Congress debated decamping for Montgomery, where the government originated. Davis insisted on holding fast, telling all that "his" army would do again what it did last year. The pro-government press picked up stories from the North charging Meade as temperamental, schoolmasterish, and unimaginative. Some said he planned to retreat after the first day's disaster at Gettysburg, and was only dissuaded by "more courageous officers." The *Dispatch* printed a copy of the Pipe Creek circular, saying "Meade is a general of the defensive. He would never have attacked but for the foolhardiness of R.E. Lee."

Miss Van Lew's letters to Sharpe, smuggled out via "Prediger's Lines," said morale was rising. Johnston's had 30,000 veterans led by Maj. Gen. D. H. Hill and Col. George Washington Custis Lee, son of the failed hero.

Tropical rains fell for a week, turning fields into swamp and roads to soup. Meade and his staff lived in the comfort of dry tents and the mess at the Crawford Plantation. Malaria swarmed through the bivouacs. Hospital tents filled with sick men, and Meade ordered boats to take as many away as possible. They would need the space.

Soldiers struggled alongside Negro gangs laying logs to corduroy the roads, repairing bridges McClellan's men had built in '62. Rail crews pushed track out from the trunk of the Virginia Central and the Richmond and Fredericksburg within sight of Rebel lines. Gangs set telegraph poles alongside.

Rebel regiments trapped a Negro detachment on Sherman's flank. "They held back six of them," Prediger told Fitz. "Shot the rest and hung the bodies outside their trenches where our men could see them." With tears in his eyes he added, "They marched the six in chains to Richmond, and executed them as fugitives on the grounds of the Capitol."

Sherman telegraphed:

These murders enrage the men. Most will fight better for it. Some Negroes feel this way too, but their officers believe they are frightened. I intend to catch the culprits and try them before military courts, and have announced the same. With your permission, sir.

William T. Sherman
Major General
Commanding

Meade's temper soured. Nothing moved swiftly. Time was the Rebels' friend. A newspaper man asked if he'd "thrown away victory." The shadows of '62 fell on them. The sniper's bullet in his shoulder from White Oak Swamp was a daily reminder. The provost marshal reported soldiers saying they ought not tempt fate twice in the same place. Disease, heat, flies, and tropical languor affected them, especially men from New England, who longed for pine forests and rocky coasts.

On September 30, Sherman said he was ready. Meade ordered the assault for the next morning. Fitz again carried the orders. At 3d Corps officers were drinking heavily. When he joked about clear heads, the commander bridled. "I know damn well what's needed without advice from a subordinate." Fitz smiled. "I'm sure you're right, general." And pressed on.

Lincoln was again a presence in Stanton's office. Within hours they expected a major battle below Chattanooga. Meade was moving on Richmond. "He tells us nothing about his plans," said Lincoln, pacing the room. "He's got two armies surrounding Richmond, and don't move. For what does he wait?"

Halleck stepped in to relieve Stanton of the constant questions. "Entrenched troops, even green men, on the defensive exact a heavy toll. Meade knows he'll lose the initiative the instant he has a setback."

Lincoln had heard it before. "I understand that." He pushed his arms out to the sides as if to force the argument away. "We've stripped every arsenal from Missouri to Massachusetts to send him breech-loaders. Richmond is flat. Davis has lost control. We waste precious time." The whine rose. And in Tennessee, Monsignor Rosecrans waltzes while the Rebels dig trenches too. We could wake up tomorrow with two defeats. The closer we get to the end, the more I worry.

He waved the back of his hand at Stanton. "I suppose you've seen The New York Herald?"

"You mean by the man who calls himself 'Historicus?'" Stanton was tentative.

"You mean by that '. . . sagacious officer General Sickles.'" Halleck quoted the article.

Stanton glared at him. He could rush in too quickly. "Yes, it does appear to flatter the good general," he said. "Still, there may be some truth in it. Meade would have ordered a court-martial if Sickles' maneuver had hurt the army in the face of the enemy."

"I agree," said Lincoln. "General Meade is not one to suffer fools gladly. It strikes me Sickles rendered a service."

Stanton wanted to change the subject. Lincoln continued to have doubts. Argument was wearing. Meade had gained a better position than anyone before, but the President couldn't accept it. *He thinks about the election next year.* "Meade was born in Cadiz, was he not?" Stanton flung out words as oil on the waters.

"Yes," said Halleck, seizing the topic. "His father lent a large fortune to the King of Spain to repulse Napoleon. Congress talks about paying the old claim. It was subrogated to the United States under the terms of the Florida Treaty."

Stanton was relieved. Halleck was learning.

Lincoln grinned. "We are all of us lawyers, general, who know about subrogation. I wonder. Does Meade take an interest in the claim?"

"He avoids any mention," said Halleck, "and thinks his brother, a Navy captain, is wrong to sue the government—an act unworthy of a serving officer. He guards his professional honor."

"So are we all honorable men," said Lincoln, "Lawyers, politicians, and generals. But, Halleck, you don't seem to care much for General Sickles. I think sometimes these volunteer men have good ideas."

Stanton thought Halleck was going to tell Lincoln why Sickles deserved a court-martial.

"To give Sickles credit," Halleck said smoothly, "General Meade has told both of us that, whatever his failings at Gettysburg, the final outcome, especially taking account of Sickles's wound, was enough to erase the need for a reprimand."

"The Committee on the Conduct are silent," said Lincoln, smiling at last. "For that we can be grateful. But I doubt Sickles will back off. His reputation rests on Gettysburg."

"Then you think as we do" said Halleck. "Sickles wrote this 'Historicus' article."

"Oh, no doubt," said Lincoln. "He's active. I will grant you he's a politician, effective in his way. He picks on Meade because he's, as you say, too much of a gentleman to fight back." Lincoln grinned, and the folds of his face rippled.

Stanton thought him happy to confound Halleck. *Lincoln has an odd streak. He doesn't care much for leaders of Society, nor for scholars like "Old Brains." He cherishes the brash. Strange man!*

★ ★

Union troops moved in the early light. Three corps, 45,000 men, attacked two miles of Confederate line north of Richmond. Hundreds of guns went to work in a concerted barrage.

Swamp and uneven ground sloped up to the Rebel trenches. Officers struggled to hold formation. At intervals between brigades, batteries belched shells onto the enemy. The first wave struck at three points. The Rebels repelled each assault. In the 3d Corps, regiments separated in the advance, and the defenders concentrated on vulnerable units one at a time. The men of the 5th held formation, fought stubbornly up the slope of the entrenchments, took hundreds of casualties, and fell back, carrying wounded and leaving the dead on the parapets.

The air filled with smoke. Meade could scarcely see through the binoculars, but he knew the time had come, and signaled Sykes. At 8:45 a.m. by Meade's watch the first rank of the reserves reached the glacis, fired a volley, reloaded, and moved up at double-quick. Rebel fire weakened as sharpshooters forced heads down. "They've got 'em!" Meade cheered.

They reached the top. A volley cut them down. "Damn! Johnston's got veterans in the rear." He saw men pull bolts from their rifles to clean them. "They're weaponless! Idiots!"

A second rank followed, and met a second volley. Survivors crouched on the outward face of the trenches, taking advantage of their new weapons to reload under cover. Groups rallied across the gap to reach the rear. Rebel fire sent them back. Meade knew they would fight back and forth for a long time. He ordered Fitzpatrick forward to reconnoiter, and waited, pondering a third thrust. Johnston had surprised him. He was uncertain.

Fitzpatrick returned in less than an hour. "The Rebels have veterans in a rear line. We hold four hundred yards of trenches, but they've built forts dominating long stretches of the line from the rear, and they are out of sight of artillery."

Meade sat silently on Blackie, his fine new horse. Finally he asked, "How many are we getting of theirs?"

Fitz shouted above the roar. "Their losses are better than half of ours, sir. We fire faster. They have better position. The reserves have lost nearly five hundred, and can't move forward to take the rear line. The Rebs move up fresh men and rotate them, like we did on Culp's Hill."

Meade returned to his vigil. Nothing seemed promising. The firing went on, Yankees and Confederates trading lives for little. After two hours the reserves began to fall back, and Meade ordered withdrawal.

A message came from Sherman in the late afternoon. The 1st Corps and a Negro division had turned Beauregard. Union regiments would reach the Weldon Railroad before nightfall. Resistance was light. Beauregard had retreated toward Richmond.

At dinner the mess was quiet. The staff knew Sherman was winning the day and were glad. But they had lost 4,000 men, and the Army of the Potomac had failed to advance. To make matters worse, copies of the "Historicus" article arrived in camp. Meyer tried to speak to Meade and got an earful of venom.

No one spoke to him if he could avoid it. Meade was choleric. Even Humphreys kept silent. The general took out a cigar and smoked in silence. Until he left the table, no one could move.

Newton of the 6th and Hayes of the 2d came in. Meade brightened and offered whiskey. They refused. He stood, motioning to several others to follow, and left for the command tent. The others stood, much relieved as they filed out.

Philadelphia
September 10, 1863
My Dear Husband,

An article in The New York World *by "Historicus" circulates in the city. People say it is self-puffery by that banty rooster Sickles, who wants to advance at your expense. They stop me on the street to say how dismayed they are by such raw ambition. You are too much of a gentleman to have to deal with his sort. Shouldn't you consider a court-martial?*

When I think that last month you invited him to the Rappahannock and offered to parade his old corps. Perhaps you are too kind, my beloved husband? I know you are at heart a man of peace, but you must know that all are envious, and they will be the more so when you destroy the wretched Confederacy.

George is well and heals. The scar is ugly, but thankfully confined to the side of his head. His bonny face is unscathed. I worry about Sergeant, who continues frail. Summer disagrees with him.

I pray for our cousins in the South, and hope you can end the war soon. Their suffering will end, and you will come home in glory.

Affectionately,
Margaretta

Johnston told Davis he had less than twelve hours. Sherman's men would be in Richmond by the next noon. The general planned to withdraw in the night and move west. Beauregard would stay to fight a delaying action with militia and a small force of veterans.

Soldiers set fires in the tobacco warehouses along the James, lest their valuable stores fall into Yankee hands. At the Richmond and Danville Depot by the river, trains came over the Mayo Bridge and left in haste throughout the night carrying troops and officials. The government was going to Montgomery.

The area around the depot swarmed with people trying to escape, but the army could spare little space. Government files were loaded in freight cars many a wealthy man would have given much to ride in. A militia regiment came to keep order. The crowd pressed dangerously around the cars and onto the bridge as trains rolled in. Fights broke out. Fumes from the fires filled the air. Ladies screamed, and several fainted. There was no room to fall or lie, and their maids struggled to hold them upright. The women slouched, eyes closed, praying out loud for the night to pass.

Bands of Negroes moved freely in the streets. No one dared stop them. Looting began late in the night. Most whites hid in their houses not knowing what to expect, but certain they preferred an army in blue to a slave revolt. After midnight the fires raged out of control and spread into town. Only a few came to fight the blaze.

Before dawn Miss Van Lew heard a soft knock at her pantry door. Three knocks, a pause, then one. She bade a servant open. A large black woman dressed in the clothes of a rich man's household bounded through and turned to make certain the door was bolted after her.

"I am Mary Bowser, ma'am, from the Davis's house."

Elizabeth nodded. "I have a room for you." She reached out her hand. Mary, hesitatingly, took it. "Did you come alone? What are the streets like?"

"They are walkin' in the streets, just lookin'. Some are stealin'. Most just don't know what to do. The Yankees are comin' in the morning. That is what they say." She forced a smile.

Mary had gone through an ordeal. "You must be relieved," said Elizabeth. "We don't have to pretend anymore."

"The Davises were good to me, ma'am. They wanted me to go with them. I ran off while they were busy arguin'."

Elizabeth marveled. Mary could not be more than 20. Her carefully written notes sent out in sewing baskets from the mansion provided detailed information about the President's disputes with General Johnston, about military plans, even fortifications. They were so clear they needed no interpretation. Elizabeth sent them straight on to Prediger.

"You can stay here, Mary. Are there others in the mansion staying behind?" A loud explosion from the Basin drowned out her last words. The women stopped, terrified, unsure whether this was the beginning of siege or insurrection.

"Not any I'd trust right now, Miz Van Lew. Three of them left last night, and some of the men are goin' now with Massah Jefferson. What's behind are local folk."

★ ★

Meade awakened at 3 a.m. and stepped out to see the southern sky lit up. Something was afoot in the Rebel capital. He called for Blackie and sent for Fitzpatrick. Troops of the 2d and 6th formed in a column behind cavalry to march around the enemy's left. Meade took command riding near the head. No one knew what to expect.

A trooper brought a message from Buford. Enemy forts were held by militia. Johnston and the veterans had pulled out.

It made sense. Meade sent word to the other corps to push straight through Rebel lines for the city. He wanted a peaceful occupation. The main objective was to pursue Johnston's army and Jeff Davis. He ordered Buford to scout the rear deeper, and sent word to Custer to enter the city from the west and find a crossing of the James. Johnston would surely take his men over the river.

By noon he was in Richmond. Large numbers of Virginia Militia had been disarmed and organized under guard to fight fires. A sharp engagement with veterans near the Mayo Bridge was soon over. Retreating Rebels took up brands to set it afire, but lacked tinder. The 2d Corps ran them off and saved the structure. Then, led by Custer's cavalry, it moved across to meet Sherman's van a mile to the south.

Meade ordered the provost marshal to deal with city officials, while he rode to meet Sherman. He wanted to catch Johnston before he could reach the mountains. He gave Sherman the job with two divisions of cavalry.

CHAPTER XVIII

Colonel Fitzpatrick searched for the remains of Confederate government. No leader stayed in town. Those who didn't find a place on the last trains disappeared. No one would take authority for transfer of power. The governor left, and the mayor spoke bitterly about "the condition of the citizenry." The city core lay in charred ruins. The flour mill by the Basin, once the world's biggest, burned to the ground. Refugees streamed south, and Richmond's wartime population dissolved. Food was scarce, and disease spread. White people kept out of sight.

Groups of Negroes lined the streets to cheer arriving Yankees. Many sought work, but with the war winding down few jobs were open. Every white Fitz met spoke about "the problem of the Negro." "What are they going to do?" "Where are they going to go?" "Would they turn on us?"

On the afternoon of October 3, Fitz, Sharpe, and Prediger called at Miss Van Lew's large house on Church Hill overlooking the river. She served them tea in fine porcelain cups in a dark, high-ceilinged parlor among lightly stuffed English chairs, arms and headrests covered with crocheted antimacassars. "Yes, they will hate us," she said, sitting up straight as a first-year cadet. "And this too shall pass." She looked into the cups as she poured. "We must go through a period of difficulty. No one knows what we have done, nor what military occupation might be, nor has given it the least thought. In June we expected General Lee to win the war." Her soft accents appealed to Fitz, final a's and r's indistinguishable. She said "out" like a Scot with the diphthong of the Chesapeake Bay.

Fitz thought the 40-year-old spinster attractive. Though she neglected her features, her strength appealed to him. Her face was almost wizened, and her body so thin he wondered if the household were starving. She served Prediger tea as if she'd done it all her life. "I will see you are sent rations. For all of you," he said, nodding toward Mary standing behind Elizabeth's chair like a doubtful watchdog. "And we'll post a sentry. Not right in front where it will attract attention, but near enough to guard you."

"I don't think we need protection," Elizabeth said with a faint smile. "Not now. We're not the ones who need help. You must make the streets safe for people to come out of doors so the markets will open." She put her teacup on a small octagonal table. "And the Negroes. You must show them by example what to do. White people think they are children and can do nothing by themselves. If they knew how Mary read President Davis's papers at a glance and remembered them like a photograph, they would know differently. You must give them work. Keep them busy, and the rest will join."

Fitz called on Custis Lee, now in custody, to give him Meade's personal assurances about his father. The younger Lee urged sending the Negroes back to the plantations. The mayor bemoaned "criminal bands of looters. The entire black population is scouring the streets." The provost marshal was concerned more about Union soldiers looting, and reported few blacks involved in violent crime. Well-to-do households refused to believe it. Tales of black roughness and threats dominated their talk.

With the Union Army came philanthropists, traders, and hucksters, some looking to do good, others to do well. Fitz found a train of brightly painted wagons beside a three-storey brick building near the waterfront. "It's old Alice," the provost said, "She's settling down, 'making an investment,' she says." He smirked. "If she'll let us inspect the place, it won't be too bad."

"Just make sure," Fitz grinned, "she doesn't come to the notice of our well-beloved boss." In his mind Maeve and Alice now lived in different worlds.

The war in the East sputtered to an end. Johnston surrendered his ragged army in Farmville a few days' march from Richmond. Desertion, straggling, and sickness depleted his force. No more than

15,000 remained in the ranks. Even so, they were a problem. Meade disliked wasting troops on guard duty. Yet with the war raging in the West and irregulars active nearby, he had no choice. He ordered prisoners sent North.

Ending the war was now less a matter of fighting than forging peace. Though no significant force remained in the field against him, Meade's army had little control of the countryside. Marauding horsemen raided supply lines and outposts, aided by diehard locals. Fitz urged using the prisoners as a bargaining tool, releasing them as a reward for accepting Union control. Meade, convinced his family ties to Virginia's prewar leaders would help him gain support, segregated the local men hoping he might free them after an early settlement.

In Tennessee a Rebel army stopped Rosecrans at Chickamauga Creek, proving the wisdom of caution. Union forces fell back on the hills of Chattanooga. The Rebels lost 10,000, and the Yankees more from a larger force, but Rosecrans would not budge toward Atlanta through the crippling mud of North Georgia. The armies in the West stalemated.

☆ ☆

Three Negroes entered the White House and walked into the President's office with an air of solemnity. They were going to talk to the one leader who could help them. Lincoln rose from his desk to shake hands warmly with each: Frederick Douglass, the Reverend Benjamin Turner, and Josephus Alexander.

Douglass came with others in 1862, when Lincoln urged them to colonize lands in Central America. They had swiftly rejected his idea, telling the President in strong terms that America had been their country for 200 years, and they weren't leaving.

"Well, since we last met," said Lincoln, motioning each to a chair, "matters have advanced a great way. Richmond has fallen. The war will soon be over."

"We can praise the Lord for that," said Douglass gravely. "But now we have to deal with peace."

Josephus leaned slightly forward because the wounds in his back pained him, and he could not rest against the cushions. "Mr. President," he said, "I'm sure General Meade has reported large numbers of our people roaming the towns and countryside in Virginia with no place to go. This disturbs everyone, our people and the white folk alike."

"Yes, indeed, he has," said Lincoln staring at Josephus. "You're the man, aren't you, who brought us such vital information at Gettysburg? I must thank you properly on behalf of the nation." He held his hand forward in a gesture that said, "Behold, the hero."

Josephus nodded and waited for him to continue. But he didn't. Lincoln seemed to be waiting for their proposition. "Our people are mostly from farms and plantations," Josephus said. "They need land. They need to be settled. The sooner the better."

Lincoln pulled his hand over his beard. "Where would we get this land?"

"It seems to us," broke in Douglass. "The Union Government can find it in the South and West. There are abandoned lands where the owners fled or gave them up. Property of Rebel leaders might be forfeit. And they say there is a lot of land that's never been touched." His voice rose implying this was common knowledge.

Lincoln was silent. He turned to Stanton, who had a committee of experts studying the "Negro problem." He was the only other official present. "There may well be some opportunity," Stanton said, "but will the Negroes be able to make good use of it, and will it be enough? We don't know, do we?"

Josephus eyed Stanton, wondering how the conservative lawyer could deal with the problems. "Perhaps, we might help your committee, Mr. Stanton. Negroes have produced most of the valuable crops in this country for centuries. We can work the land all right." He turned to Lincoln. "I think we can agree the matter is urgent. The more time goes on, the more trouble with the white folks there's gonna be."

Lincoln nodded. "You are most certainly right about the latter, sir. I will ask General Meade for his ideas, and we shall talk again."

★ ★

For the women at the settlement house, work in the slums was hard, but Maeve hardly noticed. It was a lot easier than what she'd grown up with, and lot more satisfying. Sigurd seemed calm and happy, though she talked about "the officers" and constantly probed Maeve about the handsome colonel who got her out of Nellie's.

She missed her "noggin" as she called it, and attempts to wean her onto pre-prandial sherry failed. She despised the small glasses of bitter wine, and bribed the Irish girl to buy a pint of whiskey. She became so drunk and incoherent Maeve expected Fannie to put them out. After a long and painful talking-to, Sigurd agreed to try to stay sober, admitting that but for the drink she was happier than ever before.

Occasionally she mentioned Colonel Fitzpatrick at dinner, which always brought Fannie into discussion. Maeve was sure before long she would say something to one of the ladies who came to call. Fannie knew very well where Maeve's heart lay. Sigurd was easier to deceive, but unpredictable. When newspapers reported the capture of Richmond, the *Bulletin*'s frontpage carried a linotype of the colonel standing side by side with Meade. People spoke of him as if he would be in the Cabinet, assuming the President would be General Meade. Some suggested Fitz would run for high office. These were people who knew him, and Sigurd listened in awe, the majesty of his position for the moment stopping her mouth.

Maeve was glad of Fitz's fortune, but knew she could ruin him if her past came to light, if, that is, they were together. She thought a lot about him, and the prospect of being together played in her dreams. Often she cursed the day she met Alice, but was honest enough to admit she'd never have met him if she hadn't.

She anguished over the "Historicus" article and agreed with Fannie it was falsehood. Nor was she happy her fame as the "Angel of Gettysburg" rested on a connection with Sickles, whose measure she took even under sedation. The two women assured callers General Meade had not flinched for an instant. The colonel's letters belittled "Historicus," noting "such slanders were the kind of thing our boss will have to deal with now he is famous. There's always someone trying to build himself up by tearing the big fellow down." Fitzpatrick wrote twice a week, always begging her to reply.

She responded with Fannie's tutelage, writing straightforward notes in a round naive hand saying what she was doing, thanking him for rescuing Sigurd, asking about his health, and telling him to keep well. She said nothing about love, though she would like to. It wasn't proper, yet. Maeve loved the colonel, though every day she believed more that they could never come together.

✯ ✯

Navy steamers tugged and huffed, clearing away wreckage before the docks for the small craft coming up the James with Stanton and Halleck. They came to talk strategy with the man who stood head and shoulders above all others in the nation. Even Lincoln could no longer challenge his judgment. The press conference Meyer arranged after Richmond's capture, with Meade in the saddle en route to join Sherman, had raised him to demi-god.

Newspapers were slow to reach the army. Ten days after the fall of Richmond, Meade was unaware of speculation about him in Washington. He mostly felt an ironic sadness that the army which gave him action and comradery would soon disband. Peacetime offered obstacles, and enemies, he would not know how to meet. He wrote Margaretta that Philadelphia looked better every day. Standing on the dock with Fitzpatrick, he felt unready for the visit and the problems it would bring.

Stanton wobbled, nearly falling into the water before managing to stagger to safety. Recovered, he greeted Meade effusively, "I've come to see the ruins of Richmond, general, and to congratulate you. The President wanted to come, but General Halleck and I per-suaded him against it. Too dangerous, don't you think?" He was oddly chipper, as if it were a brisk fall day and not a parboiler.

Halleck approached with dignity and saluted. "I have the honor to inform you, general, that the Congress of the United States has made you Major General in the Regular Army to date from October 2, the capture of Richmond."

Delighted, Meade returned the salute. Until then formally hold-ing a temporary rank, he was now the senior general in the entire U.S. Army, a position beyond hope four months before. He thanked them, seemingly unmoved, and bade them climb into the open car-riage for the ride to headquarters in Jeff Davis's former mansion. Groups of Negroes came onto the streets to cheer them as they went. Other than soldiers, not a white man was in sight.

Their talks lasted for several days, by design. Stanton wanted time to sound out Meade's ambition. Military questions were not

218

complicated—Meade would continue southward, taking the ports and state capitals down to Savannah, then turn west to meet the Army of the Cumberland at Atlanta. The Western army would strike for Montgomery, while Admiral Farragut could seize Mobile. Meade insisted on retaining his cavalry to fight bushwhackers and marauders, a growing problem, but conceded two infantry corps to the west.

More difficult was peace. Even if the army took Montgomery along with Jeff Davis and all his ministers, Lincoln would not treat with them. He insisted on no recognition of the Rebel government. At Meade's suggestion they decided to work state by state. Each would have to accept the 13th Amendment abolishing slavery, repudiate Confederate debts, and pledge loyalty to the Union. What to do with former leaders was left in the air. Meade pled for leniency, but Stanton said the *ultras* in Congress were strongly opposed. They settled by agreeing to release military prisoners as each state came to terms.

As for former slaves, all agreed it best to keep them out of cities. Stanton said finding land was difficult. Lincoln wanted the so-called abandoned lands, which the Radicals wanted to seize, returned to their owners, except where they belonged to prominent Rebels.

Matters stood without solution until Fitzpatrick, standing off to the side, spoke for the first time. "What about a Freedman's Bank to support the purchase of land for settlements?" Meade nodded, meaning "Proceed." Quickly, Fitz outlined a plan to buy land and finance it by selling bonds against a government guarantee and "hypothecation of the properties." The others weren't sure what the terms all meant, but agreed the proposal, if feasible, could be a solution. "It's better than anything we've thought of so far," said Stanton. He and Meade both knew Fitz had ties to the financial world. They urged him draft a minute for the President.

On the third day Stanton told Meade quietly, "The President feels General Rosecrans may not be ready for the job of ending the war." He said no more.

The Commanding General of the Armies of the East pondered, not wanting to judge a brother commander, though he had anticipated the question. "Rosecrans needs a goad," he said. "Perhaps

Sam Grant ought to take command out West. Hooker could take the Army of the Tennessee."

Stanton smiled. "You would not object then, General Meade, if Grant were made commander in the West, while you commanded the East?"

"How can I?" Meade answered. "We have more than enough to do here. The war isn't over by a long shot."

This was the deal Stanton came to make, Fitz thought. *Meade could demand the supreme command, but Lincoln didn't want to give it. Washington, or Lincoln, favors Grant. Does he naturally prefer Westerners? Maybe he trusts them more. That could split the country again. We can hardly afford that.*

★ ★

In the afternoon, Stanton took Fitz into the cozy library. Knowing Fitz since his days at the War Office, he claimed credit for sending him to Gettysburg. They sat over whiskey and water beneath the red, cut-velvet walls. "You know, colonel, the President would like to recommend George Meade's promotion to lieutenant general." He stared into his glass. "There is a difficulty, however."

Fitzpatrick kept silent. Stanton rarely drank. More would come.

The Secretary looked up. "Politically, the President would be foolish to promote an opponent in next year's election. He's never said a word about that, mind. But I think I know his view of the matter. I know, for example, he doesn't take seriously the idea that the general's foreign birth would bar him from taking the highest office." Stanton looked straight at him.

It was time for Fitz to speak. "You mean not everyone in Washington thinks the general can't run." He smiled, and put his glass down. "I haven't known him for long, Mr. Secretary, but I know one thing surely. General Meade has little interest in politics."

"Ah," said the Secretary, dragging out the sound like a sigh. "It would be a matter of benefit to all of us if he could put that in writing to me, or preferably to the President, as a matter of a senior officer discussing his immediate personal plans perhaps." His voice rose making it sound like a question.

Fitz smiled. Nothing could be easier. He would arrange the letter. *They're afraid of Meade. How powerful, and vulnerable, is our well-beloved boss!*

In early November Sherman entered Wilmington and sent his columns on to Charleston. A column of three corps under Slocum went through Raleigh, then Columbia and into Georgia. Grant sent the Army of the Cumberland south of the mountains. He and Meade were both learning that destroying the enemy and taking territory wasn't enough. New marauder bands appeared every week led by Rebel cavalry officers at the head of mounted infantry and local guerrillas. The Union assigned large numbers of men to suppress them, and successes were few.

On November 30 Lincoln summoned Meade to Washington. They had not spoken for four months. Meade's small party arrived at the Anacostia docks on a clear, cool autumn day. A few copper maple leaves clung to the twigs. A large crowd waited before the White House. In the park a military band played marches. Cheers went up when Meade and his men on horseback swung around the corner by the Treasury. People swarmed to catch a glimpse of the man who had won the war.

The President met him at the massive front and brought him into a crowd of favored citizens inside. Lincoln held up his hand. "Gentlemen, I present the victor of Gettysburg, the captor of Richmond, and conqueror of the Confederacy." He paused to turn to Meade. "I have the honor to announce, sir, that I have this day sent your name to the Congress to be the first to bear the rank of lieutenant general in the field since George Washington." The crowded applauded and shouted, "Bravo!" while the President leaned forward in a half-bow.

Meade clutched the handle of his sword to steady himself, and managed to say. "You take me unawares, Mr. President. I am very proud indeed, and thank you very much." His face bore a public smile he had learned to wear—half-grin, half scowl of authority. After what seemed to him a long silence he added, "Let us hope we can now end the war well and truly." He wondered how he sounded, thinking he hadn't made much sense. Lincoln had caught him, and he felt trapped.

The President smiled graciously and beckoned. Meade with Fitzpatrick and Sharpe followed into his office. "You will forgive my directness," said the President inside in a friendly voice. "I wanted to announce the business to you before the press did. That's part of the game, I've found, haven't you—keeping ahead of the newspapers?"

Meade softened. "In camp, Mr. President, we have a little more say so about such things, and I've been blessed with good advice." He smiled at Fitzpatrick, and Lincoln followed his eyes.

The President motioned them to chairs beside Stanton and Halleck. "I would very much appreciate," he said as he sat behind his desk, "to hear, General Meade, how we can bring about peace. What do these marauders mean to gain? How long can they keep it up?"

Meade sat rigidly in a straight wooden chair. He was not comfortable. Fitzpatrick had predicted his promotion, and he was pleased, but he remained ill at ease with the ways of Washington City, a different place from camp or a Philadelphia drawing room. He cleared his throat. "The marauders, or 'bushwhackers' as some call them, want to frustrate the pacification. Colonel Sharpe here has evidence that Confederate officials encourage them in order to keep any leader from coming forward to play a responsible role with us.

"It's a losing game, I think. As their ports close and factories shut down, they run out of supplies and must forage among their own people, who are already hard-pressed. When they first appear in an area, they meet enthusiasm, especially for bands led by famous veterans like Hampton. The thing appeals to the young. We've captured boys thirteen years old carrying flintlocks. Inevitably they will fail because people run out of patience. That's why young Mosby surrendered last week. He knows the war is over, and he was doing more harm than good."

Lincoln leaned forward on his desk, head propped in his hands, and listened. "That's very interesting, general. I'm glad to hear your optimism. Yet I find it a potent mixture—the bushwhackers on one side and roving bands of the colored people on the other. There must be a link, don't you think? Surely these irregulars promise protection from the former slaves, and play on the fear of them."

"Yes, that is so, Mr. President," Meade answered. "That's why we are trying to settle as many of the Negroes as we can, or put them in camps and have them work with the army. But whatever we do, the whites resent it, and the marauders take advantage of their feelings."

"So it's urgent we find a solution for the Negroes as soon as we can," the President said. "I have read Colonel Fitzpatrick's highly original plan, and have asked for comments from the Secretary of the Treasury, Mr. Chase, whom I think you know, general."

Meade laughed. "He was my old schoolmaster. It's a small world."

"Small word, indeed," said the President with a knowing grin. "Mr. Chase and his advisers don't much like the idea of a government guarantee, nor putting up ten million dollars, but that's to be expected from money men. I think they understand the need of it. Mr. Chase is a staunch abolitionist."

Meade kept silent. Chase was not someone he cared to know. This was new ground. "Then you think, Mr. President, we might proceed. There is land we've found, unoccupied or abandoned, and I suppose we could claim the land of Rebel officers who don't come in to surrender. That ought to give Wade Hampton something to think about."

"Yes, proceed by all means," said Lincoln. "But be careful about seizing property. The higher-ups in the Confederacy must sacrifice, and I'm sure the bushwhackers ought to as well." He stopped and continued as if thinking out loud. "We can get the money out of the Congress as a matter of military necessity." He turned to Stanton, who nodded agreement, then to Fitzpatrick. "Colonel are you prepared to be the head of the Federal Reconstruction Land Bank?"

The announcement stunned Meade. He had never considered losing Fitzpatrick. Discipline held him silent. Fitzpatrick had every right to move up.

Fitz nodded assent.

Flossie Muelheim seldom looked at her diary after the summer. On All Saints Day, dusting her room, she found it again:

Toddy Bates has left for Low Water, Tennessee. The provost marshal in Harrisburg sent us a note saying he could go. We wanted him to stay for the winter, but he said he had "the homesickness" and must look after his mother. All the men taken at Gettysburg are to be free. I miss Toddy. He has promised to write, but I don't expect him to.

Southern grief over defeat turned to white hot outrage as the Yankees handed lands to former slaves. Many called it an unpardonable violation of their liberties, though few said so in public. Some said, "The Yankees have come just to give our land away to the niggers," and "If they love niggers so much, why don't they take 'em up north." Or, when speaking to a Yankee, "We understand the black folk. They're children. They can't read or even count. How are they going to know when to plant?"

Propertied men spoke continually about the labor shortage. Slaves had been their working assets. Especially for those who gambled on Confederate bonds, their prospects were grim. Hired labor was expensive, and greenbacks were scarce.

Bushwhackers seized on the discontent. They got food, fodder, guns, and blankets, as well as concealment and intelligence from many planters. In South Carolina, the war flared up when Sherman's men showed special anger for the home of Fort Sumter. The army burned the houses where bushwhackers were said to find support. Meade considered courts-martial for the arsonists, but judge advocates were overburdened. Burning continued.

Lincoln ordered the Virginia prisoners sent home. Meade agreed, though he worried about the cavalrymen, and hoped senior men who were former federal officers might work for stability.

In November a delegation of planters called on him in Richmond. "We will swear allegiance to the Union," declared a florid spokesman from North Carolina, "and we expect life to be difficult for awhile, but we can't survive unless we can work our lands. When all the Negroes work their own, no one works on ours. And let me add," he wagged a finger, "they aren't goin' to plant cotton. They goin' to sit on their land and grow corn, beans, and hawgs. Cotton will da-ahh." The last word dragged into a long double diphthong, and Meade had trouble understanding the rich drawl. He guessed the man meant the cotton trade would die.

They met around a long polished table once used by the Davises in the large, plush dining room. Meade sat at the head in dress uniform with Fitzpatrick by him. "The labor of the Negro is available on the free market," he said. "I understand that poses a burden when funds are scarce."

He paused for effect. With Lincoln's agreement, Fitzpatrick had negotiated a broad charter for the Land Bank so it could lend money for any "lawful purpose of the occupation."

"Many of you are eligible to borrow from the Land Bank." Meade waited again, looking down the row of faces. "Have any of you visited Colonel Fitzpatrick here in town?"

No one spoke. No one expected this, and they sat chewing on the general's words. "What are the terms?" A man spoke in clear military voice from the end of the table.

"Depends upon your collateral," said Fitzpatrick. "We offer New York market rates to property owners who take the oath of loyalty and are not prevented by Act of Congress." He grinned at the man. "We can finance your crops through the growing season. Our aim is to help put the economy back on its feet."

"I'm sure we can all agree to that," Meade broke in with a laugh. He motioned to a black servant to offer sherry.

"We still don' know wheyah weah gonna git labah," came a voice, soft but loud. "We haven't been able to ship cotton foah yeahs. We kin turn ovah a good profit if we git help, but if the nigras cost too much, we cain't do it."

Meade sat listening to Fitzpatrick answer questions one by one. It wasn't talk he could easily follow, though he knew a little about the give and take of finance. Most important, it wasn't war. If these men found self-interest tied to federal money, they could make progress. Fitzpatrick's idea was brilliant. Lincoln would be very pleased. Meade wondered what sort of medal they could give him.

When the meeting broke up, Fitz jumped up and moved quickly toward the tall man at the end of the table. "Edward," he called and got no answer. "Edward Alexander," he shouted, moving past planters eager to catch him and talk. Finally, someone pulled the Georgian's sleeve.

"Jimmy Fitzpatrick, by God! I heard you went for a soldier, but I sure don't recognize you in that Yankee get-up. They said you caught Pete Longstreet. He's mad as hell about it." Alexander laughed, and a smile lit up his face. Others nodded knowingly, and parted for them to meet.

"When did you get back?" Fitz asked, as if Alexander had been at school instead of prison camp. The older man had been Fitz's idol in summers up in Rhode Island.

"I was only home a few weeks when I heard about this meeting," Alexander said. "I'm hardly used to the new life, and must offer a thousand thanks to your family. Mr. Fitzpatrick came to see me twice, and brought fresh food and blankets."

Meade watched the two greet each other with a pleased smile. *Bringing men of quality together is no problem.* He envied Fitzpatrick his energy and exuberance.

Three weeks before Christmas Sherman telegraphed:

Bushwhackers attacked Negro settlement near Barnthistle, S. Car., yesterday burning all houses, barns, and tents. Three men dead, twenty-two injured. Have offered help and am pursuing raiders. No help from locals. Have posted thousand dollar reward for capture of criminals and notified whites this is a hanging offense.

Sherman

Major General

CHAPTER XIX

Fitz sat at the edge of the canopy bed searching through Maeve's letter for hints of feeling, anxiety or love. Her writing showed growing confidence. At night he returned alone to the house on Union Hill after long hours appointing managers, overseeing lawyers, cajoling politicians, and sorting out borrowers. The work tired him, and he found solace in thoughts of her.

> *Philadelphia, November 30, 1863*
> *Dear Colonel Fitzpatrick,*
>
> *We had a wonderful Thanksgiving dinner celebration at the Horace Morris's farm in Bucks County. They had turkey and a lot of other dishes, including cranberry which I never tasted before. Snow fell last week, and winter comes rapidly. The poor shiver in huts. We carry around food baskets, hardly enough.*
>
> *Miss Morris says we will go to Europe in the spring, and I must have French lessons. We leave as soon as the sea calms. I have never even seen the sea. I fear the voyage, and so does Sigurd. She doesn't want to come with us. She fares well, and loved the farm, which is where in truth I think she would be happiest. . . .*

Her words were nothing, and everything. They came every two weeks. He begged her to write more often, and couldn't understand why she didn't. He now wrote almost every day.

Evening callers were expected. He reached for the glass on the night table and finished his whiskey.

William Stanton was not elated, not exactly thrilled to receive his former client. But since the man was a major general, a war hero who had lost a leg defeating the Army of Northern Virginia, he couldn't very well avoid him.

Dan Sickles clumped in out of breath in full uniform. "Those stairs ain't made for a veteran, Bill. I'll bet I'm not the first hero to stump his way up. And complain about it, too." He laughed. "Time was I'd run 'em up in a leap, or so I remember."

Sickles knew how to charm, a politician's skill Stanton took as a piece of local scenery. "Finding something for Sickles" had become an issue. Senators, congressmen, Ben Wade and the Committee on the Conduct, Lincoln himself, all pressed to know what it would be. Sickles demanded a return to the 3d Corps, "his corps," and had the gall to go see Meade about it. The Commanding General gave him a parade with ruffles and flourishes. *It was generous after all Meade's taken from the little fellow. Still, he sent him away with nothing, and it's back in my lap.*

Stanton was philosophical. This morning the President had signed the money bill for the Land Bank and confirmed young Fitzpatrick as its head. *With good men to hand and Lincoln's sure-footed ways maybe we can settle things down.* He stepped away from his easel, and helped Sickles to a chair.

"I guess I've had all the glory I'm going to get," said Sickles falling back into the seat. "But I'm still on the rolls. Ain't I? And I'm ready for a little work. I got a letter from Joe . . . uh General . . . Hooker." He pulled a paper from his coat and handed it over. "He wants me on his staff as a counselor for dealings with the natives. Needs a lawyer, I guess. What do you think?"

At the height of the war such a job would have been dubious indeed. Generals, especially political generals without work, always demanded things. Usually Halleck insisted they oughtn't to abuse the regulations. But Halleck was gone out West.

"Not a bad idea," said Stanton, standing with an arm stretched over his easel. "I'm sure an occupying army could use your skills." He smiled. *Not a bad idea at all to send him a thousand miles away. Meade would be pleased.* "Good, then." He looked back at his papers as though spotting something relevant. "We can arrange for that. When would you like to leave?"

"As soon as you can draft orders, Bill." Sickles grinned. "I'm sure you'll be glad to see the back of me. George Meade will be here soon to collect his money. We can't have two heroes in town at once, can we?"

The audacity amused Stanton. "And so you will absent yourself for the good of the army." He shot back. "The President will be grateful. He's running again, and he wants quiet on the front lines, so to speak."

Sickles's smile suggested a truth privy to a few. "And with seven hundred fifty thousand dollars for the Meade claim to repay his pa's loan to the King of Spain, old George will be more interested in going back to Philadelphia than running against old Abe."

Stanton started, and Sickles saw it. "Oh, don't fool me, Bill, I'm a local, remember? If the public wants Meade, no politician in the land will dare raise the foreign birth issue, and no court would sustain it."

Stanton relaxed. "No, you're perfectly right, Dan. Seward says Meade's father had a diplomatic appointment in Spain. One could say he was born under the flag, the same as native birth." Stanton pulled on his whiskers. "The Democrats are pushing the Meade claim. They're courting him. The President remains carefully neutral. The Radicals are furious, of course, but there's nothing they can do. The government owes the Meade family a large sum, and no one dare stand against a legitimate payment to a legitimate hero. And, in any case," he sighed. "Meade's certainly no politician."

Sickles struggled to his feet. "Well, so much for contemporary politics, Bill. I won't detain you." He grinned at the relief printed on Stanton's face. "Tell them to send my orders over to F Street, and I'll be off." He stumped to the door at the speed of a normal man. "So it won't be President Meade," he said over his shoulder. "Tell the President I, too, am grateful."

Toddy Bates came home to a sad welcome. Older brothers were not back. No word from either in months, and one was almost surely dead, probably both. Toddy's mother and sisters scraped a patch of hill land, probing eroded soil for corn, beans, and poke. The hogs were taken by the soldiers.

He spent his greenbacks on food, tools, two pigs, and a cow, fixed the porch and the roof, and spent his spare time searching for news of men from the 7th Tennessee. Two, one missing a leg, the other, a hand, lived off families barely able to feed themselves. Gray, sunken faces of the wives betrayed deadly poverty. The men had lain in hospitals since July and knew nothing about others.

One old woman had a letter from a grandson in Georgia who'd found work in a sawmill. Another man was with him. "They wukin for Gin'ril Gordon," the woman said, "Gin'ril Gordon who fought to the bittah end."

People told stories about Gordon—how he fought on into the dark night of July 3rd when everyone else surrendered. A dozen Yankee officers had to hold him down, had to put him in chains even after he was wounded. Gordon was the one man, they said, aside from the martyr Early, who fought with honor.

Toddy tried to figure out what to do. He'd done what he could for the womenfolk. His sisters could work the land as well as he. Finally, he decided—better go away, find a paying job, and send money home. The only men who might help him were from the regiment—the only ones who even knew he'd fought. Best he'd go down to Georgia.

In late December Union soldiers entered Atlanta and pressed on to Montgomery. The final victories belonged to U.S. Grant, and Radical Republicans, wary of Meade, sang his praises. In the lame duck session, Congress passed the Meade claim unanimously, granting restitution for the diplomat Richard Meade's *noblesse oblige* to the King of Spain. In a generous mood, the legislators went on to order gold medals struck, one each for Meade and Grant. They voted thanks to Sherman, Hooker, and Hancock. At Meade's insistence Lincoln got them to pass a memorial for Reynolds, but they pigeon-holed his request for a medal for Josephus. In the final days, Congress made Meade Commander in Chief of the U.S. Army, and Grant his deputy, also with the rank of lieutenant general, to have responsibility for the Mississippi and the West with headquarters in St. Louis.

Meade looked forward to meeting Grant, and was sorry the first occasion would be a White House reception. He wanted a professional talk. They had much to say, stories to tell, and ideas to exchange and needed to spell out working arrangements. Meade was anxious to give him as much occupation duty as he would take. He wouldn't order him to take it, though he could. Halleck had complained long ago about Grant's skill at skittering around orders from Washington.

At a reception in honor of the army the President and Mrs. Lincoln stood in a receiving line, the generals and their wives *en suite*. Margaretta spoke convivially with the shy Grant next to her. His terse words carried a spark of charm. She was amiable too with the taciturn Julia Dent Grant, whose crossed eyes disconcerted most who talked to her.

"Well, Sam," Meade said during a lull, "is this what we're condemned to, now the fighting's done?" He towered over his wife to look down on his colleague.

"I hope not," said Grant. "At least I can get out to the frontier, and the fighting's not over in Texas. There's consolation in that." He paused. "Odd, how we miss the war."

Margaretta tugged Meade's arm to aim him at an approaching ambassador. He could only nod a grinning assent. *Damned impertinence, these affairs.* Meade saw a vision of a cornfield at Antietam strewn with bloody bodies, blue and gray lying together among the stalks. *What the Hell are we doing here? I need to talk to Grant man to man. The President doesn't seem to have any sense about this at all.*

Lincoln looked back. "General, you see what we have to put up with here. This is called 'peacetime.' I'm sure you'd prefer Rebel bayonets." He turned to an urgent summons from his wife. "Duty calls." He grinned.

Meade didn't see the receiving line break up.

Philadelphia is more attractive every day. We can buy a palace along the river, retire, and I'll be a country gentleman, ride to the hunt, and entertain the Sargants, the Biddles, and the rest. Mary Lincoln walked past to greet Margaretta, and ignore Julia Grant.

"Mrs. Grant and I were just saying how elegant is your new drapery, Mrs. Lincoln." Margaretta tried to repair the insult.

"How would she know?" said Mary Lincoln. "Surely you don't find them out in the West." Her minimal chin rose as she picked up her skirts. "I'm sure you have the finest in Philadelphia, Mrs.

Meade, and I'd be interested in your opinion, but I must be gone. We have guests to make welcome." She pushed off like a carriage and four at a rural coach stop, with a smile for Margaretta and nothing for Julia Grant.

Meade watched in horror. Mary Lincoln could be cruel. She intended to be cruel to Julia Grant, while nice to Margaretta. *Pure snobbery! If we weren't from Philadelphia, how would she treat us?* He turned to speak to Mrs. Grant who had gone into a corner where Sam was trying to console her.

"Did you see that? She cut Mrs. Grant dead, absolutely dead."

"A difficult woman," said Margaretta. "Greatly admires 'Eastern Society.' I can't imagine he gives two pins about it." She nodded toward Lincoln talking gaily with a pack of politicians.

"I worry about Sam Grant," said Meade. "This gets us off on the wrong foot." He offered his arm, grateful to have a wife capable of dealing with a regiment of Mary Todd Lincolns.

The tall man coming down the aisle in the gray tunic of a Confederate officer caught the eye of everyone in the congregation of the First Baptist Church of Brunswick, Georgia. Ramrod straight and solemn, a raw scar across his left cheek, he held his hand gently behind his pretty wife's narrow back to help her into a pew. "Gin'ril Gordon!" they whispered before the hall fell silent when the beadle came to place the Book on the altar. The black-frocked minister stopped to shake the hero's hand. Gordon stood, unsmiling, and bowed slightly from the waist.

"My sermon this bright sunny morning is about honor," said the minister at the pulpit. "We need to remember our honor, how we sacrificed for it, how our God-ordained freedom depends on it, how it shall protect us in these dark days.

"We who have been free men serve a new master, and institutions ordained by God and bespoken by St. Paul and the Hebrew prophets are destroyed in the wreckage of cruel war. . . ."

Men nodded to their wives. No doubt he spoke about slavery. No Yankee came to church. No soldier in town was a practicing Baptist. Captain McCarthy, the commander, was said to be an Irish Catholic. The presence of General Gordon gave them hope, and pride.

The Episcopalians and Presbyterians couldn't boast the like of him.

In the narthex after the service, the general shook hands with each. Some made Masonic signs with their fingers, and he acknowledged them. They were glad the Yankee commander wouldn't be coming to Lodge meetings. In their homes, in church, at the Lodge, and at every social gathering, they spoke of protecting themselves. They had all, since childhood, understood the unspoken fear of slaves. They knew as a matter of scripture that the black man was a child needing the guidance of whites. Yet the Yankees were giving good lands to the Negroes, who built their shacks on plantation fields in the ruins where great houses stood.

Gordon owned a sawmill on the bay, cutting the tall coastal pines into lumber and shipping it off by sea and rail to rebuild burnt-out cities and country houses. Business was good, and he had hired a large crew, all veterans. The local folk were pleased to see them riding through town four abreast. When they walked they swaggered like bushwhackers.

"That's a fine group you've got there, gin'ril," said a white-haired man with a knowing grin. "I hope you're trainin' 'em proper."

Gordon smiled. "I like taking on the veterans," he answered, and said no more. Secrecy was a watchword. Secrecy!

"I see 'em hangin around that Freedmen's Bureau all the time," said a woman in black. "They've got nothing to do. One wonders what they'll find. Mischief, I'm sure."

"Patience, Madam," said Gordon with a solemn face.

"Yes, we must be patient," said his wife, reaching a hand to the widow. "All will all be well in the end."

Philadelphia
January 5, 1864
Dear Colonel Fitzpatrick,

It is colder since you were here at Christmas. I am glad for the warmth of Miss Morris's house, and I only wish our people in the settlement were so blessed. We do what we can, but there is never enough, and I fear many good veterans of Gettysburg and their wives are starving. Several big factories have closed that made things for the army. There is no work, and life is very hard for the poor.

Sigurd has gone. To go where I do not know and cannot learn. She stayed out at the Morris farm after Christmas and took up with a boy who worked on the place. I had hoped they might marry, but that is not her way. They ran off. I pray for her. Please don't think I'm asking for your help. She will turn up, I know.

I think often of our talks at Christmastime, but the future is frightening. With best wishes,
Maeve

As with everything in life, Josephus planned carefully. With the help of Henry Prediger he searched out six families from the old Fairfield and Ashburn Plantations. They were spread out among contraband camps, shanty towns, and military barracks. He told them of his plan to acquire land on the islands off the Georgia coast and to grow its highly valued long-staple cotton. It seemed impossible, but hope was alive, and the prospect was the best they could find. So they waited for Josephus to do his work.

Fitzpatrick employed a small army, many of them Southerners eager for paying jobs, to acquire land and match it with settlers. When Prediger came with Josephus to tell Fitz of their plan to buy lands abandoned on St. Simons Island, he quickly fell in with it.

Josephus said he knew of several good farms where members of his family once worked. "Anyone of 'em would do," he said. "Henry Prediger and Sally will come, and I think we have two families near Fairfield and two more from out on the islands."

The Ashburn Farm on a low plateau sloping down to the Altamaha River was Josephus's choice. His mother, before the Alexanders bought her at age six, had lived on the place. He found men and women who had worked the land. Some had saved precious seeds of Sea Island cotton, and were happy to talk about the soil and what it would grow. The aging owner had ignored the place, leaving the land fallow. When the islands were taken by the Yankees during the war, former slaves grew vegetables and grains for the Union Army. The soil, he believed, was likely to have recovered somewhat after years of depletion from "cotton-mining."

Josephus carefully read back copies of *The Cotton Planter's Manual* and drew up a scheme of production. He brought six families to

Ashburn in early February and began repairing the manor house, where he settled four of them. The rest spread out in the old cabins. They set about preparing the fields. Life was good. Most could not believe their luck. When Josephus announced that he had ordered machinery for a cotton gin, it made them laugh and shout as they worked. Spirits ran high.

★ ★

Meade and Grant met in early January and agreed to divide the duties of military government. Meade took the East Coast down to Florida, leaving the rest to Grant. Each would be sovereign in his domain with powers of a dictator under martial law.

Reconstruction was underway. Officers of the Land Bank spread out from its Richmond headquarters swiftly to fashion Negro settlements, wherever possible lumping them together apart from the whites to be independent and able to protect themselves. From frequent reports of attacks on ex-slaves, and not a few cases of revenge, Meade, Grant, Fitzpatrick, and others concluded that separation of the races was the best course.

The army shrank—from over a million in the fall to less than a quarter of that early in the year. The large majority wanted to go home as soon as possible, though a surprising number wanted to stay. Jobs grew scarce as military purchases ended. There was a surfeit of officers, especially volunteer generals.

"We're going to have to reduce them," said Grant grimly staring at a roster. "Look at twenty-five-year-old Major General Custer here. In the regulars he's a captain. What do we do with him?"

"And he wants to stay," mused Meade. "Cavalrymen will be useful in the occupation, and then they're going to have to go out West. You've got forty thousand men in Texas. A large number ought to be cavalry."

"True," said Grant thoughtfully. "Unless we have to go into Mexico. Then we'll need infantry."

"Sam, did you ever think out in Illinois three years ago you'd be sitting here after leading armies in battles bigger than any ever fought before and deciding on the future of the U.S. Army?"

Grant snorted, "No, George, I was a ne'er-do-well, none too good a ne'er-do-well at that. If someone had shown me a vision, he couldn't have done better."

"Sometimes I feel the same," said Meade. "I was a surveyor becoming a scientist." He paused. "I'm damned if I care much for occupation duty."

They chuckled together.

"We've got to appoint military governors," said Meade. "You have a list, I suppose." He pulled a paper from a leather case.

"It's not difficult," Grant said, "mostly regulars by order of rank, I'd say." He paused to look at his list. "The best are older heads like Bill Sherman, whom I'll be glad to have back."

"I hate to give him up" said Meade. "He and Hancock are two with a flair for this sort of thing. Bill has a perverse love for Charleston. I thought he might take both the Carolinas. He'd like that."

Grant pulled on his chin. "I won't argue for his sake. I'll put Joe Hooker in New Orleans. Thomas can go to Texas. The President keeps after me about Sickles. He doesn't fit, not being a regular and all. But I have to admit he's seems to understand the problems of the occupation."

"The Radicals love him," said Meade.

"True," said Grant. "And he's a jolly sort of a chap when he wants to be. Quite humorous. I can see how he ingratiates himself." Grant paused and looked at Meade. "But I'd rather you had him, general."

Meade sighed. He wanted no part of Dan Sickles, but he knew Lincoln's mind. "All right," he said, "I'll keep Bill Sherman and take Sickles in the bargain. He can have Georgia. I'm going to tell the President he'd better damn well behave."

The rest of the meeting passed smoothly. Meade felt he knew Grant's mind and believed he had begun to build the bridge of trust needed to reach all the way across from Washington City to the Mississippi. *Well, better Grant out there than I. Margaretta wouldn't care for it.*

"I've got to tell you," said Grant at the door. "Julia is very happy in St. Louis. I doubt we could ever adjust to Washington."

"Don't worry about it until I retire." Meade grinned. "Then perhaps she'll have to." They laughed loudly, standing on the open threshold. Twenty heads of junior officers turned, seeking to join the high level hilarity.

☆ ☆

Josephus took three children on the ferry to Brunswick to buy supplies and lumber. Time had come to build a foundation for the machinery. Local merchants were sometimes unpleasant to Negroes, and he wanted to show the youngsters how to deal with them. Many tried to pass off shoddy goods and fool them on the accounts. Josephus turned aside their sallies as he completed purchases of staple foods, cloth, and a few tools.

He knew as soon as he saw the sawmill it wasn't merely a place of business. The men, in their late teens and twenties, behaved like soldiers in garrison. Many wore remnants of rebel uniforms. Josephus half expected to see guns, and decided they probably had some hidden away.

"Whadd'ya want," shouted a tall man on the loading dock in a gray coat with sergeant's stripes.

"I would like to buy some lumbuh for a foundation we ah buildin." Much as he wanted not to, his tongue thickened, and he fell into a slave's deference. The man's anger seemed to demand it.

"What sort a lumbuh?" the man mocked.

"I need eight or ten four-by-four posts, tha's all, suh."

"Oh, you fixin' up a cabin. We got somethin' you can use." The sergeant looked behind where several others sat on a bench. "Hey, young un, take this nigrah over to the slash pile and see what we got that suits him." He turned with a sour grin. "Toddy'll take care of yuh."

As they walked away, Josephus heard the foreman say, "Ordinarily Gin'ril Gordon don't like doin' business with niggers. But if we take some of his dollars fer the slash, he won't mind." They passed ten-foot piles of sawdust and scrap and huge long decks of pine logs. Toddy was glum. "Suppose, Mr. Toddy Bates," Josephus said when they were out of sight. "Suppose we didn't want to buy slash but wanted good lumber? Would they sell it?"

"I doubt it, Mr. Josephus," said Toddy, who seemed glad to speak freely. "They don't take kindly to coloreds."

"I guess we better pretend not to know each other for your sake,"

237

said Josephus. "You can sell me a couple of dimes' worth maybe we can use, and we'll be off."

After loading two knotted four-by-fours onto the cart, and paying Toddy a dollar, he asked, "Now tell me, if you please, just what is this place?"

"Gen'ral Gordon, he hires veterans. Some are from Tennessee. That's how I got on. But a lot of 'em were bushwhackers who come in with horses and guns. They keep 'em hidden, and drill out at Gordon's three mile north. I don't go often, cuz I don't ride good.

"They call me the 'young un' like they did in the army. It'd be worse if a couple of 'em weren't from the 7th and knew I was in Pennsylvania."

Josephus came home with a grim face, and the young people were quiet.

CHAPTER XX

For Abraham Lincoln, re-election posed a delicate problem. He had decided long ago to run, and cleared from his way the military men who might stand against him—all but one, the incomparably egotistical McClellan, blunderer of the Peninsula and victor at Antietam. "The Democracy," as Democrats were more than ever careful to call themselves, wooed "Little Mac," and found no trouble persuading him to take a soft line with the South. He would stand resolutely for the rights of property (meaning compensation for slaves) and staunchly urge "peace" (meaning back to the old days). Lincoln hoped to exploit Meade and Grant and take over the peace issue. He opposed compensation, but would be gentle toward the South and risk the wrath of Radicals, like Thad Stevens and Ben Wade. What he feared most was a fight over the fate of the Negroes.

Unfamiliar with Africans, white Northerners were unsure what "emancipation" meant. Many thought the Union could abolish slavery and leave them as they were before the war. Men complained about "giving out land and money to slaves" and "lending to Rebels." Lincoln gambled the settlement program would find support so long as it meant keeping blacks from coming north.

McClellan would run as he fought—move slow, take the defensive, and wait. Lincoln planned to appear with his heroes wherever he could. The North had yet to drink its fill of patriotism. He would wave the flag without the "bloody shirt." Meade was his man, a gentleman, modest, conservative, and supposedly a Democrat. The war had blurred party lines.

The Meades and the Lincolns saw much of each other in early 1864—Mary Todd soaking up the social wisdom of Margaretta

Sergeant, while Lincoln courted his general. For his residence the Commander in Chief chose a large house on Lafayette Square, from which he could walk as easily to the White House as to the War Office.

"He wants me to go to Chicago with him," he told Margaretta on a warm May evening in the library. "For the election. He said something about my having to learn about these things. Sometimes I think he baits me."

Margaretta, glasses at the end of her nose, sat in a Shaker rocker, a book in her lap. "He's only saying what everyone else does. In time, George, you will be President. Of course he wants you along. You're his stalking horse for little McClellan. Lincoln wants him to come out and fight." Margaretta put a small round glass of port to her mouth and pursed her lips around it.

"Little Mac won't come into the open," said Meade. "He never takes the aggressive even when the odds are three to one. We're to meet Grant in Chicago. I can't think why." He stared absently out through open French doors into the walled garden. "Lincoln doesn't have to deal directly with my deputy, does he?"

"Don't be officious, George. Grant is a hero out West. Can't you see what Lincoln's doing? He's wrapping himself with heroes to match McClellan's uniform."

"I miss Fitzpatrick," said Meade, squinting into the fading light. "He does well with his bank. Never makes a mistake. The men who've borrowed prosper, and he's settled thousands of Negroes. Critics become admirers when they meet him. He knows politics by instinct. Never had any training I know of. . . . the Fitzpatricks are financial people."

"You were fortunate to find him." She put her book on the table. "You could talk to him. He's our kind. But you have others—that German Fannie brought, what's his name? Meyer? I hope you're keeping him on. The press was never your cup of tea."

"We've had a talk about that. Stanton says he don't have the money. I could put some up myself I suppose. What kind of a precedent would that be?"

"You mustn't hesitate, George." She took her glasses off. "If you don't decide where you're going, someone else will. That's what

240

father said. Politics is in constant motion in this town. You have supporters—many Democrats and propertied people look to you for protection. Mary Lincoln is absolutely your partisan. She can't abide Grant, and thinks he's going to set the blacks over the whites on the Mississippi. People are afraid of the Negroes, George."

"I know." Meade held his glass to the light, "We don't know much about them. Lee told me they're children and can't learn to behave like white people. But in the war I saw them do prodigious things. That fellow Josephus, black as coal, not a drop of white blood in him, he's a military genius. And Prediger and Douglass and many others. I don't believe they can't do for themselves." He put his glass down, and grinned behind his spectacles. "And, I'll tell you I'm damned glad Congress passed the Meade claim without debate. Somebody could ask embarrassing questions about where our money came from."

Margaretta looked at him like a school mistress. "Someone will bring up the slave trade eventually. It's your deeds that count, not your forebears. Your grandfather won't be standing for office."

"I don't envy Lincoln." Meade was gazing again out the doors. "Yet I admire his skill. He was against slavery long before he became President. Once elected, he concealed himself, like a hunter stalking game, even put on disguises. I think he probably believed in colonization, sending the Negroes away. In the end, he came out for their full rights, which, as far as I can see, is the only choice."

"Equality!" humphed Margaretta. "It's a fine principle, but it doesn't mean they can marry into the family." She put her book on a side table.

☆ ☆

Vichy, France
May 25, 1864
Dear Colonel Fitzpatrick,
We have been here for a week drinking the water and going to concerts. Fannie insists my French study makes progress, but my tongue doesn't turn around the words. And its seems so useless. I can't imagine I shall ever speak the language at home.
I did not write to you for a long time because I have thought a great lot about our conversation before we left Philadelphia. The newspapers in France

write often about la guerre civile aux Etats Unis. They write about le maréchal Meade and sometimes about son jeune confidant très intelligent, le colonel Fitzpatrick. You stand on the stage for all the world to see. It leaves me breathless.

That is why I must tell you that we cannot marry. I can never be a suitable companion and wife to a man like you. In the salons I see women who play musical instruments, draw, sing, write, and speak about the great issues, as I cannot. You require such a woman, and a woman without a past, as they say. It's as simple as that.

At this great distance it doesn't seem so difficult to write, though I know it may hurt you. I'm sorry, and I wish to add that it takes nothing from my love and respect. I wish you well, mon ami.

Yours very sincerely,
Maeve

Fitz carried her letter in his vest for weeks, rereading it, hoping to find a glimmer of an opening through which he might find his way back to her. But none appeared. As the days passed, the warmth of love, which had wrapped him like a cloak, no longer clothed him. Emptiness filled his thoughts in the dark nights riding alone on unknown streets. Loneliness absorbed him.

Calvinist discipline urged him to work, travel on business, and dine and drink more often with clients. Pleased to meet good society, Southerners opened their homes—the Moultries in Charleston, the Alexanders in Georgia, the du Villiers in New Orleans. They served up daughters as on silver trays—chaste, pure young women skilled in talking to men. Fitzpatrick became the most sought man south of the Line.

Often at night he rode through the streets of Richmond, sometimes at a trot, sometimes at a canter, never at a walk, forcing air into his lungs and his brain, trying to purge the picture of her face and the soft feel of her flesh, which he knew better than he dared remember. He spun out a thousand scenarios how they could be together in New York City, London, or the South Seas.

As the army shrank, few comrades remained. Hancock, recovered from his wounds, came as Governor of Virginia. Fitz sometimes went to the weekly dining-in at the former Davis mansion, where he looked for Sharpe, who was often down from Washington. Now a brigadier general, Sharpe was ferreting out secret remnants of Rebel activity.

The bushwhackers had gone to ground, but in the western mountains a few Scotsmen formed secret clans dedicated to white ascendancy. Fitz and Sharpe heard from Elizabeth Van Lew the continuing rumors of Rebel plots in Richmond's netherworld of the theater. The famous, and reckless, Wilkes Booth was said to be involved. During the war his patriotism was all noise and brag, she told them. Still, one couldn't be sure.

Many late nights Fitz rode past Alice's Hotel, a quiet, proper-looking building standing almost among the ruins at 15th and Cary Streets, where a liveried Negro stood to take the gentlemen's horses. Union officers emerged as he passed, often drunk, always jocular, sometimes singing together arm in arm. The scene did not tempt him. He had not met Alice, nor any of her girls. His rendezvous with Maeve occurred in a special place apart, unconnected with trade.

The "niggers' gin on the old Ashburn place" was the talk of Brunswick. Josephus got materials for it with the help of the Freedmen's Bureau. Yankee soldiers led by a fuzz-faced lieutenant rode out to Gordon's mill to buy solid timbers needed to hold the machine as well as studding to support the roof. They didn't say it was for Ashburn, but the mill hands knew, and grumbled.

"Niggers got no business with machin'ry," growled the sergeant from the dock as the wagons snaked out of the yard. "They don' know a damn thing 'bout machines. They jus' gonna cause a whole lotta trubba for decent white fokes." He spat.

General Gordon watched from his office window, stern and angry. The Yankees had forced him to do sell where he never would have. His men were raging. Every day people told him they wanted protection from the black hordes. He knew their fears weren't justified. Yet he had to give his men their pride, and the Yankees had shamed them.

"Sergeant," he called, "Get the men out for drill this afternoon, and send me that young fellow from Tennessee—the one knows something about the gin." He'd scarcely spoken to Toddy since he'd come.

When he appeared, Gordon asked about his war service. Toddy answered, "7th Tennessee, Archer's brigade, last Fry, gin'ril, sir."

"You were in the last assault?" Gordon's voice softened. "How far did you get, son?"

Toddy relaxed. No one could fault him at Gettysburg. "I got to the wall, gin'ril. A Yankee held a gun on me about to shoot. Saw I was a young un, I guess, and told me to clear out."

"What did you do?"

"I ran like Hell, gin'ril," Toddy grinned involuntarily. "But I kept my gun. Found some of our'n down in the trees. Hill sent us to the back ridgeline."

"How long did you stay there?" Gordon asked.

"Cain't rightly say, gin'ril." A mountain accent gave comfort. His body was tense. He knew this wasn't about the war. "Seemed like quite a spell. We didn't have more than a hunnert men in the reg'mint by then." He paused for breath. "Along about sundown they came at us from all sides."

"Where did you go?"

"I went with two others toward town. One got hit. I turned to help him, but he wuz gone. When I turned I wuz alone. So I found a barn and hid out."

"And you fell asleep," said Gordon knowingly. "We were all pretty tired by then."

"Young German girl found me, gin'ril. Family made me pris'ner. Kep' me to look after wounded in the house. I never did get sent to camp, on accounta ma age, I guess."

"And so you lived with the Yankees. Were they good to you?"

"Well, yea, fer Yankees I guess ya might say," Toddy looked at his feet. He was going to have to shade things.

"Who did you see on the Yankee side"

Gordon's smile invited him to relax, but he remained tense. "There wuz a number came to the house to see the wounded."

"Any generals?"

"Well, yessir, Gin'ril Meade come to see the nigger." He wished he hadn't said it.

"What nigger?"

"They say he rode through Rebel lines with a message just before the Yankees attacked. Gin'ril Meade 'peared to prize him highly. . . . And there were others too, both niggers and whites." Toddy tried to steer the talk away from Josephus.

"What was his name, son, the man General Meade prized so highly?" Gordon looked at Toddy through close, narrow eyes, face cold as an ironclad.

"Why, Mr. Josephus, gin'ril," Toddy blanched and looked at the floor.

"He's the one came to fetch wood a few months ago, wasn't he?" asked Gordon, his voice again soft.

"Yes, gin'ril." Toddy wished to God he were somewhere else. "The one's building the gin."

★ ★

The special cars were comfortable, but the West was hot, and even with windows open the humid air was boiling on the train. Lincoln urged Meade and his staff to take off their coats. Meade demurred at first, but seeing they would all suffer in following his lead, relented. He felt uneasy, half-dressed in the presence of the President.

"We stay at the Windsor House near the lake shore," said Lincoln. "There should be a breeze, and it ought to be pleasant, if the wind is from the water."

Meade wondered what it would be like if the wind weren't—stench from slaughterhouses, slums, and factory dumps, no doubt. He didn't care for the hinterlands, though his years in Detroit had been happy enough. Yesterday, when they passed through, the people cheered him grandly. They were warm and friendly, open-faced, the good common folk of the country. Lincoln was at home, and much preferred them to sophisticates of the East. His stomach was upset. He drank milk at breakfast. It didn't help.

"Grant will meet us, I expect. Then we'll all go to see the town fathers," Lincoln told him. He seemed to relish the prospect. "They will have a banquet, and you will have to say a few words, general. They'll expect to hear all about the fighting, I'm sure."

Meade hesitated. "We didn't have a lot of Illinois men in the Army of the Potomac, Mr. President. It won't be like Detroit where

I could sing the praises of Custer and the Michigan Cavalry." He forced a smile.

"The 82nd Illinois in Krzyzanowski's brigade made the final attack that forced Gordon across Rock Creek, did they not?" Lincoln stared at Meade as though he ought to have this fact at the top of his mind. "And there were a couple of Illinois regiments in Buford's charge, I recollect."

Mead smiled. Lincoln's knowledge of minutia was acute when a speech was to be given. "You amaze me, Mr. President. The 8th and 12th Illinois Cavalry rode with Buford. I stand corrected. Those men won the war. I ought never forget." Meade's smile turned to a grin. "I know what to say." Lincoln knew exactly how to address a group—a skill of his trade, like picking the point of attack.

At the hotel Meyer knocked on Meade's door. "I have an amusing story to tell you, Herr General," he said. "The newsmen say much about Herr General Grant." Meyer's accent was heavy. He had been tippling.

Gusts blew through the windows of the sitting room. Meade was wrapped in a dressing gown, sitting in a stuffed chair, trying to recover from the noon banquet. He had talked war with city officials, party leaders, journalists, men of religion, business and the professions, all speaking with Lincoln's nasals. He was more at home in Richmond. "What is it, Meyer?"

"Perhaps I disturb the general?"

"No, no." Meade waving him in. "A little bit too much heavy food."

"German cooking can be *schwer*, heavy, as you say."

"What is the news, Meyer? I haven't heard any in so long I'm eager to get it."

"It appears, Herr General, "that the General Grant and his wife ride in a private car that belongs to a rich New York millionaire, a Mr. Vanderbilt, *ein Hollander*."

Meade grinned. "Cornelius Vanderbilt, a railroad builder. Rich as Croesus."

"Well, they traveled to the Grant former home, a river town called Galena here in Illinois. The city's leaders would give them a house. *Aber*," Meyer paused for effect. "The house was not to their taste. In the town it was not the best or even the second best. Herr General and his wife walked through, looked at each other, and politely said 'thank you.' Within an hour they got back on their car, and left the town. Are you not amused, Herr General?"

"What are you telling me, Meyer? Herr General Grant didn't like his house? There must be others in the town, *nicht wahr?*"

"I don't think, Herr General, that General Grant and his wife want to go to Galena, Illinois. My newspaper friends agree that he looks for a better house, a white house. He can't go home, so he goes to Washington City. Comical, no?"

Meade rubbed his nose at the bridge where his spectacles chafed. "Because Grant can't go to Galena, he has to go to the White House? I don't follow." He paused to look out toward the lake, and resumed slowly. "You mean it's like the child who tastes cream. He don't want to drink milk anymore."

"Ja," said Meyer, exhaling sharply. "I think that is the point. You should know that General Sickles accompanies General Grant and will be at the dinner tonight. The General Grant now listens to him very carefully about politics, I'm told."

Meade's insides churned, and he stood to ease the pain. "This damn heat. It takes getting used to." *Mustn't show Meyer what I think about this last news. What the Hell is Sickles doing here? He's supposed to be in Savannah. Is he still pushing for court-martial?*

"Thank you, Herr Meyer," he said after a pause that was probably much too long. "I appreciate your services very much. Please keep me informed." He nodded in dismissal.

"Of course, Herr General."

In Brunswick people spoke of little else than "that damned gin," or "that infernal nigger gin." Negroes called it "God's engine" and "God's gift." Captain McCarthy reported the danger to Savannah but got no response. General Sickles traveled a lot. McCarthy wrote a second, full report, spelling out who the antagonists were.

Gordon knew little about Yankees and their Negro clients. His time in prison camp taught him about the North only that he hated it. The abolitionists, the Freedmen's Bureau, and their garrison troops were uneducated idiots. A college man with strong convic-

247

tions about the economy of Georgia, Gordon knew a thing or two about business. He saw the Yankees' Negroes creating a monopoly over long-staple cotton by means of the steam gin. He would never concede Georgia agriculture could prosper that way. Slavery had been the natural order of things. It had given God-fearing folks their freedom.

He lectured the Masons. "That wily Negro built his factory right on the shore where boats from other islands can unload raw cotton alongside," he told them. "They don't need to come anywhere near a road, even a house, frequented by white men. They've got the whole thing under their power—all the long-staple cotton that's selling in London for five times what it was before the war."

The leading men of Brunswick were stunned. The war had cost them dear. They had lost sons, and property. In the absence of a strong banking system they had put everything in Confederate bonds. True, the new Land Bank financed many a white farm, and some owners said hiring Negroes was as cheap as using slaves so long as the price of cotton was high. The Masons respected Gordon. They were privileged to have him, a man of great courage, and vision.

Fitzpatrick was angry as he threw the reins to the groom. The night was dark after a thundershower. He had dined with the officers, and they had drunk several bottles of wine. He wished he weren't in uniform. He did not know why he was at Alice's, nor much like himself for being there. He didn't know whom he would see, or what was going to happen, and he felt a rush akin to going into battle.

The lobby was an ornate wood-paneled room where an olive-skinned mulatta girl in a black dress and white apron greeted him with a soft smile. She motioned toward an adjoining lounge, where a half-dozen soft chairs were arranged so that no more than two faced each other. Windows opened onto a garden. The room was cool and empty. He sat.

"Can I get you a drink, sir?" she asked.

"Whiskey and some water." For what seemed a long time he sat alone. He heard distant girlish laughter and footsteps on loose floorboards.

Alice appeared in a black velvet gown with lace at the neck carrying a bottle, two glasses and a pitcher of water. "Welcome to my hotel," she said, setting them down and sitting on the arm of the chair opposite. "I am sure we can offer you amusement."

"Thank you," said Fitz. An inner voice told him to run, but carnal pleasure held him.

Alice waited for him to open the bottle and pour a drink. She accepted one herself, then, allowing him barely time for a sip, stood and invited him to follow through a door into a long corridor. Along each side were rooms with most of the doors open, a girl standing at each, smiling, grinning, or laughing, some beckoning—one of every hair shade, two striking mulattos, and another dark girl in Indian dress. "Just step in wherevah you please," Alice crooned, attempting a local accent.

Nothing tempted him, though one Negro woman struck him as wicked. He grinned back, unready for experiment. At next to the last, he stopped before a small, well-made blonde in black tights, bodice pushing up provocative breasts. Her smile looked like Maeve's.

"Here. I would just like to talk, here."

"Yes, this is Flame," said Alice. "May I send you champagne?"

"No," said Fitz then changed his mind. "All right." He hastened in, as Alice closed the door.

"Flame?" grinned Fitz. "You look like someone I know."

"Perhaps," said the girl, "because I am someone you know." It was Sigurd.

Astonished, he sat on a sofa along the wall opposite a low double bed. She sat beside him. "Flame is my professional name, you know, like 'Maizie.'" She took his hand in both of hers.

Hearing her voice, Fitz stopped and fell back against the cushions. "Maeve won't marry me," he said. "I don't know what to do."

"Don't worry, colonel," she said putting a hand on his knee. "You can always come see me, and I will not betray your secret." Her grin looked more like Maeve than he remembered.

"Why?" he asked. "Why did you leave her?"

"The same reason you're here, colonel." She giggled. "The farm was boring. I like meeting men, and no one tells me how to behave."

Her laugh ran on softly as she appraised him.

Fitz took one of her hands and held it, looking down at her bare legs. Her laugh seemed forced, and she probably wasn't going to tell him the truth, yet he felt he could talk to her. They drank wine, and spoke for nearly an hour. At the end he felt calm enough to leave, ride home, and sleep. It was probably unusual just to walk out, but he felt good about it. Kissing Sigurd on the cheek, he paid for her time and left.

Josephus had dreamed of buying Ashburn Farm since he came back to life at Gettysburg. His mother told him of the huge, sprawling oaks with limbs drooping moss on hills rolling to the water, of the rich smell of the soil and the sea air, and cool ocean breezes. For years no owner lived at Ashburn. The overseers were cruel, and his mother was glad to come to the Alexanders. Still she spoke fondly of the place. It was not a large spread, but plenty for his two score people.

He hadn't expected General Gordon in Brunswick, nor Rebel veterans riding out to harass Negro settlements. "Keep 'em in line," was the phrase heard in town. Raiders came at night without warning, wearing kerchiefs over their faces. They carried torches, burned buildings, fired shots in the air, and sounded Rebel yells. They had hurt no one, but they threatened to, and Josephus knew the cotton gin would be a target. It had to be because he planned it to take the harvest from other Negroes' farms—to gin out their beautiful cotton and make them all as prosperous as whites.

Women from Brunswick households heard the complaints. Townsfolk said "niggers got no business taking white man's position. Bad enough we lose our slaves. The Yankees set 'em up like lords of the manor." A few Unionist families spoke against the malcontents, but they were few.

Josephus felt angry eyes on him when he came over to buy supplies. He tried to teach young people about white anger. "Freedom is not a gift. We may think the end of the war gives us everything, but we must stand up for ourselves. In time they'll accept us." He was confident.

Gordon and his mill hands would be the center of hostility.

Thirty men worked for him. All had horses, not the usual property of mill hands. Josephus was sure they had guns, in spite of federal authorities. At the farm he had three Springfield rifles and two horses—not much, but properly used enough to hold off marauders until help came. He posted night guards with a spare man sleeping in a hut near enough to hear an alarm and far enough away to get quickly down to the end of the island where Union soldiers held a lonely post. Lieutenant Rothwell knew about the tension.

The gin was important to all Negroes on the offshore islands, and Josephus thought about asking for soldiers. But he knew troops would be only a temporary help. They might encourage the bad folk to bring on reinforcements.

"Men like Gordon's don't stay in one place for long," he told his people. "They'll leave after awhile. We must deal with them. And we will be stronger."

At the sawmill off Bay street Toddy Bates lived in a new pineboard bunkhouse. He didn't like being called out to the farm for drills. The war was over. Some of the others were cavalrymen and could do trick stuff, make their mounts dance on hind legs while they shot dead accurate from the saddle. Toddy could barely hang onto his horse. When he was lucky, he stayed at the mill.

Work was not hard, though they shipped a lot of lumber, and the hours were long. It chilled him to hear the sergeant brag about, "Going out to get the nigger." He knew they meant Josephus, and probably meant to kill him. They said they would, saying how they'd make a purse out of his ball bag.

The more they talked, the more inevitable was the day. It was only a matter of time until they'd had enough liquor, someone would challenge the sergeant, and off they'd go. Toddy thought about speaking to Gordon again, but knew it would do no good, and only make trouble for himself.

In early August Gordon stood on the dock to address the men, "We're going to go fix that gin so it won't ever run, and we're gonna fix the strutting black bastard that built it." They cheered.

They'd been given orders. Toddy thought about warning Mr. Josephus, and reasoned against it. *He knows what's happening as well as anyone. He was the smartest nigger in seven counties. And if I got caught I'd lose my job. Gotta keep earnin' wages for ma's sake.*

Island cotton was ready near harvest. Gordon calculated "Fire would ruin the gin machinery, and the Negroes, once run off, would not have the stomach to rebuild it."

It took several days secretly to ferry a dozen horses to friends on the island. Men left in groups of two or three. They were ready. A half-dozen stayed conspicuously in town to support a story that none of Gordon's men had come near Ashburn. Both in Brunswick and on the island the men spent the early hours of the night drinking.

The general stayed behind, but sent Toddy with them. "This young 'un knows a few things, sergeant," he nodded at Bates. "Can't ride worth a hoot, but he may help. Remember now, I want that gin burned down. Nobody will fault us for that. Don't shoot anybody if you can help it."

"What about the head nigger?"

"I'll leave that to you," said Gordon.

Toddy remembered he didn't say not to kill Josephus. His heart was in his mouth, and he almost spoke, but the men were too stirred up. In any case, no one ever corrected the general.

They arrived in a small boat in the dark, landing where they saw a signal light at a dock up from the village. After midnight eleven men rode toward Ashburn through a hot night with no moon. "Gin'ril's smart," said the sergeant. "He knew it'd be black as pitch out here."

They met a lookout a mile from the farm. He said all was quiet. The sergeant ordered four men to go around west of the big house and start a fire in the cotton. They had rags and coal oil, and promised to have a fair blaze going in a half-hour.

"Now, young 'un, you put on a kerchief like the rest of us." The sergeant pulled a kerchief over the lower half of his face. A man broke out a Confederate battle flag. "We're stayin' away from the house," said the sergeant. "We don' wanna be spotted 'til we get things lit up. The fire in the fields 'll draw 'em off, but they'll be headin' our way fast when they see the gin's on fire."

"D'ya spose, sarge, they got rifles?" a man asked.

"Oh, I wouldn't be surprised to see a pistol or sumthin', but none of the niggers had any trainin.' We known that much."

A fire roared in the west fields on cue, and they followed the lookout toward the gin. Toddy rode beside the sergeant, wishing it were over. It felt like the first day at Gettysburg, and he prayed someone could send him to the rear.

When they got to the gin and lit their torches, they saw Josephus standing before the gin, a much younger man by his side aiming a rifle. "Git outa the way, nigger," yelled the sergeant. "Jes' git, while we burn your gin here, an nobody's gonna git hurt."

"You are on private property," said Josephus. "I suggest you take these men off, and, as you say, no one will get hurt."

The sergeant signaled a halt. A standoff appeared for a moment, when he raised his whip, "Damn yer impert'nance," he shouted, and charged at Josephus. A shot rang out from the dark beside the gin as Josephus and his mate went for cover. The sergeant fell from his horse and struggled to remount. Gordon's men raised carbines and fired at the men they could see—Josephus and his partner—hitting both. The younger man scrambled under the foundation posts out of sight. Shots came from the woods at the side, and from the gin. Two Gordon men fell.

Toddy decided the fight was over and turned his horse along with some others. The remaining men cursed them, calling on them to stand and fight, until one was hit and fell. At that they all went off in disorder. Galloping away, Toddy decided he'd had enough of General Gordon, hung back, separated, and picked his way toward the Yankee outpost.

The fire burned in the cotton for an hour before it went out. At the plantation one man had a superficial wound, but Josephus lay in the dust by his gin.

★ ★ ★

Book Three

THE WAGES OF PEACE

★ ★ ★

After the end of hostilities, the illustrated press abandons images of war for such lustrous scenes as the White House portico before a soiree.

The President & Mrs. Lincoln

request the honor of

General & Mrs. George Meade's

company at dinner on

Easter Sunday April 16th at 7 o'clock

An early answer is requested.

CHAPTER XXI

Meade stared out the War Office windows across the muddy street through a light summer rain at the White House, where a few minutes before Lincoln had offered him the Vice Presidency, and the eventual Presidency of the United States, on a silver salver. "General, you will succeed as a matter of nature taking her course," he said. "That's what the public wants, nay, demands. And it will free you a mite from partisan back-biting along the way."

Almost without thinking, he refused, saying he'd reached his life's ambition as Commanding General. "A sound military man, Mr. President, does not favor mixing the army into politics."

Lincoln, fingered his beard and grinned. "Oh, that all generals felt the same. Sadly, sir, they do not. The Democrats will nominate McClellan, and Mrs. Grant has ambitions one hears about, though I couldn't guess by looking at her."

The President knew he disliked Grant's ambition and had a perverse way of playing on it. Lincoln might be toying with him. He was firm. "I have no desire to sit all day facing an empty Senate."

"Or empty senators," Lincoln laughed.

That had been the end of it, and Meade wondered whether he did right. For all his denials he believed he must become President, if only to please Margaretta. *She thinks no other job suitable. But meanwhile no place is better than where I am. I have respect, men around me I trust, and I do fairly what I please.*

He smiled. These were not the thoughts of the science-inclined surveyor and family man of 1860. Success was corrupting him— and, much as he hated politics, the conquered South fascinated him. Perhaps it was his grandfathers' tie with the slave trade, or his sisters' marriages to Hugers of South Carolina and Ingrahams of Mississippi. His own daughter was married to the son of the man who proclaimed Virginia's secession, the final act that assured war. His mind wandered. Many from Philadelphia had links to the South and its "peculiar institution." These connections were now painful. Meade tried to befriend his relatives, sending money—a small adjunct to Lincoln's policy of charity. *But they murdered Josephus! At the hands of a Rebel general. Gordon is no career man, nor all that much a gentleman as far as anyone knows. Probably an opportunist with a war record trying to build power. That's what Sharpe thinks.*

And now comes Sickles to take advantage from the thing. He's put dozens in the local jailhouse. Meade smirked. *One budding politician at the mercy of another.* He pictured an imperial Sickles stumping down the gangplank of a Union gunboat, taking charge with a regiment at his back, the Radicals cheering him on like an avenging angel.

A knock preceded Hardie's soft tread coming to announce Senator Van Huysen of Delaware, a Democrat become a particular friend of Margaretta. "I surmise, gin'ril, he's here to talk about the Gordon affair."

The soft burr delighted Meade as Hardie dragged "affay—iir—ir" into three syllables. *Why doesn't someone come about the "Josephus Alexander affay-iir-ir?"* he mused, and answered himself immediately—*Because few care, or even know, the Negroes lost a champion they can't replace.*

Van Huysen, all smiles, greeted Meade effusively, asking about Margaretta, and shaking hands as though he wanted to dispense with preliminaries as soon as possible. "I've come to talk about conditions in the South, general. I have a letter from Alexander Stephens, a former colleague who, as you doubtless know, served the Confederacy, though he opposed secession. He is a force in Georgia. Therefore, I listen to what he says."

"I see," said Meade and, wary of getting too close to a copperhead, did not reach for the letter Van Huysen held out. *Should I remind him that Stephens was the Confederacy's Vice President who said slavery was its cornerstone? Surely he knows.* He waved the senator to a chair.

"This may seem untimely, sir." Van Huysen was smooth. "But a number of us are concerned about the behavior of our Occupation

Forces. General Sickles has put prominent men in jail, and in Savannah John Brown Gordon sits in prison, held *incommunicado* without even the benefit of counsel. I wonder if this is Mr. Lincoln's policy of a generous peace?" *How does he say all this with that benign smile? Politics is always a puzzle.*

"General Sickles acted for the safety of Negro settlements financed by the Federal Government, and to put down bushwhackers who have fought the peace ever since the war ended." Meade decided to teach him the realities of military government. "We find it hard to be generous to an armed and treacherous enemy." He waited until he was sure the senator was about to speak. "According to many reports, and not just from General Sickles, Gordon planned a local insurrection. We don't provide counsel to prisoners of war."

Van Huysen stifled his rejoinder, if he had one. "I am sure you know best, general. And in broad outline we all approve of the President's policies. I shall not defend traitors, though I fear that misunderstanding over General Gordon may cost Mr. Lincoln support he may need should Southern voters divide inexorably along lines of race. Our Republican friends court the expected Negro vote, and they goad General Sickles. Of that we are certain."

How much of the "we" is "I," and exactly who are his allies. . . . How deep is his good will toward Lincoln? . . . I won't defend Sickles's rushing in like a mad bull and making an enemy of every white in Georgia. . . . Fitzpatrick says Gordon is a cause célèbre. He's their champion, and Sickles has contributed mightily to their opinion. . . . Damned fool! I ought never have accepted him. Meade held his face taut as if at a review, unwilling to share his least thought. "I understand your concern, senator. The case of General Gordon must not be allowed to undo the President's policies. But you should be aware that the man killed was the very person who brought me victory at Gettysburg. There is little doubt Gordon's men shot Josephus Alexander." He took time to watch the senator control himself.

"I have dispatched General Sharpe, a fine lawyer, to investigate. The evidence strongly supports the case, including eye witnesses." Meade stopped. Perhaps he'd said too much.

"Negro witnesses?" asked the senator dubiously.

"Both black and white, senator." Meade caught himself. *Must pro-*

tect the white man.

The senator shifted on the edge of a low leather chair. "I'm not here to give you worry, sir. I only come to tell you of conditions from, let us say, another point of view. As a politician, I am a realist. Peace in the South with Negroes becoming the equal of their former masters will be most difficult to achieve."

The man's voice was steady, and he seemed to offer a strange good will. *But with what condition? I wish I had Lincoln's skill.* "I accept what you say, senator. This is a hard business, and I am guided by the President, whose abilities I frankly admire." He was being partisan, but perhaps it would clear the air.

"Oh, General Meade, I quite understand," said Van Huysen, now singing in the same key. "I for one have no great faith in my party's candidate to resolve the peace question. I would much prefer we in Delaware had joined the National Union to support Mr. Lincoln. But we were a slave state until recently, though not much dedicated to the institution I'm happy to say."

"Thank you for your honesty," said Meade, wondering what he meant by it. "I speak of the President strictly in my official capacity. I don't comment on General McClellan, under whom I once served. My view is that military professionals do better to leave politics to the politicians."

"I appreciate your sentiments," said the senator, smiling broadly and holding his hat ready to rise and leave. "Yet I rather hope in time you will change your opinion. In a few years our party would be more than happy if you did." His smile broadened.

There it was again, an invitation to talk about my future. It pops up every time I meet a member of Congress. What are they looking for? Their own preferment? . . . Probably. He let time pass without speaking or changing his expression, another commander's skill applied to politics. Nonresponse seemed to work, much as he hated incivility. "I have enough on my desk at the moment. I take note of your concerns, senator, and think it best we leave it at that." He smiled.

Van Huysen rose, grinning. "If you ever change your mind, general, I can assure you the number of grateful men will be legion."

The railway into Brunswick needed repair. In wartime the

Confederates took the rolling stock and even took up some of the rails for lines nearer the fight. Now the workforce had fled. A few sad men stood by the track as the train passed. Fitz wondered whether they had once worked on the line, and whether they would work again for wages, as free labor. Tension was high. The Gordon affair stirred up the planters and scared the bankers, and that was nothing compared to the fright it gave the black folk. As his father would say, the financial climate had gone to Hell.

No one wanted to take risk, though cotton prices were higher than ever. Henry Prediger had gone to take Josephus' place at the farm. Fitz encouraged him. *Worth my loss to make the effort succeed. Every Negro seems to know about the St. Simon's experiment, and watches to see whether whites will let it work. If Prediger restores confidence and gets the cotton to market, he'll prove families can make a living on their own lands.*

A stretch of open water came into view on the right as the train lurched into rail yards past empty cars standing by decks of lumber. The mills stood still and empty. Woodsmoke mingled with the odor of turpentine and the faint warm scent of the ocean. Fitz felt the languor of the seaside under a bright wide sky.

At the terminus soldiers in blue stood guard while others worked as yardmen, and a fat corporal whose stomach hung over his belt paced the platform trying to be the stationmaster. The building was weathered over years of neglect.

A soldier greeted him as he stepped down and led him to the large brick house Sickles made his headquarters. Fitz hadn't seen him since Gettysburg. Both were in constant motion. Fitz visited farms and bank branches. The general's absences were undefined, but in the looseness of military occupation no one, least of all Sickles, felt accountable for his whereabouts. It was rumored he frequently went over to the Mississippi to see Grant. Fitz wondered why Meade didn't tighten up.

Sickles sat in glory reminiscent of the 3d Corps, shouting orders, and keeping a room full of Negro petitioners and white townsfolk waiting on his favor. Animated as ever, he seemed determined to ignore the heat. Except for wincing when he banged his leg against a table by mistake, he seemed to feel no ill effects of losing it.

"Colonel," he bellowed loud enough for the entire building to hear, "We are honored by the man who took Lee and Longstreet. By God, Fitzpatrick, you've aged a bit."

The camaraderie of battle was beguiling, but Fitz was on guard, glad he'd chosen a dark business suit and neither the military uniform of a subordinate nor the light linens preferred by planters. "I'm a banker now, and must try to be serious." He grinned. Crossing swords again with Sickles roused him, and for a few minutes they reminisced—Meade, Historicus, politics just beneath the surface.

Yet for all the tension, they had a common interest. Fitz had no doubt about punishing Gordon and his men. White borrowers might complain, but they wanted order too. And Josephus's plan had to succeed, or former slaves wouldn't work their farms. "I'm here to protect our investment," he said at length. "I'd be obliged for the soonest transport out to the island."

"Done!" said Sickles, faster than good hospitality might suggest. "I'll send you off on the afternoon steamer. You can put up with Captain Rothwell, our commander over there. I'll scribble him a note." The general reached for pen and paper. "He's a decent sort. Don't know what kind of a mess he has."

"I'm going to stay with Prediger." He paused for Sickles to take in the idea.

"Not bad," said the general with a puckered grin. "But a bit dramatic don't you think? I mean, we want the darkies' support, but we don't have to live with 'em, do we? What will you eat? They don't like the same things we do. And what about the bugs? A white man gets fever, and there's a helluva lot of snakes in the brush."

Fitz grinned. "The war seasoned me, general. I can manage, and have done before. Black folk always do the cooking in the South. Some of it's pretty good."

Sickles winced. "Not always to my taste, okra and greens. I'll miss you at my table. There's something I must ask you." He shifted uneasily, scraping his wooden leg on the floor, and motioned to Fitz to shut the louvered door. He continued in a lower tone. "You knew this man Josephus, I gather, and of course you know Henry Prediger?"

Fitz nodded, wondering whether Sickles's leg ached.

"In Gettysburg did you meet a young Reb prisoner by the name of Bates?"

Fitz answered slowly. "I met a lad from Tennessee by that name who worked in the house where they put Josephus. A very young, obliging boy, not a man, a boy though he was in Lee's final charge."

"That's the one," said Sickles. "He's our chief witness. Says he was there when our man was killed, and knows who did it. Do you think he's honest? Or is he just saying all this to save his skin?"

"I've no way of knowing," said Fitz. "It's hard to understand how he got involved with Gordon. He didn't serve under him, did he?" He paused, then brightened. "Bates struck me as a decent young fellow who'd scarcely grown up. I'd have to say, though, any youngster who held his place in that charge up Cemetery Ridge wouldn't be such a coward as to lie to save his skin, especially if it meant death to a Rebel general."

"Good," said Sickles, striking the desk with his fist. "That's exactly what I think. Your friend Sharpe thinks the same."

☆ ☆

Fitz could not understand how Prediger knew exactly when he was coming, yet there he was on the dock, waving. He must have had lookouts. Everyone is a little scared, I'd guess. No one knows where this trouble comes from. The more frightened the blacks are, the more the whites intimidate them. Henry needs help.

"Colonel Fitzpatrick," shouted Prediger as the boat docked. "Welcome!"

Fitz waved. A score of Negroes, surrounding a few glum whites, waved excitedly. Two soldiers with rifles stood guard.

Captain Rothwell appeared. "We have a wig-wag across the channel," he chirped. "The darkies started coming to the dock the minute we got news you were on board. They think you've come to save the plantation."

Fitz smiled. What could he say? Josephus's plan was a long shot even when he was alive. Sea Island cotton hadn't turned a really good profit in years, and no white planter he'd met thought Negroes could get it to market without white help, much less run a steam gin. Still, he had to encourage them. Henry's bright face gave hope.

"With this man in charge," Fitz said, pointing, "things should work out." He grabbed Prediger's outstretched hand in both of his own. "It's good to see you, Henry. I'd like to go out to the place before it gets dark."

Prediger nodded agreement, and, after a farewell to the uncomprehending Rothwell and a raucous send-off from the crowd, they found horses and hurried away.

By now Fitzpatrick had seen hundreds of farms owned by former slaves. Most, only a few acres, but some were big enough to rival the old plantations. Every one had more people living on it than listed in the loan papers. Men and women without other prospects hung about as occasional labor. Fitz was not surprised to find twice the number Josephus had planned for. Many were old, crippled, and incapable.

"We have to take them," said Prediger as they sat on the verandah of a decrepit plantation house. "They have no place to go. We pay some, when we can. Right now it's all right. When we sell the cotton, we're going to make some money. Handing it out is gonna be the problem. Thank God we're on an island."

Fitz frowned. "Then you have a crop? I thought it was burned."

Henry grinned. "No, the newspapers missed some important facts. We lost very little. We'll have thirty-three bales. Not too bad, if you can help us sell it. Mr. Josephus had a dock built so we can ship it right out North. We don't have to send it to Savannah."

Fitz calculated. Anxious buyers from Rhode Island were paying more than $300 a bale in Savannah. Some were under investigation for trading with blockade runners, and would be only too glad to have the Ashburn cotton straight off the dock, if the government would let up on them. The farm might take in nearly $10,000, Fitz calculated, as much as the mortgage.

"How are you going to handle the money?" Fitz asked carefully.

"Josephus had it worked out," said Prediger. "Half is set aside for debt and capital. The rest is distributed. They should get maybe $150 each, after selling costs. Maybe it's not a whole lot, but it's more than they've ever seen. Some will waste it, but nobody's gonna starve. We have animals and a good corn crop in the barn.

"The problem is next year. We haven't got enough seed, and I don't know where we're gonna get it. Some talk about going into rice, but nobody wants that dirty work, and we don't have the capital. Our hope is the gin, taking fees from others who bring their cotton. That should make the difference."

"Do you think that's why they tried to burn it?" asked Fitz.

Henry took off his black broad-brimmed hat, and used it to swat flies. "These darn bugs bother me. I'm not used to the South," he laughed, and turned serious. "I don't think white folk know anything about how we think. As best I can determine, they think we've got no business owning machines. I don't know why not. We've been workin' 'em for years. But there you are. They just don't think we're good enough." He spat over the edge.

Fitz could feel the anger. "Well, Henry, you'll prove them wrong. He stared off over the fields in the late afternoon light. "That's what you're here for."

He was glad Henry changed the subject to hiring a school teacher, someone who might be their preacher as well. What he thought, but didn't say, was that the island people had to learn a lot of things fast, before white people convinced them they were too dumb to succeed.

In early September Savannah was almost as lively as before the war when cotton was high and money was free. Crowds gathered daily under the canopy of oaks in the square before the Court House, where the Yankees held Gordon. The soldiers permitted a few visitors each day in a concession made, people said, on orders from Washington City. No one knew yet how the trial would be held—a federal court surely, but would it be military or civilian? And would there be a jury? Murder, and conspiracy to commit it, were hanging offenses. The citizens were outraged that the Yankees might deny the general his constitutional rights.

Returning from Brunswick, Sickles called for reinforcements. Yankee regiments camped again in the cemetery they'd vacated six months before. They slept in the tombs and built fires on headstones, smashing up a good number, so reports went. Sickles published an order demanding his men respect the dead, which, Savannians joked, got as much respect as the graves.

In the square a dapper short-legged man moved from group to group listening, occasionally adding a touch of humor or, more often, a telling jab at Yankee barbarity. Wilkes Booth appeared nightly at the better watering holes and stood drinks. He had no particular business in town until some of the ladies persuaded him to hold readings in their homes.

On one evening he met the military governor in the house of a former blockade runner who kept his history quiet enough to win Yankee contracts. Booth and Sickles drank together and found much in common. Sickles spoke of his great admiration for Grant, and contempt for the "haughty" Meade. Booth knew little of Grant and kept silent on him, but joined roundly in condemning Meade and "upstage Philadelphians."

When they met again he told Sickles, "I want to know how a man like Gordon thinks. The mind of the conspirator is good fare for 'the Thespian.'" At last Booth got what he was after, a pass to visit the general.

Gordon expected him. His wife had spoken of him. Booth sought her out at his readings. He flattered her with special attention and sought her trust. A large number of Southerners were collecting funds for Gordon's defense. The help was needed. Booth, she told her husband, could raise money.

The guards allowed him a half hour. He entertained Gordon with comedy routines from his early days as an itinerant actor. Gordon, a strong church man, seemed to care little for low humor but passed over it good naturedly, finally asking, "Have you a purpose in seeking me out?"

"I do," said Booth. "You know that many of us are behind you. We will avenge you. We want you to know whatever happens that the spirit of the Confederacy will not die."

"No," said Gordon, puzzled. "I don't think it will. But I can't do much about it sitting in jail."

"Of course not. We're going get you free," Booth reassured him, and winked. Shortly afterward the guard came to the cell and ordered him to leave.

Gordon was perplexed by Booth's visit and tried to remember what he had said about vengeance and being avenged. The general shuddered. Dying in battle was glorious, but he had no interest in martyrdom.

★ ★

Gordon's trial was delayed while Meade and others in Washington City debated how to conduct it. Sickles reported the government's case ready in the second week of September, and urged haste. He was concerned about the safety of his white witness and about seething resentment in Savannah.

Sickles's worries were not so great as to keep him from a week's trip via the Central of Georgia and the Memphis and Charleston Railroads to meet Grant on the Mississippi. Lincoln's re-election, he told his fellow hero, was assured. McClellan would win a border state or two. None of the Confederate states eligible to vote would fall to him because of their large Negro franchise and because most Rebels were ineligible to vote.

"We must look forward to 1868," he told Grant, sitting in the narrow saloon of the *Wapsipinicon,* a side-wheeler Grant used to tour his huge domain. "And I'll wager a barrel of the best Kentucky whiskey the Democrats get Meade to be their candidate. He's a doughface at heart like the rest of his family, and the Democrats are already courting him. They know this one's lost, and they look to the future. With Mrs. Meade's aristocratic attitudes and his Southern relatives, they'll win him. That means, general, you run against Meade, and you'll win."

Grant wondered aloud at Sickles's certainty. They could agree, he said, that the Republican nomination was the only one worth having. "As a man of the West, I might be able to get it."

"You will carry every state west of the Alleghenies," said Sickles. "The veterans' organizations are forging strong links with Lincoln's party."

"I can see how that might work out," Grant said thoughtfully. "But the party has few resources in the East outside New England, and that's not enough."

"You have Commodore Vanderbilt and his friends," Sickles crooned. "New England abolitionists will give you six states. And the South depends on how many Negroes vote. They will be the key to your victory."

"But how many will get the franchise?" Grant looked at the ship's rug. A tumbler of water sat in front of him. Sickles took whiskey.

Grant did not. The cabin was hot, and he loosened his collar, running his index finger underneath around his neck.

Sickles looked away, out the cabin door toward the stern. "Leave the Negro vote to Thad Stevens and the Radicals. They'll push Lincoln into it. He wants to go that way himself. By '68 the darkies will vote in every state in the South, and the Republicans will carry them."

"I don't like going behind Meade's back," Grant scowled. "It hurts the army." He looked hard at Sickles. "Does he know you're out here?"

Sickles raised a hand in denial. "In Savannah they think I'm in Birmingham. In Birmingham, they think I'm up in Tennessee, and in Tennessee they think I'm in Savannah, which I will be soon after the next train leaves Memphis."

"Then we'd better send you back down river," said Grant with a smile. He liked Sickles well enough, but the growing number of people who came to talk about politics was a bother. Perhaps he ought to find some reason to talk to Meade. *He can't be happy about all this. Why can't they let time deal with these matters?* Grant smiled at Sickles. He admired the man's courage, though his insolence wasn't to his taste. *Still, he'll be loyal,* Grant thought. *His hatred of Meade guarantees that, and he may turn out to be the best weapon I've got in the East. I just wish he wouldn't go to shooting his guns before the enemy gets on the field.*

☆ ☆

Returning to Richmond Fitz found a chatty letter from Maeve telling him she was back from Europe, feeling "much educated," even struggling at last through a bit of French. She looked forward to work in the settlement house. He was delighted to see her hand again, though the feeling was momentary.

The thought that she would never have him, that he would never make love to her again, stuck like a knot in his brain. It stopped him short at odd moments when everything else was going well, when he was enjoying his work and the rest of life very much. He would think of her and turn sad. Hostesses would ask him about it, and young women would try to comfort him.

He was a disturbed man. He took long rides through the city at all hours, and on fine days out into the country to look at battlefields around the Chickahominy and as far as Petersburg. At night he stayed late at the mess, sometimes drinking so much he couldn't remember the ride home.

One evening late in September he stopped at Alice's hotel, and again went through the ritual of walking past the women in their perfumed little rooms. Another mulatta, flicking her smiling tongue around the tips of large white teeth, nearly trapped him before he got to Sigurd. He persevered, telling himself he must give her news of Maeve.

He told her Maeve was back in Philadelphia and offered to arrange for her to visit her sister. She scoffed. She seemed slightly wild and kept pushing her bosom towards him. "La, with all her good works I don't think she'd want to see me now. And anyway," she turned her pretty chin in a pout. "What would I be doing in Philadelphia when all the handsome men are here?" She put her hand on his shoulder, moved toward him and planted her mouth on his. Her tongue penetrated, and for a moment Fitz lost track of where he was. Her body began to writhe on top of him, and she fumbled with his clothes.

Finally, in what seemed like a supreme act of will, he pushed her away. "I'm not here for that," he said, glaring at her.

She recoiled, and smiled willfully. "Then, for God's sake, why are you here? You're a man. I can feel you."

The coarse reference tipped the scales in his fuddled mind. He stood up, fumbled for money, threw ten dollars on the settee, called for his cape, and left.

Alice was in the room in a trice. Sigurd, tipsy from champagne, had a skewed smile on her face.

"Don't worry, honey." Alice put a black velveteen arm around her neck. "He'll be back, and you'll have him." She smiled and chucked her chin. "We'll both have him."

CHAPTER XXII

Fitzpatrick enjoyed the rail trips to the mouth of Acquia Creek, then onward via the slow steamer up the Potomac to Washington. The decks were crowded with military men and their families going back and forth. Though he seldom wore a uniform, many recognized him and bowed or saluted. Traffic between Richmond and the capital had grown tenfold. Soon rails would punch through the forest directly connecting the cities. River travel would be abandoned. Fitz reflected on progress. The war had changed the face of everything.

Meade was glad to see his protégé, and anxious to hear news of the South, of the progress of the occupation, about families he knew, about the pioneering effort to get Negroes onto their own land, and particularly about the trial. "I don't understand," he said, as they sat in his office by the cold iron fireplace, "why Sickles presses so hard. Surely, Gordon has his rights no matter what he's done.

"Both Stanton and the Attorney General worry about constitutional procedures. There's no avoiding a military commission, of course, but that doesn't mean Gordon won't have the right to appeal, to the Supreme Court if necessary. If Sickles jumps the gun at any point, and the South thinks at all Gordon has been hijacked, hotheads will stir up trouble everywhere. They'll never forgive us. It will be worse than any wartime atrocity."

"Well," said Fitz with a sigh. "You know Dan Sickles loves attention. If I were John Gordon, I wouldn't want my life in his hands." He paused as if he had prepared something to say. "Perhaps, general, it might be wise to replace Sickles. He's been insubordinate with his trips over to see Grant. All the world knows he's scheming against you."

Meade turned to stare out the window. Fitzpatrick was one of the few, beside Margaretta, he allowed to speak so frankly. "No! It would be petty of me to dismiss him on suspicion of plotting about something four years hence. I'd be no better than he." Meade brightened. "I've got Sharpe down there keeping an eye on things. Perhaps I should put the case entirely in his hands." He pulled his hand over his nose, a gesture he'd picked up from Lincoln.

"Grant, on the other hand is an honest fellow. He may want the Republican nomination. He's not alone, and that's his business. But I have no cause for complaint. He's handled the Mexican border beautifully, and the states under him do as well as mine. Lincoln thinks the world of him."

Fitz wondered at Meade's calm. Men conspired all around him, and he didn't notice. Even Lincoln's preference for Westerners worked against him. Fitz made a silent vow to defend his well-beloved boss against his own innocence. He smiled. "General Hancock plans to visit Robert E. Lee soon. Perhaps the old man might help."

"Good idea, Fitzpatrick! I'll ask Win to sound him out. Lee might write his former officers to urge calm. Southern politics right now hinge on the views of the Confederate officer corps." Meade smiled. The mention of his former enemy seemed to cheer him.

★ ★

The trial opened in early October before a seven-man commission of Union officers. Sharpe had found no way to reconcile the code of military justice with the constitutional requirement for trial by jury. He rejected a proposal to impanel one, since the most it could do was to recommend a verdict. The decision lay with the officers of the commission.

The chairman, a brigadier from southern Indiana, was adamant. "The regulations," he argued, "require a jury to include Negroes. That would be a travesty of justice, and would inflame the South more than none at all."

At the opening Mr. Cuyler Rutledge raised a strong objection, citing the general's constitutional right to trial by jury. The chairman overruled him, handing down as his opinion *verbatim* a statement sent from the War Office. "The trial will proceed before the commission," he read, "under the laws of the United States, taking in view the fact that civil jurisdiction is not re-established in the state of Georgia." He passed over the fact that Gordon, a former Confederate officer, had not been restored to his rights as a citizen.

The Federal Government charged John Brown Gordon with conspiracy to commit murder on a "person under the protection of the U.S. Army, namely, Mr. Josephus Alexander of St. Simon's Island." Sharpe had convinced the commission to drop the incendiary charge of treason and insurrection by arguing that conspiracy to commit murder was itself a hanging offense.

The members, from the junior captain to the general, were lawyers. Three commanded infantry units in the war, and one, a major, fought under Howard against Gordon's brigade at Gettysburg. The chairman did not think he need stand aside.

Cuyler Rutledge was a 55-year-old Savannah lawyer with excellent family and no military experience. He knew nothing about the members of the commission, nor did he try to learn. He told friends confidently that, since the men on the commission were not from Georgia, they could in no way be the general's peers.

Gordon stood in a separate box guarded by two sentries. Disorganized thoughts went through his brain. *This Yankee court can't render justice. Rutledge is absolutely correct to insist on my rights. My best hope lies in appeal to the Supreme Court . . . The commissioners have no evidence of conspiracy. I specifically told my men not to kill anyone. . . .*

Booth worries me. Too much talk about vengeance. Justice is what we need. Sometimes I think he wants me hanged so he can enflame everyone. . . .

I don't like that chairman. He doesn't know anything about us . . . At least there're no niggers on the panel. He's smart enough to avoid that . . . Why do I have so little to say? I read law like he did. Rutledge acts as though I know nothing about it.

In opening arguments the prosecutor, a junior colleague of Sharpe, told the commission he had two eyewitnesses "to the murder of Mr. Josephus . . . and also to the criminal conversation between John Gordon and the men who committed this evil act. The latter men will be tried separately, and one, as we shall show, has confessed to his acts. . . . The government will present evidence both from associates of Mr. Alexander and from men riding out to

Ashburn farm under orders from General Gordon."

Gordon's face did not change. He had heard one of his men had turned, but was convinced he couldn't tie him to the killing. Rutledge had witnesses to testify that the niggers fired first. *That ought to be enough in the State of Georgia, but in this crazy world the Yankees have made I can't be sure. The sergeant says it was a fair fight. I couldn't possibly be involved.* Gordon wracked his brain to remember what he had said when he sent the men off to Ashburn. *I told 'em not to hurt anybody. I'm sure I did.*

☆ ☆

Win Hancock gained weight during his long recovery. At the crest of the charge on Cemetery Ridge a bullet struck his saddle and drove splinters into his groin. He ordered his men not to carry him away so he could watch the counterattack, but lost consciousness before Meade gave the command. Hancock's brilliant career came to a quick end, and he saw no more fighting. Healing took time. Splinters emerged one at a time over weeks and months. As he waited, unable to exercise, his girth began to grow. He could mount a fast horse again, but it had to be stouter and stronger.

A long ride beside the lines of the defunct York River Railroad out to White House Plantation on a soft fall day was an effort. But he looked forward to meeting Bobby Lee, who never came to Richmond. Southern hotheads blamed him for defeat. Ten months after the war, newspapers continued to castigate him, though the men Hancock met in town, Ewell, Hood, and others, revered "the old man." Even Longstreet, they said, respected him. Only that fool Pickett went on about "the charge."

Win Hancock thought Lee's final attack was a glorious thing. He wouldn't have ordered it himself, yet he admired its discipline and spirit. Only a leader like Lee could get men to move like that.

An old Negro in a faded coat that must once have been his livery took his horse, as he dismounted before the sagging porch. Though the house had been spared by order of McClellan and then Meade, years of neglect had taken a toll; its paint was flaking and its shutters awry

Hancock barely reached the first step before Lee stood above him, white beard, gray coat and black cravat, bidding him with a benign smile come meet his wife. He was courteous and affable, pleased to meet a peer from the battles.

The war was over, and for both men it had been a better time. They sat in the parlor, talking over the Gettysburg campaign as if working through a textbook problem. They spoke with fondness of Academy men fallen and surviving, regardless of where they fought. Even the interruption of refreshments brought by another aged servant man did not stop to the flow.

Lee seemed to relish the chance to talk about Gettysburg, and no man save Meade himself was more conversant than Hancock. "I find it odd," he said. "When I first met Union officers, we talked about Mexico. That served well enough to warm conversation. Lately I find it an actual pleasure to speak about this war, how they saw it, what mistakes we made, what chances we missed."

"There were plenty of them," snorted Hancock. "I used to think war was scientific. You put men in the right places and you win." He spoke with hands on his lap in front of him. "But looking back I wonder if it wasn't all luck. I never knew where my men were, or where they were going, except in a roundabout way."

Lee smiled. "The Union always seemed to have men like that fellow Sickles who didn't like to follow orders. We had them too, but for some reason they didn't cause so much damage."

Hancock was seventeen years younger than Lee, though he had spent twenty-five years in the army. For him all history culminated in the war. Politicians like Sickles, Butler, and Garfield would use their war record as a lever to hoist themselves. He was sure a professional like Lee would condemn such behavior.

"I regret so many officers have decided to get involved in politics," he said carefully. "Both Northerners and Southern. It uselessly carries on the conflict."

"I agree," said Lee, "Yet it's unavoidable."

"General Meade has asked me to speak to you about Georgia. He fears events there might become a renewed *casus belli* if we're not careful." Hancock described the legal situation and assured Lee Gordon would have a fair trial.

"It is awkward the state government is not recognized," said Lee. "I did not know General Gordon well, though he showed promise.

He surely would have had a division, in time."

Hancock chose his words thoughtfully. Lee did not care for Lincoln's policies. Nor did he. Still, he was a realist. The result of the war meant Negroes were to be free and equal. "We're trying to keep officers out of politics, at least those on duty. The task would be a deal easier if professionals who served with you thought the same." He avoided Lee's eyes.

Lee stared at him. "And what would you have me do, General Hancock? I know you didn't ride all the way out to White House Plantation just to talk about the war, pleasant though that may be."

Hancock suggested Lee write his former officers, particularly those in Georgia, to help cool tempers before they got to the boiling point.

A long pause followed. Lee looked thoughtfully at his hands. "I doubt it would be much use," he said. "I don't know a great number of Georgians, save General Longstreet. He had several prominent men serving under him, but he would very likely ignore any request from me."

Hancock decided not to press. Lee seemed sad, as though all of his officers had left him. Hancock dropped the subject, and Lee offered to show him a fine view of the river.

☆ ☆

Gordon fought back anger when he saw Yankee officers bring out young Bates. He had forgotten about the boy, and tried to remember where he had been on the night of the raid.

"Do you solemnly swear . . . ?" The voice of the clerk sounded as Toddy stood in the box, face sober, eyes avoiding Gordon and the counsel for the defense.

The prosecutor carefully laid a trail of questions leading to the night to the raid. Bates answered with spare words. "Yes, sir" and "No, sir" were most frequent.

Gordon saw Bates was uncomfortable and decided to stare at him, dare him to tell anything but the truth of his innocence. He had done nothing to encourage the killing of the Negro.

"And were you present when the accused gave his orders to the sergeant?"

"Yessir."

"What did General Gordon tell him?"

Toddy hesitated and looked toward Gordon, this time directly. He took a deep breath. "'Remember,' he answered, 'I want that gin burned down.' And then he said, 'No one would fault us for doing that.'" He looked away from Gordon at the prosecutor.

"Is that all he said?"

"No, he said, 'Don't shoot anybody if you can help it.'"

A sigh came from the audience, and the chairman banged his gavel.

"What about Mr. Alexander? Was he mentioned?"

"Yes, the sergeant said something like 'What about the head nigger?'"

"He referred to Alexander?"

"Yessir."

"And what did the accused respond?"

"He said 'I'll leave that up to you, sergeant.'"

Noise broke the calm as men coughed and scraped their chairs. A few in low voices said, "My God!" "Well, how about that?" and "That's it." The chairman banged his gavel. Mr. Rutledge got to his feet objecting to "heeyah sa-ay." The chairman smirked, and overruled him.

Gordon scowled, taken by surprise. He hadn't remembered Bates was even present. Clearly, Rutledge was unprepared.

The prosecutor pressed. "What do you think the accused meant by that phrase, Mr. Bates?"

Gordon was tense. Here was a chance for Rutledge to intervene if the witness offered a conclusion. The defense counsel pushed his chair back ready to stand up again.

"I don't know," said Bates. "But those were his words exactly."

Rutledge remained in his seat.

The prosecutor asked about later events.

Bates said Josephus carried no gun. "He was hit, sir, trying to find cover."

"Where did the first shot come from?"

"I can't be sure. I think it was fired toward us. Our men fired back."

"And they aimed at Mr. Alexander and the man with him, even

276

though they were unarmed?"

"Yessir."

Cuyler Rutledge rose to cross-examine. Gordon silently urged him to attack. *They told him what to say, damn it. Destroy that testimony! You've got to wipe it out!*

Toddy Bates, in a slow, careful way, would not be shaken. To every attempt of Rutledge to suggest he may not have seen things as he had said, he refused to give way. Rutledge persisted through dozens of questions. He asked about Bates's relationship with Josephus Alexander, but found no opening. Finally, he turned to Bates's war record, asking about Gettysburg and what he had done there.

Gordon watched in horror. *Stop you fool. Don't you know what you're doing? You're building him up!*

"And so on the final day of the battle where were you?"

"I was with my regiment in Archer's brigade under Colonel Fry, sir."

"And did you advance to the Union lines?"

"We did, sir."

"And were you wounded?"

"No, sir"

"Were you taken prisoner up on the ridge?"

"No, sir"

"Then you ran? Didn't you?"

"I reached the wall, sir, and a Yankee had his rifle on me. He said, 'You better skeedaddle, young Reb, if you know what's good for you.' And I did." The courtroom, including officers of the commission, broke into laughter.

Gordon's scowl was later reported in the papers. None of the sympathetic reporters fathomed what he was thinking—*Not one of those wattle-bottomed men on the commission saw anything like that kind of action. Rutledge has made him a hero. Damn him!*

☆ ☆

The early morning air was damp and cold as Fitz rode up Union Hill. Deep gulps of it revived him. He had drunk a lot. *Wine only?* he wondered. The memory was vague. His coat buttons were out of order, and a cold draft pouring into his groin told him his trousers were undone. His head was clearing, but he wasn't sure where he'd been.

The next day he remembered little. The night had started at the mansion where they drank champagne. One of the senior men urged Fitz to join his crew for a little fun down in the town. Fitz went along.

Several days later when he went to see Hancock on business, a staff officer joked about their "outing." Fitzpatrick laughed and said he couldn't remember much, except he knew he'd drunk too much.

A week later he sat at dinner beside the colonel who organized the evening. "I don't remember much," Fitz offered.

"Probably as well you don't," laughed the colonel. "You weren't the gayest in the bunch, but you brightened up well enough when Alice brought her girls in."

"Did I?" said Fitz, beginning to fear the truth.

"Well, you were a stick-in-the-mud about going off with one of them. We left you alone in the lounge with that big-breasted blonde who seemed to know you. She was trying to pull you down the hall."

"Do you remember her name?" asked Fitz, feeling his way over thin ice.

"A German name, I think."

"But I stayed in the lounge, you're pretty sure."

The colonel laughed. "How do I know? Don't worry. Nobody remembers."

Vaguely now, he recalled Sigurd. She had got him down to her room. He remembered putting his nose in her curls. They smelled like Maeve's. He didn't recall details, though he had a vision of her slipping magically out of her gown. One minute, dressed, the next naked—bare, all of her. He had visualized it before, and he could not be sure he had actually seen her.

"You don' care foh the soup, Cuhn'l?" asked the waiter.

Fitz came back to the present. "No thank you, Jethro," he said and tried to talk with the major on his left about horses. It didn't take his mind off Sigurd. *She must've pulled off my clothes. That's why they were in a mess. She would know about those things. She laughed and poured champagne in my glass. I sat on the couch with my pants half off, a goblet in my hand, giggling like a kid.*

He could barely get through the meal. Fitz wanted to have that night back and change it. He had made few false steps in his life, and no longer counted his time with Maizie-Maeve as one of them. He was determined not to touch Sigurd, just to see her as a reminder of Maeve. But he had touched her, and in a drunken stupor.

Over the next days details came in a rush. Finally, he recalled the feel of her tongue coursing over him, a lascivious smile on her face. She toyed with his body, and he made no effort to stop her. The memory was pleasurable. She was so much like Maeve. The thought had struck him that, since he had done it, he might as well go back again. His flesh against hers, just like Maeve's when she was Maizie!

His member coursed inside her, and she giggled. He kissed her lips. "I knew you'd come to me," she said.

For a second day Toddy Bates resisted Cuyler Rutledge. The defense counsel tried to confuse him, suggest he'd misheard Gordon, get him to draw conclusions he might challenge. Toddy stuck to his guns, saying what he knew and no more, insisting on his version. By the time he left the box, no one doubted he had reached the crest of Cemetery Ridge.

Sharpe doubled the guards. Threats came on Toddy's food tray—"Were gonna get you. Your life ain't worth a cent." A second, said, "Yer as good as ded." All were signed by "The Order," a term meaning nothing to Yankee intelligence.

The trial went forward. Rutledge tried to prove Gordon had never given orders to kill anyone, and hence no conspiracy could exist. Members of the commission were in a strange land. The ways of the South were odd—often pleasant, at times pernicious. They knew about the threats to Bates. Conspiracy was a likely feature of the place. Rutledge seemed to come from another world.

Gordon watched in anger. Yankee officers treated Rutledge as a relic of a bygone age. His manners did not impress them, and his lack of experience disqualified him from talking about anything military. Gordon knew he'd been better off with a man out of the Confederate Army, *a lawyer like Kemper or Kershaw. There were dozens of them. Hire 'em cheap. Rutledge was an expensive mistake.*

Gordon, too, received messages on his tray and from visitors. They urged him to keep up his spirits, said they we're going to appeal to the Supreme Court. Most said, "You will be avenged!"

"I don't want to be avenged, so much as I want to be freed," he told his wife.

"But don't you see, ma darlin'? You're Sir Lancelot, riding out to destroy evil. Their champion."

"Dearest, you don't understand how fast this thing is moving. I am in the hands of Yankees who don't know where they are. All this talk of vengeance is going to get back to them, and it will only make them believe in conspiracy. It will convict me, and, by damn, I'm not guilty." Gordon stepped to the barred window of his cell to look away at the sky. It was too high for him to see the ground outside. He pointed where he knew people gathered. "These people may want Galahad chasing after some phantom. Too much damn Walter Scott! I'm no Galahad, but I am political, and I know Yankee *ultras* wouldn't mind making an example of me. For God's sake, woman! Let's not play their game. Find out who's sending these messages and tell them to stop. Tell them for John Brown Gordon, the war's over."

★ ★ ★

CHAPTER XXIII

Southerners meeting Colonel Fitzpatrick saw him as a mature and seasoned financier, as a compleat man with the glow of military accomplishment and a lingering blush of youth. At 26 he disdained the face-hair preferred by military officers. Nor did he gain weight. Exercise on horseback and moderation with food kept him fit, though around his eyes tiny lines and dark bags appeared after a night's drinking.

Fitz looked forward to seeing Fairfield. He'd heard about the Alexander planation since summers in Rhode Island, when the older and wiser Edward taught him about life. In late October he rode up the long road between rows of red oaks to a freshly white-washed brick house framed by holly and cypress and draped with ivy. A Negro in clean work clothes took his horse. Fitz strode into the house to receive a welcome of a half dozen of the family.

Although he was used to a warm reception from borrowers, often their greetings struck a false note where former hatreds were barely concealed. Not so at Fairfield. He felt years melt away as he took the good will of people he had long loved and respected.

Fairfield was not the showplace of the cotton kings. It had always been a working farm. Inside, were no clashing floral patterns nor dark cut-velvet. The rooms were full of books and musical instruments. Outside, white fences were straight, and outbuildings were in good repair. Fitz saw few weeds.

"It's all because of your money," said Edward Porter Alexander as they walked out to the fields after dinner. His gait betrayed stiffness in his upper body. With a short gray beard, he looked much more than three years older than Fitz. "Father was too old for the war, so he could borrow from you all. Our crop was a bonanza." Almost reluctantly he grinned. "With ten bales in the shed, we got enough to put this farm back in operation and make a start on my place down on the river. We put the darkies on a share system that costs less than working them as slaves." He pointed toward fallow fields with a riding crop in his right hand. "We have fewer assets, but our income is good. I could be a sight angrier after four months in prison. We don't complain."

"I wish there were more like you," said Fitz, aware that Alexander's shoulder hurt. *That's the reason for the riding crop. It keeps the arm from going stiff.* "It's plain the economy can revive without slavery as long as everyone works," he said. "A lot of people want to keep Negroes from having land, or even working in towns. I don't understand it entirely."

Alexander struck the crop on a gate post. "I am opposed to all those equality notions, and a little surprised I have to explain it to you." His teeth clenched. "We see crowds of 'em in towns or around shanties in the woods, and we wonder whether they'll ever work at all. Of course, ours have mostly done well, those who stayed on."

They walked further, and Alexander seemed to cool. "Mind you, the darkies aren't as smart as we are, in spite of what you preach, but I'll grant they can farm and trade. My father trained the household to read so they'd know the Bible, and you know what that got us. I suppose in your eyes we ought to be proud of Josephus." He frowned. "Around here, you know, they say we hatched a devil. Father's oldest friends don't speak. If I hadn't been in the war, they'd say we were Union, I swear. I am very careful to be called 'Cuh'nel Alexander.'"

"Social life is difficult since the trial. People say Gordon's going to hang. There aren't two men in the county believe he's getting a fair hearing. We've sent money for his defense, of course. It was father suggested Cuyler Rutledge. I doubt that was wise. Men down here don't know about Yankees, any more than you know about us."

They moved in silence. Alexander poked and struck with his crop, sometimes as a toy, sometimes as a blade. "You may wonder why I carry this," he held it up. "Well I enjoy it and it makes me use my arm. It also reminds people I fought." He stopped to stare over a stone fence, and resumed slowly. "General Longstreet sent a letter last week suggesting a group get together in Atlanta to talk about the 'situation.' I'm sure he refers to the new secret societies. Bedford Forrest is their leader. I don't know him. He was a slave trader, you know. Didn't go to the Academy."

"I've heard about Forrest," said Fitz. "His men fought in the mountains well into last spring, and held up reorganization in half the old Confederacy. I didn't know Forrest's men were active here."

"They're not, yet," said Alexander. "Longstreet thinks we can form a counterweight by organizing officers of the Army of Northern Virginia against them. He wants us to meet in Atlanta, and says Lee favors such a plan, but I doubt the old man wants to encourage that, not now at any rate."

"Are you going to go?" Fitz asked, and looked away. He knew Alexander might hear about Longstreet's meeting. Little would come of it unless men actually got together.

Alexander swung open an old wooden gate leading into a pasture and motioned Fitz to pass. "I'm not sure. We'll have to stand up for Gordon. That I can foretell. We really can't do much about calming things down if he's going to hang.

"He's our hero, you know. The trial has made him greater than any of the others—Johnston, Beauregard, Lee. They're all failures. Gordon fought to the end, like old Jube Early. You're making an example of the wrong man."

"It's accidental, I assure you." Fitz looked at the sky. "You don't think Longstreet can do anything, then?"

"No," said Alexander, "I don't." He looked sadly at Fitz. "Like most of us, he's a very different person from when you took him at Gettysburg. I remember that day. He was full of energy and anger. Nothing could stand in his way. Damned if I know how you did it." He smiled at last, like the older boy praising his brother.

"Today, Pete Longstreet tries desperately to make a living in New Orleans with few assets other than the fact that he and U.S. Grant were classmates. He's not the man to move the South, not now."

They resumed walking over the field. Alexander stopped and turned to face Fitz, a low plowed furrow between them. "I'll tell you who can make a difference. That's General Meade. He has the power to stop this nonsense. He's the man decent people look to down here. You ought to tell him."

Dan Sickles liked Savannah. The Gordon trial kept his name in the New York papers. Local ladies were pretty, often lonely with so many men lost in the war, and sometimes receptive. He discovered that a gallant wound drew concern and was less a drawback than he'd feared. The food was amazingly good, upsetting a false notion, and the enormous power of his office helped him influence events.

"The politics of the United States for the next decade will be determined by the South," he told a Northern visitor. "The Negroes will keep the Republican Party in power with the electoral votes of Southern states." Sitting in a cushioned chair behind a writing table, he paused to anticipate an objection. The man said nothing. The general continued, "Or will depend on the darkies' vote, if we're vigilant."

The man was about 40, dressed clean-shaven in a dark, unpressed suit with a red, white, and blue medal on his lapel indicating membership in the Grand Army of the Republic. "This trial ought to put the fear of God into 'em down here." He took an unlit cigar from his mouth and stared at the end as though debating whether to light it.

Sickles propped his wooden leg on an ottoman underneath the desk. The move forced him to sit upright in a position suitable for dictating a lesson. "When you get back to Saint Louis, I want you to give this to Grant." He handed over an envelope. It contains an article in the *New York World,* saying our Commanding General is ineligible to run for President by virtue of foreign birth." The man nodded and grinned.

"Tell Grant I know the argument don't hold water, but it serves to keep people away who want to support him. McClellan is so unpopular the Democrats don't even campaign in the West. They're looking four years ahead. They want Meade to run and win with support of the white South. It might work, if Meade wasn't so inept." He chortled.

The other man laughed as if celebrating common wisdom.

"Tell Grant," Sickles continued, "I've got another something else coming out about Meade's Benjamin, Fitzpatrick. It'll blow that young man's gilded career right out of the water. It'll leave Meade helpless. Believe me, he'll miss him. Left alone, he's lost. Fitzpatrick has the instincts, and he's tough—for a dandy. The sooner he's out of the way, the better."

"What are ya gonna do?"

"Just tell General Grant to keep his eyes peeled for 'Historicus.' He knows where to look."

"Yer not gonna say what this is all about?"

"Not exactly. Just this. Hancock up in Richmond closed down a fancy whorehouse his officers used. Some of the wives must have gotten wind of it. They got the provost to close the thing down and run the girls out of town. The madame is destitute. You can draw your own conclusions." Sickles laughed. The story would be far better than his visitor would ever imagine. He grinned, and the man laughed out loud.

"There's another thing to tell Grant," said Sickles, turning serious. "We're going to convict this Gordon fellow, and it's a hanging offense."

"The South will be up in arms." said the man, repeating what he'd heard in a local barroom.

"We can handle that," said Sickles raising his hand palm out to deflect argument. In the months since he lost his leg, his arms had strengthened through use, and his shoulders and chest had filled. "A little trouble down here's no problem. We've got enough troops. A good hanging will clear the air. Somewhere along the line it has to be approved by the Commanding General."

The man took awhile to respond. "You mean Meade will have to approve it. But he doesn't have to, does he?"

"No, he doesn't," said Sickles as though he were talking to a pupil. "But if he doesn't, he's a doughface, and the North won't forgive him. The Negro Gordon killed gave him the victory at Gettysburg. Meade must avenge him." The military governor paused.

"Lincoln can pardon Gordon," said the man.

"He won't," said Sickles. "Meade will be the last to act. And he'll have blood on his hands in the states he needs to carry four years from now." A grin stuck to his face.

The man protested, "They'll be all kinds of back and forth, even after Meade approves execution. They'll debate it in Congress, the press will get involved . . . It ain't a simple thing," he said, voice rising to higher notes as he ran out of breath challenging Sickles.

"Might be," said the general, toying with a pencil in his hands and looking down at his desk. "But that depends on who's in a position to act." He snapped the pencil in half.

Fitz agonized for weeks over his carouse in Richmond. He was sure he had made love to Sigurd in the fullest sense. He'd "fucked her," as soldiers said, and he had sunk to their level. The man who captured Lee and Longstreet, who at 26 was one of the leading financiers in the nation, was a whoremonger and a slut-chaser, no better than a cad. It made little difference that he was drunk and didn't know what he was doing. He knew Sigurd was there and what she would do, and he had wanted it. Even now he thought about her white, soft flesh. He shivered as he rose in his bed. He wanted it again.

In bright morning sun, astride a good horse in fresh air, life seemed more promising, and his brain took control. Hancock closed Alice's so the men would stay with their wives. They'd have no business at her place, anyway, if they had women. Nor would I. He began to form a plan.

In early November he took leave, left Richmond by train for City Point, and caught a military steamer up to Annapolis, arriving in Philadelphia within a day and a half. He kept out of sight, staying at a club, sending no word to his parents, but a note to Maeve, only delaying long enough to include a large bouquet, to tell her he would call.

Fannie could read portents as well as any woman, and greeted him at the door. She brought him in to Maeve. "I'm going to leave you two alone." She left, sliding the parlor doors shut.

Maeve wore a white dress with light blue ribbons at the sleeves. She seemed perplexed, but her manner suggested she was not displeased.

"I know you've sent me away," Fitz began. "But I have to tell you," he paused. "To say." The hero was tongue-tied. "Certain facts have made it absolutely clear to me that I can never love another woman, nor would any other woman understand me." He looked at her for sympathy, and then brightened. "That's selfish, I know. And you might say foolish, but I think it is true. I want to marry you, and the sooner the better."

"You can't," she protested, as if it were decreed by law. She said no more while they stood a few feet apart at the parlor doors. "You will throw away everything you stand for. They won't let you stay at your bank. General Meade. What will General Meade say? He won't like it at all, and colonel, he needs you. Even I can see that."

Maeve has a natural sense of things. She sees my link to the general, and knows what it means. How can she feel she's not in the right? The matrons of Philadelphia and the tattle tales of the world can go to Hell! "General Meade and the world will just have to accept us. I have no fear of that. The war has changed many things, especially you and me."

He paused gazing at her. "There is something I must tell you. Perhaps we can sit?" He glanced toward a couch by the windows.

"Yes," she said, taking his hat. "How uncivil of me, and I must thank you for the flowers. They are amazing for so late in the year."

Fitz sat on the couch several feet away from her. "You may know. I guess I've told you that Sigurd went to work at Alice's Hotel in Richmond." She nodded, and he went on. "I saw her there several times." Maeve smiled knowingly. "I thought I was just looking after her." He sighed and looked at Maeve. Knowing she knew what would come made it seem easier.

"I often dine at the mess in the old Rebel President's House where we have a club," he said. "Sometimes we drink a lot. I seemed to have gotten into the habit." He stared at the floor, then looked up to gauge her face.

Maeve watched him patiently. She would know the scenario. She knew about men, and she knew Sigurd.

"Well," said Fitz. "I really didn't know what I was doing. But the last time I saw her, I'd had a lot to drink. I don't remember exactly what happened, but I'm pretty sure I went off with her."

Maeve moved over to sit beside him, putting a finger to his mouth. "Whatever happened must be left aside," she said. "You mustn't blame yourself entirely. Men are men. I know that, and you were lonely. Of course, Sigurd would do everything she could to get you." She laughed. "Just to prove she's as good as me.

"That's the way we used to think. We competed to show Alice who was best. So you see you can't blame yourself."

"You're being kind. Men are supposed to be made of tougher stuff."

"Well, you aren't," said Maeve. "That's one thing every girl in the trade knows."

"God, I love you," said Fitz. "I could never live my life with a woman I couldn't talk to." He paused, and scowled. "I'm sure you've seen enough of the world of elegance to know I'm not likely to find another so honest." He smiled.

"Perhaps not in Philadelphia," she answered, "but maybe in New York or Paris. Women here are held back somehow. I don't want to be a local matron."

"But you will marry me, Maeve? I'm damned, if you don't. There are places for us. We can go to New York, or Europe if you like."

"It wouldn't be fair for you," she said, frowning.

He saw pain in her face and moved to take her in his arms. They kissed. "Can you honestly say that anything else matters?"

☆ ☆

Toddy Bates remained unshakable. He would say no more than what he thought he knew to be true. The veteran cavalry sergeant was less constant. From the outset the prosecutor regarded him as uncooperative. He nonetheless put him on the stand as a means of clarifying Bates's testimony. The sergeant said he thought Gordon had ordered them to kill no one. Gordon had said, "No, do nothing about him," when asked about Josephus.

Cuyler Rutledge rose to cross-examine, wondering why the prosecutor had called the man. "Now, sergeant, you ah sure General Gordon gave orders against killing of any kind?" He spoke in the soft Coastal accent of a man used to hearing what he wanted to hear.

"That's right," said the sergeant, brightening. "He was clear 'bout that." He spoke as if that were the end of it.

The surprise on his face was plain when the prosecutor came at him again for re-cross-examination. "Now, you say, sergeant, you are sure about General Gordon's words. You are sure he said specifically in relation to Josephus, not to kill him?"

"Yes, suh, I am." said the sergeant with defiance.

"And you asked about the "head nigger," I believe you called him?"

"Yes, I think I did."

"And that was in regard to violence, killing, was it not?" The prosecutor's Illinois nasals contrasted with the sergeant's back-throated tones from lower Appalachia.

"Yes, suh."

"And what did General Gordon say?"

"He said, 'No killin.'"

"Did he say that exactly, when you asked about the 'head nigger?'" The prosecutor raised his voice.

The sergeant shuffled his feet. "I don' remember word for word."

"In fact," said the prosecutor, pouncing. "He didn't answer. He said nothing."

"That's possible."

"Possible, or very likely, sergeant?"

"He didn't say nuthin' I kin remember."

Cuyler Rutledge was quick to come back. "Did the prosecutor speak to you before the trial?" He looked over his shoulder expecting an objection. None came.

"Yes, suh."

"What did he tell you?"

"Nothin'. He just asked some questions, and told me the best thing for me was to tell the truth."

"And what did you say then?" Rutledge was expectant.

"Ah didn't say anythin'. But I figured he was prob'ly right."

Several of Gordon's men and two civic leaders from Brunswick testified that the general had never discussed killing anyone, and that horseback drills among his men using guns were meant to be ceremonial and peaceable. One conceded under questioning that they might have been partly used as training to keep public order. But all witnesses, including the Baptist minister, said Gordon was a "peaceable" man.

Rutledge could not shake the prosecution's version of Gordon's last orders, and as the trial ground to a close after ten days, his failure was the talk of Savannah. Gordon himself became agitated and refused to see Booth. He urged Rutledge to appeal to the higher courts as soon as possible. "The Constitution is our hope," he told his wife.

On November 2, just before election day in the North, the court reached its verdict. Gordon was guilty.

Savannah kept calm, waiting for the sentence. The local people expected imprisonment, not death. They had become accustomed to Lincoln's soft approach. Surely, General Gordon's life was not in danger.

Lawyers in Washington City filed an appeal asking the Supreme Court for *certiorari*. The powers of the military commissions had not been tested. The Supreme Court was not in session, and the vacancy after the death of Chief Justice Tawney left it divided between senior men with sympathy for the South and four Lincoln appointees. The Washington lawyers were confident, however, and wrote Rutledge the Court would very likely overturn the decision on the constitutional ground that there had been no trial by jury.

In the second week of November the military commission met to pronounce sentence. Gordon stood before the bench in prison garb.

"John Brown Gordon," read the chairman from a prepared text in a strong, tense voice. "You are sentenced to be taken from this court to a place of execution and hanged by the neck until you are dead."

Observers were stunned in disbelief. After several minutes they rose and silently, perhaps fearful of speaking, left the room. Outside, screams from women pierced the quiet. Gordon could hear his wife's wail above the rest.

News of the sentence cut through the South like a tornado. Where it came, it upset the peace. Bedford Forrest's following grew tenfold. It was a call to arms. Men said it was like the beginning of the war all over again.

Meade sent reinforcements and instructed his governors to tighten laws on weapons. In Georgia, Sickles declared all side-arms and rifles illegal including hunting weapons, except for those few who needed them to feed themselves. Negro enclaves reluctantly turned over guns to the army for safe-keeping, fearful they would disarm and the whites would not.

Lincoln's re-election was overwhelming, as Sickles predicted. Shortly afterward, he nominated Edward M. Stanton, exhausted by endless months in the War Office, to be Chief Justice. Salmon Chase, who had expected the job, resigned from the Treasury in anger, but he could not stir up his Radical friends, who were happy with Stanton.

For Meade, the loss of a trusted friend at the War Office was a blow, particularly since it meant he would be alone in deciding on Gordon's sentence. Postwar military justice required approval of capital sentences by both the Commanding General and the Secretary of War. The new man, Francis Blair, a conservative facing a difficult confirmation in the Senate, told Meade he would defer to his judgment.

In the South, Forrest's legions paraded through towns carrying the Stars and Bars, officers wore swords on their old uniforms, and troops of men on foot, many on crutches without limbs, followed in tattered uniforms. Sickles banned the parades in Georgia.

Forrest's organization began holding ceremonial "campfires" in the countryside at times unknown to Yankee authorities but well advertised to local citizens. Some men appeared incognito, covering their heads with bed sheets so no one would know who they were. The idea caught on. If no one saw anyone, men reasoned, no one could tell any tales to the Yankees. And so the custom grew, and the campfires were known among the Scotsmen attending as the "call-in' of the clan."

CHAPTER XXIV

As a matter of custom and protocol, the Secretary of War received General Meade in his office. Today, Edward Stanton made an exception, and strolled down the high-ceilinged hallway to the door where a sentry stood guard. The Commanding General repeated congratulations saying he, most of all, would miss him.

Stanton sank with a tired sigh into an overstuffed leather chair by the fireplace and began speaking almost at once, "This Gordon business is what I've come about, general. You'll have to work with Blair, but I feel I ought to give you some lawyerly advice. I'm not sworn, so I can.

"The Supreme Court avoids interfering with military justice where civilian rule has not been re-established. In other words, whatever the military commission decides in Georgia will stand. I doubt the Court will review the case at all, though the pressure be strong."

"That means," said Meade, "that we are the final arbiters, unless the President will grant a pardon."

Stanton, looking into the grate where four large logs smoldered. "Just so. I don't think I ought to say more. I'm sorry you've got to face this alone."

The trial record took over a week to come. Newsmen gathered in the hallway. Meade cursed the events that brought them, and the frequent pleas from Meyer to speak with them. He kept a strict isolation, and methodically read the papers. Sharpe came to report that the commission had conducted the trial according to regulations. The Attorney General advised that the testimony of key witnesses, Bates, the sergeant, and the young Negro who stood with Josephus, was compelling. Neither the Attorney General nor Sharpe saw any legal ground to overturn the conviction. The sentence was another matter, and Meade pondered it. He could not seek anyone's counsel. Any thought he uttered to anyone would be in print in the flick of an eyelid. He wished Fitzpatrick were there, but he was in Richmond and in any case, Meade thought, too closely associated with the victim.

Shortly after Stanton's visit, three members of the Supreme Court, acting in recess, refused to hear the Gordon case. On a gray morning at the end of month, Meade walked through the muddy west garden to the White House to speak with the President.

"I have to ask myself," he told Lincoln, "How can I spare a Rebel general who connived in cold blood to kill a brave and loyal man, a hero, because he was a Negro? I have ordered the death of dozens of deserters whose chief offense was no more than a wish to go home."

Lincoln pulled on his beard standing beside Meade in the middle of the room, two tall men leaning toward each other weighed by a common problem. "I understand you, general. It's an awkward business. Our people in the North demand Gordon's blood. The South wants their hero spared. They don't see why a black life is worth a white one." He paused and stepped back. "Have you thought what would happen in the South if you put him in prison somewhere?"

"They'll continue to agitate," said Meade. "Eventually, someone down the years in this office will let him free, I suppose."

"We have to accept that it's easier to hang a private than a general," said Lincoln. "But we don't have to agree that it's all right to kill a colored man. What does General Sickles recommend?"

"He favors execution at the earliest date to show an example."

"What do you think about that, general?"

"I have no faith in the argument, Mr. President. Setting an example for men close-confined in a barracks is one thing, but I have no experience with a broad populace." Meade saw Lincoln grin, and wondered what it meant.

"You're right to doubt it, I'm sure, general. I hate executions."

"Perhaps, Mr. President, the best outcome would be a pardon, which only you can give. That way, it comes as a matter of grace. He'll still have been found guilty under military law."

Lincoln frowned "Yes, you may be right. We won't have a martyr, but with a pardon he goes scot-free. Do we want that? I will consider the argument, slowly and in good time. Don't rush the matter, general. I am sure we'll see our way, as events unfold."

Meade felt no relief. The President knew how to handle these matters, but he had to make the first decision. Never far from his mind were thousands of men with their lives ahead of them who died for the Union, men who sacrificed themselves, like Josephus.

On December 10 he approved the sentence, and informed Lincoln. To Sickles he sent a courier carrying the formal confirmation along with a sealed, hand-written order telling him to delay execution until the President had time to consider a pardon.

A fresh-minted second lieutenant traveled seven days on rough seas to deliver the pouch, and suffered agony from the motion of the ship. He could barely get down the plank after the steamer docked on a winter evening in Savannah. He took a carriage to the military governor's office, signed over his burden to the duty officer, and hastened to a steady bed.

Sickles the next morning opened the pouch and saw two messages—an order affirming sentence and a sealed hand-addressed letter to him from the Commanding General. He guessed the letter contained an easement, a plea for delay, probably word that Lincoln planned pardon. He had long since run through all possible scenarios, and would let nothing interfere with his plans. Replacing the sealed letter inside and unopened, he put the pouch in a desk drawer and called for the provost marshal.

To keep Gordon away from an adoring public, Sickles had confined him to a makeshift prison down river at Fort McAllister, once an array of Confederate earthworks defending Savannah against naval attack. He held a tight rein on the city, stationing armed men in each of its tree-covered squares. Unable to exploit the tension, agitators had no place to rally.

In the fog of an early winter morning, a week before Christmas, the prisoner, heard his fate read out to him three hours before he was to march in chains to the scaffold. The sergeant and two others struggled behind.

Accompanied by a Methodist army chaplain, Gordon rattled forward repeating the Twenty-Third Psalm . . . "Yea, though I walk through the valley of the shadow of death, I will fear no evil, for Thou art with me."

Soldiers on the parapets heard him as he climbed the wooden stairs. Even after a man in dark uniform without insignia put a black bag over his head, they thought they heard Gordon chant "The Lord is my shepherd, I shall not want. . . ."

Boards strained, the trap dropped, the general's voice stilled. Men groaned. Execution was done.

☆ ☆

Headquarters U.S.Army
Washington
December 20, 1864
Maj. Genl. William T. Sherman
Military Governor
Charleston
Proceed at once Savannah assume command as Governor and secure public
order. relieve Sickles on arrival and Ensure his immediate departure for
Washington City by Naval vessel. Report conditions daily until further notice.
Humphreys is enroute Charleston to act as your deputy. Acknowledge receipt.
George Meade
Lt. Genl
General in Chief

Bill Sherman had no more use ☆ ☆
for Dan Sickles than did any other Academy man. He read between the lines: Sickles had kicked over the traces. He held no brief for Gordon, and thought he probably deserved hanging, but Sherman had been in the South long enough to know Sickles had put a match to a powder train.

Many in Charleston despised Sherman for the special hatred his men, who proudly called themselves "bummers," showed South Carolina. Though he liked the city and met charming people, he was glad to leave. Savannah, he heard, was more hospitable. Tales of Sickles's conquests among local ladies circulated through the orderly rooms. They did not endear him to Sherman, who was angry he had made the city hostile.

He enjoyed turning Sickles out. Yet, gruff as he was, he knew the army could ill afford to give Savannans a glimpse of their differences. Together they did a short *pas de deux* at a farewell dinner attended by tame locals. Formalities were observed, and Sickles left on a steam cutter directly for Washington—in a storm, Sherman reported to Meade with glee.

For all Sherman's sensibility, he was no star at diplomacy. In the city squares anger dripped with spite from the Spanish moss, slithered off shiny magnolia leaves, and seeped up through wet ground. Rebel flags flew from dormers of vacant houses, forcing soldiers to come take them down to the jeers of large crowds, who seemed to know when to gather. Horsemen late at night rode through the streets covered in white hoods, carrying the Bonny Blue flag and calling on Gordon's name. Outposts reported the same in other Georgia towns, and in South Carolina. Armed men harassed Negroes, urging them to go back to their plantations.

☆ ☆

From Richmond, Fitzpatrick took the rails to visit the settlements. Everywhere he saw fear and despair in men and women who once had hope. Some told of visits from former owners urging them to "give up and come home," meaning work on shares. Many plantations were failing for lack of labor, and owners were desperate.

He was astonished in Atlanta to find Negro militias deprived of weapons and wired an appeal to Sherman to reissue the guns. In the company of soldiers from the Freedmen's Bureau, he wore his uniform. Not far from Savannah he found a community visited two evenings before by white-sheeted night riders. They had fired guns to round up the men, and chained them two by two as if to march them off. They herded women and children into one small cabin while they set fire to the plantation house. After hours of terror, and beating the men with barrel staves, they had left, telling them to go to their masters, and shouting they would be back.

Fitz spent more than an hour convincing the leaders he was not an army lawyer come to turn them out. Most sat on the edge of low cabin porches. Some lay flat on the boards—men, women, and children motionless, faces dead blank. Women shook when they tried to talk, if they could speak at all, and would not look at him. Some moaned, "Don' send us back. Don' send us back." Older people, unable to walk, tried to crawl away and hide.

Fitz knew more about slavery than most Yankees, but he had not seen fear so deep. Clearly, they couldn't work. Fences broken stood unmended. Mules and oxen ran loose in the fields. Men and women stared at him, and, if they answered questions at all, fell into the obsequious cadence of slaves, "Yes, massah. Sho' nuff, massah. You right, massah." No one looked him in the eye. He had seen fear on the battlefield when men couldn't move. He'd assumed much of it was shamming. Here there was no doubt. These people were paralyzed.

Shaken, he saw the collapse of his program if the terror spread. He had not understood how much former slaves feared their masters. There was a lot he didn't know. The gulf was wider than anyone thought. "I've got to see Sherman," he told his companions, "I'm going to ride directly to Savannah."

They protested. Savannah was 35 miles away over rough roads and unknown obstacles through country where a lone Yankee officer would find no welcome. Fitz ignored them. He needed the ride to clear his mind. "If someone wants to take a shot at me," he told them, "Let them try. There's enough daylight left, and I've got a pistol."

Fitz wondered whether peace would ever come. Why hadn't he seen how far apart the races stood? He cursed himself. Maeve had told him there was a lot he didn't know about people. Her image raised new worries. Could he bring her South? Could she exist between two cultures, black and white? Would Southern families accept her? Maybe not. How much would the two of them care? How long must he stay to assure the settlements survived?

And what about the Commanding General? He thinks he's going to be President, but he has no sense of politics and counts on my help. How can I stay in the South and be useful? Sickles knew no one would ever hold him to account. He planned a swift, humiliating death for Gordon, knowing it would anger the whites and force the Negroes to look to the Republicans for protection. Can Meade scotch a snake like him? What can I do about all this?

On the fourth day after his arrival, Sherman was sorting through reports of what were now officially called "clan raids." "I got your telegram, colonel," he said as Fitz stood before him. "A little unusual, considering your rank. But I suppose, strictly speaking, this is a civilian request. You aren't in the army anymore, are you?" He stared at the uniform as if it didn't fit, or Fitz oughtn't to wear it.

"No, I'm not, general. The uniform tells my borrowers I'm on their side. The men in the Bureau thought it useful. After what I saw, I think they're right. The countryside is more than just unsettled. We're at swords drawn with the planters."

Sherman saw Fitz was exhausted. "Better get some sleep, colonel. I got your message, and I've given the order to re-arm the militia. Maybe they'll drop one of those bastards in a sheet, and we'll find out who they are—if the niggers don't kill him first.

"The so-called 'clan' parades around Savannah late every night, even though we've forbidden it. No one talks. They have 'a code of silence.' But I'm damned sure the rich folks are behind it. I disbelieve the Savannah ladies when they tell me it's just the lower orders."

★ ★

Meade left with Margaretta two days before Christmas for their estate outside Philadelphia. He would not return for several weeks and took with him a small retinue, including Colonel Hardie, a bachelor who had no other place to spend the holidays. News from the South was bad. Margaretta had strongly favored pardon for Gordon and was outraged by his hanging. In Philadelphia, ties to the South remained strong. Many friends condemned Gordon's humiliating death and blamed Meade.

Nothing bothered him more. He could not understand how people so recently hailing him as their savior could be so irate over the death of a Rebel general guilty of a serious crime. Hardie suggested it had to do with the colored folk. "They dinna see they're people." But Meade disagreed. The good men of Philadelphia stood for the Union. They should know better.

Sharpe passed through after Christmas en route to New York to resume his law practice. Margaretta made him welcome. He was one of the few wartime officers she approved of.

He had news from Richmond, where he had called on Miss Van Lew. Her Negro friends—many still worked in houses of former masters—said the white folks ignored the Gordon affair, because it happened far away. She said Virginians didn't like hearing about the white-sheeted night riders.

"That's the sort of thing I hear from Hancock," said Meade as they sat in the library at afternoon sherry. "The trouble comes from Georgia westward where this Bedford Forrest fellow is raising Hell."

Margaretta frowned, and Meade corrected himself, "Raising Ned, I should say."

Sharpe seemed embarrassed and changed the subject. "Sickles is active, I'm told, writing another political piece. I'm sure he'll be soon out to see Grant about the grand gathering of veterans in New York City next month. He's trying to set up Grant in your territory for the next election."

Margaretta's frown returned. "I keep telling George he mustn't let the grass grow. General Sickles deserves a court-martial. At the top one's bound to have enemies, and one must deal with them."

"Well I should be glad of Sickles then," said Meade calmly. "I'm not going to fret about everything he does. He always manages to entangle himself. Grant will soon take his measure."

"Perhaps," said Sharpe, "but I think, general, your friends who want to see you in the White House one day ought to go to that rally in New York. Sickles is not as strong as we are. No sense in letting him steal a march."

"You're very right," said Margaretta. "I'm glad you're speaking out." Her frustration with Meade's nonchalance was obvious.

Sharpe turned to her, "I've heard from Fitzpatrick. He's going to come up, and we'll get other men from Gettysburg, like Humphreys and Doubleday. We won't leave the platform to Grant, whatever Sickles tries to do."

Meade offered more sherry and suggested Sharpe stay over for New Year's. Margaretta smiled approval, but Sharpe declined both, saying it was late and he must leave early in the morning. He had much to do back in civil life.

Before Christmas Flossie Muelheim wrote:

Toddy Bates is back. The trial of General Gordon was terrible for him, and Papa says he's lucky to get away alive. The newspapers say armed men go to colored houses at night and beat them. The South seems to be going wild. Don't they know the war is over?

Papa says we shouldn't care a fig about old Gordon. He was a nasty Rebel. Yesterday he went with the men over to Benner's Hill where he was captured. They told about how he hovered behind his men like a night phantom, urging them not to surrender. Papa says he was a fanatic.

Some people don't understand how Toddy could come back here after fighting for the Rebels and riding with Gordon. Mama tells them he's a good boy, and did the right thing by telling the truth. It took courage. He stood up against the general. In the South they'd like to hang him. Papa put him to work in the store and says he does well.

✮ ✮

The Freemasons of Brunswick took charge of the funeral of John Brown Gordon. A large group of veterans of six Georgia regiments who fought at Gettysburg would march in uniform behind the coffin. Burial would take place two days after Christmas. The Masons needed time. Extraordinary measures were taken to preserve the corpse after it arrived by coaster.

The Union commander reported anxiously to Savannah. The timing could not be worse. The event would come in the midst of the Christmas holiday season. Sherman knew newspapers would report this irony widely, spreading anger and bitterness. He was still trying to understand the situation. He had no choice but let plans go forward, and sent an order to arrest anyone carrying a gun.

A large crowd boarded trains in Savannah for Brunswick on Boxing Day, among them John Wilkes Booth, traveling with three widely suspected night riders. The latter were young property owners, not wealthy, but articulate and ambitious. Newspapermen watched them closely. At times they seemed uneasy with the attention, as though it were better their exploits went unmarked. But they loved Booth and his stories, and his ways with women. He spoke freely about the "dastardly cowardice of Yankee generals," frequently mentioning Sickles, Sherman, and Meade.

December 27 broke calm with a line of light yellow sky at the edge of the eastern water under a low bench of gray clouds. Directly overhead the sky broke in places into puffs of gray against a cold blue background. A Union regiment formed on Main Street at sunrise and took up positions between the Baptist Church and the cemetery on the northeast side of town. Every black person left who could find a place to visit. Even Mrs. Gordon's people asked for the day. Only one lifelong servant, an old lady on wages, stayed to help.

The service was traditional and religious. The eulogy stressed Gordon's "righteous patriotism," his "zeal in the defense of all honor," his "passion for the obligations of work," and his "dedication to the truth of the human order." In attendance in uniform without side arms were Generals Ewell and Johnson and Col. E. Porter Alexander. Gen. Nathan B. Forrest and several of his officers wore swords.

The procession had a short way to go, but so many groups formed behind the coffin that it took an hour and a half for the graveside ceremony to begin. At the end of the line in full sight of the Union troops came three men on horseback in white sheets decorated with black crosses carrying the forbidden stars and bars. Booth waved to them as if pointing out special friends. Several men urged him to keep silent, but he ignored them. The Yankees were dumbstruck and took no action. Newsmen gleefully wrote about the "three visitors covered in white."

★ ★

In early January, a Negro orderly at Sherman's headquarters found the pouch holding Meade's sealed letter in a dark corner of a supply room. Sherman had already received a full account of it from Meade, and suspected Sickles of trickery. It was too late to do much about it. Gordon was dead, and little good could come from telling his wife and friends that Sickles foreclosed a possible pardon. That was hardly news.

As for Sickles himself, Meade considered a court-martial for disobeying orders, but decided against another open trial. He ordered his discharge on the day he arrived in Washington City, refusing to grant him a final interview. Lincoln agreed.

Sickles told the press he'd been "persecuted just for doing my sovereign duty," and left for New York City before Meade's friends could issue a riposte. Newsmen were accustomed to sudden comings and goings among generals, and the story died.

Southern papers, outraged by Sickles's behavior, saw through his sudden departure. Some suggested the Commanding General was better disposed than generally known. A few emerging politicians with links to the old Democratic party confidently told friends, "General Meade is indeed well disposed toward the South." Indeed, they didn't know what he thought, but they knew it was better to pretend to have a champion at court.

Other papers reflected the view of a majority of planters who blamed the army, and Meade in particular, for "the hasty and unspeakably cruel death of General Gordon." They looked past his alleged crimes to the issue of fairness of Gordon's trial and the "shameful absence of constitutional procedures." Many approved of the clan and founds ways to support it.

CHAPTER XXV

Fitz spent a week in Washington City meeting with the President and the Treasury about expanding settlements on lands in the West and finding more credit for white planters. Meade offered his quarters on Lafayette Square, but Fitz preferred the hotel. He wanted to talk to newspapermen and politicians in the Willard bar, where he could pick up the latest rumors from the Grant-Sickles camp, listen to members of Congress, and get the mood of the capital. He also fed their curiosity about Meade, soothed their worries about the South, and joined in raucous humor over whiskey at the rail.

The Commanding General was famous, popular, often revered. He was hailed everywhere in the North, wildly cheered by veterans, even in the Republican-run Grand Army of the Republic. Fitz knew Meade was not the only hero of the war and that ambitious men would find ways to attack him. Four years was a long time to wait. Fitz worried about the general standing as a motionless target on a national pedestal.

Speaking in public, Meade was good on the war and the South, but gave vague answers about silver, the transcontinental railroad, and Free Labor, issues taking more space in the newspapers every day. An increasing number of things that moved the nation were alien to him.

Meade could offend an audience with his high-born condescension, especially on the subject of the Negro. While most Northern men applauded the execution of Gordon as well-measured justice, many disliked black people. Meade seemed unable to grasp their race-born fears. He fervently believed every good Union man ought to favor emancipation and Lincoln's plans for reconstruction.

Grant, men said, showed remarkable savvy. He seemed to have the West in his pocket, and, with Sickles at his side, was quietly wooing leading men in New York and Boston. Still, wisdom in the Willard barroom said the West didn't count for much, except for states like Illinois and Ohio which had gained a fair population. Grant had to make a showing in the East.

Itinerant journalists at the bar said Sickles pretended to Grant he was a political magician. He joked with the general, offered him fine cigars and liquor, bragged about the war, flattered and convinced him that he, Sickles, knew how business and politics were done in the East, and how political campaigns were fought—fought, not conducted.

After a few days in the capital the turmoil in Georgia fled from his mind. Fitz was easily immersed in politics. Events were moving. He had business in Philadelphia. When he climbed into a hack for the B&O station to catch the morning cars, the house porter saluted. At the station, people stood aside to let him pass. A young veteran brought his son to shake his hand. In the first-class car others gave him room.

Staring out of the freshly washed window, he reviewed the business ahead. Everything had to be done quickly, a meeting with his parents, a more serious one with Meade, and, most important, a long call at Fannie's to see Maeve. Hardie would tell him first thing whether Meade had read the day's papers. Fitz smiled at the plush interior of the car. Less than two years before Hardie brought him over these same rails in a filthy wreck of a wagon to find Meade and tell him history was waiting. Hardie was the only one who hadn't changed, the sharp-minded staff man. He would give him the word about that damned letter in the *New York World*.

Fitz reached down and took from an open portmanteau the front page of a newspaper displaying the latest letter from "Historicus." Sickles was the only man close to Grant nasty enough to try to drive a wedge between Meade and Fitz. He read it, concentrating on lines he had memorized:

Your readers will be amazed and outraged to know that the so-called "Angel of Gettysburg," who made a great name for herself nursing the wounded, even attending the amputation of brave Sickles's leg, was brought to the job by her madame from a traveling brothel. This woman, this viper at the breast of the brave, was no more nor less than a trumped-up prostitute presented on a shell like Venus on the eve of battle to serve along with other whores from her stable. . . .

Madame Alice has since decamped for the gold fields of Nevada, but before departing she gave us this explicitly clear testimony. . . .

Fitz winced at "whore," and smiled grimly as he thought how Sickles would have obtained Alice's confessions. He had paid her well enough to go where no newsman would find her. Sickles would not want her hanging around to tell the press, in exchange for drinks, about being bribed.

Meade would be shocked when he told him about Maeve. He wouldn't like to think of Fitz being involved with such a woman. Sickles counted on his high morality. Meade must have known Alice's girls were working with the wounded. Fitz wondered whether he knew "The Angel of Gettysburg" was one of them, and not the chaste settlement worker living with Fannie. Fortunately, Sickles's latest "letter" did not mention her proper name, "Maeve McConnaughy."

The train rattled slowly into Baltimore Station, where Fitz stepped out to breathe fresh air in the cold morning. No one recognized him. Newsboys hawked their wares, but none carried papers from New York. Perhaps Meade hadn't seen it. Fitz would have to tell him. In the best of circumstances, Meade would never understand his reasons for wanting to marry the woman.

The Meade property stretched for a quarter of a mile along the Schuylkill, enough to give all the privacy his stature required. George, almost fully recovered, set up a home with his young wife in town. The general and Margaretta had the immense house to themselves—and a dozen servants, plus a detail of orderlies who followed him about. They were enjoying a pre-inaugural winter holiday.

Fitz stayed with his parents on Chestnut Street, and spent the evening debating whether to speak of Maeve. They knew the girl as a ward of Fannie who did settlement work. They liked her. His mother was not the prude his father was, and might well understand

305

a romantic attachment—after all, Fitz wasn't poor and could do what he liked. He didn't have to live in Philadelphia, where society posed a high barrier to women without family, whatever their virtue. He'd never considered pushing Maeve into those stuffy rooms. There were other, open places like New York, even London, the Continent, or the West.

Fitz knew it was wise to take matters one step at a time. His father was ebullient, sure Lincoln's policies would assuage hostility in the South, and believed Meade would be President, a great thing for his son, "the Commanding General's right hand." In the study on the white marble mantle behind his desk he kept a large Brady photograph of Fitz standing alone beside Meade before the ruins of the Confederate capitol.

"A brilliant career lies before you," he said as they settled into the room for tea. "Everyone says so, don't they, mother?"

"Yes," she said softly, "People expect you'll be in the Cabinet one day." A wide smile lit her face.

"What portfolio do you want, son? You'd still be a bit young for foreign affairs, but you could do the Treasury in your sleep."

"I don't think it will work out that way," said Fitz, struggling to evade talk about the future. "I think there is a lot of opportunity in finance, possibly in New York."

"Not a bad thing," said his father. "We could do a bit of business up there once this slump is over. You're making the South safe for Northern money, my boy. I should think you'd be as welcome as the flowers in spring."

Fitz didn't want to disturb their dreams, and hated to disappoint them. That is what Historicus's revelations surely meant—taking Maeve far away from any kind of Society with a capital "S." He sipped his tea and said crisply with an English affectation, "Yes, that's the thing."

"And the general," said his father waxing to the subject, "He'd be pleased to have you up there, an anchor to windward. Indeed, an anchor to windward." Mr. Fitzpatrick was a keen, if occasional, sailor who spent four months a year at their brown-shingled summer cottage overlooking the rocks of Newport harbor.

★ ★

Elizabeth Van Lew sat at her writing table near the fire in her dressing room. Richmond was freezing in its second postwar winter. A few buildings had been rebuilt, but the town center lay in ruins. Tobacco growers who had loans from the Land Bank were spending money, and trade had picked up, but many of her friends lived on charity, and she herself had only three servants.

She wasn't thinking about her own position. She rarely did. Word from the cotton states was that Gordon's execution would produce more violence against the Negroes. People commonly said too many were flaunting their freedom, lording it over the whites. They were an excellent target, she mused. And resentment could turn hot into vengeance.

She pushed the lace back from her cuff and extended her right arm over the paper:

Dear General Sharpe,

Reports from our friends now speak of revenge since the hanging of General Gordon. Much anger is now aimed at General Meade and at President Lincoln. Some speak of a plot to kill high officers in Washington. These reports often sound fanciful, as if some down-at-the-heals gentleman spun out a yarn of what he might do if he could. I would pay no attention if I had not received an unexpected visit from one Captain Harrison, a former Confederate officer and admitted spy during the war. He told me one of his former acquaintances from the stage was plotting to kill Mr. Lincoln and other prominent men in the capital.

I might ignore his words if I did not respect Harrison's courage in coming to me, and if I did not know the wild and unpredictable character of one of the plotters, the actor John Wilkes Booth, who now spends much of his time up there. Booth is rash. He is accustomed to men, and especially women, following his lead or, should I say, whim. Early in the war he wanted a military career, and joined the mad rush to Harper's Ferry to capture John Brown. But later he drifted into darker areas, I believe including espionage, though I can't be sure. He moves back and forth often between Richmond and Washington, and is implacably "unreconstructed."

Booth bears watching. I can believe he intends to kill the President.
Sincerely,
Elizabeth Van Lew

The sentry at the foot of the gravel drive pulled to attention for the approaching carriage. Fitz arrived early in the morning, knowing the general's habits. He would be at the top of his day in good spirits and least cantankerous.

In an outer room Hardie greeted Fitz and told him of recent events, as always both guarded and optimistic about his chief. "The Massachusetts trip was a success, I suppose. The veterans greeted him well enough, and so did the Irish, though I wasna sure they liked him talkin' about the darkies. The old Yankees were to the contrary. They wanted to know why he hadn't done away with Gordon long ago. They're fer havin' the black man in charge down there. They think he's been soft on the planters."

"The abolitionists can be hard. Massachusetts is not an easy state," said Fitz soberly. He waited and asked, "What's on his mind just now?"

Hardie looked at him from the side of his eye. "Yer askin' about the thing in the *New York World*. He's read it all right, and figures it's Sickles tryin' to do mischief. I wouldna give it a lotta thought, laddie. The girl has nothin' to do with us, after aw."

"I suppose you're right," said Fitz as he stood to put his hand on the door handle, pushing it open to see the tall slim figure in an unfamiliar dark suit standing behind a massive table that served as a desk.

"Halloo," shouted Meade. "Good to see you, my boy. I suppose Hardie's told you all about our triumphs in Boston?" He laughed.

Fitz stepped forward to shake his hand and felt a tug as though the general wanted to pull him to his chest.

Meade was clearly delighted. "It gets a little isolated up here, you know. We think of Washington City as a small town, but it's a very active place. Up here if one's not in business or an active club man, which I am certainly not nor ever shall be, it's dead slow. If it weren't for a long ride everyday, I think I should never want to live here again."

Meade sat down in a broad-backed winged chair covered with cut velvet. "Well, there's still a lot to do back in the capital, eh? The President likes your idea of expanding the reach of the Land Bank.

The planters will do anything for credit. Of course, it's hard to sort out who ought to be eligible. I have made some suggestions."

Fitz wondered whom the general would support. It wasn't wise of Meade to get involved in choosing among people in the South. On the paper Meade handed him were the names of Virginians Miss Van Lew listed among the die-hards. He knew she was right. Some of the chosen Georgians were involved with Forrest.

Meade pressed on. "I've taken quite a fancy to young Alexander. Do you think it's too early to employ a former Southern officer?"

Fitz wished mightily he would concentrate on the army and leave the politics of reconstruction to Lincoln. Meade seemed to prefer this to the hard work of military government. He despised reading reports from governors and making tours of inspection.

"General," he said, standing up to explain as though he were a young aide. "I've been talking to my father about going to New York to start a branch of the business."

The general's jaunty affect collapsed. "But, my God! I need you, Fitzpatrick. How are we going to get along? I have never thought for a minute of doing this work without you. I could never be in politics, Lord knows." He sat down quickly, looking stunned and sad.

"You've seen the letter in *The World*, general?" Fitz knew the moment he mentioned it he shouldn't have. There was time enough to talk of Maeve.

"I suppose," said Meade awkwardly. "There's no truth to it. This is just Sickles's ranting, trying to cause trouble. It has nothing to do with us. Anyone can see that, can't they?" Meade stood, came quickly around the table and, motioning to a Chippendale chair for Fitz, dropped into one for himself.

"Yes, that's true," said Fitz. "It won't do much damage. But you must understand, general. This woman, Maeve, is important to me."

"But, my God! Fitzpatrick, Sickles says she's a . . . ." Meade stopped, "was a . . . . Well, wasn't she?" Another pause. "No, don't talk about that." He waved his hand in front of his face. "What are you trying to tell me, colonel?"

"Well," said Fitzpatrick. "I think she is a pretty fine woman. She did extraordinary things during the war, and continues to do so with

Miss Morris in the settlements."

"That's all well and good, Fitzpatrick. I can understand your affection, but you have a fine career ahead of you." Meade's face flushed, expressing irritation and some anger. He held tight to the arms of his chair. "No other man in the country has your prospects. You could be President one day. Is this woman the equal of all that?" Meade stopped again. He was in unknown territory. Other men's emotions were something he didn't talk about. He tried to smile.

"I'm sorry, colonel. You have to do what you think best. I would miss you very much. One day we'll all be there in the White House. You'd better come."

The room was quiet. Fitz spoke of conditions in the South. "After Gordon's execution, general, I think we have to be especially watchful. They are talking about killing people in Washington, including the President."

The general smiled as if he were aware of the threat. "The President has heard these stories and dismisses them. Still, I suppose we ought to be careful. Yes, additional protection is probably necessary until the Gordon thing passes."

Maeve was glad to see the colonel, and flattered by his continued attention in spite of her refusals. He was the only man, of all the men she had known, whom her body craved. Even if the colonel was beyond her reach, no one else could replace him.

To be sure, he had again spoken of marriage, had offered a handsome proposal. Fannie, the realist, had said, "Young lady, there's no reason why you have to live here. Colonel Fitzpatrick is quite capable of finding a solution to the problems of society. You just won't live in Philadelphia. I doubt he cares tuppence about that."

Local men who came to call acted as though they were courting. But Maeve received them dressed in a plain smock with her long red hair pulled back in a bun or tied with a bow. She never looked them in the eye, or gave them encouragement. Still they came to the row house on 19th Street below Rittenhouse Square bringing flowers and invitations, even though she regularly turned them aside.

Now came the letter in the *New York World*, by the hand of

General Sickles, whom she disliked the moment he was carried into the field surgery by his crew of flatterers. *Sooner or later everyone in Philadelphia will know what I've done.* She flayed herself, *I've had more men in a day than any of these women have in a lifetime. I'm stained, not chaste, and can never be. Why on earth would he want such a person?*

Fannie stood looking out the front window. "Well, here he comes, my sweet, and it looks to me as though he wants you, no matter what the papers say. So you must deal with it. He proceeds like an impresario. People don't know who he is, but they stop and tip their hats because they think they ought to. He's gained a presence, your colonel."

Maeve was about to say he wasn't hers when the bell rang with authority, and shortly afterward Colonel Fitzpatrick strode in with a bouquet of hothouse roses, which he held out casually as though he called everyday.

Maeve held them to her face. "They smell so sweet," she said with sadness.

"Nothing's changed," he said, moving to put an arm around her shoulder, while looking at Fannie. "You and Fannie should both know we are going to marry, if I have to kill that man." His face reddened, and he seemed to have trouble choking his rage.

Fannie smiled softly. "It's about what I'd expect from a slithering type like General Sickles. He means to make a career of the war and his lost leg in spite of all the nasty things he's done. I've often thought about accusing him of denying care to his own wounded men when he took the surgeon off with him. But it would do no good. Heroes are allowed their faults." She smiled as if to imply such amnesty applied to Maeve and Fitz too.

Looking at Fannie, Fitz spoke, "He'd have had Meade drawn and quartered by that damn Committee on the Conduct of the War, if we hadn't destroyed Lee's army."

"Sickles won't give up. Grant's future is the high road of his vendetta. Well, he won't do it at Maeve's expense, not if I have to call him out, the little . . . ." Fitz stopped short.

"Yes, the little bastard," said Fannie quietly, "All those nice male words apply to him. But none of this helps our girl here. She doesn't deserve a bit of it."

"Oh, stop, both of you," said Maeve. "I can hold my head high. People don't necessarily connect "Maizie" with "Maeve," and I'm not the same person. I don't feel the same, and I don't want to hurt you, colonel." She turned to him with a determined smile he'd have been happy to bury his face in. "This isn't your fight, sir."

"I've an idea to present to you," he said. "Fannie, you and Maeve can come to New York next week, perhaps?"

"Certainly," said Fannie, "We often take the cars up. We've been working with the immigrants in the lower island. Sometimes I think we might decamp to New York City altogether."

CHAPTER XXVI

Elizabeth Van Lew's letter arrived in February to the office of Lieutenant-Colonel Baker of the 1st District of Columbia Cavalry, in charge of intelligence since the departure of General Sharpe. Baker was a policeman who loved crime. "The Gordon Conspiracy," as the press called it, held his attention, and his mind turned on it. He looked for potential violence, and set his men to watching for signs of trouble in the capital. They began interrogating unrepentant Rebels they had considered irrelevant.

Baker wondered if he ought to open the letter, and feared it might be personal. You never knew what the higher-ups were doing, and it could bring trouble to poke his nose where it didn't belong. Elizabeth Van Lew was a complete mystery. Sharpe kept her activities and her correspondence to himself. *A secret bastard,* Baker thought, *maybe he had something going on in Richmond. He went there enough.*

The letter sat on his desk. The duty sergeant reported a lookout had seen strange activity around Mrs. Surratt's boarding house on H Street, unusual people coming and going. She was from Southern Maryland, a Rebel hotbed. The actor Wilkes Booth was going in. He was an outspoken Rebel, a wild card, who spent his time between the stage and a wide circle of women, from Hooker's division to respectable parlors. And bedrooms. The Surratts had no business with the likes of him. Baker ordered a closer watch.

Baker was immersed in the details of security for Lincoln's second inauguration, and too preoccupied to think about Miss Van Lew. Finally, two days before the big event, he marked the letter "Personal" and sent it to New York.

313

As part of the patriotic festivities leading to the inauguration, New York's veterans planned a war memorial conclave at the Armory on 39th Street in Manhattan. They negotiated for weeks and agreed finally that the City Encampment of the Grand Army of the Republic would act as sponsor. Its leaders, mostly former officers, knew that the rank and file of New York's veterans were immigrants with views at odds with those of men from the West and New England. They strove to prove neutral in the growing disputes between the Grant-Sickles camp and men loyal to Meade. They wanted also to avoid the derision heaped on Western posts as the "Grand Army of the Republicans."

Sickles's old cronies met with Meade men from the Army of the Potomac led by Sharpe. They agreed their champions would be on stage in equal numbers with no more than three to speak for each side, General Sickles to be the final speaker, preceded by Colonel Fitzpatrick. Sharpe and his friends were astonished by the hostility of the Sickles's men, "one of whom," he wrote Fitz, "stated it as a matter of honor that General Meade had betrayed the little fellow at Gettysburg."

Dan Sickles's allies were sure they had the best of the bargain. Young Fitzpatrick would stand on strange turf and hold small appeal for an audience of men largely from the old 3d Corps. The general would be on home ground, where he had close ties to Tammany leaders who knew how to manage affairs like this. Local leaders assured Major Tremaine. Torchlight parades in loyal precincts would turn out large followings. The men in the hall would be primed for their one-legged hero.

Fitzpatrick and Sharpe sought out men of the Irish brigade, from the 63d, 69th and 88th New York, who had fought under Hancock, urging them to come early, and take prominent places in strength. Generals Andrew Humphreys and W.S. Hancock agreed readily to come from the posts in the South to stand with the Meade men.

On the evening of March 2, veterans in fading blue uniforms bulging at the seams filed into the great hall, shouting, chanting and singing the full repertoire of war songs from the bawdy "A Rovin'" to the haunting "Lurena." Red, white, and blue banners poured down each column. Bunting dropped from the rafters and covered the bare masonry behind the gaslights. They stood shouting and stomping in a heaving sea of blue caps, as though waiting the order to march back to the Rappahannock. In plain suits, journalists, city officials, and gawkers below the raised wooden platform seemed isolated, intimidated, and out of place.

Above them a master of ceremonies in full civilian dress introduced distinguished guests one by one as they climbed up. A rousing cheer went up for Dan Sickles as he clumped up the steep stairs and came forward to take his bow. The shouting lasted for many minutes while the marshals banged for order. They cheered the others, greeting Fitz handsomely, considering his status as an out-of-towner. Humphreys, and more familiar heroes received a rowdier welcome.

Speeches by the first two on each side took more than two hours. Sickles's allies extolled his heroism, and carefully rang the changes on Grant's victories from Island Number Ten to Atlanta. They spoke of "true faith in the Unionist cause" (meaning abolitionist Republican), dwelling as little as possible on issues of the day, except for the Transcontinental Railroad, where Sickles and his associates had invested heavily. Sharpe and his friends extolled the Army of the Potomac and Meade, citing the general's great military achievements ending the war sooner than any had thought possible. "Think of our brave comrades who might have fallen, or, worse, suffered lifetimes of endless suffering and pain if the war had gone on." They extolled Meade's fairness in seeking peace in the South (a subject the general insisted they raise) and his loyalty to President Lincoln.

Waves of cheering greeted every claim. By the time Fitzpatrick rose, he thought the two camps shared the audience about equally. He was a good storyteller but no great speaker, and struggled to breathe deep and swell his chest to get out the first few words in a voice loud enough to be heard in a hall that was never quiet. Military training helped. He found a command voice and, after a few references to the Commanding General, who, everyone knew, was his patron and professional father, and after he read a telegram from Meade (a trick Sickles missed), they set up a roar that came booming from all sides. Whatever their views, these were men of the

Army of the Potomac. Most had fought with Meade in the triumphal march to Richmond, Charleston, and Savannah. Fitz concentrated on the last days of the war when Sickles was inactive and Grant was a Meade deputy. At last he sat down to a storm of cheers.

As Dan Sickles pulled himself forward, he brought forth wild shouting and stomping, a release of yelling perfectly timed and seemingly endless, as though, Fitz thought, the men had been paid for it. He wondered how Sickles went about hiring a crowd, while the general in his new, well-cut uniform began his harangue, dwelling on his own exploits, talking about his famous leg and how he forced the Army of the Potomac, virtually against the Commanding General's will, to win at Gettysburg. Fitz decided Sickles had probably plied a few sergeants and corporals with whiskey—and maybe a few women.

After 20 minutes, Sickles got around to Grant, who made, he conceded, a contribution to victory greater than his own. No more mention of the Commanding General. That would be Sickles's style, to act as if Meade, the cold, distant professional, was somehow never there, and then to go on in rich color to tell anecdotes about the convivial Grant and himself, two fellows ready to share rations around the campfire with any worthy veteran.

They loved it. Sickles made himself a giant before their eyes. His speech was powerful, skillful, and sly—Fitz was sure he heard Sickles say Grant was born in the Bowery. Sickles said he thought so, and then hurried on as if it wasn't important. He generously offered rewards from a future Grant Administration, including a Uniform National Pension Law "which will make '40 Acres and a Mule' seem like beggary." Sickles spoke of Grant as the greatest friend any veteran could possibly have. After a peroration of rich periods evoking hallowed symbols of the war, his name, Grant's, Atlanta and Gettysburg, he stumped back to his chair, bowed to peers on the platform beaming smiles all around. Cheers exploded in the hall.

If the night ends here, we're going to lose. Fitz turned to look toward the wings. He didn't see them.

The master of ceremonies and the marshals, after many minutes of gavel-banging aided by commands from former drill sergeants pressed into service for the task, managed to quiet the hall. "Men, our program is not quite over. We have a surprise for you."

Fitz watched astonishment distort Sickles's face, as his eyes shifted quickly from right to left to find out what was happening. "And now," said the master of ceremonies, "It is my great honor and wonderful privilege, not to bring forth another great man, but the greatest, I'm sure you will all agree, lady of the war, the woman who saved so many and stood by you in the darkest hours, who nursed our own beloved brother General Sickles . . ." The general was searching around, as a sense of expectancy engulfed the hall, and the men stood up waiting, curious and ready for a surprise. "The young lady we all know and love as the 'Angel of Gettysburg.'" Applause, cheers, yelling, and whistles greeted these last words, drowning out the final mention of her name, "Miss Maeve McConnaughy."

Maeve, escorted by Sharpe and Fannie, slowly made her way up the side stairs of the platform while the veterans stretched their necks to leer at the only women in the house. Hypnotized by the stunning redhead, they continued to yell and cheer. Sickles looked furiously at Fitzpatrick, who smiled back impudently, as Maeve gracefully walked to the front with her escort two steps behind. She was dressed in a plain dark blue gown gathered at the middle and covered by a white apron from neck to hem. Her long hair hung well down her back, tied loosely in a large red bow. On her head she wore a white peaked cap.

The effect was perfect—simplicity, modesty, decency—things Maeve had every right to claim, though Fitz was surprised by cosmetics featuring her eyes in a dark outline, reminding him of the first time he saw her in the back of Alice's wagon. The mascara along with subtly reddened cheeks projected her appeal into the large hall, as she and Fannie must have anticipated. The whistling, cheering, and stomping kept on without anyone trying to stop it.

The men on the platform rose, the Meade men noticeably quicker. Sickles, using crutches, pulled himself grudgingly onto his feet and stepped forward. Fitz could see him fighting back anger. A drummer boy in uniform presented her with a large bouquet of red roses. Maeve kissed him on the forehead to the delight of the audience, smelled the flowers, and handed them to Fannie.

The master of ceremonies lifted Maeve's hand to present her to the audience, and with his other hand beckoned the men on the platform to gather round. Sickles clumped forward forcing a smile and took his place beside the master of ceremonies. Fitz stood next to Maeve. Neither looked at the other, though Fitz saw the trembling in her hand. She had the little smile that he loved, and he was sure that in spite of the raucous male behavior she was prepared.

The master of ceremonies stepped back between Maeve and Sickles, holding up their hands signifying a reunion of the stricken hero and his nurse. Fitz held his breath. Sickles contrived a smile, helpless to resist as Maeve stepped over, spread her white arms around his shoulders and embraced him. The cheering reached pandemonium. Below the platform the press corps, at last entertained after hours of repetitive rhetoric, peered upward, scribbled, and looked up again, twisting to catch every detail.

Sickles at last rose to the occasion, returned the embrace and stepped to the side holding Maeve's hand up to the grateful audience. *He's a performer*, Fitz thought. *We counted on it. And so is she.* Fitz fought for self-control. He wanted to grab Maeve and hug her, and he wanted to tell Sickles, "That does you, you little bastard!" But all he could do was wait for him to drop Maeve's hand—it took forever—and turn to bow, while Maeve withdrew in the company of Sharpe and Fannie and quickly left the hall before any newsman could get close to her. Fitz had stationed Meyer below to keep the journalists busy and ensure their stories had all the necessary, and only the necessary, details.

The hall slowly emptied after the speakers left the platform. The men offered to stand each other drinks at nearby saloons, or left one another pledging to keep in closer touch. Fitz and Sharpe met to review the events with Meyer at a German restaurant run by a kölnischer friend. Meyer reported the newsmen enchanted with Maeve.

The next day's papers carried full coverage, including lengthy accounts of the speeches, and featured Maeve's arrival with special attention to her reunion with Sickles. Several editorials, including one in the *Times*, dwelt on the role of women in the war and on Maeve as a fine example. Even the *World* had a good word for her. Fitz's only concern was that in using the occasion for Maeve might have slighted Meade, but Meyer assured him the reportage was highly favorable.

✩ ✩

All Washington knew by now that Margaretta Meade was the only woman Mary Todd Lincoln genuinely liked. They talked endlessly about their children, about relatives in the South, about their husbands, and occasionally about politics. In the latter, Margaretta was in some ways the more skilled, but she was careful always to cede to Mary Lincoln. The consequence was a happy symbiosis the capital had not seen since the presidential family came to town.

The Meades had gone with the Lincolns in February to see a series of Shakespeare plays featuring the eminent actor Edwin Booth. The President liked the Elizabethan language. He and the army's chief general recited passages out loud to each other in the carriage on the way back to the White House. The theater parties were festive, and Meade was delighted to find Lincoln had a flair for the great bard, whose language often inspired his own.

Meade rarely thought of himself as a public man, though he understood it was now his duty to be one. As the two couples rode in a carriage down Pennsylvania Avenue to yet another play, Meade realized that he constantly found more to admire in the President. Far from reviling Lincoln as a hayseed, as so many did in Philadelphia, he saw the subtlety of the man. "He may pick his nose and break wind in public," he once told a horrified Margaretta, "but he uses those things. The common touch serves him. Sometimes I wish I had it. His political instincts are as sharp as my barber's razors."

Politics for Meade was a new school. *Fitzpatrick takes to it like a duck to water. He knows right off what course to take. The Land Bank was sheer genius. Lincoln thought so, too. Fitzpatrick is a golden boy. How could he throw his life away on a prostitute? It makes no sense. Damn it! He'd be in my Cabinet. He can be President some day. Lincoln has said as much, himself.* Meade frowned and glanced at Margaretta sitting beside Mary Lincoln. The carriage slowly pulled through the mud. She smiled back affectionately. *Bless her, she knows I'm thinking about him.*

"We're meeting Senator Harris's daughter and Major Rathbone at the theater," said the President with unusual gaiety. "I'm sure they'll be there ahead of us. The play's supposed to be entertaining, *Our American Cousin*. This is Laura Keene's last night."

Mary Lincoln frowned, "That's all very well, Mr. Lincoln, but my nerves would be a deal calmer if you had brought extra guards this evening. I feel tense. The air is heavy."

Lincoln took a deep breath. "Nothing more than the usual mix of mud and offal we suffer in the capital, mother. Possibly a little refreshed by the rain. The comedy will relax you. I'm always amused by the English presumption," he laughed.

Earlier in the day he had discounted urgings from both Blair and Meade that he stay away from the theater. The "Gordon conspiracy" had become an unhappy turn in the course of the reconstruction. Meade thought of his own presence this evening as partly a matter of protecting his President. To a soldier such duties came naturally.

He lapsed into thought. Again, he missed Fitzpatrick. The old South was by no means conquered. The business with the Negroes was not easy. The President had to carry water on both shoulders. Whites in the North were often as unhappy about freedom for the black folk as the Southerners. It would take a genius to make this work.

The South consumed the Lincoln Administration a year after the war ended. Lincoln dedicated himself to "knitting up the raveled sleeve of state," as he termed it. *It is more than raveled*—Meade held a smile on his face for the ladies—*It is rent in two, between realists who accept peace and firebrands like Gordon who could never believe their army failed.* Not for the first time Meade considered whether more troops should be sent. *We've reduced strength too fast. I've told the President.*

They arrived at the theater on 10th Street with Meade in reverie. "Come on, general," called the President in happy voice. "We're missing a good play." Lincoln dismounted and stood in the street to hand the ladies down.

Young Major Rathbone and his fiancée were waiting in the presidential box and immediately moved toward seats at the side. Lincoln and his wife took two chairs in the fore. Margaretta sat behind the Lincolns in the second row next to the rail with Meade on her right near the door. They stood as "Hail to the Chief" was played, then settled silently as the actors carried on.

The guard outside the box, after an hour, grew weary and told a White House clerk to take his place at the door. A few minutes later a suave man, whom the clerk remembered seeing at the inauguration, offered his card to gain admittance.

John Wilkes Booth waited in the anteroom, then slipped into the box silently and unseen. Lincoln and his party were intent on the play. Booth stood in the shadows until his eyes adjusted to the dark, then placed a bar across the door to prevent interruption. He waited for a laugh line he knew was coming in the script, and knew would divert the audience. The one unforeseen circumstance was the very tall man in uniform sitting in the back row. Booth was unsure of his skill with the Derringer. He had but one shot.

Determined, excited, he drew the pistol and almost spoke, then paused as his actor's instinct took command. He would play the scene as it ought to play, as dramatic and more real than any role he had ever played. He would strike with lightning speed, then leap from the wing to center stage. He took one stride, two—as Meade turned his head and looked directly at him no more than three feet away. Booth feinted to the side, a fencer's move, seeking to pass and reach the President. Meade rose, the soldier seeing his duty, and stepped in to shield his Commander-in-Chief. Booth feinted again, Meade parried with his right hand, grabbing at the pistol with his left, twisting the shooter's wrist in a warrior's grip. The Derringer exploded. Meade fell.

Rathbone stepped over Meade to spring at Booth, who now held a dagger. Booth stabbed; Rathbone dodged and reached; Booth stabbed again, slicing the soldier's arm, to the bone, but lost his grip. Mrs. Lincoln screamed and lept to the President, demanding his protection. Now disarmed with the door barred behind him, Booth stepped up on the low front rail of the box and jumped for the stage, catching a foot in the red, white, and blue bunting. He landed awkwardly on the apron, missed a step, stumbled and fell.

He stood, the instant pain of a fracture bone ruining his composure and pace. He stumbled off, eyes flaming, and limped past a gaping Laura Keene and her troupe.

Meade lay on the floor, the blood spreading over his chest. "Mr.

President," he gasped, "please escort Mrs. Meade home."

A doctor appeared as the President ushered Mary out of the box. Paying no attention to anyone else, she screamed repeatedly, "He meant to kill Mr. Lincoln! He tried to kill Mr. Lincoln!" The President hurried her away, saying over his shoulder that he would send the carriage back for Margaretta.

She refused to leave the box. The doctor ordered the unconscious Meade carried to a quiet room in a house across the street. A large crowd gathered. Margaretta waited outside the room, keeping people away while the doctor worked. A major general she did not know came, and she asked him to find men to handle the crowd.

Hours passed. Finally the doctor emerged and said, "The wound is mortal."

Meade was staring expressionless at the ceiling unable to speak as she entered the room, She took his hand and felt a squeeze. She held it tight. George Gordon Meade, Lieutenant General U.S.A., died shortly before 3 a.m. on April 15, 1865, 21 months and 17 days after taking command of the Army of the Potomac.

In April Flossie wrote:

Todd says even in Tennessee they mourn General Meade. Here in Gettysburg, we don't understand it. No one believes he's gone, just as we couldn't believe at first the Rebels were gone.

No one knows anything about General Grant. He is a Westerner, and Papa says he will almost surely be the next President. I hope this doesn't mean more trouble. General Meade was the proper gentleman. He stood by the Union, the whole country, and President Lincoln.

The Hofmuellers have finished their new hotel. They've made a museum out of the room where Lee surrendered to General Meade. It is very popular. The hotel's trap goes by every hour back and forth to the railroad station. Only five vacant lots remain where houses once stood. The rest is rebuilt as good as new. With all the people coming to see the battlefield, the livery stables and the boarding houses do a good business.

Papa's store is busy, and he thinks about building a factory to make kitchen tools. Todd has ideas about this and even a few inventions. Father smiles at him and says he must be German. Todd says he isn't sure. Mama says one day he will ask me to marry him.

★ ★ ★

EPILOGUE

Abraham Lincoln served out his second term in a continuing struggle with the South. His hair turned white within months of General Meade's death. Booth and his conspirators were quickly caught, and executed. Lincoln spared Mrs. Surratt's life and eventually pardoned her. The President led mourners at an elaborate funeral, and was relieved that Margaretta Meade rejected an offer by veterans to build him a tomb in Arlington on the model of Napoleon's. She returned with the body to Philadelphia for a large civic funeral. George moved out to the estate to raise his family.

Thanks to the Land Bank, credit and trade revived in the South. White vigilantes were suppressed, as enclaves of blacks in adjoining settlements worked out means of protection. Henry Prediger ran successfully for Congress from Georgia in 1868, serving four terms until appointed Postmaster General by President Tilden.

Colonel Fitzpatrick remained at the Bank until June 1867 and saw to the settlement of more than one and a half million former slaves on their own lands. Two months later, he married Maeve McConnaughy onboard a steamship bound for Europe, where they spent a year-long honeymoon in Italy. They settled in San Francisco, and built a large mansion on Nob Hill after he made a fortune by anticipating Grant's demonetization of silver. James Edward Fitzpatrick, Colonel U.S. Volunteers, died at his ranch in Marin County in 1895.

The Fitzpatricks' wealth and fame combined with Philadelphia credentials easily established an unassailable social position. Maeve became a prominent figure in San Francisco. She was only once dogged by her past when Alice briefly appeared on the Barbary

Coast. But she was old, ill, and too far gone with drink to be dangerous. In the '80s Maeve established a Home for Unfortunate Women on Stockton Street a few blocks from the stews of the port. She was an early advocate of the conservation of nature, a sponsor of John Muir, and in 1919 a silent founder of the Save the Redwoods League.

President Grant failed to continue Lincoln's balancing act, and veered sharply toward the Negro voters as a means of building the Republican Party. He alienated much of the white population and by 1873 announced he was "weary of the South" and would get on with the business of the rest of the country.

Grant did not bring Dan Sickles into his Cabinet but sent him as ambassador to Spain, where he spoke the national language. Sickles's charm did not fail in Madrid. He became one of the lovers of Queen Isabella, who seemed to prefer her one-legged American to others, and took him with her when she went into exile in Paris.

Returning to the United States, Sickles resumed an active role in veterans' organizations, and was a member of the New York State Monuments Commission until removed in 1912 on accusation of embezzlement. He played a major role in organizing the Gettysburg National Battlefield Park, where he often addressed veterans' meetings on the "vital importance of his advance on the second day of the fight, assuring Union victory and settling the fate of the nation." He was eventually supported in this claim by his former adversary, James "Pete" Longstreet. Both men lived on into the twentieth century, outlasting their peers and putting a strong and bitter spin to the public memory.

By demand of the veterans, Sickles's amputated leg was preserved, and remains on display at the National Museum of Health and Medicine at the Walter Reed Army Medical Center in Washington D.C.

AUTHOR'S NOTE AND ACKNOWLEDGMENTS

———————————— ☆ ◄———————————

First among all those who helped this story to evolve, I thank my wife Caroline who has corrected drafts and offered criticism and fresh ideas regularly ever since that weekend in June 1995 when we rose early in Gettysburg to see the fog in the fields and try to understand how it was. (We were amazed to find the statue of Meade green with age and ignored not far from his headquarters at the Leister House, which was also ignored and unremarked.)

Among the people at Gettysburg, I want especially to thank the Battlefield guides Hans Henzel, Jim Clouse and Tim Smith, and others who patiently if skeptically heard my fantasies and helped me spin them out. Special thanks to Tim Smith, Park Ranger Eric Campbell, Professor Ervin L. Jordan, Jr., of Charlottesville, Virginia, and Col. B. Con Anderson, Jr., (USAF-Ret) for reviewing parts of the draft manuscript. My gratitude also goes to Anthony Waskie, president of the General Meade Society of Philadelphia, and to the Society for its support and for its efforts to revive the general's good name. I also thank my mentors Professor Janette Turner Hospital of the University of South Carolina, and Margaret Blair, and not least Philip Kopper, my thoughtful editor and publisher.

And a sentimental salute goes to the U.S. National Park Service, in whose bosom I was raised, for persevering in helping us to hold onto our heritage in nature and in history.

In the richness of Civil War literature, the pinnacle of Gettysburg fiction remains Michael Shaara's *Killer Angels* (Ballantine Books, 1974). As I began researching the battle for myself, Shaara's images were the most compelling. Shaara wrote essentially from the perspective of the South, I from the North, and Meade appears only once in his classic.

Sadly, much to the Civil War's "historic fact" is nearer myth or invention than truth, thanks not least to Daniel Sickles and other survivors who spent decades rewriting what they thought they saw or did. With a certain faith in General Meade's veracity, I have relied on his published letters, which are available in the original by application at the Pennsylvania Historical Museum in Philadelphia, and as published with editing and comment by his son Captain George Meade and grandson (Scribners, 1913), as well as the letters of his aide, Richard Lyman, written after Gettysburg and most recently published with the misleading title, *Grant and Meade, From the Wilderness to Appomattox* (University of Nebraska, 1995), along with Freeman Cleaves' 1960 biography *Meade of Gettysburg* (University of Oklahoma, 1960).

My principal source for Sickles was W. A. Swanberg's *Sickles, the Incredible* (Stan Chase Military Books, 1956). For data on military movements, I consulted Edwin B. Coddington's *The Gettysburg Campaign, a Study in Command* (Scribners, 1968), and well as John Batchelder's semiofficial battle maps, though the latter were published in 1876 and are now often challenged. (Batchelder's principal advisor was that indefatigable self-promoter, Dan Sickles.) For the color of Lee's final attack, I found nothing better than George Stuart's *Pickett's Charge, a Microhistory of the Final Attack at Gettysburg* (Houghton Miflin, 1959). For troop strength and casualty figures I relied chiefly on John W.Busey and David G. Martin's *Regimental Strengths and Losses at Gettysburg* (Longstreet House, 1982).

As for the moods, atmosphere and trivia of Washington City during the Civil War, nothing surpasses Gore Vidal's classic novel, *Lincoln* (Ballantine Books, 1985). Josephus and his spies were inspired by Edwin C. Fishel's monumental *Secret War for the Union* (Houghton Mifflin, 1996) and David Ryan's diary and biography of Elizabeth Van Lew, *A Yankee Spy in Richmond* (Stackpole Books, 1996) and David Robertson's novel *Booth* (Doubleday, 1998). For details of the immediate post-war period, I drew on Eric Foner's fine 1998 work, *Reconstruction*. I also drew insight about the South from Fanny Kemble's *Journal of a Residence on a Georgia Plantation, 1838-39* (University of Georgia, 1984), Mary Chesnut's war diaries, *The Private*

Mary Chesnut, edited by C. Vann Woodward and Elisabeth Muhlenfeld, (Oxford University Press, New York, 1984), and Ernest B. Furgurson's *Ashes of Glory, Richmond at War* (Vintage Books, 1996), as well as Ralph Lowell Eckert's biography, *John Brown Gordon, Soldier, Southerner, American* (Louisiana State University Press, 1989). Finally for a survey of early Union Civil War literature from U.S. Grant to Ambrose Bierce, still nothing beats Edmund Wilson's aptly titled *Patriotic Gore* (1962).

Georgetown, D.C.
April 6, 2002

Meade's Reprise, A Novel of Gettysburg, War and Intrigue was designed by Susan Lehmann of Washington, DC. To resonate the era of the narrative, the text is set in Baskerville, a serviceable and enduring face that was highly popular in the late nineteenth century. It was originally designed in 1734 by the eponymous English writing master, letter cutter and printing innovator John Baskerville. The titles are set in Bodoni Ultra Bold another classic typeface. The first edition of the book was printed and bound in Iceland by Oddi Printing.